Alter

C000060933

Kenn Gordon

Copyright © 2017

Kenn Gordon

I grew up in the Highlands of Scotland. I became a musician whilst still at school. Then I made my first musical instrument, at the age of 13. At the age of 18, I joined the Royal Air Force. I served for 9 years, and worked at numerous secret establishments. During my military career, I continued to play in bands and to write music. When I left the RAF, I still played music, forming my own bands and recording over 32 Albums, under various names. I also created Gordon Guitars, making high end and bespoke guitars. As I grew older, I looked for a new avenue for my creative juices. It is because of this, that I have decided to become a writer. The first novel entitled 'Altered Perceptions' is the first part of a Trilogy featuring. Andy McPhee and Team Seven, of the SIS Black Door Operations. SIS (Secret Intelligence Service) do exist, as do Black Door Ops. What goes on at CDE (Chemical Defence Establishment) Porton Down, is part factual and part fiction. Although this story is fiction, or you could say factional. The Enriched Uranium and Plutonium did go missing from FBR (Fast Breeder Reactor) Dounreay. The Secret Royal Navy program, the Vulcan Project, did take place between the RN (Royal Navy) and Rolls Royce. There were two major accidents at FBR Dounreay and they were covered up. There still, to this day, remains two mile of off-limit shoreline. Where pieces of Plutonium are being found, on the beach near Dounreay. Much of what happened in this first book, did happen in real life. Some is of course pure fiction. Real names, have been changed. The Majority of the places exist. Gruinard Island, was used by the British Government, to test out Bacteriological and Viral spores of Anthrax. The Island, remained uninhabitable for almost 50 years. The UK has signed up to the Geneva Convention, that bans the use of Chemical and Biological Warfare. Yet it continues to make these banned items. The UK is not alone in this. The USA, France, Belgium, Germany along with the majority of countries in the west. Yet we first world countries, condemn the third world countries, who try to make them. Worse still, in some cases, we even supply these countries, with the parts required to make these weapons of mass destruction. That is a fact.

Kenn Gordon

44-12053592007
Kenn.gordon@yahoo.com

DEDICATION

I dedicate this book, to my Mother and my Father who have always encouraged me in everything I did. To my long suffering wife Susan, who has put up with my childish tantrums, when I cant find a way to express, the ideas that are flying around inside my head. To all of my sons from both my marriages Yjan, Lachlan, Mark and Adrian. I hope that I have provided the tools that you require, to make a way for yourself in life. To My family and friends who have supported me, by buying my Music and now my Books

Kenn Gordon

CONTENTS

ACT 1

I was not athletic, in the standard sense of the word. I was fit though. I took part in a lot of sporting pursuits. I loved to swim, along with long distance, cross country running. I was not really interested in the formal competition of it, it was more of a way, to relieve the boredom, of a mundane life as a medic. I was stationed at R.A.F. Brawdy, which is located in the South West of Wales. Apart from the rare major incident, this usually meant working with a Station Medical Officer, treating hangovers, or servicemen with a dose of the clap.

I also enjoyed an adrenaline rush. Whilst I was stationed at R.A.F. Abingdon, I took up free fall, parachuting. Even on occasions I completed jumps, with the R.A.F. Falcon's Parachute Display Team. This team was also known as the Big Six, strangely because most of the team, were under six-foot high. This in itself, made me stand out from them. I was six foot two inches tall. I always liked to take everything in life to the limit, at least as much as I was able to. When parachuting, I used a variety of 'chutes.' over the following years, from the 'Para Commander' in the mid 1970's, to the later 'Strato Cloud Ram Air Parachute'. I think more out of a combination of vanity and ability, I went to the extreme length, and had my own custom made 'Chute'. This parachute was loosely based upon the 'XL Cloud'. Over the subsequent years, I completed more than 1,000 high level jumps. This would have gained me a place, in the Falcons Display Team, had I wished it. That said, I was in it for the thrill, and not for the job. So over the years, I continued to do it just as a sport. That is, whenever time or location, would allow. On one of my annual leave breaks, I went to the USA and completed an Oxygen assisted, free fall jump, from a 'PAC750'. This was from a height of thirty thousand feet. I completed this jump with my lifelong friend, Lachlan Henderson. Lachlan, who was better known to his friends, as Lachie. We both grew up together in the Highlands of Scotland. We first met in the Strath of Kildonnan. Both of us boys, were from the tiny hamlet of Kinbrace. We even went to school in Kinbrace and as we grew older went to the High-school in Helmsdale. The pair of us, enjoyed the same sort of things, as young boys. Swimming, shooting and fishing, whenever time between chores, and schoolwork, would allow. Lachie was a stockily built lad, with a shock of curly blonde hair. He seemed more Icelandic, than Scottish in origin. He always stood a good four inches taller than me. Whilst I, with my jet black hair, and a slight throwback, to some far off distant relative, of Indian origin. I always looked as though, I had a great natural suntan. Of all the things that we enjoyed most, was shooting. Not just because of the thrill, of actually shooting, but more the excitement of the hunt. As youngsters, we would pretend, to be in the real military, and the enemy would be a Stag, or perhaps, a Hare. We stalked our prey carefully, whilst traversing the Highland mountains, then creeping up on the 'enemy'. Sometimes we would just stalk, and not even bother with the kill. Attempting to get as close, to the prey, as we could. The keen competition between us as boys, continued into our teenage life. On one occasion, we got within three feet, of a Hind and her fawn. Then we gently slithered, down the side of the mountain, on our bellies, without even having fired, a shot from either of our rifles. I say our rifles, they of course belonged to our fathers. Lachie's was a Remington Triple Two, which we used for hares and rabbits. The rifle that I carried was a Mannlicher Thirty naught six, this we used for long range shots, when shooting the Red Deer, that roamed, just about every mountain, hill and valley, of the Strath. Both of us, had managed kill shots, at over a thousand yards, using standard telescopic sights. The rifles, were old bolt action models, and had been well used. However, they had been well looked after, by our parents, and probably our grandparents. Always taking the strictest of turns, as to which of us, would take the shot. We had the one rule when out shooting. We would never shoot anything, which would not be taken home and then eaten, by our families, or their friends. Unlike the rich folks from the South, that came to shoot in the Highlands. We were not trophy hunters.

Lachie and I were also keen fishermen. To us, this was almost as much fun, as shooting. Often, we would go fishing, in the river Helmsdale, or one of the many tributary Burns, that would flow into it. We would fish for either Salmon or Rainbow Trout, which were plentiful in the clean and clear waters of the Highlands. We combined this activity, with swimming, in the icy cold, but crystal clear water. Sometimes we would see, which of us, could stay under the water, the longest. We would hold large rocks in our arms, to prevent us, from bobbing up prematurely. This competitiveness ran through our school years and then at the age of 18, we joined the Royal Air Force together.

ACT 2

After we signed up, we were sent to R.A.F. Swinderby, in Lincolnshire, in the East of England. This is where we completed, our basic training. Or as it was called by those, who had already completed it, Square-Bashing. Swinderby, was nothing like our homes in the Highlands. We had never seen such a flat, and unexciting piece of land. Lincolnshire, was flat as far as the eye could see. It was pretty much, all arable land. However, that said, because of our fitness, from running up and down mountains, we found that running around the Perry Track, of the airfield, was really easy for us. The pair of us, excelled on the rifle range, using the S.L.R. (Self Loading Rifle)7.62 rifle. To get a two inch grouping, at twenty five yards, posed little or no challenge, to either of us. Lachie, when told to do his grouping shots, asked the instructor?

"Is that a two inch grouping, on a moving, or a still target?"

Then Lachie, promptly fired, of an entire magazine of twenty rounds, into the centre, of the 'Soldier' target. All twenty shots, were confined to a round hole, of somewhat less than two inches. This was Lachie all over, he was always quick of wit, but sometimes too quick with the mouth. This little stunt, saw us 'Guarding the Perimeter', of our training camp, as the rest of our squad, slept soundly in their beds. After our six weeks of basic training, and prior to our 'Pass out Parade'. We were all given, our training awards. We never made, best cadets, or most improved, however though, we were awarded our 'Crossed Rifles,' for perfect shooting. I however as a medic, would never be allowed to wear them on the sleeve of my uniform. The Geneva Convention forbade it. After the Pass out Parade, all of us were rewarded, with one week home leave. Lachie and I, went back home, in our full Number One's. (Dress uniforms) We boarded the bus from R.A.F. Swinderby, to the historic City of Lincoln. It was there, we caught our train, to London Kings Cross. Then from there, we took the overnight train, to Inverness. We had a coffee and a curled up British Rail sandwich for breakfast. Then we boarded the train, from Inverness to our final destination, of Kinbrace. Kinbrace railway station was at the time, and I and sure still is, 'a request stop'. This is primarily due to the small number of people, that ever use this remote station. At Kinbrace Station, we were met by our respective fathers, and taken to our homes. One week later, we met up again, to go back South. This time, it was to be to different destinations. Lachie was off to R.A.F. Catterick, to train with the RAF Regiment. I was off to learn medicine, at R.A.F. Halton. It was at this point, that our lives, that had been joined, for so many years. Saw us split company. Over the years, we would see each other occasionally, when home on annual leave. However, we were destined to be reunited, some years later. I was by now a Sergeant, and stationed at the combined U.S.NAFAC (United States Naval Facility) and R.A.F. Station, Brawdy. Lachie was a Corporal, and was stationed at R.A.F. Saint Athens, as part of their R.A.F. Regiment, Ground Defence Force (This was a glorified title, for the R.A.F. Regiment, or as we called them Rock Apes. A title given to the R.A.F. Regiment, for their defence of the Rock of Gibraltar). One day, in early spring of that year. I was sent out from R.A.F. Brawdy, along with the Senior Medical Officer. Our instructions were, to bring back to base, an injured member, of the Special Air Service. The man, had apparently been injured, in a training exercise, on the Brecon Beacons. We flew out from R.A.F. Brawdy, in a Sea King, Search and Rescue Helicopter. From 2.0.2. Squadron. This search and rescue squadron was also stationed at R.A.F. Brawdy. Upon landing the S.M.O. and I, were directed to a waiting A.P.C, (Armoured Personnel Carrier) with R.A.F. Roundel, painted on its side. We went over, and clambered in, with our equipment. When the driver turned around, it was Lachie.

"Where are we going too, gentlemen? I have another pickup, in twenty minutes. They are both far better looking than you two."

His mouth, was still that bit quicker, than his mind. It would seem, that time and punishments, had not cured it. The S.M.O, who I was travelling with, was a Wing Commander, and whilst laid back with his own lads, at the Medical Centre, he was in no mood, to put up with Lachie's irreverent quips.

"That will be, I will take you to the patient SIR, or I will have those stripes. Now get a damn move on Corporal" replied my boss.

Lachie did not bother with a reply, but shifted the A.P.C. into drive, and started off with a solid jerk, and a spin of the wheels. This was followed by, a quick wink at me.

"Why could the chopper, not take us right to the patient?" I asked

"Oh apparently, he's stuck, in a deep and narrow gully. Now what's worse, is he is in a tree. If we took the chopper anywhere near. Then the wash of the chopper blades, would like as not, blow him right out of the tree, and further down into the gully."

We travelled, without any more conversation, for about fifteen minutes. All the time, the terrain was getting rougher and steeper. On arrival at the incident site, initially, there was nothing for us to see.

"Walk this way Sir." Lachie said, and then under his breath said.

"If he could walk that way, he would not need talcum powder."

He then pointed over, what looked like a small crest, in the rolling Welsh countryside. Lachie led the way. When we reached the crest, it was more like looking down a cliff face. I looked down, and there, laid on his back, was the injured soldier. The trouble was, he was snared up, in a large tree, which was also, leaning over the sharp drop. Its roots, having been, all but pulled clear of the soil, which was all, that was holding it down, to mother earth. There was another soldier, crouched down, at the base of the tree. He was fixing ropes, and staking them into the surrounding area.

"How did this happen?" the S.M.O. asked Lachie.

"Sorry sir. I have all the info, that you have. Which I am guessing, is none at all."

I knew Lachie, was just pushing the officer, to see how far, he could take his own sense of humour. Whilst the S.M.O. said nothing, I knew, he was not happy, with Lachie's sarcasm. This under normal circumstances, could have been treated as 'Rank Insubordination'. The uninjured soldier from below, shouted up.

"Are you guys, here to help, or to watch?"

We carefully slid down the side of hill, towards the tree. Initially it seemed quite obvious to me, that there had been some sort of explosion, near to the tree. This had resulted, in this unfortunate individual, ending up clutched, in a bosom of branches, about eight feet from the ground.

"Grenade went off." The soldier roping the tree said, pointing to a medium sized hole in the ground, about 8 feet from the side of the tree.

"Well, I have no intention of climbing up there, to treat him. So you lot, had better get him out from the tree, and up to the top of the ridge." The S.M.O. said

Then he turned, and started back up the slope, that we had just come done. Lachie and I, helped the other guy, secure the tree. Then between the three of us, we managed to attach a short neck and back board, to the injured man. After which, we carefully extracted, the man from the branches. Then we gently lowered him to the ground. He was breathing, but very pale. I did a quick check, and most of his major bones, seemed to be unbroken. The only sign of any injury, was some minor bleeding, from both of his ears. There was little or no response, to light from his pupils. He looked, a bit like death warmed up. After getting him onto the stretcher, we got him up to the top of the slope, and to the awaiting Medical Officer. I rattled off my basic report.

"Neck and Spine, along with all major bones, look OK. Blood pressure is a little low, as is his pulse. He has shallow breathing, and has shown no signs of consciousness, Sir".

The S.M.O. started his own check, of the patient. I walked over to the other soldier, who wore no insignia, or rank badges.

"So, how did he get no external injuries, from a blast, that looks to have thrown him up into the air, and then dumped him in the branches of a tree?"

"I don't know Sarge. It happened well before I got here, and I was just told to call it in, then secure the site." He replied

"OK Mate, I need some details. Like who is he? What Unit?"

"I refer you, to my first reply, Sarge"

I started to think, he was another Lachie, a smart mouth.

"And you are?"

"Sorry Sarge, I can't say."

"Don't be a tosser, all your life. We are not some sort of enemy" I replied to him. In somewhat harsher tones, than I had intended.

"Sorry Sarge. Was not being a gobshite, just none of us, on this training course, know any of the others, and I am on orders, not to give out my details"

"Who's Orders?" I asked

"Sor.............."

I cut him off "Can't Say, OK I get it. But for us, to be able to treat your man over there. I am going to need. a few details. Like blood group etcetera, etcetera."

My boss, called me over

"He has a tag around his neck, which has a bar code, and just his blood group, of O-Positive. What did you get, from his mate?"

"Less than you Sir, it would appear, to be some sort of SAS 'hush hush' training shit"

"OK, let's get him down from here, after we get a line into him"

Lachie and I, put the stretchered patient, into the back of the A.P.C. I turned around, to get the other soldier, to give him a lift back, and he was gone. Fuck it! I thought, and closed the back door, of the A.P.C. Then I got in the front, with Lachie. We chatted on the drive back, and he told me, he was actually planning, on joining the S.A.S. He had come down, with some other Rock Apes, who were providing logistical support, for the S.A.S. this week. He had volunteered, for this duty, so he could have a look, and check out, what it would be like, being a member, of the most elite fighting force, in the British Army.

When we reached the chopper, we loaded up our patient. The flight back R.A.F. Brawdy, was uneventful. We got him down to the medical Centre. My boss asked me, to get on a computer, and get the medical records, belonging to the patients Bar Code. So I scanned it, and sent it off, to the Military Records Department. I had expected a quick reply, just not quite as quick, as it came. The phone on my desk, rang.

"Station Medical Centre, Sergeant McPhee speaking. How can I help you?"

"You, have one of my men there. We are sending a chopper, to collect him"

"Sorry, who am I speaking too?"

"That does not matter. What matters, is this. You have one of my men. You picked him up, on the Brecon Beacons. We will be with you, in about ten to fifteen minutes. Can you have him ready, for transport?"

"Please wait. I think you need to talk, to the Senior Medical Officer, as he is treating this man"

The Phone went dead.

I went and told the S.M.O. of my brief telephone conversation. He was interrupted, by his phone ringing. The S.M.O. motioned for me to stay, and answered his phone.

"Sir, Yes Sir, yes Sir, Sir? Are you sure? Sir, yes Sir, but.... but, OK, but I want you to sign off on this. OK Sir. Yes, Sir" and he put the phone down.

"That was the C.O. (Commanding Officer) He says, we are not to interfere, in any way, with this patient. We are not to ask, any questions. Just make him ready to go. And Andy, not a word of this, to anyone."

Ten minutes later, a Gazelle chopper, landed on the Helipad, outside the medical Centre. Two soldiers, in full Nomex, complete with balaclavas. Came in, and took the stretchered patient,

"One of you, wants to sign for him?"

They never even broke stride, and just took him outside, and loaded him, along with themselves, into the chopper, which took off immediately. Leaving me standing in the dust cloud, that it left behind there.

"I Guess not" I muttered to myself and walked back inside. I was trying to sort out an order in which things had happened today, when my boss stuck his head around the doorway to my office.

"Andy. Can you come to my office please"

I followed the S.M.O. to his office.

"Take a Seat, please Andy. I don't know, what happened here today. But I just got orders, for you. I am guessing, it probably has something, to do with today's incident. I am also, being posted out. You are to report, to the C.O. at The Centre for Defence Enterprise. Porton Down. You are also to receive, a promotion to Flight Sergeant, effective immediately. I am apparently off to Strike Command, at R.A.F. High Wycombe, with a promotion to Group Captain."

I think my mouth must have dropped, but he went on.

"You are not due for a promotion Andy, nor am I. But I

will take it, without question. And I would strongly suggest, that you do the same"

"Not a problem, for me Sir"

"That's it. You best go pack. Its been nice working with you. Perhaps we'll meet again. Best of luck, in your new post" He put his hand out, and I shook it

"You too Sir"

I walked out, and cleared of my personal possessions, from my desk. Then, I went over to the Sergeants Mess, and packed my Kit Bag. By the time I got to Administration, I was handed my travel warrant, along with the Crown, to go on top of my three stripes.

ACT 3

On arrival at C.D.E. Porton Down, I reported to reception, and was pointed immediately, to the Commanding Officers office. I knocked and waited.

"Enter"

I did so, and was faced with a Group Captain, who I saluted and spouted off

"Flight Sergeant McPhee reporting for duty Sir"

"Have a seat"

I did

"Now before we start, I need you to sign, the Official Secrets Act. I am sure you have already done this, on many occasions, but this one, carries a RED SEAL. Effectively this, takes you, to a top secret level. That is to say, that it is the extended version, of the Official Secrets Act."

I signed, and he countersigned, then put the folder down on his desk.

"I have your service record here. I don't know, the whys or the wherefores, of your promotion, and posting to me. It looks like, you either shagged the wife of someone, very high up, or saw something, that you should not have seen. I shall not ask you, which it was, as I really don't want to know. The official line, for this place is, that we are all working on the cure, for the common cold. I am quite sure, that you already know, that is bullshit. So to cut the crap, we work on Chemical, and Biological warfare. This does also include, finding treatments and vaccines, for all the nasty shit, that THEY have. As well as creating, our own nasty shit, to use against THEM."

He paused, and I guessed he was waiting, for some kind of response from me.

"What is my position here, Sir?"

"You are to work in the Medical Research Treatment Centre. We have volunteers, from across the Armed Forces, and we patch test things, like Blistering agents, on them. This is for us to be able to determine, which of our NBC Suits, is the least impregnable, to these agents. Occasionally, there are some minor incidents. When this happens, you will be required to treat patients, who have had reactions."

He continued "Now get yourself over, to the Sergeants Mess, and get settled in. Then, you are to report to your section, tomorrow, for induction."

"Thank you Sir"

I stood up, and stood to attention, and offered up, one of my smartest salutes. Then I turned, and exited the office. I found my way, to the Sergeants Mess, and there I was allocated a room. After I unpacked, and put everything, that someone, who lives out of their Kit-bag, has, away. Then I went downstairs, to the Bar.

"Large Jameson's please, and no ice"

The steward, brought the drink over. I sipped it. I tried to process, all that had happened, in the last twelve hours.

The following morning, I went to where, I had been told to report. The Medical Research Centre. This was massive, and full of various sub sections. I went to reception, and woman in civilian clothes, pulled open the glass sliding window.

"Your name and rank please?"

"Flight Sergeant Andy McPhee."

She gave me a blue Radiation Monitoring badge and another yellow, and undisclosed monitoring badge

"You are to wear these, at all times. Please sign here" she passed a clipboard over, and I signed. Then attached the two monitoring badges to the outside of my uniform.

"Down to the end of the hallway, and take the lift to S3"

"S3?"

"Sub level three."

I did as I was told, and took the elevator down to S3. The lift doors slid open, into a narrow corridor. This was lined, with thick glass windows, that made them look green. I went to the first door, which was fortunately labelled 'Office'. I knocked, and then entered. There were two other people in the room, an older gentleman, with a white lab coat, over an army shirt, but without insignia, or rank showing and a slightly younger man, who was dressed, in a Saville Row Tweed suit.

"Excuse me, I am Flight Sergeant Andy McPhee, and I was told to report here today."

They both looked at each other, and then at me.

"Or I can just wait outside, until you two, are finished."

I turned, and walked out, closing the door behind me. Then I waited, in the narrow corridor. From time to time a, variety of people, would go from one door to another. Some, were dressed in civilian clothes, others in various Military Dress Uniforms. Then occasionally, some were dressed in protective clothing. No one talked to me, not even to say Hi, or to ask, what I was doing here? After about twenty minutes, the guy in the Saville Row suit, came out from the office.

"You can go in now." He said

Then he left, and entered the lift, and was gone. I went in, and waited for the bloke in the lab coat, to finish writing. However he continued to do so, seemingly, blissfully unaware, of my presence. I coughed a few times, just for good measure, then waited some more. Eventually he looked up, and closed the folder, he had been busy reading, and adding notes to the margin.

"You're the Medic from Brawdy?"

Personally, I kind of thought it was obvious, that I was a medic, standing there in my number one dress uniform, and wearing my gold RAF Medical badges, on both my lapels.

"That would sound about right, yes, and you are?"

"Edwin." He rose and offered his hand, which I shook.

"We just use first names here, and we don't bother, with all that rank stuff. It gets so confusing, with all the services, and various nations military, that we have here as well." he said and then he sat back down

"So you are Andy. You and your Station Medical Officer, were called to an incident, on the Brecon Beacons yesterday? Is that about right?"

My internal alarm bells, were going off big time, as I was trying to figure out, why a soldier who had apparently, been blown up with a hand grenade, would cause my sudden and immediate posting. To this place, where no one really had a name, rank or service. I decided to keep my answers short at least until I knew, what was going on.

"Yes"

I had not been offered a seat, and being as I was not being held Rank accountable. I removed my Cap and sat down.

"Did you get a good look, at the patient?"

"Yes" I replied

"Andy. What was your medical opinion?"

"Someone, tried to blow him up, however his injuries, were not consistent with the story. In fact, I thought, he was having some form, of brain haemorrhage. Though, I am not fully qualified to answer that question"

I was not sure, if this guy was being friendly, or just yanking my chain, so did not reply using his name

"And was this the opinion of the Medical Officer with you?"

"I really can't say. You would have to ask my boss"

"But in your opinion, would you say his injuries were inconsistent, with being blown up?"

If I told him the truth, which was, I don't know how the guy ended up in the tree, but he sure as hell was not standing next to a grenade, when it went off. No fractures, no massive blood loss, (except from the ears) no tears to his uniform, and his boots were clean.

"I would have to say, that a concussive blast, could have ruptured both of his eardrums, and sent him flying up into the tree. There was a small crater, similar in size, to that which could have been created, by a grenade"

"Andy, have you and your medical officer, discussed this with anyone else"

"Nope"

"Or with each other"

"Apart from the basics, like he was unconscious but alive, and we took him back to Brawdy, for full examination. But as I am sure you know, we never had a chance, to do that"

"Any others, see this injured man?"

I knew the question was coming, to be fair. That said, I really did not want to involve Lachie, in whatever shit, was going on. No one, gets a promotion overnight, without apparent reason. So by that very reasoning, there must have been an important reason, and it must have been very time sensitive. I decided to hold back a bit.

"Not that I am aware of, Edwin."

"OK Great. Thanks Andy."

Then, he went back to his folder, making more notes. I just sat there, and waited some more, and some more, until he looked up.

"Is there something more, you wish to tell me Andy?"

"No I don't think so"

"So?"

"So?" I replied

Another pregnant pause, I gave in first

"Edwin. What am I doing here? I was posted to this Unit? Who is in charge? If you could tell me, so at least I can get to work, or get a coffee."

"Sorry Andy, I thought you had been told. You are to go to the S.S.T. Unit, on the Ground Floor, and report to their reception"

"Right" I replied. Fortunately I knew that S.S.T. meant that I was being sent to the Specialist Safety Team. I knew that this unit normally dealt with Biological and Chemical spills, but occasionally they also worked with radioactive contamination.

I stood up and walked out, leaving the door open and headed for the Lift. I entered, and pressed the button marked <G>. Once again in the reception area, I asked the woman, behind the glass window, for the S.S.T. UNIT. This time she handed me a Visitor Tag, and pointed down the hallway, and through the double doors, to the room, at the extreme end of the corridor. I clipped on the Visitor Badge next to the tow monitoring badges I was now wearing, then headed on my way. As it turned out, it was a long walk that seemed to slope gently downwards, taking the occasional turn, to the right, and then up a small flight of stairs. At the end there was a door, Emblazoned with the letters S.S.T. and all sorts, of Hazardous Warnings, Chemical, Radiation, Biological, Fire and a few other symbols, that I did not instantly recognize. I had no doubt, that at some point, someone, would tell me what they all meant. I opened the door, which looked like a classroom, filled with multiple services, not to mention a good variety of ranks, as well as what looked like, a few civilians. There was a General, from the Royal Army Medical Corps, talking and pointing, at an oversized blackboard, with an old snooker cue. Every eye in the room, turned in my direction, and the General stopped talking, and glared at me

"Yes? is there something, I can help you with Sergeant?"

"Hi I'm Andy, and I was told to report here"

It seemed that the hush, had become even more hushed, if that was even possible. I looked at the General, and the veins and arteries, all over his neck and face, looked like they were about to explode!!!!His mouth, moved but nothing came out for a bit, and then it exploded, in a torrent of spittle and expletives, most of which, I had previously heard, but there were a few in there, that were new to me.

"Well Sergeant, Andy Fucking Pandy! You little badly spent piece of cum, that managed to get into your mothers, poor forlorn and damaged womb. From which she spewed forth, your little fucking shit for brains, out, onto my highly polished, and well educated floor. You Sergeant Andy Fucking Pandy, are less than the total, of an amoeba's sex life, and without the singular brain cell, to go with it. You, were to report here YESTERDAY!"

"Finished?" I asked

This brought forward, another mouthful, that would have been respectful, from some drill instructor. However, it was a tad more, than I had expected, from an officer and a General at that. The veins by now, were threatening to detonate, and his eyeballs seemed, to be trying to extricate themselves, from their sockets.

"See this Rank on my arm, I am a FUCKING GENERAL!"

"Yes Sir, Sorry Sir"

I wasn't but said it anyway. He stalled for a moment, so I thought just for fun, a bit of tit for tat, was in order.

"See these three stripes? Now that would make me a sergeant. Now you see this fucking gold crown? Now that would make me a fucking Flight Sergeant. Now we are even."

I was really starting to have a bad day, I continued.

"Sir I was just down at S3. There I was told, that it was all first names, so I was unaware, that the rules changed with the floors. I was only shipped out to this place, twelve hours ago. This was about thirty minutes, after I got the posting notice. Those were handed to me, by my S.M.O. who was, in turn posted to Strike command, with the same speed. So, I am really fucking sorry. Because I don't have a clue, as to what the fuck is going on. Being as no one here, will fucking tell me, Sir!"

The silence was palpable, and then he stuck out a meaty hand and said

"Welcome aboard Andy."

Then the entire classroom, burst into hysterics at my expense.

"Andy, Take a seat please"

There were a few empty seats, along the side of the room, and so, I walked on to the end of the front row, and sat down.

"For the benefit of our newest member from the Royal Air Force, Sergeant Andy Pandy, with the Crown"

I guess, I had asked for that slice of sarcasm

"I shall quickly, go back to the beginning"

The lecture proved to be about the dangers, associated with the different levels of contamination, and how these contagions, would normally be directed toward an army, or Country. So the lecture, was at the basic end of the scale. When the lecture finished, I followed the rest of the sheep, out of the room, and down the corridor, to what was a dining hall, for all ranks. I joined the line, and grabbed a tray and went to the servery, where I chose steak pie and mashed potatoes, along with a mug of coffee. I found an empty table and sat down to eat.

ACT 4

"Hi Andy"

I looked up, and Lachie was standing there.

"What the fuck are you doing here Lachie?"

"Nice to see you too mate. I suspect we are here for the same reason Andy"

He sat down and I looked at him, I noticed that like me he had received a promotion and was sporting a new set of stripes on the arm of his uniform.

"And the reason for that would be?"

"We were in the wrong place, at the wrong time. They probably think that we may have seen, or heard something which folks don't want to be made public knowledge?"

"If that's the case. Why put us with so many other folks? And on a camp with mixed civilians and armed forces? Why not ship us off to Benbecula or Sax Vord? I can understand the promotions, as that gives them a reason for posting us from our regular duties. You know as well as I do. When you get a promotion, you get shipped to a new base."

"Andy, perhaps a lot of these folks here, are here to spy on us. To see if we will say anything, they don't want to be said. And the promotion could be a bribe of some form. You know like a sign of good faith on their part?"

"Could be" I replied. Then I continued after a swig of my coffee.

"So if we are here, why did they ship my boss off to High Wycombe? By the way, he got a promotion too. There are senior ranks here. Why not send him here along with us?"

"I don't know Andy. What I do know is, I don't like this place much. Too many people here, with too many secrets. And everyone here is just 'TOO' nice".

After dinner, we followed the herd back to the class room. Then settled down, for what I imagined to be another boring lecture on NBC (Nuclear, Biological and Chemical) Training, by an Army Medical officer.

I looked up and was surprised to see the man in the Saville Row, Harris Tweed, Suit, standing at the podium.

"Gentlemen and of course Ladies" he began

"You are all here for one reason, and that is because we have a problem. We believe we have a serious problem"

Although no one said anything and apart from 'The Suit' talking to us, no one else was talking or even whispering. The room seemed to have grown quieter.

"Some material was taken from here. We have already seen it used twice, on service personnel."

Lachie and I exchanged glances and even raised our eye brows.

"Some of you will have seen something of it first-hand. Some more of you, may have accidentally been involved in some way, with the people behind this. You have all been drawn here, so that we can find out the following. One, who took it, Two, why he, she or they took it? Three, how do we stop it from being used for whatever reason it has been taken for? All of you have signed an extended version of the Official Secrets Act. This means if you speak of any of this to ANYONE, outside this group. You WILL be incarcerated for the rest of your life, in solitary confinement. Or you will simply disappear. I do hope that I have made this very clear. Most of you are NOT volunteers, and in fact many of you, until now did not really have a clue, as to why you were sent here. Some of you may have seen things, that shall we say gave rise to you questioning incidents around you. Others may have been working alongside, and without the knowledge of those who have taken these items. For whatever the reason you are here, does not really matter. What does matter is that YOU ARE HERE. From now on your ranks and positions that you previously held, do not count. There are reasons for this which I cannot disclose to you at this time. None of you will be privy to the complete picture, unless it becomes operationally necessary, for you to do so." He paused for breath. And then continued

"All of you will report directly to me, or any person that I instruct you to do so. You will not have any outside contact, unless I deem it to be within the remit of this operation. Who and what I am is not important. In a moment I will be handing out mobile phones to each of you. There is one number logged into it, and that is my number. You will NOT use this phone for anything other than to contact me. They are the very latest in Field satellite telephones, so whilst they look like your average Nokia. They are not. Being satellite phones you will never be out of range for contact."

He passed a large box, to the guy on the far end of the front row, and said

"Take one and pass it on to the next"

There were murmurs as the box of phones, was passed from one person to another "Thanks" "Here you go Mate" "Cheers" "Ta" etcetera, etcetera.

When everyone in the room had their new Satellite phone, 'The Suit' continued.

"After some intensive training, some of you will be sent to other bases around the World. Some of you will remain here and some of you will be posted in the field. Each of you will be told personally by me, where you are to be"

He walked from the lectern to the black board and wrote 'EBOLA' on the board

"Many of you will already have heard of Ebola and some of you will know, that it causes a break down, on a Bio Cellular level. Resulting in the bodies organs, turning to 'Mush', for want of a better word"

He paused for a moment. I was pretty sure most of us were aware of what Ebola was and what it did. As over recent years, it had been in the news, due to various outbreaks in Africa.

"The Ebola Virus, is part of a group of Viruses known as V.H.F.'s"

He took the chalk and wrote this under

EBOLA

V.H.F.'s

"VIRAL HAEMORRHAGIC FEVER'S"

He put the chalk down and stood in front of the board.

"There are many of these little bastards".

He went back to the board and picked up the chalk and wrote

CRIMEAN-CONGO HAEMORRHAGIC FEVER.

DENGUE AND SEVERE DENGUE.

EBOLA VIRUS DISEASE.

LASSA FEVER.

MARBURG HAEMORRHAGIC FEVER.

RIFT VALLEY FEVER.

"All of these little bastards will kill you, given half the chance. They all are very contagious" he continued whilst walking up and down in front of the black board.

"Most of these are passed on via direct contact. That is via body fluids, or drinking infected water. But in some cases they can become airborne. Most of what is done at this research establishment is to find cures, or ways to kill these Viruses. However, saying that like most Countries we also are looking at ways of using Biological Weapons, in other words Weaponising Viruses and Bacteria. It is somewhere within this system, that we have suffered some form of a breach"

He stopped and then turned back towards the blackboard. Then with his back towards us continued the talk

"Let's assume that we have managed to do this, and I am not saying we have, but for arguments sake, lets suppose we did and then we gave it a shortened lifespan, by adding a Bacterium to that virus, which in turn would kill the virus in a set time span. That is to say, that if a person were exposed to it. Then it would kill them and those around. BUT only for a short period of time, say eight hours or less. That would make it a Weaponised Virus" he wrote.

BACTERIA + VIRUS + G M

"A Genetically Modified Bacteriological Virus"

"Assuming this exists, and once again I am not telling you it does, and that it has a life span for infecting of just eight hours. Then this sort of weapon 'Could' be used to clear an Area or a Country, in order for it to be invaded, without the loss of life to the invaders. Lots of Countries have looked at the use of Chemical Blistering Agents in ways of debilitating the others armies. However, imagine again if we rather than using a Chemical Blistering Agent changed that"

He took his chalk and wrote in the board again

NATURAL   BIOLOGICAL   RECURRING BLISTERING AGENT

"So it is a GM modified Viro Bio Chem."

FURANOCOUMARIN

"This is found in giant hogweed can inflict painful burns and blisters, on anyone who touches it. The sap contains a phototoxic chemical that becomes active when it's exposed to light. The activated chemical damages the skin, on a genetic level. Grapefruit juice is known to interfere with the action of many medicines. It increases their absorption through the lining of the small intestine, which can result in an overdose by increasing the efficacy. The plant chemicals responsible for both the hogweed and the grapefruit juice effect are known as Furanocoumarins" he paused again.

"Now imagine that we, then genetically modified this Hogweed sap so that it became strong enough to act like an acid on our NBC suits. Not to burn holes in it or anything like that, but to make the molecules small enough to get through the microscopic weave and then to deliver the Virus of Ebola but with a shortened lifespan and a version that was so modified that it only attacked a specific part of the body, in the same way that the meningitis virus tends to do by attacking, the membrane of the brain. So turning the brain to mush in minutes rather than hours, but that the virus would die within the host, because of the added Bacteria. Why would we want to create such a monster as this? Because, our Country is no longer in a Nuclear race. We, that is, all the major countries, of the world are in a BIO-CHEM Race. Where the deadliest and most indefensible bug becomes the one thing, that stops the other side, from either attacking or retaliating."

He put the chalk down on the lectern and

"We are at war with an unknown enemy, who has managed to either get our weapon, or get the information on how to fabricate it. We have to get it back at all costs and we have to ensure that no one else can have it, or any knowledge of it. Some of you are involved in medicine and are technically Non Combatants. However, this is NOT a normal situation. Some of you were part of the program to create our defensive and offensive weapons. Of which many of you, are also Scientists or Doctors. Some of you are just Soldiers, Sailors or Airmen. As of now NONE OF THAT MATTERS. As of now, you are part of a team that may have to save mankind. There are three ways it can end for all of us. A lifetime in Jail, Dead, or We win. So let's have a coffee break. Obviously you will want to talk about what I have said here, but do so ONLY with the people inside this room. Later I will assign each of you, to a more specific task. Then from that point on. You are not to discuss it with anyone, other than me, or if I have set up teams, then with your team members. I will choose from the personnel, within this room. You will work this project together, and then report back to me. Now get a coffee from the machines at the end of the room"

He wiped the board and put away some files he was reading from. I held back with Lachie.

ACT 5

"What kind of shit are we in now Andy?"

"I am sure you and I both know, it is the worst possible kind of shit. It has to do with that bloke, we pulled from a tree yesterday Lachie. But he was alive, when they took him from Brawdy."

"Andy. Who were 'They'? And why did they take him?"

"I have no Idea Lachie. They turned up shortly after we got back to base, and took him off in chopper. A few minutes after that, I was promoted and given the boot from Brawdy. After that I was posted to here, and my boss got the same thing, except he was posted to Strike Command."

I pointed at his newly acquired third strip

"And it looks like you and I got the same thing"

"Aye"

"So, what do you think happens now? Lachie"

"I have a feeling we are about to find out Andy."

Most of the folks in the room had their coffee and were sat back down, although some were huddled in small groups around the edge of the room, probably discussing things, like Lachie and I were.

"Can you all, please take your seats"

The 'Suit' was standing at the lectern again this time with a clipboard in his hands.

"I am going to split you into groups for your various assignments. When I call your names if you stand with those who you have been patched with"

"Group one. Robert Weston, Mark Shallows, Jane Miller.

Group two. John Roberts, Martin Wilson, Rory McKay, Ian Watts.

Group three. Mary Morris, Millie Wyatt, Susan Randall, Steph Brown

Group four. Brian Robertson, Andrew White, Stephen Munroe,

Group five. David Heinman, Mick Jay, Peter Humphries, Jayde Smith, Yvonne Harper, Jennifer Harper

Group six. Alun Verne, Colin Eccles, Eric Slow, Gordon Andrews

Group seven. Andy McPhee, Lachlan Henderson, Jon

Steinman, Hans Gunnerson.

Those of you who have not had your names called could you please exit this room and enter the second room on the left where another person will assign your various tasks. And thank you all for your patience."

We went over and shook hands with the other two men in our group, and said our polite Hello's. Those who were not selected were shuffling out of the room.

"Right folks I gave you a brief outline, of the sort of thing that goes on around here and what it is we are trying to find. Each group is to be given specific agendas as well as training that will be specific, to their operational duties. You have already been grouped by certain skills that you either already have or have an aptitude to take on board. Each of your groups will be barracked together and will no longer have contact, with any of the other groups, or for that matter with any other person, other than those I arrange to be with you. These would be the training instructors, who will only be training you. They will know nothing of your objectives. Should any person outside your group, try to involve themselves in your project? You are then to immediately inform me. So keep your phones charged, and with you at all times. First briefing will be arranged for you tomorrow. I shall then arrange for each team, to have a leader that is suited for the group's role. It will not be based on Rank, but purely what I deem to be the right set of characteristics and skill sets. For today that is it. Tomorrow we begin our journeys. Go to reception and tell them your group number and they will arrange for you to be taken to your accommodation. Thank you.

ACT 6

The place where we were barracked, was more like a small private hotel. Each of us had our own en-suite rooms. Downstairs, there was a large dining room, which had a fully staffed kitchen off from it. We had our own private bar, with barman. Also a soundproofed lounge area. What it did not have, was outside access. No Windows, No TV, No Internet, No Phones, apart from the ones we carried with us. We ate pretty much in silence, and the food was great. Then we all got a drink and went into the lounge and closed the heavy doors. We sat around in the plush leather arm chairs. It was Jon who broke the silence

"Do you think someone has stolen something, from the Frankenstein's that work here?"

"I think we have a lot more to learn. Before we actually know who, what, and if anything has been stolen. I don't think we have had much of the truth told to us so far. I mean that 'The Suit' never told us who he is. Let alone who he works for. We don't know what each group will be set up for, or how our roles, will interact with theirs. Hell we don't know a damn thing, apart from what we know about ourselves" I said.

I was careful not to let the others know, that Lachie and I actually knew each other as lifelong friends. This could just be some weird form of military exercise. Just to see how we worked under pressure. The RAF is very good at doing that sort of thing. I was sure the other services also did the same sort of thing. We called it TAC-EVAL or Tactical Evaluation. Although if this was one of them, it was a lot more complex, than the ones I had been used too. In a normal TAC-EVAL, the whole military station would be involved in a series of scenarios. In order for the Tactical Evaluation teams, to see how the camp would perform in the event of a war. The initial start would be station alarm being sounded and all personnel would report to their place of work. Then the camp would go into lock down. After that there would be a huge selection of exercises. Each designed to test individual sections. Security of the camp perimeter would be tested with attacks by ground forces. Then there would be an Air Raid Warning RED in which the camp would be subjected to a simulated, attack using conventional weapons (the TACE-VAL personnel, usually from strike command) would place flash bangs and smoke flares around the areas that had been "Bombed" and then the station emergency services, would go into operation. We would go and collect the injured and take them back to the medical Centre. There, we would TRIAGE them. Proffer theoretical medical treatment, and then assign the wounded to other medical establishments. After this attack exercise, there would be an Air Raid Warning Black (the warning of a Nuclear, biological or Chemical attack) We would all then put on our NBC Suits and Gas Masks and take to our Nuclear Shelters. In my case, it was directly under the medical Centre. We would take all the 'Patients' and 'walking wounded' down into our shelter. After which the thick blast proof doors would be sealed shut. Then we would then await the all clear siren. After a full series of these tests, which could last for up to two weeks. The base would then be told the exercise was over and every one would return to a normal regime. So this situation we were involved in, did not feel like a 'Normal' Exercise to me.

"So where are you guys all from?" Jon asked

"I am from Iceland, but I was on attachment to your Army" said Hans Gunnerson.

He was a giant of a man. He must have been six foot, six or seven inches tall. I would guess his weight to be somewhere between fifteen and sixteen stone. He had broad shoulders. He had crew cut ginger blonde hair. His skin was almost white, but for the freckles that covered all the exposed skin. Hans was definitely Nordic in origin. His voice was deep and bass like and seemed to come from below his boots. There was also warmth to that voice, that made him instantly a really likeable person.

"I have come to teach your army, how to Ski and Kayak. Also to show them, how they can survive in the cold. Unfortunately, you don't have much snow here in England, so your Regiments travel up to the Scottish Mountains. There is a little snow there, but not as much as my home."

"Where's that" asked Jon

Hans looked up at Jon. He seemed to choose his words carefully,

"I am from a small village, on the North East coast of Iceland. It is called Bakkageroi. It is a fishing village. But there was no real work so I left and joined the Army."

"What about you Lachlan?"

I asked hoping he would get the message that I did not want everyone seeing or knowing a deep insight to our friendship. When he answered it was with a lie, as I hoped it would be.

"Oh me, I'm from an Island too. I am from Benbecula. It's a small Island off the west coast of Scotland. I left to join the RAF Regiment".

That was the thing about Lachie he could make a lie from the truth and vice versa. Although Lachie was now from Kinbrace his parents had moved there from Benbecula when he was about five years old. Then they split and his dad stayed in Kinbrace. He still maintained that lilt, of the Hebrides accent. I jumped in next before Jon could ask

"I am also a Highlander, but from a Village Keiss"

Like Lachlan I threw in a half truth. My family had lived there for a very short time. It was a small Fishing Village on the East coast of Caithness. Where the coastal area is rugged and was windblown from the cold North Sea, combined with the Northerly wind from the cruel North Atlantic.

"I am a medic in the RAF, but I guess most of you know that as I was one of the few folks that arrived in Uniform"

I looked at Jon,

"So what's your story mate, where you from?"

"I am from Israel. I joined the Israeli Army right out of school. My family is from Jerusalem. My father was killed in the Six Day war. So since I left school the Army has been my life. I don't know why they sent me here. I was working with the SAS teaching. I was with them on temporary assignment."

I noticed that he gave more info than the rest of us. However he did not say what he was teaching the SAS or where, he was working with them.

"Nice to meet you all" I said

Then I raised my glass of Jameson's Irish Whisky. We all clinked our glasses. I looked at Lachlan and caught what would have looked to most folks as a slight twitch on his finger as he raised his glass to ours. That twitch was a signal we had used when stalking Red Deer, as lads. It meant 'We can't talk as we are too close to the deer, and that we did not want to spook them with any sounds.' After we had some small chit chat with the others, as folks do when they have a drink in a bar. Then I decided to call it a night, so that Lachie and I could have our private chat. I didn't know what 'The 'Suit' had in store for us tomorrow, and wanted at least to be semi awake for whatever it was.

"Night all, I am off for some shut-eye, it's been a long day for me. See you all in the morning"

ACT 7

I stood up and went upstairs to the room I had been allocated. I really was actually tired, but I knew it would not be long before Lachie, would knock on my door. I did not have that long a wait. I had just finished emptying my kit-bag and hanging my uniforms in the wardrobe. I had had to rapidly re-pack them from my room in the Sergeants mess, when I had been allocated to team seven. So now most of my previously, neatly ironed and folded items, were somewhat rumpled. There was a soft knock at the door. I Went to open it and was surprised when Hans was there.

"Uhh Can I help you Hans?"

"I need to talk to you please"

I opened the door then looked up and down the corridor. There was no one else there. So I motioned for Hans to enter. He came in and sat down in the lone armchair. After closing the door I sat down on the edge of the bed and looked at Hans.

"What's on your mind Hans?"

He said nothing for about thirty seconds and I wondered if he had come because, he liked me or he hated me. Either way I was starting to worry.

"I have seen him before" he said

His voice was such a quiet whisper that I struggled to hear it. I waited for more but it did not come so I asked the obvious question.

"Who is it you have you seen before Hans?"

I too whispered, though was not sure as to why, as there were just the two of us in my room. It was the sort of reaction that you automatically do when someone whispers to you.

"Andy, I don't know where I have seen him, but my mind is like a camera. I just need to remember where" he whispered again.

Another thirty seconds of waiting. I was just about to ask again when he said

"Jon, I have seen him."

He was whispering so quietly that I had to move closer to him, in order to actually hear.

"What do you mean Hans? Have you seen him in

Iceland, or here at Porton?" I whispered

"No Andy it was before Porton, and I think it was not a long time ago. But I know I have seen him. I recognise him for sure. I don't think he knows me, but I have seen his face before."

"So why are you telling me Hans? Why not tell the guy in the Suit?"

I was worried that we were whispering like co-conspirators. This alone, was liable to get you locked up around here

"Because Andy, I have seen him also."

"OK Hans. Tell me truthfully. Who you are? Because I know you are holding something back. Like WHY you were sent here? If Porton Down has some problem with their security why would Iceland need to be involved? Who were you working with before here? What were you doing with them? And why are we whispering when we are alone?"

He got up and went to the Fridge and helped himself to a bottle of water, unscrewed the top and took a small sip.

"You might think I am crazy"

He said as he walked up and down on the floor. All the time looking at objects, in the room. He stopped every now and then, to take a closer look at some items. By now, I practically had my ear to his lips, when he spoke. I was patiently waiting for him to open up to me. He put his fingers to his lips, I thought he wanted me to be patient and wait for him to come up with a question, or a statement for me. He switched on the Camp's internal radio system, and an old Marc Bolan song, played 'Ride a White Swan'. Then he turned the sound up a little, and went to the bathroom where he turned the shower on. I was actually beginning to think he was crazy. I was formulating a plan, in my mind's eye, as to how I could take down this giant of a man, with my bare hands. When he came back into the room I stood up, thoroughly expecting to have to fight for my life. With the fight or flight question, banging around inside my head. He unplugged the Bedside lamp. This is it, here it comes, I was thinking. I flexed my mussels and started to ball my hands into fists. When again, he put his fingers to his lips and then pointed to the inside of the lamp shade. There stuck to the inside, was a small square circuit board, with a wire trailing out from it.

"OK Andy" he mouthed

Again he pointed to the shower. He carried the lamp towards the shower.

"I will say Goodnight Andy" In a louder voice than he had been using.

He put the lamp gently down on the bathroom floor.

"See you in the morning Andy. I can see you were just getting ready to shower."

He shut the bathroom floor. Then he whispered

"Say Goodnight to me please" I was thinking weird or what!

"OK Hans. Goodnight. Try not to drink too much. See you in the morning"

I opened the Door to let Hans out and Lachie was standing there, ready to knock. Hans put his fingers to his lips, and Lachie looked at me. I just shrugged. I guessed that now Lachie was here, at least I would have a fighting chance against the man mountain that was in my room. Lachie came in and I gently closed the door after him. Hans made sure the Camp Radio was loud enough to cover all but a shout. Then he took his fingers from his lips.

"Hi Lachlan. Fancy seeing you here?"

"Andy. What's going on?"

"I am not sure but I think Hans, was just about to tell me"

Hans now sat back down in the chair and Lachie sat on the bed end, which left me standing.

"Can you trust him?" Hans asked pointing at Lachie

"Why?"

"Can you?" he hissed

"Again I have to ask you why?"

"Because I think your life might depend on who you can, and who you can't, trust around here" He replied

"Let's assume for the sake of argument, that I trust him more than I do you, at this moment Hans. On account of he is acting a little saner than you."

I waited, looking at Hans, and waited some more. It was like playing cards against a stone cold card sharp. This was becoming a bit of a habit for me of late. Once again I gave in first.

"Yes I trust him."

I did not really want to give out more info than I had already done so.

"What's this all about then?" said Lachie

"Hans thinks he knows Jon and the guy in 'The Suit'"

"How does he know them?"

"Don't ask me, ask him" I said shrugging my shoulders and pointed to Hans.

Hans stood up and looked first at me and then at Lachie.

"I don't know" he said and continued "But I am one hundred percent sure, I have seen both of them before. They were together in the same place."

Lachie looked at me and I gave him my best 'What the fuck. You ask him, stare'

"When did you see them? Was it here or somewhere else?" Lachie asked

"No it was not here, but somewhere before and sometime before today. I am just trying to remember where" Hans answered

"Hans also found a bug in my room Lachie"

It was out before I could stop it. I had not called him Lachlan I had called him Lachie. I was not sure if Hans had noticed but Lachie had. The dagger stare told me so. Shit I was not a spy. I was a fucking Medic!

"You mean like a cockroach?" asked Lachie

"No an Electronic sort of listening device, Hence the Camp Radio System being on and the shower running without me getting wet!"

"So what is going on Andy?"

We both looked at Hans. Who once again appeared to be deep in his own personal thoughts?

"I am Icelandic, as I told you. I am in the Icelandic Army. This is to say I am also in the Icelandic Special Forces. I am under the command of The National Commissioner's, National Security Office. We do not have a normal standing army. But we have a Coast Guard and a sort of Army for defence. But we also have a Special Forces unit. That unit, is only supposed to operate inside Iceland's borders. I was on an exchange with the SAS and I was training them in how to survive, in extreme cold climates. I was also teaching, skiing and Kayaking. I was attached with G Squadron 22 troop. There was some kind of accident two days ago, on the Brecon Beacons. We were working with a multinational force, under the command of G squadron. It was a mountain top hostage rescue exercise. I did not see the accident. Then they sent a Chinook helicopter and they collected only me. I was flown to a military base near Manchester. My belongings had also been sent there and then the next thing I know is that I had been seconded to C.D.E. Porton Down. I also received Orders from my Director General in Iceland. Stating that I was to do, what they asked me to do. On top of that, I had been given a field promotion to Acting Colonel in the I.D.F. There is something wrong here and I do not want to be involved, in something that might look bad on my Country. Yet, I know Jon, and the one you call 'The Suit'. Because I know I have seen them somewhere before today. Then earlier I went to my room and just out of habit I did a security check. I found a listening bug, just like the one I have found here in Andy's room. I suspect we will find the same in your room too Lachlan. I also suspect, that from the little messages that you two give to each other, I suspect that you are also friends or comrades from before today. I see these things because it is my job. To be not just a soldier, but also part of my job is to be a policeman too. The Icelandic Defence Force covers all sorts of duties as our Director dictates. So I have been honest with you. Can you two, please also be honest with me?"

"WOW. That's kind of a big pill, for me to swallow. But yes Lachie and I do know each other. We grew up together, but I had not seen him for a long time, apart from when we meet up on our annual leave. That was until yesterday, when we met on the Brecon Beacons. I was sent there as a medic from RAF Brawdy. Brawdy is the nearest military base with full medical facilities and is also the home of the 202 RAF Search and Rescue Squadron. I was sent with a Doctor to assist in the recovery of an injured soldier. But the Helicopter could not land near the site so we landed further down the Mountain and that was where we were met by Lachie in a A.P.C, which he was driving. He was also on Temporary attachment to G Squadron of the SAS, as a Driver. Like you we were given field promotions and dispatched here. My boss was sent to RAF Strike Command at RAF High Wycombe, also with a Promotion. So now you know pretty much what we know.

Although I don't think, that 'They' whoever 'They' be, know about Lachie and I being good friends. But of course I could be wrong" I replied.

"So let's assume that is the case here" said Lachie and then continued

"We all know that the one thing that links the three of us in this room is an injured soldier, on the Brecon Beacons. But what about the rest of the folks here, on Teams one, two, three, four, five and six? How do they fit into this picture? More to the point, how do Jon and 'The Suit' fit in. Are they Spooks? And if so who are they spooks for? Let's just wing it at the moment. And see just where all this shit takes us."

"OK I can work with that" I said

"OK we will all talk later, tomorrow, but for now do we tell 'The Suit' about the bugs?" said Hans as he got up to leave.

"I say we don't actually say anything to 'The Suit'. If he and Jon do know each other, and Jon is on our team. Then he is probably here to spy on us. Hans? See if you can remember where you have seen them before and if so, were they together or just in the same place at the same time?"

"I will, Goodnight Andy, and to you too Lachie"

"Goodnight Hans" Lachie and I said together, as Hans left.

"What the fuck is this shit?" Lachie asked to no one in particular, even though I was now, the only other person in the room.

"Do you trust him Lachie? Or is he just spinning a tale?"

"The jury is out on that one Andy. He seems sincere, but I am sure we will know a bit more tomorrow"

"OK Buddy it's great to see you again mate. But I am shit faced tired and need to sleep."

"Yeah me too Andy. I will see you at breakfast and then see when we can get a chance to chat."

"Night Lachie"

"Night Mate" He said and closed the door.

ACT 8

We had breakfast pretty much in silence and then waited for the transport to pick us up to presumably see 'The Suit'. Just after breakfast all of our mobile phones, vibrated at the same time I pulled mine out and looked at the text message

'Your training today will be S.S.T. and whilst this course is normally a full five day course you will receive intensive training and the course is now a single morning'

Lachie showed me his phone and it showed the same message.

"Your transport is here" the receptionist announced

The front door opened and a black mini bus was waiting with the engine running. As we climbed in, I noticed the windows were blacked out and that there was a black privacy glass between us and the driver.

"They either don't want us to see where we are going, or don't want others to see who is in the bus" said Jon

"Or both" said Lachie

Nothing more was said for the next twenty minutes of the journey. There was an internal light and some nondescript music was playing from speakers in the doors. We stopped and the doors were opened and we found ourselves inside a large hanger. With several screened off area's

"Put these on please"

A young woman said as she handed out some blue one piece suits, which appeared to be similar to the NBC suit but more flexible and less charcoal like inside We put the suits on over our uniforms.

"Now if you would please follow me"

She led us into one of the screened off areas, which was set up like a classroom. With a large white screen and a projector set up on a table. There was also a large speaker next to the screen.

"Please sit"

We all took a one of the chairs provided and sat down facing the screen. By the chairs there were blues boots and gloves that matched our fetching blue N.B.C. suits. The slide show began first explaining that these suits were the new and improved version of The Nuclear Biological and Chemical Warfare Protection Suits they carried the acronym of A.N.B.C-W.S. for Advanced Nuclear Biological and Chemical Warfare Suits. Just like the military to come up with a jazzy name for our Blue Men outfits. They were now also water resistant and whilst the suit itself was made of a breathable material. It now had a hard plastic collar that was fitted at the neck, also attached to the 'New Improved Gas Mask' which was now called an R.B-D.C.F. or Re-Breather Double Carbon Filter which was loosely based on the type used by deep sea divers. With the exception, that not only did it allow us to breathe, BUT that it would also allow the moisture from our bodies to escape without misting up the Viewing Glass. This Viewing glass also housed a heads up display. This would show the levels of Carbon Dioxide, RAD Counts for Radiation, along with other poisons. When put on in an emergency the air trapped within the suit and large full face mask would last for up to five minutes. This according to the Sideshow was ample time for us to attach a small Oxygen Bottle to the Utility belt supplied with the suit. Also if correctly worn, the Suit has rubber gaskets that fitted around the Gas Mask making the entire suit and mask a self-contained completely safe breathing module. Apart from that, it was pretty much self-explanatory. There were neat blue boots and gloves to go with it. The Manufacturers 'Claimed' that it was impregnable to 'All Biological and Chemical weapons' and that the new improved anti-radiation shielding provided by the Polymer lead compound would give the wearer, up to one hundred times more protection, than those wearing a standard NBC Suit. They further claimed, it would give as much protection to the wearer, as those worn by the people, who worked at the Cores of Nuclear Power plants. (This I did not want to test).

I wondered, if it would give protection to the 'Nasty Bastard' that the suit was talking about. But being as how they probably created the 'Nasty Bastard' I had to assume that they were wearing suits like this when the made it.

The lights went on, and we were asked to get out of our nice blue suits. Then almost immediately, a Klaxon sounded and we were instructed, we had one minute to get the suits and masks, complete with the gloves and boots on, before a gas would be released. Like most servicemen I had done this. Once a year, on my Ground Defence Training Course. Using the "Gas Chamber" on the camps. Where we would get the same warning and have to get our suits on, before they would release Tear Gas into the chamber. This time though, we were in complete darkness with only a guess as to where we had laid our suits down. Mine was by my chair, that I had been sat in, just as the Klaxon went off. The Klaxon was still sounding at a DB Level, that threatened to burst our eardrums. I struggled into my suit and pulled the mask on. Even before I had put my gloves and boots on, which was just as well. After about thirty seconds, gas poured down into the room, from two vents above us. The Gas was thick and white making visibility impossible even seeing my gloved hands in front of my mask was a non-starter. I was pulling my boots on when I heard someone choking beside me. I shouted to them to stop breathing until they had their Gas Mask on. I reached over to help them. Totally unaware, as to who they were? After about three minutes the extractors and lights came on and we were all standing fully suited, except for Jon. Who was busy puking, his technicoloured breakfast, all over the floor. This whole process was repeated five times over the next hour until we could rip open a pre-packaged ANBC-WS and put it on in under a minute. We had all figured by now the best bet was Mask first, then rearrange the seals once we had the suit on. On to the next screened off area for SST How to mop up a spill. I had my own feelings on that. Don't touch the fucking stuff. But I went along with the game anyway. We learned about Foam barriers and how to spray down. What to do in the event of a spill or a radiation leak. This was followed by intensive Q & A session.

The next section one was not one I had expected it was a small Coffee room where folks could smoke if they wished. Jon was looking a bit better, than he had a couple of hours previously. I know how he felt, as I remembered my time, in Basic Training. We had to enter the Gas Chamber and Stand there, waiting for the CS gas Grenade to be thrown into the room. Then, we would have to get our gas masks on and suit up, then wait another five minutes. After which, the Drill Instructor would call our names and have us remove our masks. For the next part of the torture, we would have to eat a Mars Bar, while we recited our names, ranks and serial numbers. Only after that, we were allowed to put our masks back on. There was a lot of puke filled Gas Masks that day. So it is not one you ever forget. Jon was having his own memorable moment.

ACT 9

Our next class, was not one, I had thought I would ever be doing. Especially as I was a Medic. Our instructor this time, was a man who wore Khakis, without insignia. We were seated next to a large desk. This was covered, in a myriad of what looked like explosive devices and triggering mechanisms. Some of which, were electronic but there were weird looking bottles of substances, with tubes coming out of them. Lots of stuff I personally had never seen before.

"Today we are going to show you how to stop an IED or at least give you a survivable opportunity" He said, as he lifted a cover on some complicated looking electronic mechanism.

"This, Gentlemen is an Electronic Detonator fitted with four Mercury Switches and also fitted with, a Dead Man's Switch. There is an Electronic Timer and just for good measure, I also have it fitted with a Mobile Phone Receiver. In other words, this device is set to explode, when the mobile phone fitted to this device, is called. It also, as I have told you been fitted with a Dead Man's Trigger, only this is in reverse. So that if it is picked up, then it will explode, there are four Mercury Switches that will detonate the device, if there is any movement. Added to this, just for good measure, there is a Countdown Timer fitted with three trigger wires. In short it is a Bomb Disposal nightmare. If this was just connected to explosives in a small amount, say less than half a kilogram, and in an open area. We would then encase it in foam, and sandbags. After which we could detonate it safely. If not, we would be forced to try and separate the explosives from the trigger. However again I have fitted Anti Tamper Needle Firing Pins. These are inside, the actual detonators. They are made up of, a slim tube with a fine needle balanced inside a magnetic casing, and should you attempt to remove the needle there is a ninety-nine point nine percent, chance that you will connect to the external sleeve and BOOM! This is the most complex detonator system in the world. I know because I created it."

He looked around the table and I am sure that all he could see were extremely white faces. He continued.

"What you have to do, is PRIORITISE the triggers. Which one will set it off first?" He said and emphasised prioritise.

I think it was meant to be a question, but it came out more like a rhetorical statement. So no one talked. He continued again

"Depending on how much time is left on the timer, will also depend on which of the triggering mechanisms you tackle first. Let us assume that it has less than two minutes. Which would you disable first?" This time its sounded more like a question so Lachie signalled with a small movement of his hand that he had an answer to this question.

"Yes?" said the instructor

"If the mobile phone is accessible, could you not simply remove the battery?"

"You might possible get away with that. Assuming that you do not trigger the mercury switches. You are on the correct track though. We would disable the mobile phone from receiving a signal thus blocking any calls. This is something that we do automatically these days, although we do not advertise it in the newspapers."

He lifted the cover on a small rectangular box and flipped up what looked like a two inch flat satellite dish. Then continued.

"Obviously it takes too much time, to shut down all the mobile phone towers and their networks. So this little baby" His finger pointed directly at the box like gadget next to the explosive device.

"It will create a dead zone of about thirty meters around the device so unless the person, who wants it detonated, is standing within the blast zone, it will kill the signal. So yes, we FIRST set the blocker up. Then we look at the timer and there are many types of timers. Unfortunately for us no one attaches a wind up clock to their bombs any more. They are Electronic and most work from a quartz crystal, that vibrates at a set rate of 32,768 vibrations per second. Stopping this normally is not an option as they tend to go right to zero when the power source is removed. As there is enough of a charge left in the quartz crystal to do that, and so we go BOOM once again. It's not like you see it, in the movies. Where the guy cuts the wire and the clock stops with one tenth of a second to go. You cut the wire and BOOM. However, that said you can slow the cyclic rate of the quartz crystal down from 32,768 vibrations per second to about 1,000 vibrations per second. This should increase the time exponentially of the count down. This effectively means a few seconds, becomes, somewhere between three and six minutes. Again this is dependent on the quality of the timer and how well it is screened. Trust me, that is a lot of extra time."

He paused, for breath and then asked a question

"So how do we achieve this?"

It was Hans that spoke up first, albeit over Lachie's muttered "Run like fuck."

Hans said "We use a powerful electromagnetic field"

"Partially correct but first we have to isolate the Sleeve and Pin detonator, before we can use the electromagnetic field and the only quick way of doing that is to wrap the area of the Pin Detonator in lead shielding before we can create our own magnetic field. So you use this stuff here as he pointed to a roll of grey tape. This stuff is made from lead particles, which are covered in a flexible poly resin. This allows it to provide Magnetic shielding, without it being conductive to electrical current. Thus not allowing it to go BOOM. Then we use this wonderful little device. This is not dissimilar to an MRI scanner that is used in hospitals only much smaller.

"This ring"

He said pointing to the six inch plastic ring, that he held in his hand which had two wires connected to a large plastic box by a long cable.

"You lay on top of the LED readout or Timer. This when activated, will slow the timer down. Allowing you time, to work on the other triggers."

He laid the ring down and then put a large spray can with a nozzle, on the table. There was a flexi hose attached, to the nozzle of the can. The tubing was not dissimilar to the type used in medicine.

"So the next item to sort, are the Mercury switches. What most people don't know about mercury, is that you can freeze it! The stuff that we have, in this deeply insulated container over here, is a mixture of Dry Ice, liquid Nitrogen and the stuff that they use to get deep freezes to go to minus forty degrees, Isobutane. It gets mixed but only in the nozzle. When this spray is applied carefully, to a small amount of Mercury. The Mercury will then turn from its liquid state, to solid form. Now by using this hose here"

He said pointing to the surgical flexible tubing.

"And carefully running it around the areas where the Mercury switches are and being careful, not to knock the needle and pin detonators. As this will also cause it to go BOOM. Now when you have the tubing around the switches you then need to make some holes in the tubing either side of the switch. I use the point of a jeweller's screwdriver, which I then heat with a cigarette lighter. Then I melt some holes in the tube. When that is done, turn the nozzle of the can on, so that you have a steady flow, of the freezing gas. Make sure you don't have a naked flame near this, or it will go BOOM. Keep the gases flowing at a steady rate, for at least two minutes! Then you can move on to the final switch. This will normally be a simple pressure switch, attached to the bottom of the device. This will be spring loaded and will detonate the device, if lifted. So at this point with the clock running slow and the phone disabled, the Mercury frozen solid. The needle pins are shielded. You can then carefully and gently, slide a thin sheet of non-conductive material under the device, if you feel it snag more than one millimetre, then you are fucked! There is only one way to move the device to a safe area and that is to take whatever it is sat upon other than that you will have to then make the choice of which wire to cut on the main detonator, which will be the Pin and Sleeve detonator. There will no doubt, be many wires, encased in some form of housing. This they will have done, so that you don't know which wire goes where? At this point you will probably have three, four or five wires going to the detonator. Two will be the actual circuit and the other two or three, will be alternative live, or duds. You will have to choose the one, which will be the ground, or the negative. Not great odds but a lot better, than none at all."

I was beginning to feel, that they most definitely had chosen the wrong guy in picking me. I was not made for hero shit. I loved my life just the way it was. I guessed that many in the other teams would be thinking the same as me, and perhaps some others in Team Seven.

"If you will follow me through here" he said

And then he walked through an opening in the partition into another area. There were four large cubicles and on each table there looked to be a similar device to the one, that he, had just had explained to us. It was sat on a large glass table. There was also a tool box on the floor. Each cubical was made from a steel frame and built using large glass panels. With one of these panels, used for a door.

"Each of you, have five minutes, to defuse these LIVE devices. They are not fakes! THEY WILL EXPLODE!"

I put my hand up and said "I am a medic and a non-combatant"

To which several large men appeared and bodily put all four of us inside our individual glass boxes. Then they locked the doors behind us.

"People this is NOT a drill, these will explode once I start the timers. Your choice stop them or not"

I stood in front of my device and looked to my right I could see Lachie was already busy working on his, as was Hans on my left. How could they do this to us? We are supposed to be on their side. My mind went into panic mode. I switched on the Phone blocker and shielded the pin detonators then put the MRI device around the digital timer. This started to slow the clock. However, I knew I could not do the mercury in the time. That's it. I die here for what, Jesus, this is mad, I thought.

Well there was no point in my crying about it, so I sat down on the floor. How the hell was I supposed to get out of this? Then it struck me I opened the tool box and there was a large hammer there. I could smash the door and then escape. Perhaps with enough time left to get Lachie out? I smashed the hammer against the door several times and all I got for my efforts was a sore wrist. I looked at the timer, which was slowly counting down from one minute and forty two seconds.

"Fuck Fuck Fuck" I shouted to no one in particular.

Then, I had a strange epiphany type moment. If the Gas in the canister could freeze Mercury, perhaps it would do the same to the glass and make it more brittle. So I sprayed the gas, onto the middle of the door until it started to frost over. Then I gave it an almighty blow with the hammer. This time the hammer bounced out of my grip and hit me on my knee.

"Shit Fuck Bugger!" I shouted and hopped around on my one good leg.

One minute and two seconds. Time was really slipping away. Of course the problem was not that the glass would not freeze, it was the size of the door. It acted like a heat sink only in reverse. The area of the door was too big. So I sprayed what was left of the gas on the door lock and handle. Twenty-three seconds I picked up the hammer and with every fibre in my body, I swung at the lock, which shattered into a million pieces and the door swung open. I went to Lachie's door and unlocked it and then to Hans and finally Jon's. Both Hans and Lachie, exited like me and we ran towards the main exit.

"Jon! Come on man. We have to go NOW!" I shouted at him.

"No, I can do this. Leave me it's OK" he replied.

"Leave him Andy" shouted Lachie "There is no time"

We had just reached the main doorway into the room, when we heard a soft thud and whoosh. This was followed closely, by three more

"Jesus Lachie. How the hell were we, as untrained bomb disposal folks, supposed to stop them from going off?"

He looked back at me and said

"We were not"

"You are correct" said the voice from behind us. It was the instructor.

"It was an impossible task" he paused and then continued.

"Have you ever watched Star Trek? The episode when Captain Kirk beats the simulator in the Kobayashi Maru test. It was designed by Spock to be an impossible task. But Kirk beats it, because he cheated. However, because the task had been made an absolute unwinnable task, the only way to win, was in fact to cheat. We wanted to see if you could think outside of the box and to improvise when the pressure is really on. Well done."

I looked at him and said

"What about Jon? He stayed in his room when the bombs went off".

"Oh yes, Aahhh well not a problem, that's life" he replied

I wanted to kill him, for allowing a man to die on an exercise. I had no love for Jon, but for him to bite the bullet on a training exercise, seemed a bit extreme. Then Jon walked into the room covered from head to toe in bright yellow neon paint.

"It was only a test and just so you know. You are the only team to ever have walked away not covered in paint. Well most of you did."

"Jon? Why did you not run when you had the chance?"

"I almost had it" he said.

Then he launched himself at the instructor, grabbing him around the throat. We managed to pull him off before he totally crushed the guy's windpipe. The instructor struggled to his feet and then said

"That will be all for today"

The bus was waiting for us and they did not seem to mind that one of us was a day-glow man. There was almost no conversation as we drove back to the accommodation. Jon was definitely sulking. When we arrived, we went up to our respective rooms and showered. I sat on the edge of my bed and thought hard about today's events. Trying to figure out just what the hell I was doing here, at this place. I came up with no answer to myself. So I dried myself and dressed in Jeans, I threw on a Ban the Bomb T-shirt, along with a pair of training shoes. My hands were still shaking from the last event of the day. I knew it was just an adrenalin rush, caused by being scared out of my wits, by the bomb disposal lesson. I combed my hair and went down to the bar.

"Large Jameson's please"

The steward poured the drink "Ice?"

"No thanks, the only thing I want in that is MORE!"

"Bad day?" He asked

I did not bother answering at first, then realised it was not this guy's fault.

"You could say that" I raised my glass to him

"Cheers" and then took a sip and let the Irish Whisky sit in my mouth before allowing it to slide down my throat and enjoying the feeling of warmth that it gave, followed by the smooth taste. I sat down in one of the arm chairs and waited for the others to come down, so that we could all eat dinner at the same time. I was sat with my back to the bar.

"Double Laphroaig Sixteen, Please"

"Hi Lachie" I said over my shoulder"

"You want a drink Andy"

"I already got one thanks" as I raised my glass without turning around

"Looks like you could use a refill Andy"

"Another Jameson's for my friend there, too please, he said to the Barman

Then he brought the drinks to where I was sat and put them down on the table.

"Pretty fucked up sort of day mate." He said as he pulled another arm chair over and sat down.

"And then some" I replied

I poured what was left of my first drink, into the glass of the second one that Lachie had got for me. Then I took a large swig and sat back into the chair.

"When did you realise that that bomb was unstoppable?" Lachie Asked?

"I never did. I just knew, that I could not do it Lachie. I was fucking scared Lachie! I am supposed to save people by treating the ailments. If I wanted to become a Bomb Disposal Expert, I would have joined REME or your lot mate. You know me mate, I am not normally an easily scared sort of person, but I genuinely thought, that the bloody thing was going to blow up and plaster me all over the inside of the glass cage!"

"Well if it's any consolation to you. So did I Andy. I had all the parts done with about two minutes to go. However, the Dead Man's Pin was impossible as they had made a slight rebate for it to sit in, on the table. So there was no way to slide anything under it. Also I noticed that the MRI device did not slow the timer as much as the one he showed us did."

"But you never went postal on the door like me?"

"No but I was planning to sit under the table when the clock got to thirty seconds. The table being made from the same stuff as the bomb proof rooms they put us in. So what gave you the idea for breaking the door Glass door?"

"I never broke the door, I broke the Lock mate. And the 'Idea' well that was just blind panic and a light bulb moment"

Hans came into the bar with Jon

"Drinks for anyone?" Hans said to us

"I'm fine thanks Hans"

"I'll have another thanks" said Lachie

"Gin and Tonic for me please and what would you like Jon?" Hans said to the barman and then asked Jon.

"Can I just have a Soda Water please with Ice and lemon. Thank You Hans" Jon Replied. When they had their drinks they came and joined us at our table.

"Are you OK Jon?" I asked him as he sat down

"I am now, but I really thought I had bought the farm, when it went off. It was pretty intense for me."

"Why did you not run when I opened your door?" I asked

"I just thought I could do it"

I left it at that, as from his tone, I thought he sounded tad bitter about it all. I decided not to push him on it. Hans said nothing. He just sat there with his drink.

"Gentlemen dinner is being served in the Dining room" said the Steward

"Best go eat then" said Lachie.

His appetite was never damaged by anything and the very thought of it made me smile. We all sat down at the same table which was set for six people

"Perhaps Mummy and Daddy Bear are coming to dinner?" Lachie said

"Nah Lachie but it could be those two over there" I said, pointing to the two men that came in the room and headed towards our table.

"Good evening folks" I said

"Care to join us"

Lachie said in his usual tongue in cheek way. As none of the other three tables in the room were set for dinner

"Thanks" said the taller of the two.

The tall one, who was about six foot seven inches, was dressed in Jeans and a dress shirt with a blazer over. He wore a pair of brown semi-formal shoes, on his feet. The other man was almost a foot shorter and looked like he did not work out too much. He was dressed in a pair of light tan chinos and a dress shirt. He wore a pair of desert combat boots on his feet. He was almost bald and about forty years old, which also made him look a lot older than his friend, who looked approximately half his age. Unlike the smaller fat guy, the tall man, had a full head of wavy brown hair. His haircut was a good bit too long, for the regulation military cut.

"Thanks that would be nice" the short one said

I kicked Lachie's foot under the table and he gave me a slight nod indicating that he was aware of my doubts over these two new folks, who had come to dinner. Because we four were sat two aside on opposite sides of the table the two newcomers had to sit at either end of the table, in the Mama and Papa bear seats.

"Hi all" said the taller of the two."

We all said hello and were interrupted by the waiter

"Fillet Steak or Steamed Salmon?"

All of us ordered the steak, and each of us told the waiter how we would like it cooked. As we were waiting for the food to arrive, I took a good look at our new guests, whilst they exchanged small talk with the rest of the table. The short bald one must work in an office as his skin was very pale and he was a bit overweight for the military. So he must either be a civilian working on the base or he worked within the intelligence services. The taller of the two could be military, but there was just something about him that did not click. In a way he was being over friendly, although neither of them had offered their names. My first impression of him that he might be a civilian contractor, working within one of our security services. The steaks came and we ate and chatted about the events of the day. It's surprising how hungry you get after thinking you were going to die! The steak was really nice and I cleared my plate, in fact I nearly ordered another but decided against it. I drank a glass of iced water that was served from a large pitcher on the table. I decided against desert. I tapped Lachie's foot again and then excused myself from the table. I got up and walked through to the bar. I chose against having another alcoholic drink, as I wanted to keep a clear head.

"Tonic Water please"

I said to the barman. After I got it, I went and sat down to wait for Lachie. I did not have to wait too long. Lachie came straight in and sat down opposite me

"What's up Andy?"

"Fancy a walk outside?"

"Sure" he replied

I quickly finished my drink and carried the glass back to the bar

"Thanks" I said to the barman and walked out with Lachie.

We went outside and walked over to the car park. There was a bench next to the Rose Garden. I sat down. The sun had set but it was not quite dark.

"What's up Andy?"

"This shit, is not for me Lachie. I am not some kind of SAS action man. I don't even know where this thing is going mate. I am going to ask to be reassigned I just wanted to let you know first mate."

"I understand Andy. It's pretty intense even for us Rock Apes too. I have never had training like this before. The closest I ever got to Bomb Disposal was How to arm and disarm a Claymore, or a Hand grenade"

"I am sorry to leave you here mate. But it's just not for me."

"That's OK Andy, I'll miss you though, but no doubt we will see each other when we go home at Christmas."

"What do you think about all that spy shit in my room last night? And those two new guys that came in tonight?"

"I have been giving that a bit of thought. If they are from our side then they obviously don't trust us. If they are from another side then our side need to step up their game. As for those two new guys the young guy could be Military but the fat guy is a pen pusher. What makes you think they are iffy?"

"I don't know Lachie, it just does not feel right. In fact, nothing feels right about this place. I know that most of what they do at CDE Porton Down is Secret. It's probably the worst kept secret in the world, when you look at it that way. Everyone in the Military knows what they do here. But I have worked in Top Secret bases before. And they have never been like this place. Also I do not like the way this training is going. I know that health and safety is a standing joke with the RAF or the Army, but that stunt with the bombs today was just plain fucking stupid"

"Like I said mate I am going to miss you Andy. But I do understand what you are saying. I am only staying because I figure that it cannot harm my chances of getting into the SAS. That is where I want to be. I fancy the Action stuff mate, besides it works great for the girls" he said with a broad smile.

"Just be careful Lachie and don't trust Jon or those two other guys. I will let you know in the morning how my call works out with 'The Suit'. I stood up and we walked back to the accommodation and went to our rooms. Just out of interest I looked inside the lamp to see if there was a replacement bug there, after I had flushed it down the toilet last night. There was nothing there.

I stripped down to my boxers and lay on the bed listening to see is anyone was hanging around my door. I fell off to sleep

I woke about five in the morning. I got up and switched off the Camp radio that I had fallen asleep too. I stripped off and got in the shower. I turned the shower on so it was steaming hot and stepped under the powerful flow. Letting it pound on my back and shoulders. I stood like that for a good ten minutes and then washed myself. Then I turned the shower all the way to cold, and like before I stood with my hands braced against the tilled wall. I stood there until I felt fully awake. I turned the shower off and towel dried myself and wrapped the towel around my waist. I shaved, brushed my teeth and splashed cologne on. Then I dressed in my number one uniform, which had been cleaned and pressed. I combed my hair and looked in the full length mirror. I had filled out since I first joined as an eighteen-year-old lad. I guess my body had reached its peak fitness. I checked myself in the mirror and felt slightly narcissistic, admiring the row of medal ribbons, none of them were for bravery. They were either long service or campaign medals. But they looked good none the less. My shoes were bulled up to a glass like shine. I remembered the first time I had managed to get what I thought was a glass like finish to my toe caps, and how the Drill Instructor at RAF Swinderby, had taken one look at them and had thrown them out of an open window. He then, had me do them again and again, each time throwing them out. This happened up to about the fourth week of basic training. He had now left me alone, and decided to pick on some other poor soul. I looked down and was happy to see the reflections coming from my toe caps. I straightened my Tie and walked over to the bedside cabinet and picked up the mobile phone. I opened the phone and selected the only name in the directory and my finger hovered above the call button. I had never quit anything before. When others had quit at basic training camp, after been called Wankers and Bastards by the Drill Instructors, having their hard work destroyed by the very same individuals. Then I suddenly realised. That these guys who I thought of bullies, had in fact made me into the man I was now. I was NOT a quitter. I also knew if it were the other way around. Lachie would never leave me, to do it all on my own. I closed the phone. Put it in my pocket.

ACT 10

I put my cap on and went out of my room. I walked downstairs and out the front door. I needed a walk to clear my mind. It was a beautiful morning and the sun was rising. There was a slight frost on the ground and the odd patch of mist in the distance. All in all it was a good day to be alive. Like Basic Training, I supposed that this regime was going towards an end point. So I decided to stay with it, at least for now. However, I still wanted to talk to the man in the suit. Whilst they had not asked me to kill anyone, I was still a Non Combatant. I was bound by the regulations, laid down by the Geneva Convention, governing medical personnel. The thing is, I wondered, if I was a medic any more. The time was now six forty-five. I could smell the coffee drifting out from the dining room. So I walked in there and helped myself to a large mug of the steaming black liquid. It was a lot better than the regular coffee, I had been used to, at other Military Bases. Normally I would have gone out for a run at six in the morning and then gone back and had a shower and changed into my uniform. Then perhaps grab a quick breakfast, before going into work for eight. The next man down to the dining room was Jon followed by Hans. Both came and sat down next to me.

"You look like you are going on parade" said Hans.

"Just got up with one idea and changed my mind, but not the uniform"

Lachie came in wearing a jogging suit and let out a wolf whistle. So I gave him the bird.

He grabbed a coffee and came over

"Who is she?"He said

"That's what I like about you mate"

"What's that then?" he replied

"Nothing" I said with a smile

"Awww you like nothing? About us Rock Apes? Now my feelings are hurt." he said with a wink.

"I was just planning a chat with 'The Suit' and did not want to be out-dressed by a fairy like him"

So I ate my breakfast, whilst bearing the butt of Lachie and Hans's jokes and jibes, about wearing my number one Dress Uniform. That was until Jon, tried to join in on our private joke. That kind of killed the conversation. We ate our bacon and eggs in an awkward silence. The two guys from last night did not appear for breakfast. At eight, on the dot, the bus arrived to take us to wherever, they were taking us this morning. Ten minutes later we arrived. Again it was a Hanger style building. Once again we went in, without even knowing, what was on the cards for us today. There were two tables set up with Rifles and Pistols as well as Machine Guns and RPG's.

"Gentlemen" said a voice from behind us

He was a tall, broad shouldered and stocky man. He was as black as the Ace of Spades. He bore tribal scars to his face, yet his accent was decidedly British. What you would call a 'Toffee Boy'. He managed to make Hans, look small. After I first met Hans, I would not have thought that possible.

"My name is Abdalla. This means Servant of God. Do not think of me as a saint, as I am not. I am with the Kenyan Elite Special Forces. It saddens me to say that in my duty, I have taken many men's lives. I did so only because, they wanted to kill my people, or have stupidly tried to take my life and send me to my God. I have been assigned to teach you how to shoot. That is to say how to shoot with accuracy, under pressure. I am sure, because you are here, that all of you can shoot, to some degree. However, you have probably not been given the choice of gun, that suits your shooting style. I want you to forget today, everything that you have previously learned. Then let me teach you in the short time I have here with you, how to shoot. That is to say, how to shoot in different scenarios. Then tomorrow, we will take that skill and make it much, much better. There is no limit to the number of rounds, that you can fire over the next two days. So unlike your Rifle Range courses, you will not be limited to twenty-five rounds each. Now please take a seat."

He walked over to the first table which was covered with a large selection of small arms. That is to say it was covered in a myriad of pistols and compact machine guns. We sat down facing him.

"Some of these you will already be familiar with."

He picked up a Small machine pistol complete with Magazine

"This many of you will already know about. It is the Israeli Military Industries, Mini UZI. It is the perfect gun for 'Spray and Run' it is smaller than the previous version with the firing rate having been improved from six hundred rounds per minute to nine hundred and fifty rounds per minute. It can do this because it works on the gas blowback system. Which really means that the gas of the first round fired is what provided the power to re-cock and reload the next round into the chamber. So it is a lot of lead going forward. In confined spaces it is a scythe. It is not a particularly accurate machine pistol and it is very easy to empty the magazine, with a couple of short bursts. That said, it can be fitted with a drum or double drum magazine allowing up to two hundred rounds to be loaded in. This firearm next to it is the Micro UZI again it is smaller but has an even faster action with one thousand two hundred rounds per minute. It can also be fitted with an extendable deep double drum allowing four hundred rounds to be loaded. The real drawback of the double drum is because of the weight you will have to extend the stock and hold with two hands. That said, fitted with its standard magazine, it will fit snugly under a dress jacket in a shoulder holster. These are the choice of machine pistol for MOSAD. Extremely effective in shoot and run situations. It fires 9x19mm parabellum and has a muzzle velocity of One thousand, one hundred and fifty feet per second. And a lot less than that, if fitted with a suppressor, but we will come on to them later."

He laid the UZI back down on the table and picked up another pistol

"This is the New Sig Sauer SP2022 9mm Semi-Automatic pistol. The SP2022 features a durable, lightweight and wear-resistant polymer frame with an integrated M1913 accessory rail. The Sig Sauer polymer framed pistols have earned an enviable reputation and proven track record of reliable performance in both Law enforcement as well as in Military Units around the world. This is probably one of the most rugged semi-automatic pistols in use these days. As you can see it can be fitted with rail devices such as Scope, Laser Sighting or Torch. Also one of the few hand guns you can get wet and simply fire without having to strip down before it can be used again. It takes a 9mm parabellum and can also be fitted with standard or extended magazine. It is made mostly from polymer and is probably one of the most versatile semi auto pistols on the market."

He put it down and picked up a weapon I was accustomed to using

"This is the 9mm Browning semi-Automatic pistol used by British forces. When it was introduced, the Browning Hi Power 9mm pistol was a revelation. It offered the perfect balance of handling, size and firepower, with an impressive 13-round magazine capacity. With this gun it does not matter if you are a novice or a seasoned shooter. It is as simple to fire as it looks. However the problems with sand and mud getting into the mechanism can cause firing problems so if you are crawling around in the mud you might want to slip a Durex over it and when asked are you happy to see me or is that a pistol in your pocket? You can say both"

This elicited a small laugh from us.

"Now let us move from the bigger hand guns to the small and easily carried pistols as we have a lot to get through today."

The next gun he picked up looked like a toy.

"I know what you are all thinking. You are thinking, this is some kind of joke. You see this little baby"

He held it up between his thumb and forefinger

"I had one of these, and it saved my life. I knew I was going to be captured by Sudanese Rebels. We were totally surrounded, with no hope for escape. So much as it hurt my pride at the time. I surrendered, but not before I had slipped this into my underpants and tucked between the cheeks of my butt. There are not many men when patting down for weapons will feel up a man's arse. There were six of us captured. We were held in a mud and stone hut. I waited until the Sudanese were making a lot of noise. They were firing their weapons in the air, as these rebels do all the time. I took the pistol and put it to the temple of the guard's head and fired a single shot which killed the man instantly with almost no noise and we escaped in our underpants. This is not a long range gun nor will it take down a bull. But it can easily be hidden and will kill, if used correctly at close quarters. There are many other compact point 22mm and 9mm pistols and semi-automatics. It the simplicity and size of this makes it a must as an emergency item of clothing for me the NAA Mini Revolver."

He put it back down on the table

"Later you can browse these pistols and chose the ones that suit your style of shooting and how it feels in your hand. Now we must move on the bigger guns the rifles."

He walked over to the next table.

"Please can you take your chairs over here, next to this table?"

We did.

"From my point of view, a Rifle, is a long range weapon. So it must be able to be used accurately, sometimes over great distances. Say two hundred to one thousand five hundred yards. I know what you are thinking, how can anyone? make a shot of over a mile? I know it can be done because I have done it and I know four other men who have also managed this. One of these men claims to have made a two-thousand-yard kill shot. But I also know of one confirmed kill shot of two thousand and seven hundred yards using an AS50. As its name would suggest it is a 50cal which is more than capable of taking down an aircraft. The AS50 more specifically, is a 50cal Snipers Rifle. Apart from being used to just kill people it is an anti-material rifle. It is manufactured by British firearms producer, Accuracy International. The AS50 enables operators to engage targets, at long range, with a high degree of accuracy. It can be used with High Velocity, Standard and Explosive or Incendiary rounds. Sonic and subsonic rounds. The AS50 employs a gas operated, semi-automatic action and muzzle brake. This allows for lower recoil than the AW50 Bolt Action rifle and faster target acquisition. This rifle is highly transportable, ergonomic and lightweight. It can be disassembled and reassembled in less than three minutes and serviced without tools. The AS50 is designed for the British Armed forces as well as the US Navy Seals, of which this rifle is deployed due to its high rate of fire. This is five rounds in one point six seconds. This high rate of fire is due to the floating barrel and the lightweight titanium frame. This rifle has an accuracy of one point five M.O.A. This as some of you might know as Minute of Accuracy. The barrel as I have already said is free-floating. The two-part machined steel receiver features an integral accessory rail for mounting optical sights. Two additional rails are mounted on the sides of the short barrel shroud. An adjustable bi-pod and rear support leg, hand grip allow for stable shooting. This weapon can accurately engage targets at a range of one thousand five hundred yards and much more with ease. For me it is my choice for long range shots, but you might like a different one from the table here. All of these have a killing zone of one thousand yards plus" He laid the AS50 back down.

"The next table as you can see contains various RPG or Rocket Propelled Grenade. These have basically replaced the Bazooka. These are not subtle weapons and will cause massive damage, when used against personnel or property. Now it is time for a break and you can view and feel the guns on the table and grab a cup of coffee from the machine down there."

We chatted amongst ourselves while we had our coffee break.

"Jon why do you think we are here?"

"To learn" was his simple reply

"What is it that I should be learning? I am a medical person and I do not see why me shooting guns, fits into my trade, nor do I think it would be allowed under the Geneva Convention" I replied

He sipped his coffee and then said

"Do you think those Doctors, making all that stuff at the CDE, conform to it? They say they are making cures for it. Yet all of us, who have had any military training know that every side has stockpiles of Biological Weapons. The same applies to the stockpiles of undeclared Nuclear Missiles and Bombs. Are these not weapons of mass destruction as well. And all of this is against the Geneva Convention. Do you think they will worry about one medic with a gun?"

Even though logic dictated that he was right. Years of being a non-combatant with a red cross on my arm, made me question, the way things were going here. I would have to get some answers to questions and I would do it tonight.

"OK can you please go to the bus and we will see who can and who can't shoot, then we will see if we can do something about those that can't"

We boarded the bus this time with Abdalla. We were in the bus for about forty minutes

"Welcome to our Private Military Shooting Range"

"Is that not an oxymoron" said Lachie and continued "A bit like military intelligence, and we all know, the cock ups that they have made!"

Lachie always knew how to get a laugh.

"It is, a Military Range. Only, it is only for specialist use. Today it is for your private use."

We were parked up beside what looked like an old Air Traffic Control Centre and a small disused village next to it. Most of the buildings were pockmarked with bullet holes.

"Looks like old Beirut" said Jon

"Looks like they did not like it" said Lachie

"Looks Like my home" said Abdalla in a sombre tone

I said nothing. We walked into the ATC Tower and then down a flight of stairs to a blast proof door. Abdalla took a card from his pocket and ran it through a swipe card reader. A panel at the side of the door opened up and he put his hand on the red screen. Which then turned green, then the panel closed when he removed his hand. He then punched a six-digit code into a key panel. This was followed by a series of clicks and then the sound of a vacuum being released.

"Can't be too careful with your piggy bank" said Lachie

The door swung open. When we were all inside Abdalla closed the door and lights came on and an air conditioning unit sprung into life.

"This way please."

We walked down a long corridor, that sloped downward for about one hundred and fifty yards. When we got to another door he once again repeated the same process as he had done at the blast door. Only this time he entered an alpha numeric code on a computer keyboard. There was the sound of a bolt being moved in the door and he opened the door and again the room lit up. I say room it was a narrow underground cavern approximately twenty-five yards wide and twenty feet high. I could not see, as of yet, how far it went. A series of lights, were going on in a chain reaction. There was every gun you could ever want, or imagine. They were fixed to brackets, on a wall behind some thick glass. Abdalla put a strange flat looking key in the wall and the glass slid down out of the way

"Blast proof and bomb proof doors. Here we have bullet proof glass over the guns, and if you look over there. Then there is another door which when I unlock it, there will be enough munitions in there, to start a decent sized war"

The Lights were still chasing each other down this vast underground hole making clunking sounds as solenoids switched them on.

"In case you are wondering? It is five hundred yards long and is the longest firing range in the UK and probably the longest indoor firing range in the world."

Finally the lights had found the end. Then there was a distinct change in lighting effect, to almost to that of natural light.

"In this range we can create any lighting condition. We can add mist or smoke, or if required rain, wind, and even snow. Most forms of weather and time of day. It is a one of a kind facility. We have units from all over the world come here to practice, as well as the manufactures, who send their guns for us to test. It probably has better security than the crown jewels or your bank of England. You don't see it up top, but it's there. Up to the first door you might just get arrested, but beyond that, without permission to be in here. You will be killed. That is not a metaphor either. Some have tried. ALL have died"

He walked over to the other door and unlocked it and swung it open. It was like a supermarket except that this one only stocked bullets. There was row up row of them stacked up on the shelves.

"It is time for us to work" he said

He then turned to us and continued.

"Most of you will have fired on the standard twenty five yard range. Some of you will have fired on the fifty-yard range. You will have been taught to fire your pistols in the standing position with feet slightly apart in the two hand mode. I am now going to tell you to forget that. It's not accurate and in a live fire combat scene, you want to make yourself as small as possible. So either crouching or laying down. This will not only save your life but will enable you to better take another's life. That includes, if you are going room to room, to clear a building. Anything you have seen in the movies is shit. I will teach you, to get a two inch grouping, with single shot semi auto at fifty yards. This is twice the distance that Police and FBI are trained to shoot at. I expect every man here to get a two-inch group with the SLR or SA80 or even a M16, at one hundred yards, and I will expect some of you to hit a two-inch target at five hundred yards, using a sniper rifle of your choice in a variety of weather conditions. I will act as your spotter and call out wind temperature and humidity. When I think you are good enough I will allow you to use this"

He showed us what looked like a Scope except that it was rectangular with a four inch heads up display on the end.

"This can be mounted on any weapon with a rail mount facility. Even on a pistol like the Sig Sauer, although putting £500,000.00 scope, on a £500.00 pistol. It is somewhat of an over kill"

After this, he asked us to choose two hand guns each, and then allowed us one hundred rounds, to get the feel of it, to see which suited us best. I tried the browning from a kneeling position with my left elbow on my left knee and my left hand supporting the wrist, of my extended right arm. By using the Browning in a totally straight line to my right arm, it was easy to sight the target allowing my right wrist to fall back into line between shots. I had never before tried Pistol shooting at fifty yards and seven out of ten times I got my two-inch grouping. Not always in the centre of the target but still keeping the grouping. Next I tried the Sig Sauer. I had never handled or fired one of these before. I found it lighter and easier to use. It also had less of a kick to it. So it made it simpler to snap off rounds, far faster than the Browning. Also my groupings were closer together. More than that, I got it ten out of ten. Although we wore ear defenders, I had thought it would be a lot louder in here being an enclosed space. During one of the many breaks in firing I said this to Abdalla

"We have acoustic dampening in the walls and in the roof. Even the 50cal cannot be heard from outside"

Next came the standard rifle shooting I chose a 7.62 SLR. This was what the RAF was using, when I first joined although they later changed to the SA80. I decided to give that rifle a try as well. With the SLR, I found that from both the crouch and reclined position I managed my two-inch group with no problems. But when I tried the SA80 my shots were all over the place. It was just not something I could get on with. Finally, the part I was looking forward to most of all. Sniper rifle, I knew Lachie would want to beat me at this and he probably would. After all, the RAF regiment shoots guns a lot more than the medical branch do. I had never fired anything like the AS50 and it was a monster of a rifle especially with its extending bi-pod legs and a basic x8 scope

"All the sights are zeroed in for five hundred yards. Obviously they are not set for individuals so whilst you may fire High or Low even left or right of the actual target. I will still expect to see something close to the centre with the first shot then I will give instructions to you so you can then adjust the scope for yourself"

I made myself comfortable using the snipers position which I was comfortable with from my days of hunting Stags in the Highlands. This was to lay down, with one leg outstretched to maintain line of fire and the other leg bent at the knee. I put the headphones on and listened for Abdalla, his voice crackled in my ears

"As there is no wind and zero humidity at five hundred yards there is only lift and no drop of so the sights set to zero just aim for the target."

I steadied my breathing and nestled into the stock, I brought the sight up to my eye flicked the Safe to Off and felt the trigger guard, all the time keeping my finger away from the trigger, until I was ready to shoot. I set the cross of my scope on the bright yellow dot, in the middle of the larger black square of the target some five hundred yards in the distance. I was never trained as a sniper but I had learned to shoot over great distance, although at a somewhat larger target than a two-inch dot, further away than I could see with the naked eye. I let my heart rate drop and gently let my finger slide towards the trigger, feeling the slight resistance with the pad of my index finger. All the time gently increasing the pressure whilst not taking my eye of the yellow dot, caught firmly in the centre of my cross hairs. The Gun exploded into my shoulder it kicked a lot harder than a double barrel shotgun and even with my ear protectors on it was loud. A blue and yellow flame, shot out from the end of the rifle. Then it kicked up a dust cloud from all around the end of the barrel, the air and dust were sucked up in a smoke ring behind the bullet which had already hit the target. A clang reverberated from exactly five hundred yards away and a ring of dust vortex, about six inches from the end of the barrel.

"Target Down" said Abdalla "Go Again"

Once more I settled in this time pulling the stock more snugly into my shoulder and set about firing four more times. Each time it seemed to get easier

"Five hits, do you want to go again?"

"No that's fine thanks I will just take the coconut"

I think I must have been shouting because everyone turned towards me

"Sorry my ears are still ringing"

Lachie took his turn also using the same rifle. When everyone was done, Abdalla told us to take five and showed us to a small office come reset area. While he reclaimed the targets by pressing a button on the wall, and all targets started on their long mechanical trek, back to the front of the range.

"That is some beast of a rifle Andy"

"It surely is. Perhaps I could use it for shooting stags"

"You could" Said Abdalla from behind me

"But with the muzzle velocity of that baby and the load it sends, at that distance, there would not be a lot left to eat, and you would probably kill some poor man, a mile further down the road, who just happened to be passing in the line of fire somewhere between four and six seconds later? So no, not unless you are planning to shoot a deer a mile away."

Abdalla announced the scores

"The winner of the Pistol shooting is Hans, Standard rifle is Lachlan and Sniper Rifle is a tie between Lachlan and Andy"

"Don't worry Lachie. You would beat me on the thousand yards and above, I am sure" I said in jest

I did not mean for this to be overheard by Abdalla

"Really? We can simulate that here by using smaller targets, with lighter powder loads and heavier bullets. Want to try for a thousand yards?"

"Sure" said Lachie and continued

"Unless he wants to walk away"

Fuck him. He knew I would not be able to resist a

challenge. The same as when we were kids.

"I don't want to embarrass a Rock Ape" I said

"I don't embarrass easy"

"OK If you are sure Lachie"

"Give me ten minutes to get some rounds from the store" Abdalla said and walked off to the stock room

I set myself up in position one and Lachlan in position two with Abdalla calling the shots for us. One shot for ranging adjustments on the scope and after five shots apiece the targets came back and Abdalla measured them.

"Andy wins"

"Whoa Ho" I shouted to Lachie

"Can we this be set up for fifteen hundred yards" Lachlan said to Abdalla

"Sure same as before, we just change the load and weights to simulate drop that would be expected in a bullets flight for that distance"

He came back with six rounds each One for sight adjustment and then five at the targets. The targets were actually big plates, of six inch thick steel that Abdalla then sprayed a new yellow dot in the middle using a stencil and a can of bright yellow paint.

Lachie won this but only just

"Abdalla what's the maximum range, that anyone has hit the dot on the targets here, assuming you are set up for the load?"

"Inside here a man other than myself. It was one thousand seven hundred and fifty yards and in this range a simulated one thousand nine hundred yards."

"Can we try for two thousand yards?"

"OK, but then we have to go as it is getting late and there is another party due in here in an hour's time"

He came back ten minutes later and handed us three rounds each.

"Two each for ranging and one for the target"

Lachie went first and Abdalla did not call out Kill shot he just said

"Your turn Andy" Abdalla said to me.

I settled in. and was getting the feel for this long range rifle, that packed a punch.

First shot, short. So I graded up for the second shot. I hit the steel target but outside the yellow dot. I settled my breathing, and several times almost took the third shot, then settled back in and it really was like in slow motion. My heart rate came down, my breath steady and gentle, pull deeper on the trigger, almost to its biting point. I double checked the target and the bullet was on its way I heard the clang. We waited for the targets to come back. Abdalla put a screen over each target it had moveable vertical and horizontal wires and 1mm incremental markings He measured first one target and then the other writing on a note pad.

"Andy wins by one point five millimetres."

I was going to dine out on that one for years.

"But remember in the range is one thing as a competition. Out there in real life, it is not the same thing. That said, you two have shown some of the best shooting I have seen in a long time. Not the best but ALMOST"

"Who is the best then Abdalla?"

"Why me of course" he said with a smile, and added

"Please go to the main entrance and wait there for the bus, he will be there in a few minutes. I will see you all soon"

There was a lot of leg pulling for a Rock Ape to be beaten by a Medic. I knew that I would not be as good as Lachie in the real world. He had always beaten me in the past and I had no doubt that he would do so again in the future. We went back to the Accommodation and I went up then showered and changed into casual clothing. Although today had been fun. I knew that I was not a combat soldier, so decided I would call 'The Suit'. I sat on the edge of my bed and flipped open the phone. Then I closed it, one more day would not hurt. Besides, I had actually enjoyed the range today and I was looking forward to doing more range work. The evening was quiet and we ate drank and went off to our respective rooms without any incidents.

ACT 11

The next morning after breakfast the bus came to collect us again. We arrived at the ATC and the simulated village. We exited the bus and it left. Abdalla was waiting for us.

"Today we have a full day ahead of us and we will start with how to correctly clear a building. After this we will also simulate, hostage rescue situations. Then we will teach you how to make good an escape, under differing scenarios. So if you would come with me please, we should start."

We followed him over to the village and when we arrived there were tables laid out with firearms and another table had protective equipment on

"We are going to be using live fire training. The specially adapted semi-automatic pistols you see before you are not dissimilar to paintball guns. They fire a wax coated paint shell. But make no mistake. They will hurt, when they hit you. This is why you will see also, that there is protective clothing over there." He said pointing over to another table. "These include padded boiler suits, as well as full face masks. The guns are modified Sig Sauer's each of you will be given a shoulder holster, to carry it in. You will have a belt with four spare magazines attached to it. Each of you will have a different colour allocated to you. Our first exercise, is to clear the cottage over there." He said pointing to a small cottage like building, which stood on its own away from the rest of the village.

"As you enter, you are to check and clear each room. There are no goodies only baddies in this exercise. So if you see it, shoot it. Some targets will be static and some will just pop up. Fortunately for you none of them will be shooting back. So please, first put on the safety equipment and then we will begin. The shooting order is Andy, Hans, Jon and finally Lachlan."

There was no getting a look at the inside of the cottage before we started, and we were not told how many bad guy targets, there were to shoot. I opened the front door and kept my body behind the front line of fire. Then I sneaked a quick peek inside. There were two targets either side of the doorway. As I already had my Sig out and safety set to off. I knelt and popped both targets in centre body. I crouched down and looked in the room on the left, there were three targets I fired three shots and hit three targets. I continued through the house clearing targets, then exited the building and allowing the next person to clear the cottage. I went to grab a coffee but Abdalla called me over.

"You are to collect new magazines and then to report to the building over there"

He pointed to another building. So I loaded up and went over. This time when I opened the door I was greeted with a salvo of 'Paint bullets'. Fortunately for me, I had like the last time kept my body close to the wall when opening the door. I fired three shots left and was greeted by a grunt. I must have struck a baddie. I was just about to enter, when another salvo of paint came my way. It was time for me to cheat. I ran around the back of the building and could see all the way through from a broken back window to the front hallway. There were two men with their backs to me. They were clad in clothing like mine. I popped them twice in the back each. Both men sat down on the floor and were no longer in the exercise. I popped out my part used clip and reloaded with a full one. Then I chambered a round and checked the safety was off. I climbed in through the broken window. As I crept past where they sat, they both gave me the Bird but kept silent.

There were no other baddies downstairs. As I crept up stairs I was shot twice in the back by the first guy that I had shot. He had not received, what was classed as a mortal wound. Head shot or chest, I had hit him in the gut and had assumed he was dead. So now I was dead. I walked dejectedly out of the house and Back to Abdalla.

Next was hostage rescue which was similar to the first exercise with pop up targets. Only this time there were targets of women and children. Then it was all back to Abdalla and a coffee break.

"All of you men did very well on test one and three. Only one of you completed killing all six men in exercise number two and that was Hans. Well done. After your coffee, you will each have a private instructor to take you through the stages where you failed. They will show you how not to fail in real life"

Each of us had our private tuition sessions. I was told not to expect the bad guys, to play by the same rules as us. We went through all the exercises again and I think I improved. Next came the Close quarters fighting. At this I was definitely the worst student, but in the end I managed to disarm the man of his knife, and knock him to the ground. Then roll him over and Zip tie his hands behind his back, while holding him down with my knee on the back of his neck. The final stage of today's training was Pursuit driving. This was split into two sections, offensive and defensive driving. This not only involved driving, but also shooting of paint bullets at the cars we were chasing, or cars that we were being chased by. This was done solo and working in pairs. The exercise involved one of us driving and the other shooting. I worked well with Hans and also with Lachie. Not so much with Jon, as he was a serious control freak. We would alternate driving and shooting. When he was driving, he would call out shots and when I was driving he would demand, the car go this way or that. Whilst the day was as much fun as anyone could really want for. I had realised that thing we were being trained for, had nothing to do with me working in medicine, in any way shape or form. Not even in medicine at CDE Porton Down. After we got back I flipped the phone open and hit the dial button.

ACT 12

The telephone connected and rang just twice before it was answered.

"Hello, who is this?"

"This is Flight Sergeant Andy McPhee, of Team seven"

"Mr McPhee, What do you want?"

"Out"

"What do you mean out?"

"I mean, I am a Medic and so far all I have learned is how to avoid being killed by Gas, how not to blow myself up with an IED and how to kill with a Gun. So don't you think that is a kind of strange résumé for a man of my trade?"

"There is no out for you"

"What do you mean there is no out? First I was told I was going to work in a research laboratory. Now I am learning how to shoot to kill. So it's against the Geneva Convention for a medic, to do this. I can only carry arms for the defence of my patients. Hell I don't even know, who you are? or what rank you hold? I want OUT and I want out tonight"

"You can't get out, and we will talk tomorrow, when I come there"

He hung up on me. The bastard hung Up. I wanted to throw the fucking phone out the window. Instead I went down to the bar and ordered a drink. Lachie looked at me and came and sat down next to me.

"Nice Shooting mate"

"Ach I got lucky Lachie. Normally you would beat me hands down"

"I can see something is bothering you Andy?"

"Everything's bothering me Lachie, but I don't think we can talk here. We'll do it later want another drink? I'll get them in"

"They are free, ya fucking tight arse" He replied.

I ordered and then brought two large glasses of whisky over to the table Laphroaig for Lachie and Jameson's for me.

"I think I need to get shit faced tonight mate"

"You sure you want to do that Andy?"

"Yea I'm sure. You want to join me and get busted down for some shit or other?"

"Sounds like a plan Andy. What do you want to drink? Your choice of Whisky or mine?"

"Fuck it Lachie looks like any sort of Whisky night but you choose"

"OK Brother, tell you what let's have both"

Lachie walked over to the bar and said

"Can I have the Laphroaig and the Jameson's please?"

"Certainly Sir, would that be a single or a double?"

"Just the bottles and two glasses"

"But sir I don't think I should do that" said the Barman

"Tell you what my fine young man. If I do it, you won't have to. That way you will not get in trouble."

Lachie walked around the bar and picked up the nearly full bottles and snagged two fresh glasses

"Come on Kiddo lets go"

I got up and followed him out. We walked for a bit and found the Football field and sat down by the side of the pitch. Lachie poured out two large measures

"uisge-beatha agus an tobar òigridh" Lachie toasted

"Aye the water of life and the fountain of youth to you an all, my friend"

"So what's got you all so messed up then Andy?"

"Don't you think it's kind of strange me being a medic, and doing this commando shit?"

"I did wonder if you had come over to the dark side"

"Lachie I don't think we have done a thing by choice, since the Brecon Beacons. Perhaps even before that. I don't like, not knowing what is going on. More than the fact, that they have asked me to shoot guns. Which by the way was a lot of fun? But to kill other people not really my style. And not so much the whole bomb thing yesterday or the gassing part either. Not even counting, the little microbe enemy stuff, well that was real ugly shit"

"So, what you want to do about it Andy?"

"I Called 'The Suit' and told him I wanted out"

"What did he say"?

"He said THERE IS NO OUT for me Lachie. Then the bastard hung up on me!"

"Oh"

"He said he will be here tomorrow morning"

"That's all right then. Andy"

"It is?"

"Yep because tonight we are drinking, on HIS time"

I laughed till my sides hurt

"You always have found a way of making a bad situation, sound not so bad my friend"

We sat there on the football field, and drank down a most of the whisky. Then we both fell asleep on the grass……..

I was awoken at about three in the morning, by a boot kicking my body and somebody shouting.

"Get on your feet. Both of you"

I tried to sit up but my head decided to stay on the ground

"Go away" I mumbled

The foot continued to kick me

"Fuck Off" I shouted at the boot

"Get them up" somebody else said

I was pulled roughly to my feet

"Get them cleaned up. Then bring them to the C.O's office" the same voice said

I was beginning to come around, as was Lachie. We were first taken to a Shower Block and unceremoniously dumped in a cold shower, with our clothes on. So I just sat there with my back up against the wall next to Lachie

"Looks like rain today" Said Lachie

"With a chance of thunder if my head is anything to go by"

"Right you two. Get out of there. Get dried and put these on" A Corporal who was a Military Policeman said. Then he threw some towels and two grey boiler suits down on the floor.

"That would be Excuse me Sergeant would you like some Coffee?" said Lachie.

"Or even better, Flight Sergeant. Can I please get you some aspirin?" I said

"At the Moment you two are drunk and disorderly and my Police Warrant, trumps your stripes" Said the MP

"That right" said Lachie and continued "In about two hours I will be a sober Sergeant and you will still be an ugly wanker and you will still be a Corporal. So be careful of that mouth of yours. It might run you into trouble one day"

"Just get dressed"

We stripped off out wet clothes and dried ourselves off, then donned the boiler suits neither of which fitted, making us look like two of the three stooges.

"What now do we get breakfast?"

"Just follow me."

We followed the M.P. to the Station Commander's Office

"Don't you think it's strange that their C.O. is up at this time Lachie?"

"You did not have it away with his daughter? Did you Andy?"

"Not me, Did you?"

"Don't think so, at least not recently."

"Will you two just shut the Fuck up" hissed the MP

We arrived outside the door of the office

"Wait here" The MP said.

He knocked on the door and entered. From where I was standing, I could the Corporal as he walked up to the desk. There was a Group Captain sat at it. I could not see his face but I could see the four rings of rank on the bottom of his jacket sleeve. The Corporal pulled of a snappy salute and shouted

"Prisoners are outside waiting Sir"

"Prisoners?" I whispered to Lachie.

"Have we been charged formally? Or for that matter when were we properly arrested? Now I know, we did not have it away with his daughter. Tell me you did not have his wife?"

"Not me. If we had been arrested, he would have been in the Accident and Emergency of the nearest hospital. So I don't think it's either of those Andy."

"Send them in Corporal" The arm with the four rings behind the desk said.

"Yes Sir" said the Corporal and pulled off another snappy salute and then an about face. Then marched to the door and then opened it wider.

"You two in here at the double" he barked

"Does he want us to march in or run? If he wanted us to

march fast surely he would have said Quick March" I asked Lachie

"He did say at the double Andy" Lachie replied with a wink

"OK Corporal anything you say"

Lachie entered the room first and jogged up to the desk

"What the fuck is your mate doing?" Hissed the MP

"He is RAF Regiment and you said on the double, not quick march just at the double"

"That's not what I meant. Just get in there with him" said the very flustered corporal.

So I jogged in and stood jogging on the spot with Lachie. The C.O. looked up

"What the in the name of God, do you two think you are doing?"

Lachie was on a roll

"Sir the MP said to Double. So I am doubling Sir"

"Stop" shouted the MP

"We are Stopped Corporal" Lachie replied.

"HALT!!"He screamed, then followed it with "Attention"

We stood at Attention

"You salute your Commanding Officer" bawled the MP

"Doh! Corporal. We are not in uniform and not at this moment wearing the Queens Badges. Did you not go to drill school? One does not salute the man one salutes the rank and badge of a senior officer. Besides the General said there are no ranks here anyway"

"STOP THIS NOW" the C.O shouted as he stood up from his desk

"AND YOU", he pointed a finger at the end of his trembling arm, at the Corporal

"Get out now, and wait outside until you are called"

"Don't forget to Salute" said Lachie

The corporal snapped to attention. Bringing the right leg up until the thigh was parallel to the floor. Then he brought his foot down hard enough, to register on the Richter scale. Swung his right arm up, again the upper arm was parallel to the floor, elbow bent at forty-five degrees and hand straight facing palm out. Pulled an about turn and marched out of the room.

"Damn He's good Andy, with almost enough brains to be a Drill Instructor." Lachie said loud enough for both the C.O and the Corporal to hear. You could have fried eggs on the face of the MP as he left the Room.

"ENOUGH!" Barked the C.O
He did not look too happy either.

"Right, I don't know what is going on my Camp. I am being treated like a fucking mushroom here, kept in the dark and fed on copious supplies of one form of shit or another. I don't like it one little bit. I don't even know who He is" He said pointing in the corner to where 'The Suit' was standing with another man.

"We do" said Lachlan "He's called 'The Suit', Sir"

"SHUT THE FUCK UP! Or I might forget my Fucking orders and have you shot or locked up for life, or fucking both and have you cleaning toilets for the rest of your miserable life" screamed the CO.
Lachie did have a way with his mouth that his brain did not always work with.

"Which of those? Sir, I mean if we have a choice…."

"Don't………" 'The Suit' mumbled
The C.O Continued

"But I have been told to extend him, every courtesy and that whatever he says goes. So I am guessing that you two are his fucking problem." With that he stormed out of his own office 'The Suit' replaced the C.O. at his desk.

"Can we stand easy as we have no shoes on and the floor is cold?"
'The Suit. leaned over the desk and looked down at our feet. He smiled to no one in particular and sat back down.

"Have a seat" he said pointing to the two chairs to the side of the desk.

"So you want out? Mr. McPhee? and that would be your choice too Mr. Henderson?"
Lachie looked and me and Nodded

"Before you reply, you will notice. I did not call you by your ranks of Flight Sergeant and Sergeant"

"Just who are you?" I asked

"I am a man who can make you a Mr, rather than a Flight Sergeant or even a convict in a military prison, for the rest of your existence!"

"That still does not answer my question. You or your section, obviously have some clout. So much so that you can get a Station Commander, out of his marital bed at three in the morning, and then take over his office for a couple of lads, who have done nothing more than have a drink or two."

"Tell them" Another man from the corner of the room said.

"Sir?" 'The Suit' Asked

"Tell them who we are"

"'The Suit' has a Boss too" Lachie whispered to me.

"We are with SIS"

"Ahhh a sissy" Lachie said

The suit frowned and continued

"Secret Inelegance Service"

"Never heard of them, so they must be good" Lachie muttered

"When you two jokers are quite finished" 'The Suit" said and continued

"You will know of MI5 and MI6 well they are just two departments of SIS. We are in fact their bosses. So when you called me and told me you wanted out of trying to find a mole, at CDE Porton Down. I find myself wondering why? CDE Porton Down is run by Doctors looking for Cures to Bacteriological weapons. Some of which yes we already possess, some of which we don't. But we still need to find vaccines for."

"Bullshit" I said

"What?"

"First you stage an 'accident' on the Brecon Beacons. Then you manage to put Lachie and me together, at the scene. Do not bother pretending that you did not know, that Lachie and I are childhood friends, or that we joined the RAF together. Even a fool looking at our service records would see this. Then you have us meet up again by 'accident' after which we are both promoted and get an emergency posting, to this shit hole. Then you tell us a cock and bull story, that something has gone missing or that info on it has gone missing. Then you put us all in teams. Again it's convenient that Lachie and I are put together. Then you train us quickly as Specialist Safety Team, which was the only believable part so far. Next you train us to disarm bombs, this was when I really realised, that there was little or no truth, to what you have told us so far. We discover listening devices in our rooms. You add two of your own Muppets to our dinner table. One of whom has never been out from behind his desk before. The other looked like he would kill everything that ever lived. Next you give us advanced weapon training, in an underground facility,, that probably is not even listed in the MOD records. The emphasis of that training was on long range shooting. Also the instructor conveniently has ammunition available to simulate shooting at two thousand yards over a five-hundred-yard indoor range. He shows us an advanced electronic gun sight that probably does not even exist on the books yet and that it is worth as much, as an Armoured Personnel Carrier. You KNOW, that as a serving member of the RAF Medical Branch I cannot carry or use firearms except in the defence of my patients and then only a side arm. So here are a few of my thoughts. I think that every person on the staff at the little place where we are staying, are 'your people' from the barman to the maids. I think the tale we were told at CDE was bull shit, I think that either Jon or Hans or perhaps both of them are 'your people' inside team seven. I think teams one to six, are also your people. And I think you really want us to be Civilians for some reason, yet to be told to us. My best guess it has partial truths mixed in with a good dose of bullshit. So the only link I can put together in this is that Lachie and I are from the Highlands of Scotland. Whatever the deal is it is around that locality, but for the love of me I can think of nothing up there that would warrant this level of subterfuge."

The man in the corner started clapping his hands

"Not bad Mr. McPhee. Not bad at all. With an analytical mind like that, you really are the sort of person that SIS requires on its staff."

He walked over to the desk and picked up both of our folders and dropped them in the bin. Lachie and I, both looked at each other and then at the bin?

"What's that supposed to mean? Are you kicking us out of the RAF?"

"In a way, yes I am"

"You had better have a lot more to say than that." Lachie

said his voice rising a bit

"If you both will bear with me, I will try to explain, some of it to you. I also hope that you will understand that for reasons of National Security, and International sensitivity. That I can only tell you parts of it. You are correct we did get you by using a little bit of subterfuge, as you so correctly put it. You were selected because, as Mr. McPhee so correctly said, you both come from the theatre of operation, that we have running at the moment. You are also known to a member of our team who has been located there. I will not tell you who they are, at the moment because, first you have to realise. How serious this situation is and that I really do have the power to lock you up forever, should you talk about this to anyone."

He opened another folder and browsed it before closing it again. Then he continued to speak.

"About six weeks ago, our man on location started to pick up some chatter about a possible terrorist attack, on a Nuclear Fast Breeder Power station. I am sure you know what the by product, of a NFB is Mr. McPhee?"

"Weapons grade Plutonium?" I replied and he continued.

"And then more recently, we were asked to look into sensitive material being taken from CDE. The NFB establishment is closed down, but the chatter increased for reasons we can't fathom. So a few weeks ago, we put a team on location. They were made up from members of the SAS and Marine Commandos'. They were all selected because they had joined the military from Caithness via the recruiting offices in Wick and Thurso. All have joined in the last three years. This unit was based in the village of Reay."

"But I thought Dounreay was decommissioned?" I said and then he continued

"Yes it has been decommissioned. As I said. We had a team was in Reay. Their cover was that they were ground force workers on the regeneration of the site. However, about three weeks ago they all simply disappeared and we have had no contact with them since."

"Why would folks want to attack a decommissioned NFB?"

"That I can't tell you"?

"Can't or will not?" I asked

He ignored my question and continued.

"We want you, that is to say, team seven, on the ground there. You will NOT be stationed in Reay but in your own homes. You will be Dishonourably Discharged under Queens Regulation Conduct unbecoming a member of Her Majesties Forces. This as I am completely sure, you know covers a multitude of sins. You will be officially charged and Court Marshalled, then dishonourably discharged and kicked out into civilian life."

"That sounds like a bad deal. What's the incentive for us to fall in with your little scam?" Lachie asked.

"Well if you agree. Then we will buy your homes that you currently rent. And we will also supply you with a sizeable bank account. We would also give you access to 'our supplies' on an as and when required, basis. This is effectively a blank cheque. That is only within constraints for carrying out surveillance and if required the resources that you may be required, to stop a terrorist act."

"And if we don't accept?"

"Look at it this way. You were drunk and disorderly whilst on attachment to an extremely sensitive and highly secret establishment. Where you were privy to operational information. Added to that, you have also signed the Extended Version of the Official Secrets Act. Which if you had bothered to read the extremely small print you would have noticed the phrase 'Including any and all 'Black Door Operations'. Well here you are, and welcome to Black Door."

"So we are fucked either way?" I said

"That's pretty much the picture"

Lachlan was out of his chair a fast as a flash and had grabbed hold of the standing man by the lapels and was busy lifting him up the opposite wall with his hands up around the man's throat.

"Mr. Henderson, please stop this now. Or I will be forced to take action against your friend here"

'The Suit' had pulled a fucking gun on me. Lachie growled and let the man down, but not before he had shoved him hard against the wall again, causing some of the Station Commanders pictures to fall to the floor.

"I am sorry we had to cheat you into joining Black Door.

But I promise you, when this operation is over you will have the means to start a new life where ever you want."

Now here is the good bit "You get to hit me, just the once and the same for Mr. Henderson he can strike my associate. When you have done that, you will be charged with being Drunk and disorderly and for assault on officers of the crown."

"What do you think Andy?"

"I think we are screwed"

"OK"

Lachie exploded his punch on the guy he had previously grabbed. The upper cut caught the man on the chin and lifted him bodily from the floor.

"He's out for the count and the crowd, the crowd go mad" Lachie said and raised his fists in the air, in fake triumphalism of a boxer in the ring.

I pulled 'The Suit' across the desk and if he thought he was going to get punched he was very much mistaken. I snapped my head back and then rapidly forward using the edge of my forehead to catch him squarely on the nose. I could feel the satisfying crunch of his nasal bone and cartilage snap under the impact. His head went back and he groaned. His hands went to the injured part of his face, his Eyes glazed over and the blood poured from between his fingers and pooled on the Commanding Officers Desk.

"You fucking bastard! You broke my nose"

"Nice one" said Lachie

"Yours was not so bad either"

We high five'd each other

"Might as well be done for really assaulting an officer of the crown and occasioning actual bodily harm, as for the pretend version".

"You wanted it to look authentic" I said as Lachie and I turned and to walk out of the office. We walked back to where we were barracked.

"Better get breakfast before they come to take us off to Colchester Prison" Lachie said with a Smile.

I went up to my room and dressed in my number one uniform, which some kind person had cleaned and pressed in double quick time. I guess someone knew I would be requiring it quickly. Then I packed my Kit-bag and went downstairs to the dining room. I put my belongings next to Lachie's and joined him at the table. Like me he was in his dress uniform. There were a few more ribbons on his left breast than mine. But he had been to more war zones than me. He was already tucking into his cooked breakfast. The steward came over

"I will have a full English with extra bacon please and a coffee"

"So what is then, the last meal, for a condemned man?" Lachie asked me.

"It could be Lachie. You get the feeling we have been fucked over?"

"And then some mate. I am sure they will make this a quick discharge. By the sounds of things, they lost their team and are going to want to replace it fast"

"Andy? You sure you want to do this?"

"I don't see that we have any choice in it Lachie. How are they going to put Hans and Jon up there with us? It will look kind of suspicious if we all suddenly appear to have been kicked out of the services and then all come together up home"

My breakfast arrived. Contrary to what most folks feel. I have always found a large fatty breakfast after a night on the town, actually made me feel better. It is that overload of carbs, that does it for me.

"Thanks" I said to the steward and then wondered what he was listening to? Well I guess it did not matter much now anyway, as we were already caught in the spider's web.

"Can't wait to get out of here anyway Andy, it's full of bugs, they should call in an exterminator" Lachie said with a wink.

So we ate the rest of our breakfast with small friendly banter and chit chat. I ordered another strong coffee and joined Andy in the lounge area. We waited and then about one hour later we were formally arrested by two military policemen.

"Flight Sergeant McPhee. Sergeant Henderson. You are both formally charged that last night, you both entered the Station Commanders Office in an inebriated state and then you were both verbally abusive to your Commanding officer, Group Captain Sealand. You then physically attacked two Civilian Officers of the Crown, resulting in actual bodily harm. You then fled the scene without summoning medical assistance. Contrary to Queens Regulations in that, your conduct was unbecoming of a member of her Majesties Armed Forces and in a manner that was prejudicial to the Good Name and Order of the Royal Air Force." He stopped for breath and gave each of us a copy of RAF Form 252, which were the charge sheets, for our crimes.

"I guess a drink before we go is out of the question" Lachie asked to no one in particular.

"If you men would collect your belongings and come with us to the Guard room" said The Warrant Officer Military Policeman.

I presume they had sent a rank senior to ours out of respect for the ranks that we still held. We went outside and threw our bags into the back of their Land Rover and then followed them into the vehicle. The two Military Policemen got in the front and we drove the short distance to the Guard House. Our Kit-bags were taken along with our peak caps. Both of us were put into the same Cell. The Court Martial was convened with alarming speed given the low nature of our crime. We were taken from our cells in the afternoon and marched into the court without our hats. We were bracketed by the same two military police, who had collected us about six hours previous. The panel of the Military court was made up of two Wing Commanders and an Air Commodore. The Charges were read out and our Guilty plea accepted by the court. (Which we had never actually entered) We both stood there awaiting our sentence, expecting at least twenty-eight days, in the slammer. Our sentences were read separately, not that that made any difference as they were both the same.

"You have been found guilty of the charges of bringing the Royal Air Force in to disrepute. As such you are to be stripped of all Rank and are to be with immediate effect Dishonourably Discharged from Her Majesties Forces. You are to return your Uniforms and any item belonging to the Royal Air Force. You are then to report to the Administration Block for Discharge papers to be signed. You will be awarded a Travel warrant to return to your homes. That is the decision of this court." The metaphorical gavel went down and the three officers gathered their papers and walked out.

We were escorted back to the Guard House, where we changed

into our own civilian clothes. Then we were escorted to the Administration Building

"Twelve Fifty's Please" said the young Senior Aircraftman, who was sitting behind the counter. We Handed over our RAF I.D. Cards.

"I never liked that picture of me anyway" said Lachie

"Watch your mouth" said the Sergeant who was our escort

"You want to watch yours too sunshine" said Lachie and continued

"We are civilians now. So show us some fucking respect. Remember that charge that we had of Bringing the RAF into disrepute. That means you have to call all civilians by their given name or refer to them as SIR"

The Sergeant did not reply and I saw the Senior Aircraftman behind the desk smirk.

"These are your discharge papers Sir" he said as he handed them to us

"I have been requested to ask both of you gentlemen, if you would wait in that room over there" He said, and pointed to a door on the left.

We went across with our escort and entered the room and sat down on the couch that was there. The Sergeant stood guard in case we stole the room. Two minutes later 'The Suit' entered the room. He was sporting an aluminium strip across the bridge of his nose, this partially hid the spot where bone and breached the skin of his nose. It could not however hide the purple and yellow bruises surrounding both of his eyes.

"Nice work Andy" Lachie said to me

"The pleasure was all mine Lachie" and then a little louder I said

"Sometimes you have to take one for the team."

'The Suit' ignored my remark.

"That will be all Sergeant. I will take things from here"

"But I have my orders to escort them off the base Sir"

"I said I will take it from here" replied the 'Suit'

"Shoo" I said

"Don't you understand Fuck Off?" Lachie said

The Sergeant left the room and slammed the door.

"OK If you two jokers would like to get back to reality?"

The suit put down two large thick envelopes on his desk.

"These are your Travel Warrants. Along with The Title deeds to your homes, which I believe you were previously renting"

I stopped him by raising my hand.

"There is no way you could get a change of title deeds overnight. So you must have arranged this weeks ago"

"Yes we did as soon as our team disappeared"

"You must have been pretty sure of yourself" said Lachie

'The Suit' continued

"Inside the Envelopes you will also find your Civilian Documents, Credit Cards, Driving Licenses, Passports, your National Insurance cards and of course some ready cash."

I looked in my envelope and whistled

"There is £25,000 each, but this is Expenses money and not to buy booze with. Your bank accounts have been given a healthy influx as well. The money in your bank accounts is yours in the form of compensation of what would have been, your expected normal service for the next ten or so years. Your cover Mr. McPhee" I held my hand up

"For this sort of money please call me Andy"

"OK Andy, your cover is that you had a big win on Football pools and then went on a bender with your mate here. We have already previously released your name as a winner. Actually we did that last week. You then shared your winnings with your lifelong friend. Anyway the rest is that after the bender, you committed the crimes of which you two were charged with after which you got the boot from the RAF."

"So what happens now?" asked Lachie

"Not a lot for now. You go home to Scotland and Live the life of rather well off civilians. But you will take those phones with you and you will keep them charged at all times. If you fuck me about I will have you inside a prison reserved for undesirables under the official Secrets Act, or the Prevention of Terrorism Act. Whichever one allows me to lock you up for the longest period of time. This really means you never get to see the light of day again. Do we understand each other?"

"Yes I do, I got the picture as well" I said.

"Then go home and relax. There is a Taxi waiting for

you outside"

"You know who we are, but we still don't know who you are. What do we call you?"

"You don't. Now Goodbye and I will be in touch"

They had allowed us to keep our Kit-bags to carry our civvies in. I took my bank card and driver's license along with my National insurance card and slipped them into my wallet. I also put five grand, in fifties, of the cash into my pockets as well. The rest I left in the envelope and put that in my Kit-bag. Lachie did the same. And then we walked out of the room and past the MP. Lachie gave him the bird as we exited the Administration block and into the taxi.

"Railway station please"

On the way to the railway station we did not talk at all. Lachie had been a military lifer and had wanted to go on and transfer from the RAF Regiment into the SAS. I could tell he was putting on a bit of bravado, in being matter of fact about this whole thing. I knew there was nothing I could done to have stopped it but could not shift the feeling of guilt. For some strange reason our travel warrants were made out for First Class Travel. At the railway station we exchanged the warrants for our Tickets. We took the Train from Salisbury to Saint Pancras. We filled the time with small talk and about what we were going to do with the homes we now owned. When we got to Saint Pancras we got off and caught the underground Tube for Kings Cross where we booked in for the Overnight Sleeper to Inverness. We had arrived in London Kings Cross at a little before 6pm and our Overnighter did not leave until 9:15pm. This gave us a little over three hours to kill. After a quick look outside Kings Cross, we decided it was time to eat. So we went into Caravan Restaurant and as it was quiet, we sat down next to the middle of the back wall and ordered a simple steak meal, with two pints of Larger. As we waited, Lachie pretended to be reading the menu

"I am sorry mate, I know you wanted to climb the ranks and join the Hereford boys and do all that exciting stuff, rather than wasting your time guarding RAF Bases. Or worse be a boring civilian"

"Not your fault Andy. Sometimes shit just happens." he sipped his beer and continued.

"Really not sure, how our parents are going to react to us both being dishonourably discharged. You know how proud my old man is. How he told all his friends that his only son was in the RAF Regiment. Good thing he is staying at my aunt's home on Fetlar, at the moment"

"I don't know what to say to you on that Lachie. I guess you are going to have to work it out with them. I don't think you can really tell them the truth of this. Not now anyway. Perhaps some time in the future when SIS have finished whatever this is"

"What you going say to your dad Andy?"

"I guess now I own the house he was renting. I will just say sorry and hope he accepts that. I am sure it will hurt him. I just hope he forgives me. And like you I hope to tell him what I can, when the time is right."

The meal arrived and we ate half-heartedly. We finished our beers and walked back into the station. They allowed us to board at 8:45 pm. They had put both of us in the one compartment. I stowed my bag and took the bottom bunk and Lachie climbed on to the top. I closed my eyes and tried to figure out all the things that had gone on in the last week. I did not really sleep deeply, I woke at every station, that the train pulled into on the way. We arrived at Inverness Railway station, at 8:38am the morning. Although both of us had been up for about an hour and had washed. We had coffee and biscuits. As the train stopped we alighted with the other passengers.

ACT 13

"Have you noticed we have a shadow" Lachie asked

"No"

"Don't turn around"

"Let's just walk down to the waiting room at the end, and check the timetable for the train North"

We walked down the platform, and looked at the train timetables. Our train North did not leave until 10:38 am, it turned out that we had just missed the connection with the earlier one.

"Let's get a coffee and take a seat facing up the platform, then I will point this guy out. I am sure he was in the restaurant, where we ate at Kings Cross." Lachie said as he pointed down to the waiting room, at the end of the platform.

"OK Lachie, works for me. I have to give my dad a call to let him know we are on the way anyway and there is a phone box over there."

I walked to the phone box and called my father, he answered on the third ring.

"Hi Dad, I am at Inverness Station and I will be home in a few hours. I have Lachie with me and he will be staying for a few days if that is OK?"

"What's this about you winning a load of money on the football pools?"

"Long story dad and by now, you will know I have managed to buy the house from his Lordship. I split the winnings with Lachie, as he came up with the score draws for me" I hated lying to my dad but it would make things easier

"Listen Dad I have to go, but we will see you soon. Bye dad."

"Bye son"

I hung the phone up. We grabbed a coffee, from the buffet and walked back to the waiting room, after picking up a copy of the Northern Times. This was the local Newspaper for the Highland region. I sat down and started to read the front page.

"He is the guy with the Red North Face backpack on. He is standing with his back to us half way up the platform"Lachie said without looking up.

I looked over the top of my newspaper and spotted him and then went back to looking at the front page.

"Can't say I have noticed him before Lachie, but I will trust your judgement. What do you want to do about it?"

"Nothing for now, let's see how it plays out. I have a feeling that 'The Suit' would not want us to show our hand at the moment."

I read the paper, pretty much from back to back. This was in an attempt to catch up on the current affairs of the Highlands. We boarded the train and took a seat at a table in the mid-section of the train. The man with the Red North Face backpack got in the carriage behind ours. This was a train journey, I had made many time before. After joining the RAF, every time I took this journey, coming home on leave. Then it just felt that a little bit of me was being replaced. However every time I returned to my base, it was taken away again. The train jolted to a start and moved off down the line towards Dingwall, Invergordon, Tain, Dornoch, Golspie, and then Brora. All the time the countryside was becoming more wild and much more beautiful in my eyes. At Brora the Catering staff, changed over from the train going south and the Buffet on our train opened for Tea, Coffee and sandwiches. Then the train pulled out and headed north again. The train headed up to Helmsdale and then to the most scenic part of the journey as it turned away from the coast and followed the River Helmsdale and the Strath of Kildonnan. The train slowed down for Kildonnan Station but did not stop. Up here in the Highlands, some of the stations are still request stops. Our station of Kinbrace would be the next and the conductor had already been around and checked the tickets. So he knew there were passengers to alight there. I grabbed my Kitbag from the overhead rack and Lachie did the same.

"There no hiding place here, if he gets off" Lachie said and I had to agree.

The train stopped and we got off. We had to wait for the train to pull out from this unmanned station, before we could cross the road to get a taxi from McLeod's Garage. We had agreed that Lachie, would stop with me for a few days, as his house was empty. His father had moved out, to be with his aunt on the Island of Fetlar in Shetland. At least my house would be warm, as dad would have a good fire going. No doubt something nice would be cooking on the Rayburn. Lachie was right, the guy had got off at the station, and was looking the other way back down towards Kildonnan. When the train pulled out of the station we crossed the track and went into the garage.

"Hi Gordon any chance of a Taxi?"

"Sure whose house we going to, Lachie's or your Dads?"

"We are both going to dads, if we were going to Lachie's, we'd walk. Are you free now?"

Lachie came and joined us

"Who's the lad with the backpack? Do you know him?" I asked Gordon

"Never seen him before, but there are a load of RSPB kids doing surveys on the Bird Life all up and down the Strath. Most of them are stopping in the Hostel in Kildonnan and some of them stop at the old Railway Station at Forsinard. They tend to come up from the Universities down South. Count birds and then bugger off home. If you ask me they are all probably counting the same bloody birds. But its great business for my Mum's shop" He said pointing his thumb over his shoulder, to what was the only shop for seventeen miles.

"No worries" I replied "So how long before you can run us home"?

"About five minutes Andy, just got to put the wheel back on this baby" A metallic green Range Rover was up on the ramp.

"Fishers or shooters?" I asked

"No rods or baskets so probably shooters" he replied

In the next week or two, the Hind shooting season was due to finish soon most of the shooters would be off the hill. Gordon finished putting the wheel back on and dropped the ramp back down, he reversed the Range Rover back out of the garage and into a parking area next to his workshop. Gordon was the same age as us and we went to school together. But he was always interested in Cars and Motor Bikes. He kind of drifted, into car repair, straight out of school. I don't think he actually had a qualification in it, but folks around here only wanted to know. Could it be fixed? A simple yes or no would suffice? They did not need to see a City and Guilds Certificate. You either paid cash or you bartered something. Bartering was still a way of life, in the more remote parts of the Highlands.

"You boys Ready?"

"Yes Gordon. Which car are we going in?" I asked

"Might as well take the Range Rover for a spin, got to check out the brakes" He said with a wink and a big smile.

We threw our kit-bags into the back and jumped in. Lachie was in the back and I was beside Gordon in the front. The Range Rover was an automatic 3.5 litre V8. Gordon reversed out of the parking area and changed it into drive and then, drove up the slope from the shop and turned right onto the A897 and back down towards Kildonnan. It was just three miles from Kinbrace, to Old Kinbrace Farm. And then another mile up into the Forrest behind that. The house had originally been built as holiday accommodation for the rich Shooting and Fishing fraternity. However, since the downturn in the market less and less people had the vast sums of money to throw away, on shooting a Red Deer or Fishing in what was now one of the most expensive rivers in the UK. The grouse shooters were mainly just up for a couple of weeks in August. So the folks that owned the estate, where we lived, had started renting out the houses as far back as the early1970's. We pulled left off the A897, on to a side road that went up to Old Kinbrace Farm. Gordon stopped at the deer fence and I got out and opened the gate, to allow us into the farm. He drove over the cattle grid and I pulled the gate closed and shut it with the bolt. After I got back into the Range Rover we followed the unsurfaced road, up to the farm house and this joined on to a dirt track road into the hills beyond. We followed the forestry road up and behind the farm, and then into the forest proper. If you didn't know the house was there, you would be lucky to find it. After a mile of being jostled from side to side and having our heads bounced off the roof lining. We were almost there. I could see the smoke rising above the trees and I knew home, was just around the next tight left hand bend. Then after that, you had to do an even tighter double back on to a grassy and narrow slip road, that then curved back around and there it was. A Granite Stone, three bed house. My father's jet black Great Dane called Raven and my own Red Japanese Akita who I had named Kyla. Both dogs sat like statues either side of the front porch. Gordon pulled up and turned off the engine.

"You got time for a coffee?" I asked him

"Sure why not, besides it would be nice to see your old man. I have not seen him for a while"

Gordon opened the door and stepped out. Both dogs growled menacingly, but stayed where they were. Gordon got back in the car.

"I think I'll let you go first." He said.

"Woosie." said Lachie and got out.

I got out and whistled the dogs over.

"You can get out now Gordon"

He did and then made a big fuss over Raven, Kyla jumped up and down and started running in circles. She was happy to see me back home. We got our bags out of the back and walked into the house with Kyla by my side. The door of the porch was open and I went in, then opened the inner door of the house, and then turned right into the open kitchen door. It was used as a working mans kitchen, come living room. So most of what happened in the house, happened in the kitchen. It was a large and spacious kitchen with a flagstone floor. A large old pine kitchen table was in the centre of the room, with six pine chairs to match. They, like the table were not varnished, but were scrubbed clean and were almost white from many years of use. Then on the central wall was a solid fuelled Rayburn. We would burn everything from Peat to coal and from rubbish to wood. If it burned it went in the Rayburn. Dad was standing by the stove.

"Coffee will be ready in a minute it's just percolating, Have a seat Gordon. How's the family?"

"They are grand, thanks for asking Mr. McPhee. How are you keeping yourself?"

"Gordon. I would have thought after all the years you have known me. You would have started calling me Craig" and then he continued.

"How long you home for boys?" dad asked

Not wanting to let out too much info in front of Gordon at this time. I dodged the question

"Oh the usual you know"

My father raised an eyebrow but said nothing in reply.

"Get the mugs from the dresser will you?"

"Sure"

I wandered over to the big pine Welsh Dresser that my mum had inherited from her mother. Her willow pattern china was on display as it had been ever since I can remember. I opened the door on the bottom and pulled out four plain white coffee mugs.

"No need to stand on ceremony lads. Take a seat"

My father motioned for Lachie and Gordon to the table. They pulled out a chair each and sat down. Raven came in and lay down on the floor next to the Rayburn.

I brought the cups to the table and placed them on the mats dad had laid out. Dad brought the coffee pot, which he placed down on a trivet next to the sugar bowl. I walked to the fridge and pulled out a large jug of fresh milk. My father milked the cow twice a day and the excess of milk that he did not need, went to friends in and around Kinbrace. My father poured the steaming coffee into the mugs. Then Gordon and dad helped themselves to sugar and milk, Lachie and I took ours black.

"Any of you boys want to make it Irish?" my father asked

"Why not?" Gordon replied.

My father produced a hip flask that he always carried with him. I knew that it had either Jameson or Poteen, in it. It was a bit of a roulette wheel as to which it was. As when it was empty, he would fill it with the other. I just hoped to hell, it was not the Poteen. We all proffered our mugs forward, I sipped mine, Jameson Irish Whisky. I guess that it was Gordon's lucky day as he was driving. The aroma of fresh coffee mixed with the sweet smell of Jameson's Irish Whisky, was in itself intoxicating.

"By the way a package arrived for you this morning."

I saw the look on Lachie's face and I just hoped that my father had not seen it. We used to play poker together when we were younger and Lachie had the worst poker face of any person I have ever played against. It almost seemed wrong to take his money when we did play. My father continued and did not seem to have seen the look.

"It's in your room. I have made up the spare room, for you Lachie. You know where it is. You can dump your stuff there when you are ready"

"Thanks Craig. I appreciate you having me here"

Lachie gave one of his legendary honest and warm smiles He had a soft spot for my old man and my father looked upon him as an extra son. We had done pretty much everything together since we were kids. This had continued into adulthood. Gordon finished his coffee and stood up.

"Much as I would love to stay here and drink your coffee Craig, the owner of that Range Rover outside is going to want it back in one piece. I fear if I have another of your coffees, then I am liable to dump it into the side of the hill or a ditch."

"Nice to see you again Gordon and don't be a stranger. Come around any time and give my best to your folks."

My father stood and shook his hand and then walked him out of the house. I heard the Range Rover turn and then move off down the hill. After about thirty seconds my father came back in and sat down at the table.

"So what have you done Son?" I exchanged a glance with Lachie

"We got the boot dad"

"How the hell could you both, get the boot at the same time? He is RAF Regiment and you are a bloody Medic at RAF Brawdy. You are stationed in different camps, at least you were at Christmas and that was only a few months ago. You were at Brawdy and Lachie he was at Saint Athens. So how about treating your old man with a modicum of intelligence"

"We were both attached together, and then we did the football pools and it came up with £500,000. Then we got shit faced and punched out, some smarty pants officers. So we got the boot. But don't worry about the rent on this place now. I bought it from the owners. Lachie did the same with his share."

A bit of truth mixed in with a lot of lies seemed to stop my dad, for now, that is.

"OK we will talk about the whys and wherefores later"

My father walked over to the dresser. There was an envelope leaning on a picture of my mother. The picture was taken when she was about twenty, she was a looker back then. Dad did not really condone gambling. That said as a young man, when he met my mother. He had bet on a horse and it had come in at two hundred to one. He had taken his winnings and gone out and bought my mother a real fur coat. Then he had bought an engagement ring.

"This letter arrived with the post this morning. It's for you"

He handed me the letter which had been rubber stamped with a Black Door on the reverse

ACT 14

Following an uneventful night we went to bed and slept soundly. The next morning, I woke and went for a short run, in the forest behind the house. I remembered as a child the contractors for the Forestry Commission, coming along with their heavy equipment and literally ploughing the hillsides with their great caterpillar tracked vehicles. The hills were so steep at points they would have to use chain winches to pull the ploughs up and sometimes slow them down on their descent. I arrived back at my home, then went and showered. First a steaming hot blast and soap, followed by standing in an ice cold shower. This was my routine and I found that it eased cramped up muscles and refreshed me. I went down stairs and sat down at the table. The letter from the previous day lay propped up against the sugar bowl. Presumably my father had put it there, after I had not opened it yesterday. I picked up the envelope and looked at the outside again. Just my name and address on the front. I turned it over there was Black Door stamped on the back. I slid a table knife under the flap and put the now empty envelope back down on the table. The letter was quite simple and to the point

> You and your friends may be in grave danger
> Some of the people that you are working with
> Are not who they appear to be.
> Do NOT trust anyone.
> Signed
> A Friend

There were no real surprises in the contents of the letter. The only surprise was where it had ostensibly originated with the Black Door stamp on the back of the envelope. There was no postmark or return address. What bothered me was if it had come from 'The Suit' then why had he not called me. Was it a friend or perhaps the phones, were not as secure as they were said to be? So was 'The Suit' was trying to contact us. The realism was, I did not trust anyone really apart from Lachie. I knew I could trust my father, but did not really want to burden him with it. I despised lying to him so decided, that I had to adhere to the original story. Keep it an uncomplicated lie (we won big, got drunk, got the boot) and in the meantime try to keep things as normal as possibly achievable. I had decided to wait until my father was out of the house, before I opened the package. I had put it in the bottom of my wardrobe. Dad was already out doing his daily chores, when Lachie came down for breakfast. He wandered over to the Rayburn and picked up the coffee pot, carried it across to the table and then walked to the dresser and grabbed himself a mug. He sat down opposite me and poured a coffee for himself.

"Want a top up?"

I slid my mug over to him and he topped me up and then put the pot down on the trivet.

"So what the letter say?"

"It said. Don't trust anyone, Lachie"

"Who was it from mate?"

"Someone at Black door" I passed him the letter to read

"Andy, this means that it could be from 'The Suit' or his Boss. Or it could be about him, or one of the other team members, I suppose including me"

"Lachie You, are about the only individual I do trust in this whole stupid thing. I am not a warrior, let alone some kind of spook. I am sure they could have found other more competent folks to do this James Bond shit."

"James Bond always got the babes mate"

"Yes he does. But this is real life and I am not him."

"What you going to do about the letter?"

"For now? I say we do nothing. Once you have had your coffee, I think we should nip over to your house and grab your Land Rover. Also some clothes, as I think it's best if you stop here. All the same, I think I need to get my father out of the picture somehow. So I'm going to give that some thought this morning, if you could think of anything. That would be good."

We finished our coffee and I washed up the cups and put

them away. Then we went outside to the barn. Inside there was my old Ford Transit long wheel base Camper Van. I had converted to carry all my bands gear. This was from a time before the military when, I had played guitar to a professional standard. So in the front, there was a single and double seat. And then directly behind that was a bench seat, with a bulkhead behind. Under the rear seat, which lifted up, was a large empty box space. It had a sliding door on the side to allow entry to the second row of seats, the double doors on the back allowed access to a panelled out space for amplifiers and speakers along with all of our instruments. The entire back space and bulkhead had been reinforced with inch thick plywood as was the entire back of the van. It was not flash by any standards but it had got us from A to B. My father used the Van to go down to Inverness every month, to do his shopping and get supplies for the few animals that he had. I got in the driver's side and Lachie jumped in the passenger's side.

"What was in the Parcel" he asked

"I don't know I have not opened it yet"

I turned the ignition on and nothing happened

"Dad must have left the lights on or something" I said

"Don't worry I'll take a look" he replied

I tried the ignition again, just as Lachie was about to get out of the van. There was a click and then a loud boom followed by whooshing sound along with a wall of flames. The van was blown through the wall of the barn, next to the house. The van rolled over twice and my ears were ringing. Then everything went black. When I came too Lachie was laid on top of me, and I could not move. We lay like that for what appeared like ten minutes, but was in all likelihood a matter of seconds. The van was on its side and warm fluid of some form, was flowing onto my face.

"Lachie, Lachie are you OK Mate?"

He groaned and started to move.

"Are you OK Lachie" I repeated though in truth I could not hear my own words. He groaned some more and then he kicked the shattered windscreen out. He clambered out first and I pulled myself from out behind the steering wheel. Then I too, with Lachie's assistance, crawled out from where the windscreen used to be. I could see Lachie's lips moving but it sounded like he was miles away, speaking through a pipe.

"What?"

Again his lips moved and this time I heard him faintly above the ringing in my ears.

"What Happened"

I looked around at where our home, at one time stood. Now all I could see was smoking debris and some burning wood. My ears were still reverberating loudly

"Are you OK?" I asked Lachie again

I must have been shouting and I am sure that Lachlan was too.

"Yes Mate it's just a cut to my head"

"What about your face Andy? It's covered in blood."

I wiped my hands across my face and could find no apparent injuries.

"I think it's your blood Lachie, when I came too you were on top of me in the van"

My hearing was starting to return. I wiped my eyes clear of Lachie's Blood.

"Let me take a look at that Lachie."

He sat down on an old tree stump, that we used as a block, for chopping our logs on. I went over and took a look at his injuries. He had a deep two-inch gash to the left hand side of his forehead. I took a hanky from my pocket and passed it to him.

"Put this over it and keep the pressure on it. You are going to require stitches on that mate. Are you injured anywhere else?"

"No I don't think so. What happened to your house Andy?"

"Not something good. I am thankful dad was out doing his chores. He'd have been dead if he had been in the house. I am also glad he has the dogs with him."

ACT 15

I looked around the carnage. The cow was dead, to be fair to death, she was actually splattered across what was left of the barn wall. She had been in the barn and bundles of hay were burning at the back of what was left of it. I think, had it not been for all the extra heavy plywood panelling inside the van, Lachie and I would be looking pretty similar to the cow.

"It's all gone everything is destroyed."

The Large Propane Gas Tank at the side of the house. It had exploded towards the house itself. This is why the house took the full force of the blast.

"Gas leak?" Lachie asked me

"I think so, but given the circumstances over the last week. I am not so sure this was an accident. These gas tanks are configured so that the weak point is either at the release valve on the top or from the pipes that come from the front."

I pointed to what was left of the tank. It showed bent metal petals, flowering towards where the house had previously been standing.

"This was deliberate, I am one hundred percent sure Lachie"

"So what do we do now?"

"First we call 'The Suit'. Apart from the house, our operational hard cash was in our Kit-Bags. They were in what was left of the house along, with all of my Dads and my belongings. And I want some fucking answers. We will also need some form of a statement for the Police and Fire Brigade. I am sure half of the Strath will have heard that explosion and no doubt seen the accompanying fireball."

Lachie took out his phone

"Might be an outstanding satellite phone, but it's not been made bomb proof."

He said, as he showed the phone that was now in two

pieces.

I took mine out and it looked to be all right. I flipped it open. Then selected the only number from the directory and pressed the dial button.

The number rang twice

"Hello"

"Andy McPhee here I want to talk to the guy in 'The Suit' with no name!"

There was a click and the phone went dead

"Fuckers hung up on me Lachie!"

I was getting genuinely fucking tired, of that happening, whenever I called 'The Suit'. I dialled again and got an unobtainable sound. I tried again, still nothing.

"What the fuck is going on Lachie? First my house blows up, and now the number in the phone no longer exists."

"I believe we were meant to die in that explosion mate. The only reason that we are still alive is that thick granite wall over there" He said pointing to the half demolished gable wall.

"That, and you having kitted out the van for your band, with all that plywood. I think the trigger was in the vans ignition. We would both have been as dead as your cow, if you had let me get out of the bloody van before you tried the ignition again. Then I would look the same as the cow."

I walked over to where the van laid on its side and had a look at the steering column. A small black plastic box had been attached below the steering wheel. There were two wires extending to the ignition.

I pointed this out to Lachie

"Looks like you were correct mate"

The phone in my back pocket started to vibrate. I took it out and looked at the number that was calling. It just showed a line of zero's

"Hello who is this?"

"That does not matter for now. But I am a friend. I will contact you later today. Do not go anywhere. Now destroy the phone" They hung up

"Was that 'The Suit'?

"No I don't think so Lachie"

"What did they say"?

"I have to destroy the phone, and they will contact me

later. What do you reckon?"

"Personally I don't trust SIS or Black Door, or whatever name they use. So if it was up to me? I would destroy the phone. Then lie to the police as much as we can. Until we know, just what in the name of fuck is going on?"

I bent the phone in two and then smashed the pieces under foot. Then threw the parts into the still smouldering remains, of what had been my home for many years. It had in reality only been owned by me for just one week!

"The package! we need to get the fucking package out if we can, before the police arrive."

My bedroom was on the only wall left standing, although the roof had come off the house, the floor of my room now lay angled downward towards the ground."

Lachie and I raked through the rubble until we recovered the package. It was an aluminium case similar to a hard case for a camera, but with combination locks. There was a sticker on the bottom with a number. I grabbed the case and got it out of the ruins of my house. After which I hid it under a large rock, behind the mangled van. Just in the nick of time. The dogs were first on the scene, with my Akita running in front of Dad's Great Dane. Dad was jogging on behind. He was a fit man for his age, although running, for my 70 year old father, would never be an Olympic event.

"Are you two alright?" he shouted through his breathlessness, when he was about twenty yards from us.

I waited until he was level with us

"Yes dad, just a few cuts and bruises."

"What happened?"

"We think the old gas tank exploded."

Dad looked at the burning remains of his existence. I could see the exceptional sadness in his eyes. I was at an absolute loss for words. He had kept all of mum's belongings, furniture and her jewellery. Along with her photos and several pictures she had painted from a time when they both young.

"But how son, how did it happen"? His eyes were glassy, but the tears of his emotional pain did not drop.

"I don't know dad. Lachie and I were just going to nip over to his home. It happened, just as we were leaving in the van. When Boom! The whole fucking thing went up"

"Watch your mouth boy. You know I don't tolerate language like that. I understand that you are shook up, so I will let it slide this time"

"Sorry Dad."

Again a part truth is simpler than a complete lie. I was starting to detest the person I was becoming. My parents were so proud of me when I first enlisted. And I wondered, what they would think of me now. One week into this mess and I was telling lies so easily, worse so plausibly.

"You positive you're not injured Son? You have a great deal of blood, all over your face?"

"It is not my blood Dad. It's Lachie's"

"Are you OK Lachie?" My father asked

"Yes I am all right Craig, it looks worse than it is. You know what the scalp is like, bleeds like a stuck pig. Even with just a nick."

"Have you called the Fire Brigade?"

"Dad, there is nothing left to call them for. But I am confident someone has called them and in all probability, the rest of the emergency services. I am thankful that you were out at your chores and you had the dogs with you."

"And the cow Andy?"

"Sorry Dad she is gone. I believe it would have been quick, as she was next to the house, when the blast happened. Lachie and I were in the Van, just about to set off when it happened. The gable wall probably saved our lives, even though it threw the van about a bit."

"You can stop at my house tonight Craig, or for that matter as long as you require."

"Very gracious of you Lachie" My father replied.

It had been approximately thirty minutes since the explosion and a siren could be heard in the distance. Roughly ten minutes later, a Police car pulled up with its lights flashing. A young female police constable got out, and came over to us

"Is there anybody still in the building?"

I stepped forward

"No. We were just about to go out" Indicating to Lachie, And my Father was out on the hill, with the dogs."

"There is an ambulance on the way, and the Fire Brigade from Golspie and Helmsdale." She said. Then she saw the load of blood and guts, at the side of the house. She turned white and I thought she was going to faint or be physically sick.

"Who's that over there" She said, pointing to the mess that used to be, Dad's cow.

"That was Gerty." said Lachie

I had to quickly jump in, before she called the Murder Squad

"Gert was our Milking Cow, and she is past any Veterinary skills"

She opened the door of her car and sat down on the seat. I knew her face, but just could not place it. All I knew is that it was a recent face. I did not want to push my luck, so I let it slip.

"Are you all right Miss?" My Father enquired.

"WPC Miller, and yes thank you, and you are?"

"Mr Craig McPhee and this is my son Andy. This is his friend Lachlan Henderson. I used to.......well my son owns this house.......owned this house and land."

We could pick up the wail of more sirens, approaching in the distance.

"I Hope you closed the gate at the foot of the brae?" My father said

"What? Oh yes Sir, I left Constable Murdoch down there, to direct the emergency vehicles up here."

"How did you find the place?" asked my dad

"Easy we followed the smoke Sir"

"Ahhh"

A couple of moments later, there was an Ambulance parked up, and the volunteer Fire Brigade from Helmsdale had arrived. But without a nearby water source, they could not use their pump. That said, there was not much left, worth saving. Some twenty minutes subsequent to that, the Golspie Brigade arrived, with their Fire Engine and smothered down what was left of the burning wreckage of our home. Not long after they arrived, a police Range Rover pulled up, and a uniformed Sergeant got out. He went up to the WPC and had a few words with her. She pointed to my Dad and then to me. The Sergeant came over to me.

"This was your house sir?"

"Yes that's correct"

"Do you know how the fire started?"

"I believe it must have been a gas leak, and something must have ignited it. Just as we were going out"

"You live here?"

"Well yes and no. I used to be in the RAF and I just got out."

"How can it be Yes and No Sir? It either is your home or it is not? Which is it?"

"Yes it is, well was. That is to say that pile of rubble is what remains of my home. My father lives here all the time. I normally would just have come home on leave. Now I am back for good. Does that explain it to you?"

"I imagine it will have to do for present. But at some point you are going to have to come and make an official statement. Do you require any medical assistance?" he said pointing to my face

"Ohh No, that's not my blood it's his" I replied indicating to Lachie. He was sat on the back step of the Ambulance. A Paramedic was applying butterfly sutures to head wound.

They wanted to take Lachie to The Lawson Memorial Hospital in Golspie, for an X-Ray. Lachie was having none of it though. He insisted he was OK. Then he walked over to us, sporting a large dressing on his forehead.

"I will leave a constable here overnight. To make sure, no one steals anything that is left here" Said the Sergeant and then continued.

"Do you have anywhere to stay tonight?"

"Yes. Thank you. We have somewhere to go. But I would be grateful if you could call us a Taxi from McLeod's Garage in Kinbrace"

"I can run you down there myself, if you like?" he replied.

"Thank you. I will get my dad and Lachie. Is it OK to put the dogs in you car too?"

"Sure not a problem, so long as they don't devour the seats."

Five minutes later, we were on our way down to Kinbrace. The Policeman dropped us outside McLeod's and then he got a call on the radio. He excused himself and said he would be talking to us soon. Being as Lachie, only lived a mile from

Kinbrace village. We walked there. This would save us, being asked awkward questions. We walked in silence, until we got there. Like the house I used to own. Lachie's home, like mine, was quite remote and hidden from view. Lachie reached up into a Rowan Tree near his front door and took down a small tin that was squeezed between the lower branches. He opened the tin and took out a set of keys. Then he put the tin, in his pocket. He opened the door and we all went in.

Lachie was a bit anal, in the house keeping manner and had dust throws, over all the furniture. He was house proud and I was not. It was not so much as I was dirty or anything like that. I could just be a bit untidy.

"Coffee?" he asked whilst removing the covers from his sofa and chairs.

"Got anything stronger" My father asked

"Sure Craig. Help yourself from over there."

Lachie said, pointing to a large glass fronted cabinet, full of bottles of various spirits. There was a complete collection of lead crystal glasses. From brandy balloons, to fine tall Champagne flutes and everything in between.

"I will get a fire going and you can pour me a Bowmore Twenty Five year old, that's the one with the Black Label and the Gold writing on it"

Lachie was a man who enjoyed his single malt whisky, this was one of his favourites. If you could tell a man's personality from what he drinks, then Lachie's would be smooth and warm and full of Scotland's rich heritage. As well as being powerful and robust. He said I was a heathen, for drinking Irish Whisky, though he always had a bottle of Middleton Very Rare Irish Whisky. This was for the times when we would have a drink simply to enjoy the decadence of something special. Just to relish the flavours and be indulgent for a few moments. Lachie returned with an armful of dry logs then set them on the kindling already in the fireplace. He lit it. I passed him his drink, which was in one of his best Edinburgh Lead Crystal Glasses. The flames of the fire were refracted from both the golden liquid and the faceted crystal goblets. Lachie always said, that to enjoy the best, you had to drink it from the best. We three gently clinked our glasses.

"Here's tae us. Wha's like us. Damn few, and they're a'

deid. Mair's the pity!" said my father

Now the fire was going and the house had warmed up. Lachie, heated up some soup

"Sorry I did not have an opportunity to get more in" He said with a smile.

"No problem" I replied

"Mr McPhee you can have the big room downstairs and me and Andy will have the two small rooms upstairs"

"Thanks Lachie. I have told you before, please call me Craig"

"OK Craig. You are welcome here as long as you like""

"When you go to bed Craig, Andy and I will give the dogs a walk and in all probability have a little chat and a drink"

My father had a coffee and went to his bed.

"Let's go for that walk and talk Andy"

We let the dogs out and ambled down to the foot of Lachie's driveway.

"Someone wants us dead and they don't mind who they have to murder alongside us. That letter you got, said"

'You and your friends may be in grave danger.
Some of the people that you are working with
Are not who they appear to be.
Do NOT trust anyone.'

"So who is it we are genuinely working for? We don't know sufficient, for anyone to want to kill us. Do we Andy?"

"Lachie how can we know, what 'The Suit' told us is truthful? It could all be bullshit. Nothing in this makes any sense. Christ they could have killed my Dad. We have to get him away from all of this. We can't go to the police. We just have to hope that the 'Friend' comes to our assistance. We should go back up to my place and get that case we hid"

"I don't think we can while they have a policeman there. Your dad can go and stop with my folks, on Fetlar. That should be far enough away, from whatever is going on here. Do you think he will go?"

"I think this has shaken him up pretty bad. So I would say, in all probability he will go. Providing we can come up with something credible."

"OK Andy I will telephone my folks, when we get back to the house. But I believe we should do a security sweep of my home first. We know that explosion at yours was not accidental"

I whistled the dogs over and we started back up to the house. Kyla was beside me when she emitted a quiet and low growl, the hairs on her neck and shoulders stood up. Her tail went down between her hind legs. I motioned for her to be quiet, by laying my hand out flat on her back. Raven stood beside her with his ears pinned back, his tail was also down.

"Whoa Boy" I said quietly.

"Something's up Lachie and my dad's in there. If they knew where I lived, they know where you live" I whispered.

"You take Kyla and go around the right hand side of the house, and I will go left with Raven, as he answers my call. Kyla only answers to you and your dad."

"OK Lachie, meet you around the back"

Lachie set off at a crouched trot with Raven on his heels. I set of to the right in the identical fashion. I was just about level with the edge of the house, when I saw a shadow move across towards the tree line, to my right.

"Stop or I will set the dog on you!" I yelled out.

The individual stopped for just an instant, then they turned to face me and then took off at the run. In the dark I was unable to see any detail of their face.

"Take them" I shouted to Kyla.

She was already off and running hard towards the person. The Japanese Akita, originates from the mountain regions of Japan. Kyla was a pure breed. They were originally bred to kill bears. Kyla was large even for her breed. Weighing in at just about nine stone and she could run in brief bursts, at almost thirty miles an hour. Akita's can kill a bear in a single bite. I heard the whine of a silenced shot ping off a fence post next to me. In the same instant saw the flash from the direction Kyla was headed. As I ran after her I could hear a scream of pain, and a man voice shouting.

"Get it off me, please stop. Get it off"

When I got there, Kyla had her teeth deep into the back of the person's thigh, and I caught a glimpse of a pistol roughly four feet from the man on the ground. I put my foot down on the back of the man's neck and said

"DON'T MOVE" "KYLA LEAVE"

She let go of the man's leg and lay down with her bloodied mouth, inches from the persons head.

Lachie Arrived with Raven who let out a growl from some place deep inside the bowels of the earth.

"Down Raven" Lachie said and Raven lay down on the earth next to Kyla.

"Who the in the name of fuck are you?" I asked the person who was still screaming

They mumbled something that I could not hear very well. It could have had something to do with their face being buried in the leaves and grass, along with my size nine, on the back of his neck. I raised my foot up, just enough for the person to turn their head, so that I could see who they were.

"Please don't let the dogs bite me any more" he whimpered

"Jon?" both Lachie and I said at the same instance as we looked at Jon and then again at each other.

I picked up the automatic pistol that was laid on the ground.

"What the Fuck are you doing here? And why were you shooting at me?"

"I was not shooting at you. I was shooting at the fucking mutt" he said

I lifted my foot from his neck and placed it heavily onto the mangled and bloodied region of his thigh. He screamed in agony.

"Then why were you trying to kill my dog you bastard?"

"Because it was chasing me, that's why"

"Why did you run?"

"I didn't know who you were, in the dark"

"Bull Shit" I said pressing harder

He screamed again, only louder than the last time.

"Shut the fuck up." I hissed.

I put the gun in the back of my jeans

"Raven, Heel" Raven stood up and moved beside me

"Kyla Stay"

I frisked Jon down, being certain not to miss his genital region and butt crack, unsavoury as it was. But he was not carrying any other firearms. I snagged his wallet and his mobile phone,

"If you attempt to move from this spot, Kyla will rip you to pieces and most likely she will eat some of those pieces. Lachie and I are going to check out his house. So now is the time to tell me if there are any surprises waiting for us?"

"Like Gas tanks rigged to blow" Lachie added.

Jon said nothing

"This is your last chance to say something? No? Watch him Kyla. She will take you down if you try to move while we are away, so be smart and lie still"

She growled but stayed still. The heckles on the back of her neck were raised to their full extent. Lachie and I set off at the trot with Raven in between us

"Find it Raven Find it" I said

Raven went backwards and forwards going all around the house with his nose pressed steadfastly to the ground. Then he stopped dead and lay down, next to Lachie's Land Rover. I whistled Raven over to where I was standing.

"Down Boy" He sat on the ground with his tongue lolling out the side of his mouth.

"Stay here with the dogs please Andy I have a Torch just inside the front door"

I waited with Raven. Lachie came out with his torch. It was more like a floodlight really. It was one of those, million candle power lamps. He shone it towards where Raven had indicated.

"We have a serious problem Andy. There is what looks like, an explosive device below the car and a sensor connected to the wheel. So that any weight alteration will make it detonate."

"I have an idea Lachie"

"Yeah like what"

"Wait there with Raven and I will be back in a minute."

I ran across to where Kyla was with Jon.

"Get the fuck up Jon"

"I can't man, my leg is hurt"

I kicked him between the legs, and he howled. However he stopped, as soon as he saw I was holding His pistol to his head.

"Wait, please. I'm getting up"

Kyla demonstrated her displeasure with another snarl. Jon got to his feet

"Start walking and don't even consider attempting to run away, because it's not the bullet that will catch up to you first, it's her" I said indicating towards Kyla.

"And make no doubt about it, she WILL catch you"

We walked over to Lachie, when I say walked, I walked, Kyla walked and Jon limped and dragged one leg. When we reached the Land Rover, I said

"Defuse it"

"Defuse what?" Jon asked.

Lachie slapped him hard on the back of his head.

"Don't be stupid. The dogs only found one scent and it was yours. My Father is in that house. So if you don't defuse it, then the dogs get an early dinner of fresh meat."

"I can't, please I can't defuse it. It can't be defused"

"You had better find a way in the next thirty seconds" said Lachlan

"Or I am going to throw you under the car and that will set it off I am sure."

"You can't PLEASE. There are others."

"Others…. People…. or Bombs?"

"Bombs" he replied "They are chained. There is one at the back door, one at the gate and another on top of the Oil Tank, plus the one under the Land Rover"

"Keep him here Lachie. I am going to get my dad out"

"No Andy. You stay here. I know my house better than you do. Don't worry I will make sure your dad is safe."

"OK Lachie. Be careful"

He set of towards the house

"Wait! Lachie Take Raven with you, just in case and let him walk in front of you. You know how good he is at picking up trails"

"OK Andy. Raven, Come Boy" They both set of again towards the house.

"You, get on the fucking ground"

I kicked Jon on the back of the knee, of his good leg, and he crashed to the ground, after which I put my foot, on the back of his neck once again.

"When we get my father out, you ARE going to defuse

the set of bombs, or just like the training session, you will go BOOM and it won't be paint this time"

Three minutes later Lachie came out with my father. Who to be fair was looking a little bit bewildered by what was going on. This was only one step behind me, in the stakes of things that were transpiring. Lachie walked my father over to the tree line. And then sat him down, on an old wooden garden bench he had there. Lachie wrapped a blanket around my father's shoulders

"Stay here with Raven. You know he will look after you. We will try and explain things in a bit. OK? Mr McPhee, sorry Craig" Lachie said as he corrected himself.

Then he came over to where I was with Jon, who was face down on the ground. Kyla was standing guard over him.

"It is time for you, to go to work Jon. We will stand over there by the Rowan Tree, while you defuse this device. And don't give me that shit, that it can't be done. Do it or Fucking Die doing it" said Lachie and then he added

"Does that work for you Andy?"

"Aye it does. So get going Jon. Fucking sort it"

Jon slithered on his belly towards the Land Rover

"I need some tools Please" he whimpered "And the torch"

"Too bad for you, they are in the Land Rover" Lachlan called out then added

"Only Kidding I will get them from the house"

He came out with a tool box. Then set it down by Jon, along with the torch, and walked backwards to where I was standing by the tree.

Jon worked feverishly under the Land Rover

"I need some Sellotape please" he shouted

"There is a roll of Duct Tape, in the bottom of the Tool Box" Lachie shouted back at him.

"I want my Father out of here, first thing tomorrow" I said to Lachie

"I hear you mate. We will either drive him up to Scrabster or go over on the ferry to Shetland. Or we go up to Wick and fly him to Sumburgh, Shetland. There he can catch an Island hopper to Fetlar. Then my father can meet him."

"OK mate. Lachie what are we going to do with Jon? We

can't just let him go, and that means we also, can't take him to Hospital either"

"I know a place, Andy, where we can take him, it's an old cottage. I don't think it's been used for years since the old fella that lived there died. His family all live in the South now. So it should be empty. There is a dirt track road that goes down the side of Loch an Ruathair. It's a few miles into the hills, up beside Loch Culadh. Where it sits nestled between Ben Griam Beg and Ben Griam Mor. It's one of those places that is about as remote a man can get on the mainland of Scotland."

"All right Lachie. First let's see if Jon is going to get himself covered in red paint"

Jon got to his feet. "This one is defused" he shouted over

"Get in the Land Rover" Lachie yelled back at him

"What?"

I said, "FUCKING GET IN THE FUCKING LAND ROVER!"

I changed my position to keep my view of him, but keeping the tree between Jon and myself, as he got into the Land Rover. I took the Sig Sauer, that I had confiscated from Jon, out of my waist Band and passed it over to Lachie, He took it, then popped the magazine out, checked it, and popped it back in. He raised the pistol then he fired a single shot towards Jon. A small clod of earth at Jon's foot, jumped up into the air.

"He said. GET IN THE FUCKING LAND ROVER NOW, or I swear to God the next round goes into your miserable fucking head"

Jon opened the door and sat behind the steering wheel of the Land Rover. Lachie wandered over, to stand beside his car then passed a set of keys to Jon. All of the time, Lachie was keeping a good bead on him with the pistol.

"I am going to walk about twenty yards down in front of you, if you even move I WILL KILL YOU. You know from the shooting range that at this distance, I can put five rounds into your eye. So when I am twenty yards away you are going to give you a signal and then you are then going to start the Land Rover and drive forward SLOWLY for ten feet. IF, you make ANY sudden moves, like trying to duck down, and mashing your good foot down on the accelerator pedal. I WILL SHOOT YOU. That is a promise the ONLY way that you get to live tonight, is by doing EVERYTHING you are told to do, and EXACTLY as you are told. DO YOU FUCKING UNDERSTAND?" Lachie said the last part slowly and with a fair amount of menace.

"Yes I understand" Jon said in a shaky voice

Lachie backed up slowly, all the time keeping the gun raised and Jon's head, in his sights. Lachie waved his hand at Jon and then made a key turning motion, with his free hand.

"Start it up"

Jon started the Land Rover and slowly drove forward. Then stopped and switched off the ignition.

"Drop the Keys out of the door Jon"

Again, Jon did as he was told. Lachie jogged up to him, picked up the keys and opened the door and dragged Jon out by the scruff of his neck, and threw him on the ground. I went over to where they were.

"And the other bombs are they safe now?"

"No, not quite" Jon replied

"They have to be deactivated by having the receive switch, set to off."

"So what are you waiting for Jon? Do it and like I said previously, don't think about running as you will get about five yards, before the dogs catch up with you, and THEY WILL CATCH YOU AND THEN THEY WILL RIP YOU APART!" Adding my menace to that of Lachie's for good measure.

"Don't worry I know"

He seemed reconciled to the concept, he knew there was no getting away from us. In a Town or a City, it is easy to run fifty yards and get lost in a crowd, or in and out of back alley ways. It is an entirely different story though, out in the wild Scottish countryside. Especially where there are only a few roads. From our location, there was a choice of just two roads. Over the next few minutes, Jon switched off the other three devices and brought them around to the front of the house. So we now had the IED's along with Jon, as our prisoner. I called the dogs and my father over. Then along with Jon, we went back into Lachie's home. I would have to tell my father, some of what had happened over the past week or so. He did not need to know all of the details, but I would give him some of the more basic elements of it. I would drive him to Wick and then get him on a plane to the Island Fetlar. In Lachie's Kitchen, I put the small IED's on the counter next to the sink. That way my father could see them. Because I needed him to believe the danger, he would be in, if he remained here with us.

"Sit" Lachie commanded Jon.

Raven sat down as well, thinking the command was intended for him. Jon sat where he was told too.

"Watch him while I go get my tool box" Lachie passed the Sig Sauer back to me

"Andy. Watch Him CLOSELY."

With that, Lachie went out the door, and returned a few moments later. I passed the pistol back to him.

"What in the name of all that is holy, is going on with you two? And when did you think it was acceptable to use the foul language like you have been using?" my father asked

"It's a protracted and convoluted story dad"

"Well let's see, if you can't make it abbreviated and uncomplicated for your old man then?"

I told him the rudiments, but left out the part that Jon, was supposed to be member of our team. Jon started to speak and Lachie slapped him hard across the face.

"You gave up the right to speak, until you are spoken too, when you blew up Andy's home and tried to do the same to mine. So shut the fuck up" Lachie smacked him again.
"Got it?"
Then he added.

"Sorry Craig."

Jon nodded. My father went over to Jon and backhanded Jon across his face

"That's for destroying my home. You little bastard"

Then he slapped Jon's other cheek

"And this is for killing my poor Gerty, you little fucker."

I had never heard my father use such language ever. Lachie then took the roll of duct tape and wound it around Jon's mouth and head twice, then used it to secure his hands behind his back. After which he then taped his legs together and then to the chair. Jon's leg was still bleeding, but he was not going to die from blood loss. Kyla must have missed the femoral artery.

"Dad I am going to drive you up to Wick, and get you on a plane to Fetlar. Then you will go and stop with Lachie's Dad.

You will be safe there."

"How are you going to contact Mr Henderson, without anyone knowing? Andy. They whoever they might be, in all probability, have all of your telephones tapped." My father asked

This was one of the things about my Father. He was old but his thinking cap was still firmly in place. He was right and I had not thought of it. If I called Lachie's dad using a phone. I would just be placing both of our parents in unnecessary danger. We took turns in watching Jon, while my father slept. I had to keep reminding myself. That whilst I had lost my home. My father had lost every part of his life, along with every tactile memory, that he had of my mother and his wife. All he had now, were his memories. Given that, I thought he was holding up pretty well, to the savage events of the last day. Somehow, I had to take my Father to Wick, and then get him on a plane to the relative safety of a remote Shetland Island. I also had to go and give my statement to the police in Brora. I don't think they would be too amused about the mini war that was being waged on their turf. The rest of the night passed without incident. In the morning Lachie shook me awake. He had taken the last shift watching over Jon. The aroma of fresh ground coffee filled the kitchen.

"Sorry Andy, I only have black coffee and nothing else"

"Coffee's fine, thanks Lachie. We can get some supplies later, when I go up to Wick."

I sipped the hot black liquid, ordinarily at this time of day, I had it with my breakfast, but the pure caffeine, would keep me going for a bit.

"I have given some thought, about how to get in touch with your Dad Lachie. Does your Father still use his ship to shore radio?"

"Yes. He uses it to listen in to his friends, when they go out to fish."

"Can you remember which frequency he uses, and what is his call sign?"

"He uses Standard Marine VHF, Channel sixteen, and I think his call sign is Sierra Lima Foxtrot Zero One." Lachie replied. Then he wrote it down on a scrap of paper for me.

"In that case Lachie I will endeavour and persuade a

friend of mine in Keiss to allow me use his radio. I can ask your father, if my dad can stay with him for the duration of this shit storm. As long as you don't mind looking after this shithead, until I get back. This will be approximately five or six tonight. I will get us some groceries as well."

Lachie emptied his pockets onto the kitchen table, and took out the money he had put there, at CDE Proton Down.

"There's about four and a half thousand here, in addition to what you have. You should be able to get a good load of food in. Get some clothing as well. If you go to Lidl's in Wick, and buy dry and canned goods. I doubt if there is a freezer where we are going, let alone, electricity."

I woke my Father

"Dad, we have to get going in about ten minutes. I am going to try and arrange for you to stop at the Henderson's house, on the Island of Fetlar. I am going to give you sufficient funds, to get there. I will also try to get Mr Henderson, to meet you on the beach at Fetlar. That is where they land the Island Hopper. I know this is all confusing for you, and you have been to hell and back in the last twenty-four hours. I really wish I could tell you everything, but I just can't. You are just going to have to trust me. You will be better off not knowing. Dad I need you to keep most of this quiet. Don't tell Mr Henderson about any of this. Please. Just tell him that I have bought our home and am going to do a lot of re-modelling to it. OK?"

"No son, it's NOT BLOODY OK! You should know better than to say something like that to me. Or to ask me to lie for you. Stop treating me like a blithering idiot. I am not a senile old fool. But I will go along with it. What kind of danger are you in? And what have you done son?"

"I will not lie about the danger we are all in, if we stay here. But I can tell you honestly. We have done nothing to deserve it."

We finished our coffee and I refuelled the Land Rover at McLeod's Garage, I paid in cash. Then headed on up to Wick, via Helmsdale. I would have to pick up some Twelve-bore cartridges. I had my Firearms License in my wallet. Lachie owned three shotguns, which were in his house and he probably had two or three boxes of cartridges. He also had his. Triple two rifle, and no doubt several boxes of bullets for the too. But the way things were transpiring, I would feel safer in the knowledge, that we had an adequate supply of both firearms and the ammunition for them. The hardware shop in Helmsdale, would sell shotgun cartridges to me, as well as shells for Lachie's rifle. My Mannlicher was somewhere under the rubble, of the ruin of my house and being guarded by a policeman. Which made getting access to it, out of the question.

"Would you not be quicker going to Halkirk via Forsinard Son?"

"We would Dad, but I have to get some provisions from Helmsdale first."

The silence between us was unbearable, so I turned on the radio and tuned it to Moray Firth Radio. When the News came on, the newscaster stated that there had been a gas explosion, at a farm house in Kinbrace. They added that the building, had been destroyed, but without injury to any person. We listened to the music and still my father said nothing. I pulled the Land Rover over, at Bal-An-Or. This had been the site of the Kildonnan Gold Rush of 1869. You could still Pan for gold here if you had the patience, that is. My mother when she had been alive, had managed to pan sufficient gold over the years, to have a large pendant made for her by a local Jeweller.

"I know you are angry at me Dad, and I am sorry, but I genuinely do not know most of what is going on. All I do know, is it is not safe for you to stay here. You know, after we lost mum to cancer, you have been my world. As such, I will do everything in my power, to protect you. Some things that I do know, for your own safety, I cannot tell you. I am going to tell you some of it, OK?"

"Son, I would prefer you told me all of it, but at this point in time, I guess I will have to settle for what you can tell me. Tell me this. You are not out of the Military? Are you?"

"That's a difficult question Dad"

"NO IT IS NOT SON! It is an uncomplicated YES or NO. You are right. I have lost everything that is, except the one thing I have left that matters. That is YOU!"

"Dad I am no longer in the RAF, that is true, and it is the same for Lachie. The trouble is, I don't know which subdivision of the military that I am in, and I DON'T altogether know, what is going on. So there you have it. I just know Lachie and I are still serving Britain. Can you accept that please?"

"So, what can you tell me of what is going on?"

"Dad I don't really know. Just that it is happening in our neck of the woods. This is in all probability why they chose Lachie and me."

"So what do you and Lachie, plan to do?"

"Protect the people I love, Dad."

"OK Son. Promise me you will be careful and make it right."

"I promise Dad"

I slipped the Land Rover into gear, and then headed on down to Helmsdale. I turned Left on to the Main Street and Pulled up at the Hardware Store.

"I will be back in a minute" I said to my Father.

The shop was empty when I entered, and the doorbell announced my arrival. A moment later, John McCormack appeared behind the counter.

"Home on leave Andy?"

"Yes John, but no doubt, you heard there was a gas explosion at my house yesterday"

There did not seem any point in concealing this fact, as I was sure everybody in the Strath and in Helmsdale, already knew about it, and in all probability, even before the media had announced it.

"Aye I heard about that. Is everybody OK?"

"Yes John we are all fine. How's your family"

"They are for the most part, away these days. Elli is at University in Aberdeen. My wife, she has a job at the Lawson Memorial Hospital in Golspie. Stuart still works on the boat, in Keiss. Like you my eldest boy is now in the military. He is a Private in Royal's"

This was a referral to the Royal Scottish Regiment. It was common practice for folks around here, to tell their whole life story, before actually doing anything. It was a way of life I grew up with and enjoyed coming back to.

"Now what can I do for you today Andy"

"I am staying at Lachie's in Kinbrace and we wanted to spend some time on the hill shooting but all my shells along with my guns were destroyed in the explosion. So I am using Lachie's guns, except we don't have enough shells or bullets. So

I need five Boxes of twelve-gauge number three's and five boxes of number two's. Also need two hundred and fifty, triple two's, forty grain. Here are my certificates."

I passed them over the counter. So that John could fill in his Firearms Ledger.

"Thanks John, Tell the family I am asking after them, in fact I am going up to wick and might as well take a trip over to Keiss. Do you know if they are in or out at sea, at the moment?"

"Stuart called this morning, so I guess they must be in at the moment. If you see him, tell him to get his arse into gear and come and see his father"

"I will do John." I paid for the ammunition, then we shook hands "See you soon Bye."

I left and put the boxes of bullets and shells into the back of the Land Rover. I jumped in and started it up

"OK Let's Go"

ACT 16

I drove down the Road and turned left and back up onto the A9, then headed up towards Wick. I dropped my father at the Airport. Gave him two thousand pounds of what was left, from the money, that Lachie and I still had. This was from what we had originally put in our wallets.

"I want you to buy a Ticket at the Logan air desk. Use the Island Hopper. It will visit all the outer Islands in the Shetlands and then take you to Fetlar. Don't forget, you will also have to check the Tide Timetables. Remember, they land on the beach there. I am going to get Mr Henderson to meet you there. I will be back here, before you go I promise. Dad I love you and Thanks."

We shook hands then hugged and I drove to Keiss. When I got there, I drove down the steep hill, to the Harbour. I pulled up next to the Harbour Wall and got out. The boat Stuart worked on, was the Wick registered WK3208A 'Catherine May'. It was tied up in the harbour, opposite the old Harbour Masters House. The Catherine May with its light blue and white wooden hull reflected in the still waters of the harbour. Stuart was on the deck, working on some Lobster creels. He looked up and saw me.

"Well Well, look what the tide threw up on the shore"

"Hello to you as well" I laughed.

"So Andy what brings you to Keiss?"

"In reality, you do mate"

Stuart wiped his hands and clambered off the boat and onto the quay then shook my hand.

"How you doing, long time no see. How is it I can help you?"

"I am doing good mate, but my dad is going to visit Lachie's dad. However the telephones are down on Fetlar today" I despised lying to my friends and it really worried me, that the more I lied the easier it became. I continued.

"I wanted to see, if I could use your VHF Radio, as Lachie's dad always listens in on channel 16."

"I can't see a problem Andy, though I will have to ask the skipper first. Come aboard."

I followed Stuart back down onto the boat.

"Hey Skip! I have a friend here. He wants to contact a mate on Fetlar. Can he use the radio?"

A big sturdy sort of man came out of the engine room through the deck hatch. His hair was curly and unkempt. It was salt and pepper grey, his face was weather beaten and looked chapped and crazed. He wore a full beard which was yellowed around the edges of his mouth, a hand rolled cigarette dangled loosely from his lips.

"Hi I am Andy McPhee" I put my hand out, "We went to school together, that is, Stuart and I did."

His hand was big and like the man himself, weather beaten by years of hard work at sea. He had not bothered to wipe off the engine grease from his hand, but I shook it none the less. His hand shake was steadfast and honest. His eyes were grey but full of experience.

"Who you want to call?" he asked

"Mark Henderson, on Fetlar"

"I know him he sits on the ship to shore and passes on communications, when we are out of range from home. He has a boy in the Army I think?"

"Yes sir that's him. Only his boy in the RAF Regiment" I replied

"I know that, I was just checking that you did too, before you fucked with me. Sure you can use the radio. Stu will show you how to use it, if you don't already know."

"Thank you. Sir"

"Stop calling me sir, I am not your daddy, at least I don't think I am, and I am not some Toff from the South. Name's Sandy, Sandy McKay."

I thought I knew his face from somewhere, but just could not place it. He seemed to be a nice, gentle, honest and friendly sort of person.

"OK Sandy. Thanks, I really appreciate it"

I followed Stuart, to the small cabin, that was the wheelhouse on this boat. He reached up to the radio and turned it on, then he picked up the microphone and passed it to me.

"Our call sign is Whisky Kilo Three Two Zero Eight Alpha. Do you know Mr Henderson's call sign?"

"Yes I do, thanks Stu."

He left me in the wheelhouse alone. I took out the scrap of paper with Mr Henderson's call sign on and unfolded it. I picked up the microphone and pressed the key on the side of it.

"This is Whisky Kilo Three Two Zero Eight Alpha, Calling Sierra Lima Foxtrot Zero One. I repeat this is Whisky Kilo Three Two Zero Eight Alpha, Calling Sierra Lima Foxtrot Zero One. Come in Please."

There was static which was followed by

"This is Sierra Lima Foxtrot Zero One, Go ahead Whisky Kilo Three Two Zero Eight Alpha. Over"

"Hello Mr Henderson. This is Andy McPhee. Over"

"Hello Andy. How can I help you? Over"

Time for part lies again

"I am doing some work on our house, and I need a place for Dad to stay for a couple of weeks. So I was hoping you would not mind a house guest, on that little bird Island of yours. Over"

"Would that be the work that involved your home, being blown sky high? Over"

News, it would appear. Travels much faster here, then I had remembered.

"Yes that would be the one. Over"

"Andy, your dad is welcome here any day. You are all family, you know that? Over"

"Thank you Mr Henderson. Dad will be on the beach when the Island hopper from Logan Air lands there today. Over"

"OK. Thank you. I will check the tides and meet him. Is Lachie with you? Over"

"Sorry no, he is at his house in Kinbrace, Over"

"OK. Pass my love on to him. Over"

"Thank you. Whisky Kilo Three Two Zero Eight Alpha. Over and Out"

"Sierra Lima Foxtrot zero one. Over and Out"

I hung the microphone back up on its clip, and left the wheelhouse.

"Thanks Sandy. Good luck with the Lobsters and whatever else you go out for, Be safe."

I declined the offer of a shot from Sandy's hip flask, then shook his hand and also said goodbye to Stuart and told him to check in with his dad. Then I climbed off the boat and got back in the Land Rover and drove back to Wick Airport. I met up with my father in the Airport Terminal.

"Did you get your ticket sorted Dad?"

"Yes thanks Son. I fly to Sumburgh and then I catch a smaller, Logan Air plane to Fetlar."

"What time do you leave?"

"In about an hour"

"OK Dad. I have called Mr Henderson, on the ship to shore radio. He is expecting you. He will meet you on the beach, when your plane lands. I will be in touch using the radio. I will try and get a letter to you soon as well."

"You know I don't like any of this, Son"

"I know dad and neither do I. But it's just the way it is. I will try and get some more money to you soon. Not that there is much to spend it on, in Fetlar. We have to stay off the grid for now dad that means all of us. So if you still have your mobile phone, don't use it, and don't answer it as I will not contact you that way. In fact, take out your sim card and destroy the phone. Do you understand what I am saying dad?"

"I'm not stupid son. I might be old, but I know what staying off the grid means. You go. I will be fine. Andy, look after Lachie and the dogs"

We hugged and I left. I got back into the Land Rover and drove the short distance to Lidl's. I bought cases of Baked Beans, Tinned Potatoes, packets of Bacon along with various tinned meats, a Tray of eggs, Flour, dried milk, Ground Coffee, packets of Dry Soup as well as tinned soup, some herbs and spices. I made sure I had plenty of bottled water and four bottles of Jameson's. They did not have Laphroaig, but I guessed that Lachie could take some of his own. In all I had to go around the shop three times to get all the goods I thought we might require. I bought a load of batteries and a couple of small but very bright LED torches. I think the woman thought I must have had a shop of my own, because on my last time at the checkout she asked me, if I was going to resell this elsewhere. So I told her a half truth.

"I don't get into town much, as we live right out in the sticks"

"Where do you live?" she was just being friendly but I did not want to answer honestly

"Just a wee croft out by Grummore" I lied again almost naturally. Grummore did exist and it was remote, so she swallowed the lie. I paid in cash. And I headed back to Lachie in Kinbrace. I pulled up in his driveway and went in. Jon was still in the chair. And his face looked a bit the worse for wear, than it had done when I left.

"He been giving you trouble?"

"No Andy. I have just been softening him up a bit. We need to get gone from here Andy. The police have been around looking for you. That Sergeant from Golspie was here. He is not satisfied with our version of yesterday's events."

"Can we talk outside Lachie?"

"Sure, he's not going anywhere."

We went outside

"I got my father sorted, and he is on route to your dad's. Your dad asked after you and told me to watch out for you. So did Stu. He still works on that fishing boat out of Keiss."

"Thanks Andy. We need to get all the supplies, transferred to the trailer. After that we get Jon and the dogs. Then get the hell out of here, before the police come back, or worse Jon's buddies"

"OK. I will load up you keep an eye on that shit. It will take me about half an hour."

I went over and hooked up the trailer. Then transferred all the provisions, I had bought along with stuff that Lachie had boxed up from his home. After I was done, I tied a tarpaulin over the top and went back into the house.

"We need to take all the guns, your shotguns and the triple two, along with any ammunition you have. Did he have any extra clips for the Sig Sauer?"

"Just, what we found on him last night. He is bound to have a car, around here somewhere. Any chance that Raven could find it?"

"I can but try" I cut off a portion of Jon's trouser leg and went outside with Raven. After rubbing it around the dog's nose for a bit, I said.

"Find it Raven Find It!!

Raven took off at the run. He then ran around the house, and then up to the tree line, where I had first seen Jon. Raven crossed over to the left and then back to the right. I followed and went around to the opposite side of the woods, where I found A Metallic Green Range Rover. The car was unlocked. The reason I had not noticed it before, was I had assumed that it was back down for Gordon to fix, and so I had wiped it out from my mind. I opened the door and looked around inside. In the pocket of the arm rest, I found a pair of spare clips for the Sig, along with three boxes of nine millimetre hollow points. The back seat was empty but in the boot there was a Black backpack similar to the now empty one that Jon had on him when we caught him. I unzipped the top and there were two large hunting knives. But the thing of most interest was the Uzi Machine Pistol, along with a twelve-inch suppressor. And four extended Magazines and another four boxes of nine millimetre shells. There was an OS Map of Kinbrace and the surrounding area, plus a Satellite Navigation Unit. In one of the outside pockets was approximately five thousand pounds in used twenty pound notes. I zipped up the bag and put it over my shoulder and went back to Lachie. I put the bag on the table in front of Jon.

"Raven found his car. It's a Green Range Rover and it's parked around the other side of the woods. I also found a stash of ammo and guns, along with a couple of knives, cash and a sat-nav. In there, is also an Ordinance Survey Map of this area, with both of our homes marked on it. I could not find a phone. But the keys are in the ignition. Do you want me to go and bring the car here?"

"Thinking about what's happened so far. I would bet that there is a locator device in it. So taking that, would only lead them, whoever they are, right to us. So we should leave it where it is. That said I think we should disable it before we go."

"OK Lachie. I will be back in a few minutes"

I unzipped the bag and took out one of the large knifes and ran back to the Range Rover. I opened the bonnet and cut as many hoses as I could find, then ripped out as many of the wires as I could reach. Then I stabbed the radiator several times, along with all four tires. After which I ran back to Lachie.

"OK Lachie, it's all done. That car is going nowhere in a hurry. It will take Gordon, a week to get the parts to fix it. If what you say is right, they will know he is here. So we have to get gone now."

Lachie cut the tape binding Jon's legs. We grabbed an arm each and bundled him into the back of the Land Rover. Then I put the dogs in the back with him and climbed in the front with Lachie.

Jon looked terrified, with his eyes frantically looking from dog to dog. He was visibly shaking.

"If you behave, they won't bite you. So if I were you I would not make any sudden moves. Kyla has already got a taste for your blood, and they do say that once a dog has tasted it, then it will only ever want it. Ohh and one more thing, Akitas don't like to be stared at. They take it as a threat, so if I were you. I would not eyeball her."

That was partially true and partly bullshit and I knew it. But from the look of things Jon did not know. Lachie drove around in semi-circle and then out through his gates. We drove up the Strath of Kildonnan, up through Auchentoul and a little bit further along the road. Then Lachie turned left onto a dirt track road for about a quarter of a mile. When we came to a set of manually operated Railway Gates. I got out and opened both sets, Lachie drove through and waited for me to close the gates behind us. We followed the dirt track road, for quite some distance and then in behind Ben Griam Beg and kept going for about another half mile or so, until the cottage came into view. It was snuggled deeply into a natural gully at just above the foot of the mountain.

Lachie did not have much of a problem with the hasp lock on the door and soon he had it opened. We got Jon in and secured his legs to an old kitchen chair that was there. Then we offloaded all of our supplies. There was a lean-to shed come garage on the side of the house. It was a bit ramshackle but we managed to get the Land Rover inside it. The trailer we had to leave outside but covered it with large clumps of heather and bits of wood that were covering the ground. Then we went back into the Cottage. Lachlan removed the tape, from around Jon's mouth and ripped the last bit off deliberately to cause as much discomfort to Jon as he could.

"Why?" Lachie asked him

"Why? What? I don't understand" he replied

Lachie slapped him hard with his open palm, and Jon and the chair tipped over. Jon's head hit the flagstone floor with a loud crack. The force of it knocked him out. Lachie lifted Jon and the chair upright. And I checked the pulse on Jon's neck. It was strong.

"Take it easy Lachie. We don't want to kill him. He's no use to us dead. Lachie opened one of the large bottles of water and took a deep swig.

"I'm going to take a good look around outside, before it gets dark. See if I can find a water source. There does not seem to be any running water or electric here. Not even a generator. Back soon."

The dogs lay down on the floor. They would need feeding soon too. The light was fading when Lachie came back.

ACT 17

"There's a burn about fifty yards away and the water is good and clear. There is also an old Tin Bath out back which I could clean out and then bring some water up to the cottage, as we don't want to be going out unless we have to. There's a disused Peat Bank down below the Burn, that we can use as a Latrine. How are we fixed for something to cook on?"

"We have an open fire with a swing arm, but I don't think we should use the fire in daylight"

"By the way Andy, watch yourself on the ground to the right of the house after about twenty feet, it turns into a peat bog and it looks a deep one. So keep the dogs away from there. How are we fixed for lights?"

"I have torches and lots of batteries, but there is a Paraffin lamp, that was by the sink. I suppose it would run on Diesel from the Land Rover."

"Great idea Andy and for now I am going to get that Tin Bath in here, and then start bringing water up see what we have to cook up, as soon as it gets dark"

I looked through the supplies and decided that the dogs could have Corned beef mixed in with some cheap dry dog food I had bought. As soon as it got dark I would light a fire and boil a pot of water for coffee after which, I could bake some potatoes by the fire, these we could have with beans. It was not great food but it would fill us up and keep our spirits going. Lachie brought the Tin bath in and started filling it with water. He filled a pan of water for me and as it was now dark I lit a fire from bits of dried wood. Then I topped it with peat from a stack at the back of the house. Soon the pan was boiling and I had added the coffee and put the potatoes around the fire. I opened a can of beans and set that next to the fire. After about a dozen or so trips, Lachie had all but filled the big tin bath. Jon had been out cold from Lachie's 'softening up' but was now starting to come around. I held a bottle of water against his lips for him to drink. He had a good egg sized lump on the side of his head.

"OK Jon. We are going to eat some food and then we are going to require some answers to questions. And the more you lie to us, the more unpleasant things will get for you." Lachie said as he came and sat down with me by the fire.

I poured him some black coffee and he laced it with a good slug of whisky, from a hip flask that he pulled from his back pocket. He offered me some and I held my own cup out. He poured a good slug into it 'Just for flavour'. We took our potatoes from the fire and laid them on tin plates that Lachie had packed to go with cutlery and tin cups for us. I put a cloth around the tin of beans and shared it out between us. Then we ate. When we had finished I washed the plates in the sink using a small amount of the water that Lachie, had brought up from the burn.

"Don't I get any food?" Jon asked

"The simple answer Jon, is no you don't. Not until you start revealing the truth about WHO you are? And WHY you are attempting to kill us? I don't even believe your actual name is Jon" Lachie said whilst topping up his coffee from the pot by the fire. It was that aroma of fresh ground coffee and a peat fire that I remembered from my childhood whilst growing up here in the Highlands. Lachie put his cup down and walked over to Jon

"One last opportunity, you talk we will sort your leg. Then we send you on your merry little way. You hold out, and things are going to get really nasty for you. Part of the training selection for the SAS is how to keep secrets whilst being tortured. Which when you reverse that, you learn how to torture. I have already done the selection course for the SAS. And have been spinning my wheels, while waiting to hear back from them. We don't have the time for the simple question and answer state of affairs. Nor do we have the time to wear you down and threaten your friends and family. And I don't have an electric cable to tie to your knackers. So Jon, that means that we have to move on to stage four. Do you know what stage four is? Jon"

Jon said nothing. He just looked at the floor.

"Andy. You might want to leave for this bit"

"I will stay"

I knew what was coming. I did not like it, nor can I say I in truth approved of it. But Jon had tried to kill me and my dad. He had killed our cow and destroyed my home. Then he had tried to kill Lachlan and me. He would have blown up Lachie's house, had we not caught him. So I was staying.

Lachie dragged the chair with Jon on, and moved it to the stone wall. Then he grabbed a pillow from the old bed at the side of the Kitchen area and he taped that to the back of Jon's head. I Looked at Lachie inquisitively?

"So his head does not smash into the stone wall. I WANT HIM CONSCIOUS."

Lachie punched Jon hard in the midriff, to knock the wind out of him, and then twice to the kidney's. Then he followed that up and punched him square in the face.

"What's your name?"

Jon was gasping for breath and blood flowed unabated from both his nostrils. He raised his head up and said

"Jon, its Jon Steinman. I am on attachment to Porton Down. You know me. I am part of your team, team seven"

"Wrong answer" said Lachie

Then punched Jon on the nose again, this caused a fresh flow of blood and snot.

"Name?"

"My Name is Jon I am in the Israeli Army"

"Lies try again Jon"

This time Lachie slapped him and then he left the house. I went over to Jon or whoever he really was and spoke to him quietly

"For Christ sakes, tell him, man. Because he will not stop until you tell him the complete truth."

"My name is Jon and I am in the Israeli Army, please make him stop"

"Jon. I don't believe you. You tried to kill me and Lachie. I don't think Israel has declared a religious war on Britain yet. So all this bullshit is just going to cause you a great deal more pain and suffering. You gave up any rights, when you blew up my house. Admit it Jon that was you?"

"No I don't know anything about that"

Lachlan came back in with his toolbox and dropped it noisily on the floor. Several of the tools bounced out. I thought that perhaps, I might want to leave the room, but stayed anyway.

"Last chance REAL NAME NOW!!!"

Lachlan grabbed him by his jaw and forced a dirty oily rag into Jon's mouth. I could see that he was already missing two teeth from the beatings Lachlan had given him. Lachlan took a hammer and without any kind of warning. He raised it above his head and brought it downward in a reverse of the arc that it had originally gone up in. Lachie smashed it cruelly into Jon's left knee. I gritted my teeth at the very thought of the pain, that it must have inflicted on this man. Lachlan pulled the rag out of Jon's mouth.

"Your REAL name because it sure as fuck, is not Jon. So who are you?"

"My name is Jon" he said through tears, blood and vomit that were piling up with other detritus, on the floor, from his body. Lachlan, rammed the cloth, back into Jon's bloodied mouth then smashed the other knee. He waited and then pulled the cloth out. I was feeling sick now especially as I realised why Lachie had filled the bath with water. He was going to water board this guy. I knew from training films what this involved. Everybody cracked under this or they died. Lachie dragged the chair to the centre of the floor, removed the pillow from the back of Jon's head and then laid the chair on its back. He then got the dish towel and wrapped it around Jon's head. Next took the empty baked beans tin and filled it with water from the bath tub. He poured it slowly over the cloth and he repeated it two more times. Jon was thrashing around, and choking. Lachie whipped the cloth off

"Name?"

"It's Jon you know me I am Jon"

Immediately Lachie repeated the process this time he poured four tins of water, over the towel on the front of Jon's face

"NAME?"

Lachie did not even wait for an answer, but wrapped the dirty cloth back over Jon's face. This time it was six tins of water.

"Name? Give up your real fucking Name"

Jon Spluttered unable to talk. He was coughing and puking up water.

"This really is your last chance because the next stage is what they call the real water boarding. We Pick you up in the chair and tip you upside down and leave you in the bath to drown. They do say that drowning upside down is the worst way to go. DO OR DIE."

"Give me a hand with this fucker please Andy and don't ask me to stop"

Lachie tied the cloth over Jon's face. We picked the chair up between us. Which was no mean achievement as Jon was screaming and thrashing about. But eventually we got him upside down and were just starting to put his head under the water.

"ALL RIGHT. ALL RIGHT. I will tell you what you want to know"

He was weeping and snivelling. I was not sure who was the more grateful Jon or me.

"My name it is Jabair Ambumohar. I am a Palestinian. But I was raised in the Jewish part of Jerusalem. My family were killed by the Israeli Army when I was a child. I took the name of the people that raised me and then, when I became a man I joined the Israeli Army to fight for Allah from within their ranks. I am not a terrorist I fight for the good of the world and for Allah. But you are all too late because they are coming for you and they will kill you all"

"Fucking Hell" Lachie said

"I never expected that. I just knew he was having us on a piece of string. I was going to give up after we were just going to dunk him the last time."

"Right we will get some more answers in a minute but I am going to tend to your wounds now. Is that all right with you Jabair?"

"You are all dead men"

"I will take that as a yes then."

I grabbed the medical bag that Lachie had loaded on to the Land Rover. It was a Med Kit That I gave him years ago. From a time when I came back from some exercise or other that I had been on. Only they forgot to ask for it back. I started with cleaning the blood from his mouth and face, Then I moved on down to his legs. I knew Kyla had taken a chunk out of the back of his leg, but that did not seem to be bleeding too badly.

"Jabair I am going to have to cut the trouser legs off so I can tend to your knees, and I am going to remove the bindings from your legs. I don't expect you will be able to get up and run away but don't try anything please."

I took one of his knives from his backpack and sliced through the laces on his boots. I removed as carefully as I could. I knew it was causing him an immense amount of pain.

"I am sorry Jabair but better that I do this now, than later"

"It does not matter my friend Andy. You are a good man, but you will all die very soon"

I ignored him and started on the left boot. As I finally got the boot off, a slim mobile phone like the 'Razor Three' slipped out and fell on the floor with a clatter.

"FUCK!" Lachie said He picked it up looked at it and said

"Get as much stuff that you can carry and pack it into these backpacks. ONLY TAKE THE IMPORTANT STUFF. Guns, Bullets and shells, cash, some water. Stuff like that. And DO IT NOW."

We packed furiously. Lachie took Jabair's phone, and threw it on the fire. He waited until it had melted then he doused the fire with water from the bathtub and then killed the paraffin lamp.

"Wait until our eyes become accustomed to the pitch black in here. That way when we leave we should have good natural night vision. We have to get as far away from here as we can and as quickly as we can. Andy we go up the mountain they will not expect that."

"What about him? Lachie won't he tell them where we have gone?"

"If I am right about this, they will not wait to ask. You ready?"

I whistled for the dogs and we went out into the night.

ACT 18

We ran from the house and around the back of Ben Graim Beg, then we started climbing in a diagonal line towards the summit. We were about three quarters the way up when we heard the distant sound of motors.

"Move faster Andy. Our only chance is to get to the top. There is a small sort of Loch. Just short of the top. Do you remember, when we were kids we climbed up here from the other side and picked the wild strawberries and mountain garlic for your mum."

"I remember it Lachie, I just don't remember it being this hard a climb"

"We were a lot younger and we climbed from the other side, it's not as steep as this side. Nor did you have a good 75 pounds of extra weight on your back"

We raced on and up and my lungs were burning, pumping my legs as hard as they could go. My thighs were on fire with pain. I could now see the lights of three vehicles which racing along the very road, that we had used to get to the cottage. By the time we reached the mountain top Loch, my breathing was laboured and my mouth was dry. It was quite cold out but I was sweating profusely. Between the weight of the two shotguns I was carrying and half the ammunition along with other supplies. My lungs were threatening to explode, my thighs and calf's felt like they were being burned, with a flaming torch. I could practically hear my heart thumping, like a bass drum. Lachie had taken even more of the supplies, guns and ammunition. I think he was carrying easily 100 pounds. He did not seem to be struggling, the same as me and still he reached down to give me a helping hand.

"I am glad we're here Lachie, because I don't think my

legs would have carried me any further. I think they have turned to jelly"

"You sit in a nice comfortable medical centre, Rock Apes play at war all the time. So I do this shit for a living. You are in truth, fit by average standards Andy, but I was training to join the SAS before we were stolen away from the Brecon Beacons." He passed me a water bottle

"Have a drink but drink it slow or you'll be sick"

I took a swig and passed it back to him. From our vantage point and location, we could see the lights of the vehicles; they were now splitting three ways. One following the road and the other two had gone either side and were fanning out.

"They must have at least two tracked vehicles. As they are now on ground, that you can't go over even in a good four by four"

The car had stayed on the road and the tracked vehicles had split off either side from it.

Lachie pointed to the area on the side of the house where there was a peat bog and continued.

"If they keep going as they are, they will hit the bog and sink. I have seen cows and even JCB Digger, swallowed up by these peat bogs around here."

They stopped just short by about fifty yards and the one on the other side did the same. The one on the road came to a stop and the doors opened, which switched on the internal lights. It showed three men had exited and were starting to walk along the road. They stopped about forty yards away from the cottage. All of a sudden there was a flash of flame from the right hand side of the house, and almost at the same time, one from the group on the left. The two flame trails flashed towards the cottage and impacted almost simultaneously. Devastating the old building, the explosions, blew the roof clean off the small house. The windows and door erupted outwards in a flaming fire. It was followed by a massive amount of suppressed gunfire. As all sides changed their spent magazines out, then inserted new full ones and continued to fire upon the destroyed house along with Lachie's Land Rover. We could barely hear the pop pop pop of the suppressed gunfire but we could see the muzzle flashes from at least seven automatic weapons. We could hear the whine as the bullets bounced off the remnants of the building. This was where we had been, for less than two hours, and where they had just killed Jabair, their own man. Although I was sure we had been the intended victims, once again. I heard it before I saw it. There was a chopper possibly two racing through the glens and up the Strath. It was coming down fast on our position.

"Get into the Loch now!" Lachie whispered to me.

I slid into the edge of the loch and Lachie followed. I called the dogs and the joined us in the water like it was some game. He reached up to his backpack and pulled a couple of aluminium chill blankets and spread them over our heads and the dogs that were snuggled up to us, sharing their body heat but not allowing it to go beyond the blankets. We lay there in the dark and frigid cold waters at the edge of the loch. There were indeed two choppers they were the small private variety and what I had seen was the red flashing lights on their underbellies. They were doing pattern sweep of the area around the house and extending their search pattern to take in the moor further around the house.

"They probably have thermal cameras on board or night vision, perhaps both, from here it will look like we are part of the water and the blankets will protect us from being seen by the thermal cameras"

The way my teeth were chattering, I was one hundred percent sure that we would not get picked up by thermal imaging. It was a good job no one had invented anything to pick up folks chattering teeth, due to the cold. After a while the choppers gave up and headed back down the Strath. The shooters had stopped and were starting up their engines, to go home too. The tracked vehicle to the right of the house started a wide circle turn coming close to the side of the house. It started revving madly and then its lights went out. The car drove up almost to the house and the doors opened. Then they switched on high powered torches, and started to walk towards the right of the house. They stopped short and swung their lights to where the tracked vehicle had vanished. There were shouts but they were too far away for us to hear. Then there were some more muzzle flashes and the torches turned around and went back to the car. The car turned around and was followed by the one tracked vehicle from the left of the house, and then went back the way it came.

"They just shot their own men" I said

"Don't forget about their man that they blew up in the house. These fuckers are serious Andy!"

"What do we do now Lachie?"

"We go back down the mountain, to that fire down there. Take these wet clothes of and dry them, while we get warm. We also see what we can salvage from the stuff we had in the cottage."

We climbed out from the Loch and Lachie folded up the thermal blankets, before putting them back into his backpack. We took a direct line to the house. Jogging down to try and keep the blood flowing in our bodies. It was the end of February and although it had been a mild winter. It was still bloody cold up here at night. I was sure that it would get frost here soon. By the time we reached the rubble of the cottage, our bodies were steaming with the exertions and the heat from our bodies on our wet clothing gave us a spectral look.

"Andy. Get some of the dry wood and pile it up over here next to these big rocks where there is a fire already burning, when the heat from the fire makes those rocks hot we can lay our clothes on them to dry."

I built the fire up a bit then Lachie went over to where the tracked vehicle had disappeared.

"Andy! Quick Over here and bring the medical bag"

I picked up the bag and ran towards Lachie's Voice

"Careful Andy There's one of their guys still alive about ten feet inside the edge of the bog. I'm going to see if we can get him out. Andy go back to the house and grab a couple of long planks and bring them here and bring Kyla"

I went back and got the planks and Kyla. When I got back to Lachie, he took the wooden boards and laid the first one on the top of the bog and then he slid the another plank over it, until it was next to the head of a man who was laying on his back groaning. Lachie took a length of para-cord from inside his backpack; he then measured it and cut it into to equal parts. The first length he made a figure of eight loop and tied it around Kayla's forelegs and shoulders the excess he passed to me to hold on to. Then he made a loop on the other one and offered it to Kyla. She just looked at him. I went to her and said

"Take it girl" She bit down on it and held it in her mouth. I guided her to the planks and said "Go on, go to him"

She lay down on her belly and shuffled her way along the planks with Lachie holding on to the harness he had made to fit over her shoulders. Slowly but surely she took the rope to the injured man. When she got to the man she dropped the rope next to his hand.

"I am going to bring Kyla back now Lachie, I gently tugged on the rope and Kyla started to back-peddle back towards us. Gradually and with great care she came, working her legs in a fashion that she was not comfortable with. But she made it. When she was on Terra fir-ma proper, I gave her a big hug

"Good Girl Well Done Good Girl"

Lachie shouted at the man

"Take the Rope it's by your left hand. Take the fucking rope and we can get you out"

Slowly the man reached for the rope and grabbed a hold of it

"Slip the loop over your head and shoulders, and do it now or the bog will take you and you will think that being shot, is a fucking blessing"

The man did as he was told. We pulled steadily and carefully until we had the man on firm ground.

"Where are you shot?"

I asked, he did not seem to hear me so I asked again. This time he pointed to his shoulder and then at his leg.

"Here and here" he said

I washed the areas with water from our canteen. The one bullet had entered though the front of his right shoulder and exited from the back it had just missed the collar bone and by some miracle exited just under the clavicle. About a clean as wound as you could get, bits of clothing and peat muck excluded that is. I cut away the clothing and washed both the entry and the exit wounds. The wound on his thigh was a flesh wound, where a bullet had nicked him. It just required a topical dressing. We helped him up to our fire. We need to get your wet clothes of and dry them. I helped to strip him down. He was in shock and did not resist. The worst thing for him was hypothermia. We had to get him dry and warm.

"Why are you helping him Andy? They just tried to kill us for the third time in twenty four hours

"Because Lachie. He just might be able to help us. They think he is dead and he knows they tried to kill him as well, which might work to our advantage."

"Anything's worth a shot I suppose, and if it does not work we can always throw him back in the bog"

"Can I have your hip flask please Lachie?"

He took a swig and passed it to me. I then poured some of the alcohol on the entry and exit wounds. The man did not move. I passed the hip flask back to Lachie, who took another swig and put it down on the ground next to his backpack. I put a field dressing on the wounds and then wrapped a bandage over and under his shoulder, when it was in place I taped the end of the bandage down and guided him nearer the fire. Lachie was going through the man's possessions and putting all the items down next to the rock he was sat upon. There was a suppressed Uzi on a strap, 6 spare clips in a belt, and black Ontario MK3 Navy Knife, A flip top cell phone, and a photo of a woman and child. Lachlan passed a field canteen with hot soup in. Not proper soup, just one of those Bachelors Cuppa Soups. It was probably not nutritious but it was hot and tasty. The man took the canteen and sipped from it. He warmed his hands around the outside of the square canteen. The man was young, about twenty-five years old. We knew he spoke English or at least understood it because he had followed the instructions to get him out of the Peat Bog.

"What's your name?" I was thinking to myself please don't say Jon

"M mm Merr Vinn" he said with chattering teeth.

"OK Mervin. Want to tell us why you are trying to kill us and anyone around us?"

"I can't fella's they'll kill me if I do"

"Look mate" I said "They just tried to kill you, already for NOT being able to. So tell us now or we'll finish the job"

Lachlan walked over in his Boxer shorts

"We will not tell anyone you told us, and as you are already dead you can just walk away and go back to your Girl and kid" he said and handed the man the picture.

The man took the picture and handed Lachie the now empty mess tin. Mervin started weeping and held the photo close to his chest. Lachie squatted down on his haunches next to the fire. He looked at the man, who was really little more than a teenager.

"How much are they paying you Kid?"

"One hundred thousand each for one month's work"

"Where are you from Mervin?"

"The USA man"

"Who hired you?"

"I never saw him. It was all done through a security agent"

"Who's the agent?"

"A guy from Oxford"

"How do you contact him?"

"He gave us all a Mobile phone with just his number in"

"Has this agent got a name?"

"No but I think he is British. I don't think he is a yank like me"

"You just said he was from Oxford?"

"Yes but that not where he is from. He just lives there"

"How do you know that?"

"Because we all had to meet at his house to get some upfront money and our initial instructions"

"So you went to his house you must have met him?"

"No he sent some other guy to pay us. I think he was like a lawyer or something, He gave us fifty thousand, up front and the rest to be paid at the end of the contract."

"Watch him" Lachie said.

He put his now dry clothes back on and wandered off towards the area of the Peat Bog. I got dressed in my clothes and helped Mervin get into his black boiler suit.

"So you and the other guys, you are obviously based in Sutherlandshire. So where is your base?"

"I have told you I can't tell you or they'll kill me"

"Mervin, they have already tried to kill you, they killed your friend that was with you on the snow mobile, we watched it happen"

"I won't say anything about you guys, you can let me go"

"That's not going to happen unless you help us, because at the moment you know that we did not die in the explosion's. We had one of your guys with us. They tracked him down using a GPS locator, on his mobile phone. So unless you are willing to help us we can't help you and your chances of getting back to your girl and baby will be dramatically reduced."

Lachie came back.

"I got that Snowmobile out of the bog. It had only gone in at the edge. They must have tried to get away from the bog, but in the dark they went the wrong way and went deeper into it and then got stuck. Then when they cried for help from their mates the ones in the car, shot them rather than help them out"

"Mervin you really only have one choice, tell us EVERY THING you know and you get to go home. I will let you think on it, until I have checked our gear and see if we can salvage anything from the cottage. Then I am going to come back and you can either help us voluntarily or I will force the answers out of you" Lachie said and then walked over to the rubble of the cottage.

I looked at the phone we had taken from Mervin. There was just one number in the speed dial but I looked at the call history and the text message history. There were several messages that I presumed were from his girl back home. But there were also two messages from another person. The last one said.

IF U WANT OUT I CN HLP U
A
FRIEND.

The previous message to it said
YOU R IN OVR UR HEAD
GO HOME
I CN GET U WHT U ND
CALL ME
A
FRIEND

There was also a call log to the same number just one call which was made before the second message.

"Stay here Mervin. If you try to run these dogs will take

you down. As if in agreement Kyla growled at him and sat down in front of him. I took the phone over to Lachie and showed him the messages.

"Do you suppose this is the same person who left the written note for me?"

"From the way it is phrased I would say that it's a good chance of being the same person, but what's more interesting is the call log telephone number 01408 code is a BRORA NUMBER. The person offering help to him is just down the road in Brora."

Lachie took a black marker pen, out of his back pack and passed it to me, and I wrote the number on the back of my hand.

ACT 19

We need to get to a phone"

"Why not use this one"

"Because they think Mervin is dead, and if they are able to track his phone, like they did with Jon, or whatever his name was. Then they are probably also monitoring all of their phones. At the moment this has not moved more than fifty feet since they shot him in the bog if it starts moving more or is used to make a call or text then they will know, either he is not dead or that we are not dead. I think you should get the snowmobile working if you can and then one of us go to a Pay phone somewhere, and call that number. And see what happens."

Lachie worked the rest of the night salvaging his tools from the demolished cottage. He stripped down the carburettor of the snowmobile and cleaned it. At eight in the morning, he came over and said

"You should go now Andy. There is a public phone box by the old school in Kinbrace. If you take the snowmobile and take a straight line, you should be there by nine. Don't stay on the phone for more than three minutes. Just find out who they are and if possible how they can help us. When we know more about who it is? We will be able to move forward. While you are gone I will make a hide for us."

"OK Lachie, watch that bloke carefully I will be back by ten, I think. If I am not back by eleven, then take the dogs and go to the old church in Kildonnan. You can follow the railway line to get to it. I will just take the Sig with the suppressor and a couple of clips you keep the rest. All being well I will see you in a couple of hours"

I fired up the Snowmobile and set out for Kinbrace. The journey was uneventful and I made good time. I got to the

Phone box by eight forty-five. I did not want to call the number until nine, in case they only worked office hours. I hid the snowmobile in a ditch and made my way to Lachie's house. When I was about two hundred yards away I saw it a Metallic Green Range Rover Not the same one I had disabled at the other side of his property that was still where I had left it. This was another one. It was parked inside the boundary of Lachie's property. I carefully retraced my steps to the phone box and dialled the phone number.

"Hello" it was a female voice I thought I knew the sound of her but could not place it.

"Who is this?" I asked

"You are through to Brora Radio Station"

I knew instantly where and what that was, because as kids we used to go down to Brora. There was a field there, which had a Car Park attached to it. In the middle of the field was a tall Radio mast. And there was a small green wooden shed at the foot of the mast. The shed was capable of holding perhaps half a dozen people comfortably. But about thirty or forty people would enter the hut. This would happen twice a day when they would come out and the next lot go in. So even though we were told it was just a radio station. Everyone in the area knew it was something to do with the military. It was something similar to GCHQ at Cheltenham. Except the Brora station was under ground, without the large Doughnut building over it.

"I need a friend" I said

"Are you team Seven?"

"Who are you?"

"You probably know me better as WPC Jane Miller"

"So you know who I am?"

"Yes and trust me we are on the same side"

"Will you be at this number all day?"

"Yes"

"I'll be in touch" then I hung up.

I Got back on the snowmobile and headed back to Lachie.

I made great time getting back to the destroyed house.

"How'd you get on mate?"

"Well it looks like your house has new residents, rats,

and they drive a metallic green Range Rover. It think they got a job lot on them. Or one fella gets around a lot. I called the number and guess what?"

"Come on Andy, it's not a good time for guessing games"

"The lady who came to my house yesterday, WPC Miller, at least that's who she was then, I don't think that is her real name, or at least I don't think she is a real full time Police Officer. The number is for Brora Radio station."

"The hut on the green? The one with the radio mast?"

"One and the same"

"So how does Mervin fit into this?"

"I don't know, but that is what you are going to find out now?

"Why me Andy?"

"Because Lachie my friend, you are the Rock Ape and I am the Medic"

"Ohh Funny."

We walked over to where Marvin was securely tied up to a fence post with the dogs either side of him.

"You tied him up?"

"I needed a toilet break, just wanted to make sure he was here when I got back! Besides remember, I am a Rock Ape we do all that tying up people shit!"

"Ohh Funny Lachie. Real Funny!"

"Mervin I can ask you questions and you can answer them truthfully, or Lachie can ask them and you WILL answer them truthfully. Now I know you mercenary types are all macho and hold out against the usual, shine the light in your eyes, sleep deprivation sort of thing. And some of you will rather die than give up what you see as your comrades. Who by the way, tried to kill you, as a comrade. So which is it? And choose fast because this is a time sensitive sort of thing. But before you, do think on this. The Geneva convention does not apply to privateers and mercenaries."

"I don't know anything other than what I have already told you. Honest I don't"

"Mervin Who was the message from? And why did you contact them?"

"I don't know?"

"Mervin you must have contacted them, or they would not have messaged you TWICE"

"I don't know what you are talking about"

"Lachie I will go for a walk with the dogs I don't want them to eat the bits you chop off."

I whistled and the dogs came to my side. See you in fifteen minutes Lachie. And TRY not to kill him"

Then I added just for effect

"Like you did to the one we caught before" then I walked away.

I came back a quarter of an hour later and Lachie was talking to Mervin.

"And?"

Lachie walked over to me and whispered

"He's talking, in fact he is spilling his guts. I can't get him to stop talking?"

"What did you do to him?"

"Me nothing, it was you"

"I don't get you, what do you mean it was me?"

"I told him you kept cutting bits of Jon or whatever his name was, and feeding them to Kyla, and that Jon cracked, when there was no meat left below his knees!"

"And he believed you?"

"When I went for one of my walks, Jon's body was in the ruin and he had no legs from below the knees. One of the blasts must have done it when the fired the RPG's, so I just took him and showed him the body. So now you could write a book, with what's coming out of his mouth. He is a wannabe soldier of fortune. And has not been battle hardened. I think he thought he could work his way back, into whatever team he is in by going back and saying he had spied on us, then he thought he would be forgiven by telling them where we were."

"Has he told us anything that can help us?"

"Like I said Andy? He will not stop. Probably best if you go ask him with Kyla"

"OK Mervin. Are you ready to answer my questions?"

"Yes ANYTHING you want"

Lachie was right. It was difficult to get him to stop. But eventually we had enough to be going on with.

Someone at SIS had reached out to him shortly after he

entered the County. They had discovered that they had a leak. And did not know where it was. And they wanted to have a man on the inside of the terrorists in order to close the leak. The terrorist cell was being funded apparently by a wealthy individual. But even Mervin's team did not know who he was. They just received cash and missions to complete. Mervin did not know the exact end game. They were sent to clean up after Jon had been caught by us. When Jon had failed to complete his second mission, which was to try once again to kill Lachie and me. They did not know that we had already killed Jon (Which of course we had not) but all of the phones they had also carried a tracker so they knew where we were holding him. They had sent a team to watch Lachie's house, in case we went back there. The person he was getting messages from, had already paid him a large sum of money (into his real bank account in the USA. HOW dumb this guy was, He thought he could just go back to the USA after this and continue his life?) He had sent text messages in reply to the message that reached out to him offering him a way out. But he had deleted his messages to them, hence only the received messages.... He was on a flow ratting out every one. But he did not know the end mission or who was organising it. Just that it was BIG. They had a total of twelve guys to start with but we had killed one (not really) and they had killed the other guy on the Snowmobile, with him. And they thought that they had killed him. They had Automatic weapons (We knew that already) they had C4 explosives (We knew that already) They had two choppers (We knew that already) Four Green Range Rovers (We knew they had some but that one was probably still out of action) and some Snowmobiles (We knew that, but they had one less now) He had spoken to the person on the phone, who offered him a way out once, when they arranged the money for him and it was a woman and had said she was with an organisation called SIS. He did not know who they were (We did and we had a fair idea who she was) It was probably time for us to have a re-union with WPC Jane Miller or SIS Jane Miller or whatever alphabet soup, she was feeding to us on any given occasion. But we would do it on our terms and when we chose to, which would be sooner rather than later. First we had to ditch Mervin, alive if we could.

"We have to contact Jane. As at the moment, she seems to be the only one trying NOT to kill us"

"Or you could look at it this way she could be trying to find us so she could kill us"

"Is you glass ever half full Lachie?"

"No way mate, it goes down in one!"

"You know we are in serious deep shit here Lachie, folks we don't know, want us dead, and the folks we do know don't seem inclined to help us out. The other side has all sorts of shit like Uzi's, RPG's Helicopters and cool cars. We HAD your old Land Rover and my beat up Trannie Van. A couple of old shotguns and your old triple two. Which by the way, we have not had a chance to shoot anyone with yet. Obviously, we now have a few of guns that we snagged off Jon and Mervin. We have some money, but most of the money got burned up, but we got Jon's five grand, which along with the stuff we had in our wallets will not buy a decent used Range Rover, let alone choppers and fancy weapons. And our phones seemed to work as trackers for the other side. Hell we don't even have proper food after they blew it up. They are probably in a hotel or a private Estate, drinking cocktails and watching Sky TV, when they are not out trying to turn us into worm fodder. And we are the GOOD Guys? So I am going to go back down to the phone box and I am going to call Jane. Then I am going to ask her, to send a team, to get us out of here. Because if they are using us as bait. I never signed up for that."

"OK"

"That's it Lachie? After all the stuff I just ranted out? Is OK?"

"Yep I agree"

"What with?"

"My Glass is empty"

"Mine too" I said

"I best get going then, try not to kill Mervin, at least until I get back."

With that I climbed on the Snowmobile and took off once again for the phone box in Kinbrace. I got there easy enough and when I was close to the phone box I hid the snowmobile in the ditch and then went to the phone booth. I went to call the number and realised that I had left my Backpack at cottage site with Andy. I had no loose change. I hoped that they would accept reverse charge calling I dialled the number and waited. It was answered after two rings. I asked the operator if they would accept a reverse charge, the operator then asked if them, if they would accept a call from a phone box in Kinbrace. Nice of the operator to give my location away. There was a very uncomfortable wait and then they said they would. So much for them not getting to know where I was. Still it would take them fifteen or so minutes, to get a team to the phone box. By then I would be long gone.

"Hello" they said

"Can I speak to Jane Miller?"

"I am Sorry there is no one here of that name"

Now that really fucked up the apple cart.

"This is Andy McPhee I was speaking to her earlier this afternoon"

"One moment please I will connect you to our Enquiry Office"

"NO don't please this is serious. I am Andy McPhee and am with Lachlan Henderson and we have a Prisoner called Mervin."

There was an even longer pause then a man's voice came on and it was vaguely recognisable.

"Where are you?"

"If you are who I think you are, then you already know to within the inch where I am calling from. We need retrieving from a hill location. And we need it NOW. We have a prisoner called Mervin, he was working with a mercenary unit. I think you had already made contact with him and made an agreement with him. He is singing like Mama Cass. But we need your help to get him out of our temporary location. I want a Chinook Helicopter to pick us up in about an hour or so"

"Why a Chinook?"

"Because, I don't think the bad guys have one of them yet"

"OK Where and When"

I gave the location and asked for it to be in exactly, one hour thirty minutes. This would allow me time to get back. Then I hung up.

I raced back to Lachie. When I got there I told him what

had been said. Then he asked me, why I did not ask for it sooner.

"Glass half full mate I don't trust anyone. They will land down by the cottage. But to be on the safe side we will be over there by the peat bank, just in case they decide to start lobbing RPG's at us or perhaps at him" I said pointing to Mervin.

ACT 20

Right on time we heard the double whoop whoop of the Chinook approaching. She was flying low up the Strath, following the train line. It came in and flew a circle around the remains of the cottage then landed on the rocky ground to the south side of it. All sorts of debris from the destroyed cottage flew into the air as well as clouds of ash from the resulting fire after it was hit with the RPG's. I waited with Lachie in our hideaway while the rotors spun down then the tail of it opened up and a dozen Nomex clad soldiers, piled out and set up a full perimeter. This was followed by two people, in civilian clothing. The first was the woman I knew as Jane Miller, the second person was a man, who I recognised.

"We're coming down hold your fire and please lower your weapons."

Their guns stayed ready. OK they did not want to do it that way, so I tried a different tact.

"Jane I want you to walk towards me. I can promise you I will not shoot you, if your crowd down there, hold their fire. But please keep your hands raised" I shouted up to them

The man put his hand on her arm but she shook it free and started to walk towards us. When she was about ten feet away I asked her to turn around. Which she did.

"OK, come to us please"

"I want you to walk us back to the chopper. We have had a trying couple of days, and are a bit short on trust"

"I understand" she replied and then added "Are you all OK?"

"We are, Mervin's been Shot, not by us. Mervin's friend is dead and at the bottom of the peat bog over there, again not by us. Jon is dead, also not by us, well not entirely. His body is in the rubble of that cottage."

All of us walked down up the hill towards the helicopter and the Nomex clad team

"See, they have cool gear" Lachie to me

The dogs were not happy at the sight of the Nomex clad guys with guns. We got to the Nomex ring and dropped our back packs and guns then continued walking to the man. Now I remembered him. It was the guy from the Station Commanders office at Porton, the one who Lachie had knocked out.

"Good to see you are OK" he said

"Really?" replied Lachie.

I thought he was going to deck him again. We all boarded the big helicopter and the dogs lay on the floor next to me. Kyla was giving the evil eye to the guy in Nomex across from me. Who made a gun with his hand and pretended to shoot at Kyla

"Just Fucking try it" I mouthed at him

"Let's get you out of here and somewhere where we can talk. We are going to fly to the Bombing Range at Tain, and then transfer to a smaller bird and go back to Brora. Then I can explain a lot more to you, as to what is going on. Get comfortable" he said as we sat down on the webbing seats.

The engines started, and soon it lifted off and cleared the hillside. The Chinook flew around the front side of Ben Graim Mor, after which it banked hard and slid between Ben Graim Beg and Ben Graim Mor then headed back down to Helmsdale and then across the sea to Tain. We were only on the ground for a few moments. But it was long enough for an argument. One of the Nomex men wanted to hold on to Lachie's Guns and Rifle along with our Backpacks.

"They are my guns. I have a legitimate license for them and the same applies for the ammunition for them. You are not taking them from me"

When it looked like there would be blood 'The Man' nodded to the Nomex man, to let Lachie have his stuff. We transferred to a modern version of a Bell Huey, painted in matt black. They had made it a lot quieter somehow, although it was still loud to my ears. We took off from Tain and flew close to the water and sped towards Brora. Then landed in the Car Park of the Radio station and the Chopper took off again and headed back the way it had come. Presumably we had gone to Tain to get rid of the Nomex crowd as well as the big chopper. As it was Just the five of us that went in the Huey plus the two dogs of course.

"This way please" said 'The Man'.

We followed him into the shed, which had been partitioned half way down its length. He opened a door in the partition and started descending a well-lit flight of stairs. When we reached the bottom, we were faced with a pair of sliding steel doors. There was a camera over it. The man looked up and the doors opened to reveal a lift, capable of holding twelve persons. Or so it said on the back wall. The man pressed a button and it started to move downwards. I had Déjà vu of the shooting range at. or near Porton. According to the lights we had descended two floors. The door opened into a large room which was filled with busy people, sat at computers and with headphones on.

Jane said "Mervin if you would like to come with me. I will get the doctor to have a look at your wounds." she led Mervin away

"Shall we use my office?" 'The Man' said

"Why not?" Lachie said

"Can you leave the dogs and the guns outside please?" please he asked

"No" Lachie and I responded together

"Very well, I can understand your suspicion after what you have been through"

Personally I doubted he could

"This way please" he said as he opened the door.

His Office was small but neat and tidy. His desk was clear of any paperwork, with a small computer and monitor on a smaller desk in the corner. There were no other chairs and I had assumed we were meant to stand here and be told off like naughty schoolboys. There was a connecting door on one of the side walls. His office would have been small with just 'The Man' and his desk in it, but with Lachie, me and with two dogs it was positively tiny. None of us were clean either, well apart from 'The Man', that is. Our boots had traipsed peat mud over his nice, clean, but threadbare carpet. Although Raven was meant to be Black, Kyla was supposed to have a white underbelly to go with her red, white and black top coat. She had become covered in oily and black, peat water. She looked more like Raven. The dogs smelled of that dank and damp, doggy smell, mixed with oily peatbog, all the more so, in the confined space, of his office.

"So?" 'The Man' said. He waited for an answer to his single syllable question and Lachie gave him it in an equally simple mono syllable answer.

"What?"

"Excuse me" 'The Man' said looking up from his desk. I was thinking WOW two syllables and wondering how long it had taken 'The Man' to get his education.

"You asked so? And I answered, what. Because I don't understand the question?" Lachie replied again.

"I'm sorry. I was hoping you could fill me in on the details of what has happened over the last forty-eight hours." 'The Man' said

"Nope" I had to admit Lachie was on a roll

'The Man' stood up with such force that his chair was tipped over. Kyla and Raven took up a defensive stance with their teeth bared threateningly and growling. Time for me to jump in again

"What Lachie means, is that we don't understand ourselves as to what is going on, we had expected to meet up with one of your agents up here and to be given some sort of plan of action, along with guidelines of what you wanted us to do. And so far all we know is, that people do not like us and they all want to kill us. I can understand them not liking Lachie, for his sense of humour but we don't go around looking for trouble. Even, if it does seem of late to come looking for us. Also 'They', whoever 'They' are, seem to know where we are going to be, even before we do. We know that Jon was not Jon. He may well have been a member of Mosad but was not working for them. He was working for the other side whoever 'They' are. But 'They' killed him, and we know that 'THEY' whoever 'THEY' are, have people inside YOUR organisation and I don't think it was just Jon. We also know that 'THEY' have money to burn as Mervin was being paid One hundred thousand, half of which, he had already been paid. There were twelve of THEM, but now there are only nine of them in their team, that we know of. We are not responsible for the death of any of them. They killed two of their own and tried to kill a third man. Who you have with your doctor now. I think that about sums it up"

He picked his chair up and sat back down.

"I realise, we have not been able to tell you much about this, and I hope you understand the need for operational security. We tend to compartmentalise, in order to preserve this. I would love to be able to give you the complete picture, but alas my hands are tied. I too have superiors and they probably have their masters."

"You say PROBABLY? Is that because you don't know yourself?" I asked

"It's complicated. Let me try to enlighten you, to what I am able to do so at this point."

He stood up and opened the door at the side of the room.

"Gentlemen please, after you. The dogs can stay here"

"No" I said

"I am sorry I don't follow you?"

Taking a leaf out of Lachie's book I answered

"No, I know. You go first, then I follow you, the dogs follow me, and of course Lachie too. The dogs go with us. I trust them but the jury is out on you"

"Why?" He asked

"Because anything you have to say to us the dogs can hear, they are very good at keeping secrets. Consequently, we trust them and we don't trust you yet" Lachie said with a wink to me.

"I am sorry, I just thought they could rest in my office. But whatever you say. Come along then"

We followed him through the door with the now, 'Secret Agent Dogs'. We entered a large room, which was like some sort of command centre.

"You were told, that we understand, there is some sort of plan to steal some sensitive material, from a now closed Fast Breeder Nuclear Plant?"

"No" Lachie and I answered together

"What about the use of biological weapons"

"No, we were just told that something had gone missing.

We were not told, what that something was, apart from it might be information or something they were working on at CDE Porton Down." I replied to him.

"Yes, Yes." he replied and then he continued with a singular word, which seemed to have been spoken absent-mindedly.

"Compartmentalisation"

There was a huge glass wall, which had a map of the entire North of Scotland on it. I could see that Dounreay Power Station marked on it. There were also rings, drawn on the map radiating outwards from it, with numbers and calculations, written in between the rings. And some X's marked way out in the North Sea. He continued.

"OK so please remember, that you have both signed the extended version of the Official Secrets Act"

Lachie as usual let his mouth get the better of him again

"Yeah yeah, you get our firstborn and the entire length of my family history, will be extinguished from any and all records. And you will stop our wages. Which by the way we no longer have? As they got burned up! Not to mention that we nearly got burned as well"

'The Man' ignored the comment and continued

"Did you not get the package?" he asked

"We did get it sort off" I said "But never had a chance to look inside it, because my fucking home got renovated by a big gas explosion!"

I decided it would be better for 'The Man' to think, that the case, even though we did not know what was inside of it, especially if it contained more money, was lost

"That's regrettable then, because we would have been able to communicate with you and you would not have been entirely blind, as to what is going on. I will try to bring you up to speed, as much as I can." he said, as he took a folder from a rack on the wall behind him.

"Please read this, I will be back in a few moments" and then he was gone.

I opened the file, it contained documents and maps, along with lists of names, some of which had been crossed out and others had red dots next to them. I did not recognise any of the names. On reading, I did however know where the 'Other

Side' was hiding out, and it was not too far from where we had been. They had set up base in a disused hotel at Altnabreac. There used to be a railway station near it but, I did not think it was used any more. At least not as a working station, Altnabreac was one of those hamlets that had died because of its abject remoteness. The estate of Altnabreac had previously been used for the hunting shooting and fishing community. The owner of the estate had died and left no will or relatives, so the land had reverted to the Crown and the estate staff became unemployed and so they had moved their families away. The Forestry Commission had taken over parts of it in the renewal of the Caledonian Forrest. Historically the entire North of Scotland had once been, a singular gigantic woodland. There used to be a small school at Altnabreac, to accommodate children from the Estate workers. Though like the Hotel, they were long gone. There was also a map of the coastline around Dounreay. It had a Zoomed in aerial photograph, that showed a walled in sort of harbour. Lachie looked over my shoulder at all the stuff in front of us. The man came back.

"Why choose us? To do whatever it is that you want us to do? Why not use the SAS or Special Boat Crew's? Why not just go in and grab them? Surely with the resources, that you obviously have, you could have used your own people?" I asked

"Because if you had opened the package that we sent to you, then you would have seen a file on this man"

He handed me thick file. Which I opened there was a photograph of a clean shaven man who I thought I recognised. Then I flipped the photograph over and it was of Sandy. The skipper of the boat, I had used to send the message to Lachie's dad on Fetlar.

"We chose you two, because you went to school with one of the men we believe to be involved in an act of terrorism, against the UK."

I turned the page and there was Stuart McCormack.

"I don't believe this for a second. Stu would never get involved in Terrorism NEVER! I met with Sandy and he knows Lachie's dad. I just don't believe it"

He took the folder back and passed me another picture

"Rosemary McKay, I know her, she was Stu's girlfriend when we were at school." I said and showed it to Lachie and he nodded

"We believe that they have her and are forcing Stuart to work for them. We also believe that they have forced Alexander McKay, or as you know him Sandy. To work with or for them as well"

He handed me another picture of Sandy, this time he had his full bushy beard, and I recognised him immediately as the skipper of the Catherine May. I had not realised that this man was Rosemary's father.

"We do not know, what they have been asked to do, so we need you to find out and then to report back to me. We also need you to try and get some pictures of the inside of Altnabreac Hotel."

"How the fuck are we supposed to do that without getting caught. You have already said that they are using it as a base of operations. Don't you think they might get a little bit suspicious if we just go wandering up to one of the most remote hotels in Scotland and say, we were just passing can I borrow a cup of sugar? I am sure we would also get the 'Sorry no room at the Inn tonight' speech and then get nailed to a cross. Metaphorically speaking that is."

"No because you will be going on a shooting party from the Halkirk Estate which is next to the Altnabreac estate."

"What about sending us in closer than Halkirk?"

"How?"

We were back down to single syllable answers again.

"You are the experts! You figure it out" Lachie said

I could see that Lachie was at the point of blowing a fuse. In all the years I had only seen him go off the reservation a couple of times. The first time we were just kids about thirteen or fourteen. There was this bully in the school, who loved nothing better to beat up on the new kids. The bully himself was smart enough, not to get caught actually doing the dirty deeds himself. He would have his minions take care of it while he stood there and watched. Then he would tell the subject of his beating not to cross him, blah blah blah. They did it to Lachie, there were six of them and they were all older being fifteen or sixteen years old. Lachie had fought back bravely but being severely outnumbered, he had come out of it with a black eye, bloody nose and a split lip. When the teachers asked Lachlan what had happened? He just said he fell on the stairs. Over the next two weeks he found each of the gang one at a time, and beat the crap out of them one on one. Then during break time one day, he had walked right up to the bully and called him out. When the teachers pulled Lachie off the boy, it looked like someone had taken a hammer and chisel to the boy's face. The bully was taken to hospital and Lachlan taken to the headmaster's office. He was given a formal warning that if something like this happened again he would be expelled. After that Lachie became the School hero. The gang never bothered anyone else again. The last time Lachie lost it was just before we joined the RAF. We were working during the back end of the summer holidays and were there to carry the Guns and reload for the rich shooters, who were too damn lazy to do it themselves. The Law of shooting is, that if the bird flies back over the line of shooters, then it is considered a 'lost bird' and no one follows it with their gun, or shoots at it. We were walking about twenty five yards, behind the line of shooters. When a Grouse rose in front of the guns, the bird flew up and left, and then it cut back on itself and came back over the line of the shooters. Lachie had seen it before me and shouted "Down" the bird came over and the guy shot both barrels at it. The shooter would not have seen us, as his vision was only on the bird. But he broke the golden rule and had fired behind the line, thus endangering us and the pack of dogs that were with us. A couple of the pellets hit Lachie on the back of the shoulder. But he was up and running at the man. Furious he snatched the gun out of the man's hands, and threw it about ten yards away into a peat bog. The he slapped the man with an open hand. The man shouted

"Do you know who I am, I will have you fired, that shotgun is worth more than you and all of your ingrate family could earn in a lifetime. And you have thrown my Purdy away like a piece of junk."

It did not matter to Lachie that the man's shotgun was worth £25,000.

"You are Lucky that I have not thrown you into the bog with your damn gun. You Fuckwit! You fucking shot me! You could have killed us and the dogs. You have no right to be on the hill if you do not know the laws of shooting."

"So long as I am paying for the privilege to shoot on this estate, then I shall continue to shoot" The man had said in a very condescending manner.

The game keeper had sent the under-keeper to fetch the shotgun from the edge of the bog where it lay

"And what's more" the man continued to rant "I will have you and your parents sacked for this, you bloody inbred simpleton"

Lachie slapped the man's face again and again. Not hard enough to cause serious damage, but there is nothing like an opened handed slap to a grown man's face to humiliate them especially in front of their friends. No matter how rich they may be. The Game keeper gave the Purdy to the man and said

"You don't ever shoot here again and when I tell his Lordship of this. I doubt that you will ever be back"

Apart from those occasions, I had never seen Lachie lose it. But he was just about to get there for another time. He made a move towards the man, as he had done previously in the Station Commanders office at CDE Porton Down. Only this time, the man moved with a speed that I would have thought impossible for a person of his age. He used Lachie's forward momentum and while sidestepping Lachie's telegraphed swing, caught Lachie's wrist and elbow, twisted Lachie's wrist and pulling it straight against his hold on Lachie's elbow so that the arm was in a straight line then the man simply pushed down on the back of the elbow joint. This caused Lachie's forwards motion to become a downwards motion. Lachie landed heavily on the ground with the man's knee on the back of Lachie's neck.

"I gave you a free shot at CDE Porton. You only ever get one free one. Try something like that again, and I promise you that you will awake in hospital. If I let you go will you behave?"

I had never seen Lachie bested by anyone before, even when the fight was three to one. This old guy just took Lachie down and it looked like could have caused some serious damage if he had wanted to, or so it seemed. It was like watching some kind of Kung Fu movie.

"OK OK," Lachlan said.

"Impressive" I said and continued "However if you had been a real enemy she would have killed you"

I said pointing to Kyla, whose hair was standing up on

her back. Her tail had dropped between her legs. This is a sure sign in an Akita, for any man to step down,

"Then she would have been dead."

He was confident and I had to admit after that last move, I did think that he could possibly have taken out Lachie and Kyla, without breaking sweat. So I had new respect for this old man, even though there was something I really did not like about him.

"Lachlan you are a good man and anger at times can keep you alive. Anger though works both ways, when uncontrolled it works against you. Do not let this hurt your pride, rather take it as a lesson."

Lachie stood up and it was obvious to me, that not only was his pride hurt but it had also been mixed with a note of respect for the way another man, had taken him down and managed to keep him down without throwing a single punch.

"So let us get back to work. We have to get eyes and ears inside Altnabreac. So I want cameras and bugs in there. I need to know who their inside man is. We already know that Jon was a plant. I have spoken with the Israeli Security Services. They have informed me that the REAL Jon Steinman was found in a shallow grave close to his home. So do not trust anyone. That is, unless you have known that person for years. As I have said 'They' have taken hostages to ensure that some civilians are working with them.

I held my hand up to stop him

"You say hostages? Yet you only talked about Rosemary?"

"Yes we believe that there may be more hostages. We just do not know who or where."

"If you don't mind my saying so, you don't really seem to know a lot about what is going on" Lachie said

"That may appear to be the case on the surface but it is not entirely true. I do have to hold some information back because of reasons of national security. Now if you would be so kind as to let me continue. I need to know what they intend to use the fishing boat for. Because at the moment we have very little idea as to who is running the show and what their endgame is. I am going to increase the size of your team, the woman who you know as Jane Miller will be embedded in your team to liaise directly between us. She will remain as a WPC Based in Brora I am also increasing our ability on the ground by sending two of my own men in with you, they are part of the team who brought you here."

"Not happening"

"I don't understand Mr Henderson, you don't want the help of some truly well trained and professional men that I have on hand?"

"I just do not like people being chosen for us, look what happened when you gave us Jon, that fucker tried to kill us not once but fucking twice. So if you will forgive my lack of trust in your choice of team members."

"Very well who would you like on your team?

Lachie and I confabbed in whispers for a short time while 'The Man' looked on.

"Hans Gunnerson and Abdalla Mohamed, and we need more money"

"Hans Gunnerson can't join you, as unfortunately, as I required him deployed elsewhere. Mr Abdalla is a training officer so he cannot be spared. You will be given more working capital along with ground vehicles and whatever munitions and other operational equipment on an as required basis. Before we move forward do you have any questions?"

"No Hans! No Abdalla! NO MISSION!"

"Very well, I will see what I can do BUT you will also then have Ms Miller from my office in the field with you. Do you have any other questions or demands?"

Lachie flexed his neck and said.

"I have a lot of questions, like how sure are you that this station is secure? Have you found out where 'They' are getting their Cars and Helicopters from? There must be a paper trail. Who is flying for them? Because if they are down three on the ground. Have you added in the two pilots? They must be in on it at some level. Where exactly are you planning to base us? Because if you will excuse me, I think that Andy and I know the area a lot better than anyone in this room here."

"To answer your questions in the order that you asked them, yes, I am completely sure that this station is secure. We posted all the original staff out and replaced them with SIS Staff who I have personally worked with. So I am sure that we are completely safe and secure here and without leaks. To answer your second question which seems to be a multi-faceted one? The helicopters were hired through a shell company. They have only ever flown in UK air space. We know that because the manufacturers have their own transponders fitted and when they are in the air they are on radar and the transponders show the identity of the aircraft. As I am sure you know that whilst as a general rule anything flying above two hundred and fifty feet shows on radar. But when they fly at low level between the Granite Mountains around here, we lose contact. It takes too long to redirect a satellite. Besides by the time we have them they are probably on the ground. Which, whilst it shows where the left from and where they landed. It does not show where they have been. As far as the cars they were all bought direct from a dealership in Inverness. They purchased four and they paid cash. The names on the paperwork seem to have been cloned from names of people who live up in the highlands. Again all the paper trails are dead ends. They are well organised and well-funded. We were planning to buy and use a Bed and Breakfast house in Halkirk, but if you can think of something that would suit the operation better then please feel free to offer suggestions"

"What is the point in putting us so far away from Altnabreac and sticking us in Halkirk, it's a small place and lots of folks will talk about the 'New Folks' surely not being seen at all is much better? Andy and I don't require luxury just a roof over our heads and somewhere to sleep and store our gear" Lachie said and It picked up the conversation from him.

"Surely, being closer to them allows us to keep a better watch on them. You could buy one of the many crofts that are for sale up there, or send us in as a forestry crew which is the better option. There is no better thing than hiding in plain sight. We need suitable transport and by suitable I mean Off Road Suitable. We have had Lachie's personal Land Rover destroyed and my van destroyed. I will arrange for our parents removed from Fetlar and taken somewhere that is properly safe. I want you then, to put three older people on location in Fetlar to act as our parents. But I will select the new location for our parents. NO one not even you, are to know where they will be OK?"

I knew once they were back on the mainland I could stash them away from prying eyes.

"I want adequate funding, in hard cash so we can do all this. Plus, we want Hans and Abdalla here by morning. Or you can find some other mugs, to run your operation up here. Without all this, we are out"

"Why do you want Hans and Abdalla?" asked the man

"Because Hans has an analytical mind and is a solid soldier. Abdalla he can shoot over great distances and because he has actual field experience. He is a battle hardened soldier. He is so good, that he trains your agents, which must mean, he must be the best. The way folks have been trying to kill us over the last couple of days, I would rather have the best at my back. We trust them. Look at it this way, how many servicemen come from this area? You want us, then we want them and this is a deal breaker. Can we have them?"

"You drive a hard bargain Mr McPhee. OK you get to choose where you base yourself, you get your choice of transport, and you get Abdalla and Hans. But you take Jane with you as she has operational experience and before you complain. She is my Deal Breaker. I shall Have Abdalla and Hans here in the morning. Read these files and rest up."

ACT 21

That night we stayed in the underground complex at Brora, I showered with my dogs as it was the easiest way for me to get them clean. Although I pitied the cleaner's task as during grooming the dogs, they had several times shaken the dirty water from their coats, so that now the ceilings of the wash room were pebble dashed, with black peat and mud. I used several of the large white towels from the big stack in the corner of the shower block to dry my dogs off. Then I washed myself. Dressed in one of the boiler suits they had provided for Lachie and myself. I took the dogs up to the surface for their nightly walk and then went back down and to bed.

The next morning after we had slept in the bunk rooms underground at Brora Radio Station. We were asked to go to a meeting in the control room. 'The Man' who seemed to be the boss of all this, had set up a basic breakfast bar with Tea, Coffee and buns, next to the main oval table in the centre of the room, Hans was there and Abdalla had just arrived and was helping himself to coffee.

"Nice to see you" I said and grabbed a couple of cups of coffee for myself and Lachie.

"Do you know where I am? and why I am here?" Abdalla asked

"Yes you are in the Highlands of Scotland and Lachie thought you would be a good man to have around in a fight" I said with a smile

"Why?"

"Because you have experience" Lachie's voice from behind me said

"Can you all please take a seat" It was 'The Man'

It seemed to me that SIS knew everyone's name but were not inclined to give out their own, even to people who were working for them. I also wondered where 'The Suit' was. Meanwhile Raven helped himself to a half dozen Croissants and Kyla stole most of the other buns. Much to the obvious destain of 'The Man' who got none

Jane who had come in with the man, sat down next to him. All of us with the exception of 'The Man' carried our breakfasts over to the table. There were no other members of staff in the room, just Lachie, Hans, Jane, Abdalla, 'The Man' and me along with the secret agent dogs. When we were seated, 'The Man' started things off.

"You have had a chance to look at the files, and you will know that this group, who as of yet we do not know who they are, as in which organisation or country they are working for. We do suspect they have something to do with Islamic Terrorists, although we have no definitive proof at this present time. What we do now know, is that they are not just well connected and have infiltrated not only CDE Porton but they have also got someone working inside SIS. We also know that they are coercing innocent civilians into helping them. They have Air, Sea, and land transport. Up until a few weeks ago, they had not committed any attacks on British soil. Since then they have attacked members of our team, thankfully with no loss of life to us. They have lost three of their men, two dead and we had one in our custody one man who was a Mercenary working for them. Unfortunately he died while being debriefed. They believed this man to already be dead. They are more than happy to kill their own men rather than have them captured by us. These are incredibly dangerous people. We do have enough information to arrest them but we would prefer not to at this moment. We need any and all material that they have stolen. We need to know who it is they are working for, as well as what is their end game. Then we will strike. You are to obtain as much information as you can and to then pass that on to Jane, she will then report back to me. I want you to come up with a plan, that will allow us access to them and to allow us to be based within striking distance. They already know that we are on to them so they will be extra vigilant. It is also suspected that they are trying to get some plutonium, or other nuclear based fissionable material, from the site of the Old Dounreay FBR Station. The only reason we can think of, is to create the ultimate dirty bomb or device. So we have to get a place to act as a base, for you to work from. It also has to be under a believable scenario. Get a list made of the equipment that you think you will require, talk to Abdalla about suitable weapons. Also Lachlan and Andy can you fill Hans and Abdalla on what has happened to you so far and what you know. I will be back in thirty minutes, and I would like to be able to go ahead with some kind of workable plan in one hour. Thank you for your time."

"When you say that Mervin died while being debriefed? Could you be a little more specific?"

"Complications with his wounds Mr McPhee"
I knew there was no way Mervin's wounds were fatal but I let it slide for now. I would try and find out from Jan later. The man closed the folder he had been reading from. He stood up and left the Control Room. We quickly filled Hans and Abdalla on what had happened to us since we got to the North of Scotland. Jane already knew.

"Sounds like you have had a lot of fun" Abdalla said

"I am happy to help in anyway" Hans said

"We need the latest copy OS Maps for Altnabreac and the surrounding areas please Jane"

"Why do you want that?" Jane asked.

Lachie glared at her. She stood up and walked to the door.

"I will go some OS maps printed off" she said sulkily

"Hans what long range listening stuff do we need? And can we get some kind if a list, of camera and audio equipment that can be used for hidden surveillance?"

"I can do it now" he said

"Lachie you are good with cars and shit like that, can you recommend stuff we can use as ATV without it looking too military"?

"Sure thing Andy"

"Abdalla we need some of the long range toys that you showed us in CDE with Scopes, also some really quiet stuff, that would be good at say up to twenty five yards?"

"These I have already brought with me last night, my friend Andy McPhee"

I did not set out with the intention of becoming team leader. It was just all the others had great skills that exceeded mine. Even Jane who it turned out was a genius with computers and radio. As well as being able to hold down the cover as a working police officer. They were all proper military specialists and I was just a medic, who was seriously out of his depth. So it was better I stay out of the way of this war type shit and do what a normal, senior NCO in the military does, Management.

Jane, who claimed, that Jane was her real first name, arrived with the OS Maps

It was Lachie who came up with the idea.

"Why don't we work as part of the Forestry Commission? They own most of the land up there and as the forest around Altnabreac, is about thirty years old. It has to be due for lumbering. They use Snow Cats and Argo's and all sorts of ATV stuff. They even have choppers. They also use Radio's to keep in touch. Surely 'The Man' has enough clout to get the forestry to start working elsewhere and let us be the Foresters. Andy, you should know enough about felling and replanting and it also lets us check the Deer fences all around Altnabreac. The Forestry use their helicopters in the more remote forests and when it come down to it, Altnabreac is remote. We could work the tree line nearest to them we should be able to put cameras in trees before we cut down the ones in front of them."

"We could also put some parabolic microphones in some of the trees as well" Jane piped in

"Not to mention the cover that a forest will provide as a physical barrier for us" It was Hans that said this

"How does this sit with you Abdalla?" I asked

"I am more used to desert type warfare with warm sunshine, but I can adapt."

"OK" I said "Do we have a plan for the Man?"

They all replied yes.

"Each of us needs to make an equipment list, not only of what is suitable for us to work as employees or contractors for the forestry commission, but for any eventuality that our own mission requires. And no Lachie, we can't have a Tank"!

We handed the plan to 'The Man' and he agreed that it was workable and went off to make the arrangements between The Forestry and whatever department of Agriculture they came under. No doubt it would come down to the promise of funding from one branch of the Government to another. I would expect the lie from ministry of defence, to be that SIS would be conducting some form of secret exercise. This was a common enough practice.

We were given another hour to create a list, for all the items needed, for a genuine logging site. We also created lists to suit our own personal specialist fields. We set to it. Team Seven had three of its original members and two new members. We had been tasked, according to 'The Man' with one of the most important and sensitive operations that they had undertaken since Iraq.

ACT 22

My personal equipment was easy. I wanted cash and lots of it, a full Field Medical Kit, along with the latest NBC kit, and from the sound of the job we had to do, I also wanted SST kits for all the team. My list seemed to be the shortest and should have been the easiest list to fulfil. I was told that they had some stuff I wanted but would get the rest shipped to me in the next twenty-four hours.

Lachie's list was pretty damn impressive though, He wanted. Two eight wheeled ATV Argo's, Four Snowmobiles, One Snow cat, One Bulldozer Fitted with a heavy duty winch, One 100k Generator. Three Portakabins, two fitted out as Dormitories with toilet and cooking facilities the other to be set up as a split unit for Jane and Abdalla's equipment. Four Husqvarna 36" Chainsaws. He also wanted tools and engine spares.

Jane wanted five High Gain five side band CB radios. 5 secure Motorola hand held radios complete with throat microphones with ear pieces and a Base Set. Then she wanted a portable radio mast along with full set of Parabolic Microphones, twelve low light cameras, with a set of Video Monitors. On top of that she desired satellite dish receivers and two secure laptop computers.

Abdalla wanted side arms along with rifles and pump action shotguns for all of us. This on top of the four AS50's with the new prototype electronic self-correcting optical sights from BAE that he had already brought with him. Not forgetting enough ordnance, for his personal war. This was all to go along with the latest Nomex suits and Night vision goggles. He wanted GEM-TECH suppressors for all firearms. I was not aware they made them for shotguns. But apparently they do. Full combat body armour, He also asked for KA-BAR Knives for all.

Hans requested survival equipment. A helicopter capable of carrying heavy loads, along with adequate cash in used notes for us to spend locally as well paid independent Forestry contractors. Rather than the wads of new notes, that they wanted us to have. (I had not thought it through, like he had) The Forestry Commission often sub contracted for remote regions where 'Men were Men and Trees were Scared'. As it was common practice, most of the equipment was moved in as close as possible by low loader and a locally contracted firm were asked to bring the equipment to site in locked containers. Lachie used the same forestry roads that had originally been cut to allow for the Highland Forest to be planted some thirty years prior. All the heavy plant equipment actually belonged to the forestry commission with the exception of the Bulldozer which had been leased from an Inverness plant hire firm. The rest of the equipment had been brought in on a container ship to Scrabster and then trucked down on a series of low loaders. Some of the forestry roads required re-cutting in places but this was not a problem for the monster Bulldozer, that Lachie would take off and then fix the road and then he would re-load it back on to the low loader until we reached the required location. Once all the stuff was offloaded and set into position the Low loaders drove off leaving us in peace and quiet. Every piece of forestry and plant equipment bore the Forestry Commission logo on its side. The first thing that was set up was the 100Kw Perkins generator, which we connected up to the Portakabins. The Helicopter was slid out on its rails from its own shipping container. And Hans who was a fully qualified Chopper pilot set about, swinging the fold back rotors into place. All other motorised vehicles were then taken out from their containers and fuelled up using diesel from the barrels that had been delivered with them. There were also extra barrels of fuel for the chopper. Fortunately, 'The Man' had enough sense to make sure all the equipment was already road worn, as nothing screams fake, like brand new and shiny equipment on a site. The Radios were set up and the CB Mast raised along with the Storno Ariel attached. Abdalla set up an armoury in one of the now empty containers, Lachie had also commandeered one of the other empty ones, for a mechanical workshop. I busied myself setting up the accommodation then checked out my medical kit. Most of it was there. It had taken almost three days to get all the equipment into location. This had also included a piece in the Northern Times Newspaper, about the area now reaping the rewards of a renewable forest from a project that had started three decades previously. They likewise had Moray Firth Radio, Grampian TV and BBC STV, do radio and television broadcasts of the equipment being ferried into place and an overshot of our site prior to the unloading of our equipment. This was to legitimise our presence in the place. 'The Man' had obviously pulled some strings. So we were on the ground and the first order was set it all up. Then we had to cut a line right to the boundary fence with Altnabreac. Over the next two days Lachie and I felled several hundred trees, whilst behind us Jane and Hans set up mikes and cameras along with sensors that were set at a height of four feet from the ground. These were tiny and unless you actually knew it was there, then you would not see them. We set the CB Radios up on FM Channel 16 and used that for chatting on anything to do with our tree felling operation. The Storno's would be used for anything of a more covert nature. Then we settled into shifts of being foresters and watching the people at Altnabreac. They had only shown interest in us on the first day and it seemed they had accepted us as bona fide workers for the Forestry Commission. The next test was for Hans to go shooting rabbits along the edge of the forest. In order to see what would happen when gunfire was heard by them. It brought out one man, who came to check Hans out. He seemed satisfied that Hans was shooting rabbits for the butcher in Halkirk in order to gain some extra black market money, whilst also working for the Forestry Commission. Hans had offered a pair of rabbits to the man, who had accepted them. Hans likewise noticed that the man was not wearing hill boots but was sporting HAIX Gortex Military boots. This was not as suspicious as the protuberance across the chest towards the left hand side of his green Bomber Jacket. We knew that this was a time sensitive operation and we needed to learn more about the nine men at Altnabreac. It was essential that we find out who they were, as well as who they were truly working for. From the microphones we knew that eight of the men there, were mercenaries. The other man we knew nothing about apart from he was not the boss, they were waiting for something or someone to be delivered but without a set date. They kept themselves pretty much indoors. Han's did a deliberate fly over with the chopper, on the pretext of picking up some more diesel barrels from Scrabster. They showed no interest in the chopper and our own on-board system showed they did not have Radar. Hans used an open radio channel to talk to Wick Air Traffic Control. He flew back with four, full barrels of diesel. Again he took the direct line over them. Then he landed back with us at the logging camp. Effectively everything we did was open and above board. We had black drapes inside the container that we used as an armoury, but this container was deliberately blind-sided by other equipment. For the greater part of time its doors were closed and locked. Lachie would leave the 'Tool Shed' workshop open. We would take the Snowmobiles out and plant lines of new trees to replace the ones we had cut down. I knew this was common practice when clearing forests, that new forests would be automatically replanted as a renewable source. Occasionally we would go into Halkirk, using one of the Argo's. This was for Hans to sell Rabbits or Venison, to the butcher. We shot a Stag, and deliberately sent one snowmobile back, to fetch the Snow cat. This served a dual purpose. One was to show that we had it to use in our 'work,' the other reason was Lachie had fitted an acoustic dampener to the exhaust. He had tested it inside our campsite and then intentionally switched it off, while out as he raced over the heather to collect the Stag. The difference was amazing. In normal mode you could hear it almost a mile away, with a simulated blown exhaust. However, with Lachie's modification, you would have to be close to hear the engine. He had replaced the Metal tracks with rubber ones, this had further reduced the noise. The stag had actually been shot from almost a mile away by Abdalla with a suppressed 50cal and they never even came out to see. I would say that it sounded like a small bore shotgun being fired from a distance of twenty-five to thirty feet. So it was a huge improvement on the noise inside the shooting range. This again was dual purpose as he had fitted the BAE sights of the same as we saw when on the indoor rifle range. He had seen the stag, as a tiny animal on the side of a hill around three quarters of a mile from where he lay in the heather. Abdalla had then pointed at the target pressed a couple of buttons on the side of the scope. The Electronic Telescopic Sight had worked out humidity and wind, along with the rise and drop of the bullets arc. So it was just a question of getting the animal on the zoom-able sights. When Abdalla pressed another small button on the fancy gizmo, the result being that the Stag had filled the entire four-inch screen. So you just put the dot where you wanted to hit. Abdalla said a novice could use the AS50 with this BAE Sight and beat the best snipers in the world. It was a game changer in sniper terms. Never before had he hit a target at nearly a mile with a suppressed rifle. This Sight even allowed for that as well. When I saw the stag, as we brought it back it was a perfect shoulder shot. Lachie cleaned and skinned the beast. Then removed one of the haunches and gave it to the man next door, who we had seen occasionally by the fence line. Once again he accepted the offer of fresh shot meat and even offered some cigarettes for it. The brand was not known to us 'Noblesse' they turned out to be an Israeli brand, which just caused even more questions to which nobody had any answers. We already knew Jon was out of the game. Could there be more MOSAD agents in on this? Lachie accepted them even though none of us smoked. The rest of the venison was sold to the local butcher in Halkirk along with several rabbits. It was ordinary activity up here for folks to do a little poaching on the ground they were clearing, then to sell the meat, on to the local game dealers. This made us look just that bit more genuine to any locals that may have taken an interest in our being there. What they did not see was the shoulder of venison that had been demolished by the AS50, this was cooked up for the dogs. Life went on fairly normally for us over the next couple of days. We felled trees, planted new ones and did a little game shooting. We used our tracked Snow Cat and Snow Mobiles as much as we could. Then what we had been waiting for suddenly happened. All the microphones that we had laid paid dividends. The overheard conversation that we had managed to capture had indicated that their boss would be arriving tomorrow. We needed to have a plan of action. The first thing we had to do was to contact 'The Man,' who we knew, was at the Brora radio station. Not wanting to have any of our radio chat listened into ourselves, we decided that the best course of action would be to send Jane, to go and see him personally. Jane took the battered Forestry Commission Land Rover which was fitted with one of our CB Radios. We chatted to her while she was in range, in the same way as any group of men would with a single woman as part of their crew, throwing in male, female banter. We then set about making sure that we would be ready for any eventuality. As part of our forestry cover, we really had felled hundreds of trees and laid the trunks in multiple piles along the edge of the forest line near the fence. This not only provided extra cover for our camp. Just in case we were being spied on but once again it legitimised our cover story. It would be about four hours before Jane returned. We had to assume that they would have nine men in there, as well as their boss. This would give them, ten men plus a minimum of one other, if he came by helicopter. This would leave them with double the manpower that we had. Whilst Jane was away there was sudden activity at their camp. The three Range Rovers that they had, filled with men and suddenly started up and shot off down the road, back towards civilisation. We counted the men and that left their base empty. It would totally have blown our cover if we had followed them. What it did do though, was to give us a chance to look inside the property, where they were staying.

ACT 23

Hans said that he would go over to the property and see if he could get a camera and microphone inside their building. Then quickly take as many pictures as he could, if at all possible. The idea was that we could then pass on further info to 'The Man' and then could make a command decision. Hans kitted up and I took him to the property border on the back of one of our Snow Mobiles. It would be a long crawl for him to their compound, but Hans was up to it. We switched all our Storno's to the same channel and like us, Hans was wearing a throat mike with a transmit button and earpiece to hear. I stayed on our side of the fence. I used an axe to sned, some of the thinner branches from the trees that we had felled over the previous days. It once again, gave me reason to be there and also I had line of sight to their base along with long distance line of sight to the road that led to both of our properties. I watched as Hans slithered over and through the wet heather.

"How's it going Hans?"

"It's going OK Thank you for asking, but if you prefer, I could come back and watch and you could do the crawling in this black mud!"

"Take it slow. Keep below the windows they may have cameras set up inside, and if you see anyone there, then get yourself back here quick"

"Andy, this is what I do for a living, that is why I volunteered to do it. I will give you a call when I get to the house OK?"

"Sure Hans, Lachie has you covered with the 50cal from the big log pile beside me. But if you see ANYTHING, call it in please"

"Will do Andy"

I walked across to where Lachie was hidden under a bunch of branches and evergreen foliage, and then sat down on a tree stump with my back to their camp. I poured a cup of coffee from my Thermos and took a sip.

"Can you see him Lachie?"

From about four feet, just to the right of me and from below his hide, he whispered to me

"It getting fucking cold here and I can't even snag a coffee."

"You are right about the cold Lachie. I can see snow coming, at the moment it's just on the mountain tops in the distance. So we will probably get rain here before we get the snow. I thought those Nomex Suits were supposed to keep out the wet?"

"They do keep out most of the wet but they don't keep the cold out. We are going to have to build a small fire somewhere near me Andy as my breath will start to show from below all this scrub. BUT do not let my hide catch fire. I mean that in both senses, as in my shooting hide and my backside hide"

"I know mate it's a dirty job and someone has to do it, however as a Rock Ape, you are far better qualified than me"

"Fucking Funny!" he snorted at me.

"How close is Hans to their gaff?"

Lachlan swung his AS50 around and pressed a button on the side of the sights, and made a slight readjustment to his position under the branches of his hide.

"He's about forty five yards out and heading towards the back windows, Andy"

I looked towards the area where Lachie had said. I knew he was out there, but he had used bits of heather along with clumps of grass stuck into the outer mesh of his camouflage suit, which he was wearing over his Nomex. I knew he was also wearing body armour, and had a reasonable sized backpack on. As such he was quite bulky. I looked hard but could not see him. Then I saw a clump of heather move near a piece of ground that had more grass than heather on it. He made it to the edge of the house and snuck around the side being careful to stay underneath the window.

"Can you give me a running commentary of what he is doing please Lachie?"

"Well it's a really close call between him and the sheep but it looks like he has them beaten, by a nose!"

"Funny!"

"OK He has the goose neck fibre optics out of his pack, and now he has the snake up to the edge of the window. He has it down and is moving over to the side window............Repeated the same process..........now he is beside the outbuildings..............Putting the snake under the door.................moving back to open ground..........SHIT! FUCK!........Their Range Rovers are back They have used a side track over the hills......................................Christ Andy, he is going to get caught in the open if he does not move fast........He has made it to a ditch and is down and out of sight."

"That was my fault Lachie. I should have known about that old sheep track. Where is Hans?"

"He is still in the ditch I think"

"You THINK? Lachie can't you see him with the Scope?"

Lachie pressed some more buttons on the scope

"I have switched it to in infrared I can't see him clear but I think I can see a slight heat source where he entered the ditch. He is stuck there for the moment, he can't risk being seen. There would be no believable excuse, as to why he would be outside their gaff with all that video spy shit. I think he left mini cams and bugs but I can't be sure."

"OK Lachie. There is nothing we can do for Hans at the moment without showing our hand. Take a look at the folks getting out of the Range Rovers."

The three Range Rovers were at the small car park at the front of the building. I could see men getting out but from where I was working and pretending not to be interested in them I could not identify any of the men. Some of whom were clad in black military style boiler suits. There was one man in civilian clothes along with a woman who was walking with him. Two of the men stayed outside the house as the rest went in. One man went to the outbuildings. He unlocked and opened the door and appeared to say something to the other man. He then closed and locked that door and walked back towards the main building, He saw me and waved so I waved back and then went back to snedding branches. All of this time trying to keep my head down, even though I was wearing a safety helmet and protective goggles. I deliberately turned my back on him and took a slip stone and pretended to sharpen my axe.

I radioed to Hans

"Are you OK Hans?"

I got no reply apart from a double click of the radio system. We had agreed if you could not talk to do just that. Three clicks would mean he was in danger, but with just the two I assumed that he was just staying quiet as not wanting to give up his position.

"Lachie?"

"Yes mate?"

"See anything of interest?"

"If I told you, you would not believe me, or you would lose it big time and start ranting. We need to all talk back in the camp and I mean as soon as we can get Hans out of there!!!"

I waited until the sun started to set and then made off for the camp. The rain has started to come down as sleet as I walked back. Lachie and Hans would have to wait for the dark of night. About an Hour later Lachie arrived and he was followed a further fifteen minutes later, by Hans. Hans arrived back at the camp, at almost the same time as Jane did.

ACT 24

"We need to talk folks" said Lachie

We all sat around the table in our Portakabin. The mood was serious, both Lachie and Hans had indicated that they had information for us. I had expected a lot of info to come our way from Jane but she let the others go first.

"When the folks over there came back, I saw a well organised team who all had proper military training. These guys are nothing like Mervin. That is not even the worst news. The guy in civvies that came out of the second Range Rover is none other than our own man 'The Suit'"

"What?" Said Jane

"You have to be shitting me mate" I said

"I am one hundred percent positive, I had him full face in that fancy scope! No doubt about it at all. He was there willingly, there was not a hint of him being under duress. He was happy and chatting and if I am brutally honest, I got the feeling that he was actually in charge. There was a fit chick with him and she was clad in one their black Military style boiler suits"

Lachie finished and pick up his coffee and leaned back on his chair while all of this sunk in.

Hans spoke next.

"The main house seemed normal and I did not see anything of great interest. Also I don't think they have any security system set up. I kept a good lookout for cameras or their own microphones, nothing. Not even a trip wire. They seem to be quite comfortable here. The outbuilding however, I am sure that they have someone held captive in there. I could see what I thought was a human shape tied up. I did not have a time to deploy a mini cam in or near it. I only just made it to the ditch before they arrived back. I thought you said I had about two hours? Anyway I have set two mini cams up; one is by the back window and one by the side. I have set up several mikes around the place as tufts of grass. That said I think we are going to be screwed on them, if it snows heavy. I have set up the video to show you what I saw. So take a look and see what you think. Perhaps I have missed seeing something."

Jane stood up and then turned towards us

"I also have more bad news for you 'The Man' has said that they have multiple moles within their organisation. Some of whom have been there for years. They knew some of their identities and have been deliberately making them potato diggers. That is to say, they are doing what the folks in Ireland used to do, to the SAS back in the 1970's. The Irish would intentionally leak information that guns or explosives, were hidden in a field, when in fact there was nothing there. But the British Army along with the RUC would come along and dig the entire field up. They would find nothing and the Irish would have the field ready dug to plant their potatoes. So these internal spies that we know about are being purposely given access to useless information. That said we know that there are others who we have not yet identified who hold positions high up in the Security Services"

"Told you Security Services is an oxymoron" said Lachie

Jane sipped her coffee and continued unabated by Lachie's quip.

"We, that is you, are to continue with your mission to observe and only IF you see some sort of device, then you are to take down the men at Altnabreac"

"If 'The Suit' is there and sees anyone of us then we are scuppered. So we are supposed to observe and not be seen, yet all those men down there have seen our faces at some point and if they describe us to 'The Suit' then we will be screwed. How in the name of fuck are we supposed to continue?"

"I am sorry Andy; I can only tell you what I have been told. You are now to work completely out with the Black Door Department"

"Just what the fuck does that mean Jane?"

"It means that all paperwork, about you men here, has been destroyed along with any computer files linking you to the SIS. It means you are on your own. This has been done for your own safety and that of your families and your friends. I will take verbal reports to my boss and he will pass them back to me. Again these will only be verbal with nothing on file or paper. Andy, this operation has gone totally Black. You will not get more supplies nor will you get more funding or equipment. What you have is what you have."

Lachie knocked his chair over in his haste to stand up.

"Jane, correct me if I am wrong, but you are saying that none of us here exist on paper anywhere and that no one will come to our rescue if the shit hits the fan? And we get no more supplies of toilet paper either!!"

"That is about it Lachie I am sorry I really am"

"Yet 'The Suit' chose our team, and he is the Bad Guy?"

"The Suit may have chosen your team, but he does not know where you are located or what part you have in this. Obviously he did know you were discharged, from the RAF. We leaked this morning that you were both killed in an explosion at Ben Graim Beg, in an effort to buy us some time."

"Jane you keep saying 'US' but so far it has just been Lachie and me, they have been trying to kill. Working for 'The Man' is a dangerous occupation. If 'The Suit' is the bad guy, why not just take him out"

"Because Andy we need to get back the stolen material first. So in the move to protect you and your families, none of you exist on paper"

"What about me" Hans said.

"There is no record of you ever entering the country Hans and the same applies to you Abdalla"

"So what happens if we stop whatever these people are doing and take them all down? Do things go back to normal? Will Abdalla and I, get to have our identities back and go home?"

"I don't know" Jane replied and sat down and then she continued

"I know none of you chose to do this and you are no longer officially part of Black Door, because Black Door also no longer exists. But I do know that this is an important mission.

One which I believe could prove devastating to this country if we do not stop whatever is going on."

"What is going on" I asked

"The truth is we are not really sure. Everything is compartmentalised in the Black Door ops, within SIS. No one really has the full picture. So in light of all the leaks that seem to have happened, no section is talking to another. Because most of Black Door people are in assumed identities no one wants to come forward and give up information. As they, don't want to give up their identities. The fear is that because there are so many leaks, that there will become a witch hunt. They do not wish themselves to be seen as leaking information, albeit internal. So the person you refer to as 'The Man' has stated that WE, as I am included in this, no longer exist within SIS. Worse is the chance that someone within one of the security services, might now tag you as part of whatever the men in Altnabreac are up too"

"What does all that mumbo jumbo mean?" asked Lachie.

"I am afraid it means that they might send a Wet Work team after you by mistake"

"What the fuck is a wet work team" I asked

"It is a team of killers sent to make you not exist in real life" It was Hans who had said this

"So Jane, who knows we are here?"

"For now, just 'The Man" and myself and I am staying here. So apart from the folks in this room, just the one man knows where we are"

"Well that's great news then" Lachie said, as he leaned on the backrest of the chair that he had now picked up from the floor. Then he continued

"Now I know who to kill, if someone other than the folks over there comes for me"

"This can't be right" I said to no one on particular and then to Jane.

"We are supposed to be the good guys, and yet we might be tagged as the bad guys because the SIS can't pull their zippers up after the go for a piss. Furthermore, because their internal departments will not share operational information, we are the only team on the ground and we are not even trained covert operatives, of an organisation that does not even fucking exist?"

"I am sorry boys; that is about the truth of it. I only report to and get orders from one man"

"Jane don't you see the problem here? 'The Suit' is with them and he chose us, that is Lachie, Hans and me. Abdalla along with you, came in later for this operation. He knows we are up here in the highlands. I am sure he knows we did not die in whatever plan he had for us. It will not take a rocket scientist to figure out who, what and where we are. He will probably know who we are from the descriptions his men will have given of us. I don't know about the rest of you but I have no intentions of waiting for them to try to kill me again. We don't even know who is in charge here with us. You say we take orders from 'The Man' and that he then asks you to pass them on to us. Yet there is no one on the ground here, making direct decisions and now. You want us to plan and execute orders without structure. You will know if you are military that there has to be order on the battlefield. Now I don't mind taking orders. But we have to know, what is actually going on and don't give us that compartmentalised shit. We probably have about one perhaps two hours, before they figure out that we are not foresters but a team sent to spy on them. When they figure that out then they are going to come for us. So you need to grow a pair of balls and tell us what you want us to do. Do we run? Or do we fight? If we run, we go now. If we fight, we need a real plan now."

ACT 25

Jane did not really look like a true Military person, and she probably had not done basic military training. But she was a spook and they most likely had some form of training. She was young and looked about twenty-five years old, but I guess that could have been with plus or minus five years. She had a confidence about herself. This would have been enough to get her by in the office place but I was not sure that it was working so well out here in the wilderness of Scotland. Lachie and I had both grown up in these hills and as boys had not only lived here but had worked the hills, during our school holidays. People from the outside look at the serene beauty of remote places like Altnabreac. What they do not see is that it takes a special sort of person to survive here. No mains Electric, no mains Gas, and most folks did not have mains water or sewage. It is a beautiful place on a sunny summer's day. However the weather between October and March can change very quickly. Some of the older Crofters would make it in to town for the Sheep sales once or twice a year. Then they would load up their tractors and trailers with dry and tinned goods, then return to their remote smallholding. They survived without all the chattels of modern day living. Jane did not have the look, of one of these people. Hans, the big man from Iceland came from a remote fishing village but even that was probably not as isolated as this place, although I was sure his village would be as bleak and cold in winter. So he would be able to cope with the ardours of this place. Abdalla was a brave and bold soldier and probably the best shot in his Country of Kenya. Yes, they have mountains but I doubt that they have the terrain that we had here or the fact that this snow would come in soon and we may even be in for a big storm. This was according to the weather man on Moray Firth Radio Station. I did not know where the mercenaries came from, nor did I know what their specialist training was. We were out manned, two to one. If it came to the crunch, we only had three professional soldiers on our side. Lachie, Hans and Abdalla, Jane was a Spook so she was probably very good at getting secrets from other Spooks and I was a Medic and had never been in a real fire fight. What I did know was, that I too, along with the rest of us in this logging camp, at some point in the very near future, was that I was going to have to fight for my life. This was to be in a situation, that I had not chosen to be in, nor was it a position I wanted to be in. There had been a huge, pregnant pause, after the "Fight or Flight" comment. It was like every one's brains had slipped into overdrive, with each of us working our own case scenarios out in double quick time.

"I say we Fight" it was Hans

"Me too" Lachlan said

"I will fight with you" Abdalla joined in

"I have no choice in this. I have to see this to the end, one way or another." Jane quipped in

The all looked at me. It was like being checked out on an individual basis. I thought even Lachie, is unsure of me. I could see that they were all worried, that if I joined in a real fight, they might have to babysit me or worse that they would get themselves killed, because of me. Those bastards had tried to kill my father along with Lachie and me. From the sound of what we had just been told, we no longer existed anyway. This truly meant that I did not have even a 'Hobson's Choice' so that was it, we had to fight. Only thing I wondered was? Would we be able to come up with a workable plan in thirty minutes or less? As that is all the time I thought we had.

"I'm in too, so we had better work fast on this"

"I say we divide and conquer" Abdalla said as he started to fill his large back pack

"So how do we get them to split their resources" asked Jane

"That's the easy part, Jane. We attack them and draw them to us, then we attack from the rear and then from the flanks that way they will have to fight on four fronts. We have the ability and we have the equipment. They might have some skilled foot soldiers but we have four skilled snipers. We can draw them out and then put them down without them ever seeing us" Abdalla answered her

"What about the person they have locked up down there, we have to get them out. We can't just take off and leave them" I said

Jane looked nervous as she, placed a sheet of paper on the table and started to draw a rough map of the immediate area.

"I know you guys are all better shots than I am, so it stands to reason that I should be the one to draw them out. You draw them away from their camp. They don't have their chopper with them this time. This gives us an advantage, because as soon as we use our chopper at night, they will immediately rush over here. But they will find an empty camp. The rest of us take the Snow cat and the snowmobiles. Because that way we will be able to carry much more hardware away from here and move faster over the hill than they can. Range Rovers work great on dirt track roads, but they are not so good in peat bogs or deep snow. We know they have at least one Snowmobile, as they had two when they attacked you before, and it would be safe to assume that they still have one but possibly more. I have not seen or heard them use anything other than the Range Rovers here. Perhaps they had the Chopper and the Snowmobiles based somewhere else. But we have to assume that they can call in their helicopters. If as I suspect, they these are private hired choppers then they will have to wait for them to come to here from either Nigg Bay or Dyce and they are both at least one hour away. They would then have to come here and load up, so again we have a time advantage. I would assume that any attack that they may be planning to make on us, they would come on foot. If we stay in the camp, we will have no more than fifteen minutes warning. This we would get from the cameras that Hans has placed. The Wind is starting to get up a bit so the microphones are picking up more wind noise than chatter. We do have our sensors on the trees. So it gives us a slight edge."

"Then what Jane" I asked

"Then we split and go five directions at the same time. Another thing that I have noticed that may be in our favour is the weather. I am sure Lachie and you have a better read on local weather conditions than me. I am told that when it snows here that it be as dramatic as the North Pole?"

"You are right about the weather turning" I said as I glanced out the window. Large flakes of snow were starting to be carried on the wind.

It brought back memories of when I was young and the winter of 1978. The Inverness to Wick train derailed the last five coaches after hitting a large snowdrift at Forsinard. This train had started out with one engine, to which was added another at Helmsdale, the locomotive having worked down from Georgemas Junction in an effort to keep the line clear, and to assist the northbound service. The pair of engine's and the undamaged leading coach were detached and proceeded forward only to become completely stuck in the snow at Altnabreac. Very careful use of the fuel supply on the engines kept the carriage heated until the next morning, when the driver, Stewart Munro and second man James Forbes struggled through nine foot drifts back to Forsinard to raise the alarm with Mr Tony McKay the Stationmaster there. By late morning another engine, stabled at Georgemas Junction off the previous day's freight train from Inverness, made an attempt to head south. It quickly returned to pick up a van, some volunteer staff and supplies for the stranded passengers. On this second attempt they reached to within two miles of the trapped train, allowing a young railway employee to reach the stranded passengers bringing hot soup. Once the exact location was known the seventy stranded passengers were eventually airlifted in six shuttles using a helicopter from RAF Lossiemouth and two commercial helicopters. They were operating in near white out conditions with the winds still gusting to sixty-five miles per hour. So things could get real hairy, really quick, in this part of the Highlands.

"Hans can you load up the chopper with as much as you can physically carry? Then fly a circuitous route and come back down the railway track, to the big clearing in the trees at the side of Loch Caise. Is there any way you could cover the chopper up when you get there?"

"Sure Jane I can take a couple of tarpaulins with me, what you have in mind?"

"I will sort the whys and wherefores out with you all in a

minute. I just want to make a quick evacuation plan at the moment. Lachie can you take the Snow-Cat, again with as much as you can take including the dogs and head up the North East Forestry road and as soon as you get a chance to come off that road and into a felled clearing, say about a mile away. Then set up a supply dump, before coming east, towards the edge of the forest on the North side of the tracks opposite Loch Caise. Abdalla can you take the hill top to the north of their place at Altnabreac. You might have to ditch your Snowmobile somewhere near where you set up just make sure it's out of sight, as you will be on open ground. It will give you a good view of their place and the high ground in this weather will give you an edge. Now Andy I want you to take a Snow-mobile cross over the railway and there is an old water tower, which was left over from the Steam Train era. Take what you need and set up a sniper nest there. I will take another Snow-Mobile and go to the north side of the Altnabreac Station near our top wood line. We all take Storno radios with throat mikes and remember, if you are in trouble go silent and just give three clicks. If you are OK but can't talk then two clicks. No one starts shooting unless you have no choice. We don't know who they have locked up down there. We don't know what kind of arms they have and we definitely want 'The Suit' and 'The Woman' ALIVE got that?"

We all nodded, but I still had a few questions. Some things still did not add up for me. Actually nothing added up for me.

"Jane? You worked with 'The Suit' right?"

"Yes Andy I did."

"So what's his name? And what's his game?"

"I was never given his name, nor was I ever privy to the full operational role. I was put in place as a Police Constable in Brora, on temporary posting supposedly from Inverness. The SIS has some serious clout and can put people in wherever they want. I know only a little more than you do. None of which, would be helpful to our situation at the moment as I think I am expendable, as the rest of you are. As you said Andy. He put you here and he put me here too. As to what is the game? I just know that we have moles and they have something that our Country wants back. What that is, I don't know. Information or something physical it could be either or both. I can't really say."

"All right Jane you're the boss, it seems so for now we follow whatever you say"

"I am not your boss Andy"

"You have been since you came up with, the escape from this place plan." I said with a smirk.

"Let's all load up and get away from here before you can't see where you are going the snow is moving in fast. Don't wait for us Hans, as soon as you are loaded go before the snow gets worse. Andy and Lachie, you two have the furthest to go time wise, so you two split next and I will bring up the rear"

"Not a bad rear Jane" That was of course Lachie but it lightened the mood a little.

As military folks, we are all good at a quick decamp from one base or another. And most of our gear was already stowed in backpacks. All of us grabbed our primary and secondary firearms and kitted up body armour we had no Snow Camouflage Suits but we did have some white Boiler suits with the Forestry Commission logo on, these we put on top of or Nomex and armour. This would also add another thermal layer of clothing, plus it would really help us to blend in with the snow, which was now starting to cover the ground. I managed to grab hold of Lachie as he was loading up the Snow-Cat.

"Lachie, I don't entirely trust Jane, what say you and I have a little side plan. Just in case things really go tits up. I can't put my finger on it but something in her has changed since she went to Brora. Also she said that 'The Suit' put her here, yet as you know it was 'The Man' who put her in here with us. Once you get the stuff to the site where you are supposed to be, set up a booby on the Snow-Cat. Just in case we are being played for fools. Also let's add another channel to our Storno's comes and use a single click to change to it and the same to go back on the station Jane has chosen. I will tell Abdalla and Hans which channel we have chosen"

"What sort of thing do you have in mind Andy?"

"For a start Lachie, if you could take the dogs with you, as the way the wind is blowing, I will be up wind of you. That way you can just let Kyla go and she will find me. Keep Raven with you and tell him to "Get down Boy" and he will stay that way until you choose to move. You know Raven as good as anyone and he will follow your commands. I want to move closer to their camp than Jane has asked me to be. She has told us not to shoot first. Now I am not a tactical fighter but I am sure you know that the Hit and Run is the best form of guerrilla warfare. I want to have a quick word with Abdalla and Hans before they go as well."

"What do you have in mind for them down there?"

"Well if we remove their communication we stop any reinforcements coming to the party. They have a radio mast a bit like ours. If Abdalla can take that out, I can take the phone lines out at the railway station. Then they will be left with short range radio and nothing else. They are all in one place and we will be split to five areas. This puts us in an outside ring. It also puts us on the high ground. So do you think we could hold them in our cross fire?"

"That is the way I would go Andy. If we take the fight to them, rather than the way it has been up to now. I would also take out their Range Rover's as well. By doing that we should have the total upper hand although we don't know what their firepower is. If 'The Suit' has equipped them then we will have to assume they have the same stuff as us. That said we still have the high ground and any advantage is an advantage. Abdalla will have a better view of their cars, and we will have a better view of the back of the property. We will also have two equipment dumps. The one with Hans and the one I will set up. So we can re-supply from either the north or the south. But let's all keep an open eye on Jane. Just in case she is playing us from the inside like Jon did. She just seems to be wherever we are, and just when we need a little help. I do agree we need to get 'The Suit' and that woman along with trying to rescue whoever they have down in their outbuildings."

"OK Lachie. I will go and have a quick word with Abdalla. And you talk Hans before he flies out of here. And see if he has any thoughts. I am sure he is our best tactical expert, no offence to you mate but he trains the SAS mountain and Hostage Rescue team. How's that sound?"

"No offence taken Andy and I agree. Be safe mate and if you find yourself in a tight spot I will always have your back."

"You too Lachie"

After I had finished talking quietly with Abdalla and Hans, I set to finishing up my own packing and weapons checks.

My AS50 in its flight case was strapped to the back of my snowmobile and everything else was in my large backpack. The others busied with their own packs and full equipment checks. I went across to Hans.

"Hi there Hans do you have anything that will jam mobile phone signals in your kit?"

"Andy I never leave home without them" He laughed

"Do you suppose you could slip one into Jane's kit or onto her Snow-Mobile?"

"I could, do you want to tell me why?"

"You know when you get a funny feeling about someone, and you just can't shake it. Well at the moment that is the way I feel about Jane. Let's just suppose for a moment for arguments sake that the plan she has put forward, is so that we are not together but if our positions are known to the other side, before we get there. Then we would be Fucked Right?"

"I see where you are going with this"

"We are all supposed to use Channel three on our Storno's let's say we use Channel two between Lachie, Abdalla, You and Me. But give out normal chatter on channel three"

"Andy by normal chatter, you mean disinformation as in Potato Digging?"

"Well sort of Hans, but if we also move our positions by rotating couple of hundred yards from where we are supposed to be as well. There is a smaller clearing in the woods east of where you are supposed to fly. But I think you are a good Pilot so you should be able to get in there. I can find an alternative location to keep an eye on the back of the house. Also we listen on channel three to what every Jane says and if she tells us to do something. Then we just Roger it but we then check it out before acting on it?"

"OK Andy we three have been together and I trust Abdalla so we will be extra careful right?"

"Take care Hans. One more thing can you split your supply dump in two?"

"Eggs in baskets?"

"Yes Mate"

I relayed my thoughts to Abdalla and although he was a bit harder to convince as he had been training SIS and Black Door people for some time. He did agree with siding on the side of caution. He also agreed about their Radio and Transport. As soon as we were loaded, Jane clicked her throat mike "Let's do it" All of us had night vision goggles so we did not require our lights on. As soon as the Rotors started turning we split from our camp in the directions we had been told to go and as soon as Jane could not be seen through the snow, which was now falling heavily. We changed direction to make our slight change in end locations.

ACT 26

We were about five minutes out when the wind started to gust and make the snow start to drift. I saw rather than heard their radio mast go down as Abdalla had agreed, he would take their radio mast out, the first clear view he got of it. I was racing to Altnabreac Railway Station as I had to remove the land line capability it took me just another minute to get there. Rather than cut the wire I chose to get rid of a ten-foot section of it, by just pulling it out. I then headed North on the train track by about one hundred yards. I hid my Snow-Mobile in a small gully and headed for the high ground working my way back towards house where they were based. I found a suitable spot and called out on channel three, that I was on location. This was quickly followed by all the others. As agreed before Abdalla, Hans, Lachie and myself. I quickly switched channels and gave our real locations to each other. Then switched back and waited for Jane.

Hans had dropped two powerful Mobile phone blockers close to their base as he flew over them. They would not have been able to see anything at that moment because of the snow. He had also slipped one right into the bottom of Jane's backpack after Abdalla had called her over to the Armoury Container on the pretext of giving her some extra magazines.

"They are out and looking to see where we have gone, but this snow is making things difficult to see anything. I suggest we all sit tight for the moment and keep radio silence" Jane said over our communication system.

"Roger that" we replied

I turned on the thermal imaging on the BEA Scope and

looked towards their base. I could make out six images but could also see three heading towards where Hans was supposed to be. We had arranged between the four of us that we would one click if we wanted to switch channel. So I clicked.

"Any of you other guys notice the three tangos that are heading over to where Hans was supposed to be. They are a long way out at the moment but their line is to where the big clearing is. The others seem to be heading back to their base"

"Can't see them from here too much snow" Abdalla Said

"Switch to thermal"

"OK I see them, they are spread out in a line but taking a direct route"

"Got them" said Lachie

"Negative from my position but I have a forest between me and them" Hans said

"OK back to channel."

I did not want to show our hand to Jane or for that matter to the enemy. Truth be told, I was becoming very confused as to who were on our side and who was on theirs. I knew they could not operate their radio and we were on a scrambled network, always assuming that this had not already been leaked to 'Them'. However even if it had we were already operating on another channel from the one they would have locked in on. They had no Mobile Phone signal and I had removed the landline. So hopefully they were cut off from the outside world as far as contact was concerned. The way the snow was coming down the roads would be impassable soon. The wind was whipping up some pretty impressive drifts, even as I lay there watching their camp. Suddenly I heard a crashing sound behind me and turned ready to fire at whoever it was coming for me. I was greeted with a hairy beast with a curly wagging tail. Kyla had made it down to me in super-fast time

"Come here girl, over here, good girl, down"

She did as she was asked and lay down next to me in the snow covered heather. I could feel her body warmth almost immediately. I had worked at US NAFAC Brawdy and had gotten a taste for beef jerky. My favourite brand being Biltong jerky and whenever I had a chance to get some I did. I had a load sent with our supplies when we arrived here. I pulled a piece out and split it with Kyla. Over the years she had built up a taste for it too. When I got the chance I made my own. This was not that often. Sat here perhaps I could settle down and just make jerky in some out of the way place and live of it, in a cottage industry type of thing. Pie in the sky I suppose. I turned and looked through my scope it seemed that the six men had returned to the warmth of their house. The other three were now showing only faintly in the thermal sights. But they had split up even further, though still heading to where the Chopper was supposed to have been. I would guess they were about two hundred yards out from it and nearing the start of the forest there.

"Jane what do we do about the three guys heading over towards Hans"

"I am sorry I don't see anyone heading that way. Abdalla do you see anything

"Negative" he replied one click

"We are being played, let me go back and ask her another question" click

"OK Jane they were probably deer. They must have all gone back to their base. What is the protocol if we get discovered?"

"Obviously if you are engaged then return fire. Other than that stay black"

"OK" click

"I don't think that Jane has one of these BAE Sights but she should have at least been able to see them heading up towards, where Hans should have been, through her NV Goggles" click

"Mr Andy, I have a visual on one of them. What do you want me to do?"

"Lachie?"

"Take him out and any others that you get a clean shot at"

"Abdalla Were those FULL Clips you gave to Jane?"

"Yes Mr Andy" But they are for the wrong gun she took an Uzi Micro and they are clips for the HK so she is not a field operative. I did not think so when we were doing the armoury as she kept asking about our gear. So it might be a good idea to check your kit. We better get back on channel" click

I was tracking the three very faint thermals in the

distance when to the right of it a bright flash to the top right of my four inch scope screen. It was just a blip. Click

"One Tango down" Click

Obviously Abdalla had a clean shot and had taken one of the three men. I knew that this meant that the other two would also have to go down. Killing animals was one thing for me but to take another human life was not something that I could take lightly. I knew there was little chance of me getting through all this, whatever this was, without having to kill someone. I still hoped, that I would not have too. The reality was different and I knew I would, to save my family and friends. So I checked my equipment and listened to the earpiece. Everything was as it should be. I turned my scope towards the front edge of Han's new position. Just in time to see another flash. Click

"Tango Two Down" Click

That just left one of their men he must have seen the muzzle flash because he was zig zagging back towards their base. Four hundred yards as the crow flies but the way he was weaving would be closer to six hundred. Click

"Abdalla do you have line of sight on Tango three"

"Negative Mr Andy, What about Hans?"

"Negative Abdalla, Lachie?"

"I see him I will take the shot" Click. Click. Click

That was the code for I am in danger. I was sure that all our rifles swung towards Lachie at the same time. What I could see in my scope was now three tangos plus Lachie. There were two behind him and the man who had been making his run for home had suddenly changed direction.

"Jane, Lachie is in trouble do we engage"

"Negative Andy, do not engage unless they fire first. We Hold repeat we all hold"

Click "Anyone else, have eyes on the two tangos behind Lachie?"

"Mr Andy I have eyes on Tango Right of Lachie, Repeat Tango Right" Abdalla said

"Andy I have Tango Left Repeat left" said Hans

"OK I have tango three centre, repeat I have tango three, centre. We go on three. One Two Three"

Three muzzle flashes at the same time, three human beings died at the same time. That was a total of five men's deaths that I had a hand in already tonight. I felt sick.

"Jane do you see them" I asked

"Negative Andy, are you sure you were not seeing deer again?"

I wish I had been but unless deer had moved up the evolution chain and started walking on hind legs. Not to mention moving up the food chain and started carrying guns. Then these were definitely men and not deer.

"I guess so Jane. Out"

"Sorry guys I thought there were some guys coming in my back door turns to be a couple of Sheep. Over" Lachie said

Click

"Where the fuck did those guys come from?" Lachie Asked on our private channel.

"I never saw them until you said something Lachie. Why don't you move your position back by a hundred yards and see what you can find? Better still go to the guy on the right behind you. If you turn around he is about twenty feet to your one o'clock. Take Raven and give him some rope and get him to back track the guy. Lachie be careful. OK?"

"No worries Andy and thanks" click

Click "Cancel that Lachie I am coming to you."

I was raised a Roman catholic. I did my Catechism, First Communion. My mother even made me become an Altar Boy. She would have liked me to become a Priest but that was never really on the cards for me. After I joined the military I stopped going to church, not for any special reason. I just sort of fell out, of the whole Sunday thing. Thou Shall Not Kill. Exodus 20.13. The sixth Commandment. I had broken a few of the others like, taking the Lords name in vain, and being covetous, forgetting the Holy Days, but of all the things I never saw in my future was the breaking of this Moral, Social and Religious Law. I felt physically sick. I guess I was going to miss out Purgatory and go straight to Hell. Do not pass Go do not collect Two hundred. As far as God went from now on I was pretty fucked!!! Perhaps by saving my friends life I might get to collect, my get out of Hell free card. So there were five men down and five to go. They must have had info from Jane, to be able to flank Lachie that could only mean one thing. She was somehow able to either hear our conversations or had the ability to see our positions and let the opposition know exactly where we were. Time for me to improvise, I moved over to Lachie's side, letting Kyla run in front of me. I left the Snowmobile where it was, as it made way too much nose even in this storm. When I got there

"Lachie we have to regroup. I want you to take raven and go fetch Abdalla and bring him back here. I will go with Kyla and bring Hans back meet back here in half an hour OK? Somehow or other, we have to let them know that we are friends going to them rather than the enemy. And we can't give it away as an open message on the radio. Do you have ANY ideas?"

"Andy, remember the Bomb training?"

"How could I forget? But I am not with you?"

"Kobayashi Maru, but the only folks that know about that were there. Hans will know but I don't know if the Bomb guy talked to Gun guy, only one way to find out?" Click.

"Abdalla do you remember the Kobayashi Maru from training?"

"I heard about it"

"Hans?"

"Yep"

"Double it one big one small" click

"Let's hope they know what the fuck we are talking about or we will be the next ones face down, Good luck Lachie see you back here in thirty minutes?"

"OK and Andy? Stay Low and move fast and keep the Dog Ahead of you and perhaps Jane will think it's her men moving in on us"

I ran as hard as I could I let out enough rope to allow Kyla to run to the front of me. Today had turned out to be life changing for me. I doubted now if life could ever return to normal. If I did somehow manage to survive that is. The wind was much stronger now and the snow was going pretty much horizontal towards me and it was make visibility extremely difficult. I was sure that Kyla was guiding me the correct direction, but I still stopped every minute or so. I used my BAE Scope trying to find heat sources. Occasionally I would find one in the direction I was going. I found myself literally praying to God that it was Hans I was seeing. 'Click'

"Contact, one Big One Small" 'click' It was Hans.

I moved as fast as I could, every now and then I would

sink to my waist in snow, that had filled the small gullies and hollows on the hillside. Even though it was bitterly cold I found myself sweating profusely. I knew that one of the problems when out here in weather like this, that when you stopped sweating then that moisture could turn to a suit of Ice. Although I was equally sure that with the multiple layers of clothing that I was wearing, would act like a Wet Suit and keep me warm. I stopped again and pointed my scope to Hans. I only had about another hundred yards to go. The Heather was deep here and with several inches of snow on top, was making things that much harder. I was fit but even so, I found this challenging. Finally, I got to Hans.

"You OK Hans?"

"Yes thanks Andy. So what now?"

"Good question my friend. I don't have an answer to all of this but when I have managed to get my breath back I will let you know what I think."

"You should drink some water Andy. Or you will find your body will dehydrate. Yes, even in the snow you can dehydrate as much as in a desert, especially if you work your body hard."

He passed me a water bottle and I took a couple of deep swallows. Then I slumped down on the ground beside him. I had not even noticed before but he had built himself a small hide around his position. Using large clumps of heather laced into each other and formed to an arc around where he was now squatted. The snow had piled up on top the heather and had the wind dropped and the snow stopped falling it would still have been invisible to the naked eye. We had only seen him due to the thermal imaging on our scopes. If the snow built up any more, then even the scopes would not have seen him. His camouflage skills were of the highest levels and it proved why the SAS had chosen him to train their Mountain Team.

"They are down five men Hans but I think Jane is working with them. 'The Suit' seems also to be working with them. We still do not know what we are chasing out here. All I know is that today I killed a man."

"Killing men is easy Andy, living with it is hard. I tell myself that if I did not kill them then they would either kill me or harm innocents. You will be a different man tomorrow my friend. You may be a better man, but because you killed a man for good reasons you will not be a worse man."

"How can I be a better man Hans?"

"Because you saved a friend, that perhaps would have died otherwise. Just now you saw a shape and you killed that. Later perhaps you will see a face and kill that. Those are the ones that you will remember"

"Have you killed many men before Hans?"

"I try not to keep count and I prefer not to talk about them. So I will say only this. I have never killed an innocent man. All the men I have killed either deserved to die because of their crimes or because they had tried to kill me or my family and friends. I chose the life I have and I knew that Special Forces at some point would require that I kill another man. You though Andy, you chose to be a medic and were thrown into this. So I am sorry that a man who should be saving lives will now have to take more. You are a good man Andy but even good men sometimes have to do bad things to help others. Be strong and think only of your family and your friends. This will help you to do what must be done and to live with it."

"Thank you Hans"

I helped Hans Pack up his equipment

"Did you split the supplies and hide them?"

"Yes Andy and I took GPS bearings on them, so we can find them again"

"We need to get going. We are going to meet up at Lachie's position. Then I guess we will decide what we are going to do. They are five men short so the odds are a bit more even now."

"Kyla go find Lachie"

The snow was blowing so hard now it had created a true white out. I was relying totally on Kyla's ability to get us back to where we should be. I let out about twenty feet of rope and Kyla led the way. I hoped she could occasionally catch his scent between gusts of wind. Hans had roped himself to me and was ten feet behind me. We made it back across to Lachie's Position. Abdalla was already there. Kyla ran to Lachie and licked his face. My dog was starting to become our dog. Lachie and Kyla had known each other for years. But this time was different Kyla who normally remained aloof and had definitely been a one-man dog, was sharing her love. It made me smile to see Lachie with Kyla sat on one side of him, licking his face and Raven, sitting down at the other side. Not so much of one man and his dog but more like two dogs and their men.

"So what happens now?" I asked

"Mr Andy. We have to assume that Jane is a hostile of some form. We also know that 'The Suit' is not playing for our side and that they have a captive in their outbuildings. I say that we do two things. One, we grab Jane if we can and two, we get their prisoner." Abdalla said between chattering teeth.

"Which do we do first" Asked Hans?

ACT 27

They all seemed to be looking to me for answers, which was strange because I was not the senior rank nor was I the most effective combatant. It was Lachie that spelled it out for everyone.

"Andy you are the best use of our resources here. Insomuch as we need someone to act as a base and as someone to overlook our positions and give directions. Also I know you are a cracking shot. So we need someone who can lead us from a base point and as we are the combat troops, so to speak. You should take up the general's position behind the desk. I do not doubt your bravery Andy. It is just that we have the skills that you do not have. I would have you lead me anywhere mate I trust you with my life."

"Me too" said Hans

"Mr Hans I agree with you but only because if I stay still watching then I would freeze to death" Abdalla said with a laugh through his still chattering teeth.

I had not expected to be appointed the group's leader. Personally I would have chosen Hans for his knowledge of fighting and all the secret shit that they do.

"Are you guys sure?"

They nodded in agreement. Then there was one of those awkward moments, the sort of one where the troops look at their commanders for orders.

"Right" I mumbled and continued

"First things first we need to have a plan I guess. So first, we take Jane. I would prefer if you did not kill her. She may have a lot of useful information, as she had inside knowledge of what is really going on. I am sure of it, even though she has previously denied it. So Lachie you go with Hans. Take Raven with you just in case she has moved position." I clicked my throat mike on channel.

"Jane?"

"Yes?"

"What are we to do? Do we still keep our positions?"

"Yes do not engage unless fired upon. Just watch their base OK?"

"OK. Do you have any visual from where you are?"

"Negative the snow is blotting everything out"

"Roger that, we will stay radio silent"

"I seriously doubt that she is still at the point where he was supposed to be. And she must have some kind of contact with them. I do not doubt that she can't see them or us in this white out and without the dogs it would have been near impossible to find our way back here. Years ago it took them two days to find a whole train out here. Abdalla can you take up a sniper spot? In the water tower over there they will have checked that out before, when we originally had the plan with Jane. So they probably won't bother looking there again. It will give you a good view of their base, between the snow showers and it will also give me cover. I will watch towards Jane's position and the open ground between where we were based and their property. Is that is OK with every one?"

As they set off I could not shake a feeling of guilt, like shooting down that man in cold blood. Now I was asking my friends to go out and face dangers and even the chance of being killed. I was safe and sound just overlooking. The one giving orders. It gave me an insight into what a General must go through, as he sends his men off into battle. He does so in the full knowledge, that some of them may not return. These would be his friends and subordinates. He himself will die a little, as each man in his command, either dies or is wounded. Not such an easy job after all. I stroked Kyla's head and gave her a hug. She reciprocated with a lick of my face. Click

"Base" Lachie's voice

"Roger"

"Sending back your dog"

"What?"

That was the most cryptic message I have ever had
"Your Dog has caught a rabbit"
"Roger"
I assumed now that meant that they had Jane and they would be returning. We would really have to work on our radio communication skills. Or I would? I guessed. Raven came in first followed by Lachie and Hans. Between them was Jane. I knew it was her even though they had put a balaclava, backwards on her head. Raven sat down on the snow next to Kyla. They licked each other in a doggy greeting. Hans forced Jane to her knees and removed her Balaclava. I could see from her bare neck that they had also removed the throat mike and earpiece. She did not say anything and just stared ahead. What was I supposed to say? We had once again been betrayed by an organisation that was so secret it did not exist, but had more moles than the old football field. Who were we working for? Were we the good guys or the bad guys? The lines that had seemed to me, to be so simple and well defined. They were now blurred and broken. My perception of everything, had altered so much over the last few days. We had been attacked in our homes, our parents had been forced to flee. We had been attacked at Ben Graim, and now at Altnabreac. We had been sold out by 'The Man', 'The Suit' and then, when we thought we were safe. We had been sold out by Jane, who had inside info on what we were doing, even after we had gone dark. We had no Idea who we were to report to? Now we did not even have a direct line to 'The Man'. Our lives had been extinguished on paper. I doubt that they would ever be returned to us in full, should we manage to somehow extradite ourselves from this mess. I got up and walked over to Jane.
"Just who the fuck, are you?"
"Jane Miller"
"Is that your real name?"
"Strange as it may seem yes that is my name"
"So what are you?"
"You already know who and what I am. I work for SIS and what was Black Door"
"OK so what really is Black Door? And how high up the secret tree do you fit in?"
"Black Door is a generic term that is used for all off the

book operations. You signed up for it"

"I was tricked into it. I signed, being told I was working at CDE Porton Down"

"That does not matter, as the only piece of paper with your real name on it now, is that Extended version of the Official Secrets Act. Not even your Birth Certificate exists any more. The deeds to your home they are gone. None of you exist."

"So once again where do you fit in Jane?"

"I was in the SIS, I joined from University. As part of my real life cover I trained at Hendon as a constable. Then I worked support for Black Door. I was posted here to oversee your operation. Then I was told that we had to go Dark"

"Just what does that mean?"

"It means we have no line of communications to anyone outside the mission"

"Why are you helping them?"

"I can't deny it, as that would just be stupid. You outsmarted me."

"Jane. Please don't be a wise ass. Sarcasm will not help. You know I killed a man today because of you. It was your fault. You gave away our positions. So to save a friend, I had to kill a man."

"They have my father"

"What?"

"They have my father. In the barn down there"

"What about 'The Suit'?"

"He really is or was my boss. But I am an assistant to 'The Man.' I did not know that 'The Suit' was involved with them until I saw him down there"

"Jane I need you to be truthful with me. What is this all about?"

"I will tell you everything I know, if you can get my father back. He is the only reason that I sold you out. Honest, as you can tell from my accent, I am really from Inverness. You get my father back and I will help you. They already killed my mother. I am in pretty much the same position as you are Andy. Please get him back"

"Tie her up and Gag her Lachie"

"What? Andy have you not listened to a word she has

said. She is a victim in this like us."

"Is she Lachie? Can you prove that? She sent men to kill Hans. Or have you forgotten that?"

"Andy mate I don't want to fight about it, but give me a reason why we should not trust her now?"

"Because today, she made me kill a man"

Lachie said nothing but he tied her up and put a gag over her mouth, using a Field Dressing from my kit. Then he came over to me and pulled me to one side

"Do you know what you are doing?"

"No mate I don't. Do you?"

"He is right Lachie" said Hans and then he continued

"We have been lied to by everyone in SIS and Black Door, since we started out on this thing, whatever this turns out to be. I for one will only trust what I can see with my own eyes. Even one of us could be a spy for them, have you thought about that Lachie?"

"Of course I have, I may only be a Rock Ape, but that does not make me stupid. I know I can trust Andy and the Dogs because I have known them for a long time"

"So the best course of action is to trust none but those who have proved themselves to us. Which means Andy is right. Until we know otherwise. Jane has been of help to them and not to us. So at the moment she is the enemy. We asked Andy to be the person making decisions. So let him make them. I trust him, to put your life before his. So you should trust him as I do"

"Sorry Andy mate. Things are getting a bit fucked up"

"Not a problem Lachie. I am on a fast learning curve here too. OK Lachie, can you wrap a thermal blanket around Jane, I will set the dogs either side of her they will keep her warm and keep he in place"

"Kyla Stay. Watch her"

I moved away from Jane and we huddled together, so that she could not overhear what we were saying to each other. If I was wrong and Jane somehow escaped I did not want her running off and warning them.

"Hans you have done hostage rescue for real right?"

"Yes Andy. And I teach it"

"Abdalla you have also taught this skill to soldiers yes?"

"Yes Andy, you know it, at the Range"

"So the way I see things at the moment is we need to get Jane's father out of there, assuming that she is telling the truth, about who it is they have down there? If Hans and Abdalla can get down there and get him out. Then Lachie and I will over watch, the front and the back of the property. What do you think?"

They all nodded their assent.

"Hans what equipment do you require?"

"Abdalla and I will only require small automatic suppressed firearms along with our KaBar knives. But we should carry some fragmentation grenades and flash bangs. We will put the Laser markers on our back packs. Just so you do not shoot us by mistake"

"If I shot you Abdalla, it would not be by mistake." Lachie said with a wink.

I was not so sure that Abdalla understood, Lachie's humour.

"He is only joking. He thinks he is funny, when sometimes he is not. OK just in case, I want us to change channels in our radios to channel nine and use it sparingly. One click to transmit, two clicks for can't talk, Tree Clicks for I am in danger and need help. OK? Everyone got it?"

They all nodded and changed their radio channels.

"OK Lachie you better head out first as you have the furthest to go. If you can find a good spot on the far side of the property. Then when you are there, Hans and Abdalla can make their way on down to the edge of the barn. That way Lachie and I can overlook your positions. We will cover you with the AS50's and I don't think there is any point in us using suppressors. They know we are out here anyway. And if we have to shoot then we will fire once and move and set up again. But you will be covered at all times."

"And if we shoot them at this range, a 50cal will cut them in half so try not to get behind one of them if it comes to a shoot-out" Lachie said

"Thanks for that Lachie, real helpful and reassuring" Hans said

"What?" he replied, with one of his big toothy grins.

"Go Lachie. Before Abdalla shoots you."

Lachie made his way to rear of the house which took

fifteen minutes.

Click

"On site"

"OK Hans, Abdalla you lads ready?"

I got the thumbs up from both of them who both disappeared in a new flurry of snow. It was a long ten minutes before I got the click

"On site and splitting up" said Hans

"Ready Lachie"

"Roger"

In all probability this was becoming the worst possible moment of my life, although I had had so many of those over the last few days. It seemed to me that each day, if not every hour, would bring some new kind of horror to my mind. I closed my mind to this and focused on the task in hand. I could see the front of the outbuilding, from my position and first focused on the door to it, the one where Hans had said, that he noticed a hostage. Then I zoomed out to include Abdalla and Hans in my sights as well. I knew that Lachie would have his rifle trained on the front of the main property, so that if things suddenly turned sour, then he could hold them back inside their own personal cage. I saw Abdalla break off from Hans and move around the rear of the barn. Then I lost sight of him.

Click

"Lachie do you have visual on our man?"

"Roger That."

I felt a rush of relief, in that I now only had one man to watch. That did not last long as he reappeared to the other side at the front of the barn.

Click.

"Ready?" asked Abdalla

"Ready" replied Hans

"Good to go" said Lachie

"Go" I said.

Abdalla and Hans slithered towards each other and towards the door. As soon as they got there, Hans stood up and forced the door lock with his KaBar, which he deftly stuck back down into its sheath at his back. Abdalla had his Uzi out with a barrel clip attached. Which if used, would apply a serious amount of lead to the front and close of any close quarters attack, should it come. I zoomed in on the doorway. A moment later, Hans was leading a Man out. He had his hand planted firmly over the man's mouth and was obviously whispering something rapidly into the man's left ear. Hans slowly removed his hand and when satisfied. Then he attached a Laser flasher to the back of the man. They moved towards Abdalla, who put a finger to his lips and then waved the man forward. Abdalla led the way and the man had his hand placed on his shoulder. In turn Hans had his free and placed on the man's shoulder. They made it to the edge of the barn. When a light appeared out of the house, I was blind-sided to its exact location. But knew Lachie had a good view of that area. I kept my scope on the three men escaping towards the side and then to the back of the Barn. I zoomed out to allow a better overall picture of the site. They clearly showed in my scope as three bright lights flashing. I had to hand it to BAE they made some good hunting stuff. I wondered when this was all over would I be able to snag one of these sights. I could always claim it was lost in some peat bog or other. In the moment of selfish thought. Click

"We're blown. Tangos at the front of the House" Lachie said

"If they try to follow or open fire on our boys, then take them out."

Did I really just say that? Take Them Out. Did I say it that way, as I did not want to say Kill the Bastards? Or did I say it just because, I thought it was a cool command sort of thing. I had said it as calmly as ordering a bag of sweets. The truth was it was the first thing that came into my mouth. There was no thought behind it. This was an automatic reaction in my brain, which sent out the command to my mouth. I kept my eye on our boys and zoomed out further, to allow a better picture of what was now happening. I saw a man running to the barn. He went in and ran back out to the door. He stood there and shouted something towards the house. I zoomed in on him. He was in Black Boiler suit and held a HK in his hands. Someone else came into view. It was the woman in the black boiler suit. She ran back towards the house. I heard some light firearms go off in the distance. I zoomed back in on the man in the doorway.

I put the dot on his chest. I flicked the safety off and gently I squeezed the trigger, there was a deafening bang the muzzle flash was picked up momentarily by the BAE Scope. By the time the screen had reset the bullet had travelled the distance to the man. The velocity of this high calibre round had struck the man where it was supposed to. He was dead even before the pain had registered in his brain. He would not have felt his body being ripped apart, nor would he know that the force of it had thrown him up against the back wall of the barn, because the bullet entered slight left of the sternum. It had smashed a hole, the size of a fist and shattered the sternum and three ribs. Then it had hit his heart which was instantly turned to mush and then boiled it in its own blood, by the following shock wave. After which it had exited in the middle of the man's spine this time the shock wave had now spread out and the exit hole was the size of a large dinner plate, ripping a large portion of the man's spine and spinal cord with it. The stone wall behind the man would have given testament to the pure killing power of a 50cal. I just thanked God, that the body had been blown back in through the doorway, so that I did not have to look on the desolation, which I personally had caused to another human being.

Click

"Tango Down" I said

"Two more Tangos out and chasing" Lachie said

"I don't have visual can you take them"?

"Roger"

Even with the snow storm and the wind I could hear two shots almost a split second apart. I knew what I had done was now repeated by Lachie. I knew him as a kind and gentle man who was hard to rile. Yet here he was killing fellow humans, just the same as I had done. I wondered if he felt as bad as I did.

Click

"Can you keep them pinned down while Abdalla and Hans make it back to us?"

"Roger that"

Three more shots in rapid succession and this was followed by a fireball at the far side of the house.

Click

"What the fuck was that?"

"That would be three Range Rovers, well to be precise three EX Range Rovers"

"Roger That"

I continued to follow Hans and Abdalla and their captive. They took a less direct route back to me but one that ensure I had them in my sights all of the time. It took almost fifteen minutes for them to get back. Hans forced the man to kneel down. He had a blindfold made of another of my field dressings. I just prayed we would not require them later. Ten minutes after Hans had arrived, Lachie arrived back.

"I don't think it is too safe around here, we should relocate somewhere out of firing range perhaps" I said

"That's a great idea where would you suggest, we can't go back there." Lachie said pointing to our old Logging Camp."

"I have an idea but we are going to have a cramped couple of hours. We need to collect as much of our supplies as we can. I want to leave the chopper where it is, as it is covered and will have a good covering of snow on it by now, so it will be invisible from the air. It will give us an emergency out, should we need to use it. We should take the Snow-Cat and cut back onto the railway. Due to the storm, they will have cancelled the Inverness to Wick run. They always do when it gets this bad. Before we move out, we have to disable the Snowmobiles, as we did with all the other transport at the camp. Once we have our supplies we follow the track up to Georgemas Junction. I know that Georgemas House is empty at the moment. The owners are not due up until the back end of March. It is very secluded. You can't even see it from the road. Another good point in it's favour, it is far enough away from neighbours, so they can't hear us. The only thing that would give us away, is smoke from fires. We will just have to hope that they have the electric working, or its cold soup for all. How does that sound?"

"Sounds like a workable plan, what about these two?" Hans Asked.

"Keep them blindfolded and gagged until we get there, then we can interrogate them." I replied.

Tonight was the first time I had killed another human. A few days ago was the first time I had witnessed a man being tortured. And yet here I was getting prepared to ask my friends to do it again. I was no longer a good man. I was no longer a man my mother would have been proud of. My father would be ashamed of the things I was doing and they way I was behaving. I never chose any of this. I know there was a good chance I would have to kill again. There would also be a good chance that one of us would end up falling victim to the mess created by SIS. Now we were heading for the relative safety of Georgemas House.

ACT 28

This is just what we did without any further incidents. We took the long way around, to where Hans had stashed some of our gear. Then after we refuelled the Snow-cat, from one of the forty five gallon drums, by using a hand pump. Lachie also filled several Jerry Cans and attached them to the brackets on the side of the Snow-Cat. We were all squeezed in like sardines. Inside the large cabin of the Snow-cat, there would normally have been plenty of space for six to eight people. Now with the two dogs and all the equipment. It was not going to be a comfortable hour or so. The going got easier, as we finally got onto the Rail line. Lachie kept the lights off and just wore a set of night vision goggles. The Snow-Cat did have a heater inside so we all started to remove the outer layers of clothing that we had on. In a confined space, it could have been classed as an Olympic sport of some form. Because, easy it was not! We followed the track until we got to Georgemas Junction. Then we followed the B874 road, which had clearly been blocked by snow. In our transport, the going was easy, so long as Lachie did not find and abandoned car in the way. We arrived at the house and turned off the road and followed the little circular tree lined driveway up to the house.

Georgemas House is thought to date back to the 1850's, with various extensions put on during the following years. It is hidden away, about five miles south of the coastal town of Thurso. In the summer months was a seriously picturesque property, in an idealistic location. Set in three acres, of its own private and very well hidden grounds. It had tall conifers around its borders. There was lots of parking to the front and the side, plus the detached garage. So it would be easy to hide away our Snow cat and gear. I knew the key to this property was always under one of the statutes by the large ornamental fountain to the front of the property. I had taken the son of the owner, back there one night after he had drunk too much at a Ceilidh. He had not wanted to wake his parents and told me where the spare key was located. After clearing the snow from the bottom of the statue, I located the key. I took it and checked to see that there had not been an alarm fitted since I was last here. Not that it would have done them any good tonight. As there was no way the police could respond due to the blocked roads. I was sure that the main A9 road to the highlands would also be blocked for at least one or two days, sometimes it was even longer than that. I hoped that we would be gone by then anyway. I opened the door and let everyone in. I then directed them to the kitchen. Which like most homes in the highlands was the hub of the household. I lead them through the front porch up through the hallway. The dining kitchen was big enough for all to sit down I went down the passage off of the kitchen to the old boiler room and into the utility room. I went to the fuse box and clicked the switch, nothing happened. The storm must have knocked out the power lines. Not a big problem here, though as I knew like our old farm house they also had a Diesel Generator in a shed out back. I went out checked it was primed and then pressed the start button. The light flickered and then came on in the shed. Then I flicked the power changeover switch for the main house and then went back in to the kitchen.

ACT 29

Although Georgemas House was unoccupied at the moment, it was fully furnished. The freezers and the fridge were open and devoid of contents. But the large walk in pantry was well stocked with dried and tinned goods. In the kitchen, the owners had installed an Oil fired Rayburn. So we could cook foods. It also had the benefit that it heated the water for washing and for the central heating system. We decided not to use lights in rooms where we did not have window shutters. The ground floor, was large and had two sitting rooms, the big Kitchen, with a scullery off from it. There was a passageway down to a ground floor bedroom with shower and bathroom. On the first floor were a further five bedrooms. The house had a wing to the side which I suppose served as a granny flat or perhaps it was the owner's side to the house, if it were used as a bed and breakfast. All in all, it was more than satisfactory for the six of us and the two dogs. We all stripped down to our basic clothing. We all sat down at the large traditional kitchen table.

"We need to sort out a lot of things. First let's separate these two" I said pointing to Jane and her father. Then I continued.

"We'll see how their stories tally up. Sorry Jane, but I am going to lock you in the pantry and we will have to tie you up. I hope you understand that we need to be sure. It does not get more serious, than folks that you know, trying to make us into EX-Folks. Hans can you escort Miss Miller, to the Pantry and make sure she can't get out, or hear anything that is said in here. Abdalla can you bring in all the guns and ammunition and set up a temporary armoury in the scullery. Lachie if you would be so kind to keep an eye on Mr Miller then I will sort the dogs out as they need food and water just as much as we do."

I grabbed hold of the large copper kettle and filled it from the sink tap. Then put it on the stove to heat. I dug into my back pack and found two tins of Pedigree Chum dog food. Ordinarily I did not feed my dogs with tinned food. They usually had fresh cooked meat and biscuits. But today was not a normal day by any standards. I filled two bowls that I took from the crockery rack by the cooker. I then filled a sizeable pan with cold water which I gave to the dogs. I waited for the kettle to boil and then grabbed four mugs from the crockery cupboard. There were three jars marked Tea, Coffee and Sugar. They were all full, I made four black coffees'. I also filled a glass with cold water. Then I removed the Gag from Mr Miller's mouth. I put the glass to his lips and tipped it up so he could drink the water, then I replaced the gag.

Now it was time to get some answers.

"Can you all come in here now please" I said it loud enough so everyone could hear.

"OK boss I's Commin"

"Funny Lachlan but I'm not your boss, and let's not forget to show each other some respect."

I moved my gaze from Lachlan to Abdalla, who was coming along the corridor from the scullery. When everyone was in the kitchen, I passed each a steaming mug of coffee.

"What no cream?" Lachie asked

"No cow mate, remember Jane's friends blew it to shit"

I removed the blindfold and then gag from Mr Miller

"I know Lachie, is a good interrogator, shall we say it does not fit with the Geneva Convention. I know he is not afraid to use violence. I don't like to do things that way. I suspect that Hans here is also very good at it. And Mr Abdalla here, well, he has expertise in interrogating rebel fighters up in North Africa so I don't think you will enjoy a private chat with him. Me I like to ask questions and try to get a direct and truthful answer. I am sure you know what I mean by that Mr Miller?"

"Y y y y yes, I do sir"

"I am not a Sir. My name is Andy. I want you to tell me what, when and most importantly of all, why you were being held captive, by those men at Altnabreac?"

"Where do you want me to start Si..Andy?"

"Let's start with where you were, when you were taken? And please be one hundred percent honest with me because if I find out you are telling me a lie, no matter how small. Then it will no longer be me asking the questions. You understand?"

His eyes darted around the room and finally came to rest back on me.

"Yes I understand"

"So where and when were you were taken?"

"I work as a driver for a private hire company in Inverness. I normally just do the school runs and care homes pickups, that sort of thing. It's not great money but I am sort of retired and it keeps me busy. My wife she was at our home. We live up by Mill Burn near the Inverness Hospital. You know Raigmore Hospital. Anyway like I said I was working as a private hire taxi driver and I get a call to go to the Airport. And there I pick up a lady. It was four times the money that I normally get, so I got another driver to cover my school runs. Then I drove to Inverness Airport. I was told to wait inside the main entrance, and hold up a card with Black Door on it. So I did. Then this woman she comes out tall, slim and good looking with black hair. She was carrying nothing more than an aluminium briefcase. She was in a Black pinstripe business suit. She got into the car and then she asks me to take her to the South Kessock Marina. I took her there. She gives me a Fifty Pound Note. She says to wait there. In my line of business, you don't often get paid a Fifty for a Twenty Pound Fare. So obviously I wait. She goes down the Marina and gets on this flash boat. Then ten minutes later she is back in the car. She claimed she is a rich tourist. But to tell you the truth I ain't never seen a tourist come to these parts in a business suit, with just a briefcase for luggage. She hands me another Fifty and says take me around Inverness and then says, I would like to go to see the other side of the country. So I ask where. She says can she see the Clyde? I say yes, but it will be a long round trip. She says OK and bungs me another Fifty. And she says she will pay for fuel and accommodation in Blairmore as she wants to visit an old friend. So I called home to tell my wife that I won't be home as I have a couple of big jobs. I told her about the money I already had and she says that's OK as Jane is working nights. So we drive down and see the Clyde go past the Shipyards and the Naval Base. Then we drive over to Blairmore. She hands me another Fifty and tells me she has me booked us in to a hotel, just down the road. The Lights, it was called. She said she would call me in the morning and then we would go back to Inverness. Then the next morning she says take me up to Fort William. I told her I would have to refuel and it would cost her more. She paid for breakfast and says money is no object. This time she gives me one hundred and asks if that will cover my time and the cost of petrol. I said yes and after breakfast we head up to Fort William. We get there and she meets up with this Arab guy."

"How do you know he was an Arab?"

"He has this white cloak on, I saw him as he was in his car with the window down. He had a black and gold rope sort of thing around his head, you know holding that white sheet thing on. Anyway she goes over to the car and gets in. Then the windows are closed so I can no longer see them. After about twenty minutes she comes back from the car and gets in the back of mine. Then she asks if I am hungry and would I like something to eat before we head back. I thought why not. She goes to this fancy hotel, The Inverlochy Castle I think is called. You know where they serve you a lettuce leaf, with an olive on and charge you two hundred quid. We ate she paid again then says I just have one more place to visit, but it's on the way back so I said not a problem."

"Where was that?"

"Gairlochy, we stopped there and took some pictures on her mobile phone while I sat in the car and then she says do I fancy a quick one, you know like a quick drink, before we head home. We have a drink at this bar by the road. I can't remember the name of it. I had a drink in the bar and then I don't remember anything until I woke up in my own home. They have my wife Tied to a chair in our kitchen. I am tied to another chair. We are both gagged. I see this smooth looking guy and the woman is there. Then they start asking me all these stupid questions about Black Door and my daughter. I tell them she is a police woman and they will be in trouble if they don't let us go right now. The woman tells me to stop lying and give it up. Then they slap my wife and make her cry. They said my daughter is not in the police she is in the security services. I told them don't be stupid, they say, call the police station and get her home. So I called and they say they don't have an officer called Jane miller. I told them it's a mistake. My wife she has a bad heart. They split us up and take her to the living room then. I hear them talking about they have to bring Jane in. The next thing I know is everything goes black and I woke up on the floor. I can see into the living room and I can tell my wife is dead. Her eyes were just dead. It was her heart it just gave out with all the stress. I hear the two of them arguing the man said something, like this has gone too far and it's time to stop. And the Woman she says it's too late to stop it now. And then she said something about the other players. I don't know what that means. Then things go black again and I wake up in a barn. I know there are more of them as I hear people working, helicopters, cars, and even chainsaws. There are more men some are American I can hear some things as they come in and stick me with a needle and I black out. Sometimes they tie me up and blindfold me. Then tonight the shooting and then the journey and after that I am here."

"Wow Mister when I asked for it all, I did not expect all that. But you know of course I can't take just your word for all of this. I have to check it out. Before we are finished can you tell me what sort of car the Arab was in?"

"Sure I drive for a living and I know my cars, you know I am always looking at them day in day out. Sort of like a bus man's holiday thing for me. You know I am a real car nerd."

"The Car Mr Miller, please?" I said as I twirled my finger

"Oh sure, sorry. It was one of the new Jeep Cherokee Chief, Cross-Over SUV's"

"Was it left or right hand drive?"

"I can't be sure but I think it was a left hand drive. It was difficult to see as all the windows were blacked out"

"And what was the colour of the SUV?"

"It was black as well. I don't know if this will help but instead of just normal alloy wheels they were like chromed alloy, real shiny, you know what I mean?"

"Yes, thanks that will do for now."

I drank my now luke warm coffee.

"Swap them over please Hans"

He blindfolded the man and put a pair of ear defenders that we had used when working as foresters, on him. Then I gagged him carefully, so he could still breathe through his nose. Hans took him to the pantry and brought Jane out. She sat her down in the chair, that had been occupied by her father just a few moments ago. The gag was removed from her mouth.

"Jane I want you to tell me everything, you know about what is going on. I want to know what part you play in it? I want you to tell me about 'The Suit'. I want you to tell me about the Smart Dressed Lady and I want you to tell me about 'The Man'. I don't want to hear any bullshit about security clearance levels or Extended Official Secrets Act or any of that crap. We just put our lives on the line to rescue your dad. I think we are all on the same side but in all honesty I don't know for sure. What I do know is, you are SIS and are probably trained in advanced anti interrogation techniques. Well I have news for you and it is not good. Lachie broke Jon in about two hours and he was MOSAD. And it took him just three minutes with Mervin who was one of their Mercenaries. So be straight with us please Jane. I hate having to threaten you, with Water Boarding and all that nasty shit. The only thing is Jane. It would not be you they would be torturing, it would be your father."

Jane looked up sullenly.

"Where do you want me to start?"

"Let's try at the beginning and take it from there. From the when, to the how? You joined the SIS and Black Door. What is Black Door, really is? What are its objectives? Who is 'The Man' at the top? What has a little radio station in Brora to do with all this?

"OK but this could take some time" She replied

"That's all right, because at the moment that is all we have. So please carry on Jane"

"I was at University, I was going to get a degree and join the police as a female officer, at least in the beginning. There I was approached by SIS, to work for them. I did some quick training at Hendon. After that I was posted to Inverness, just not to a physical station. I was asked to provide information on Nigg Bay and anyone who was working with rich foreign nationals. Then about a month ago I was sent to the Black Door program at and told that there had been a theft of materials, that were of a sensitive nature to the British Government. I was sent to join the person you know as 'The Man' and then attached to work with the person you know as 'The Suit' I was told by 'The Man' that there had been information flowing out of not only CDE Porton Down but also out of the Black Door program. I was put through the same training program as you at CDE Porton with the exception of the Bomb Training and advanced Firearms Training. I was to be a field agent so to speak, but to work on a white collar level. It was not expected that I would actually end up with the bullet flying sort of thing. Like I said, I was originally in the Police Force but like you, they got me discharged from my position there. I was asked to keep my parents and friends under the impression that I was still a uniformed officer and on occasions, I would actually use a police car and go out. It is strange that spy's don't think they are watched, by the uniformed Bobby on the beat. They are more worried by a tramp in a shop doorway. As you know I was up at your house after the bomb went off, this was because you were already under the watchful eye of 'The Man'. You know that in Black Door every one with the exception of the people running it, are expendable. Sometimes people get used as pawns in a big geopolitical spy thing. But I will come on to that later. I reported back to Brora and even handed in a report to the Golspie Police. While I was on duty at Brora, a man and a woman visited my parents' house in Inverness. They tied my parents up and my mother died of a heart attack. And they took my father. I did give information to 'The Woman' as she said she was going to kill my father. At that point I did not know that 'The Suit' was working against you, I genuinely believed that he was running some kind of Black Door Operation himself. So yes I was passing on your positions to save my father. Then you saw through me. I thought I actually worked well with you."

That got her a slap on the back of her head, from Hans.

"Enough! Carry on Jane" I said

"Well that is pretty much my part in this thing, but I did overhear 'The Suit' on the phone to someone when we were at Brora. The conversation I heard was obviously just one sided. From what I gathered though, was that there is a link between

Blairmore and Dounreay but for the love of me I don't know what it is, and there is a link between that and this leak or theft of material of a highly dangerous nature. Then 'The Suit' left Brora and then 'The Man' came to Brora. I have told you the truth. I know it sounds like a load of hogwash and yes, I would have killed you to save my father, especially after they caused the death of my mum. He is all I have left in this world. I never really wanted to be anything other than a police officer. I guess it sounded a bit more romantic, being in the SIS. I wish I had just said no, but I am sure they would have found a way to involve me in it. They needed a police officer from this region to be on your wing and to report back. If not me, it would have been some other innocent they would have tricked into this."

"I think we were all tricked into it. Right Jane. I need to put you back in the pantry and bring your dad back out some things I want to clear up with him."

"No don't, please don't hurt him I will tell you anything you want, do anything."

"Sorry Jane he has to answer these questions himself and if he tells us the truth then he will be OK. But if he lies then that will be his choice. Put her back please Hans and gag her"

She went quietly but I could tell she was very unhappy about her father being questioned again.

"Mr Miller. Please have a seat. Would you like a Coffee? Sorry we have no milk."

"Black is fine so long as it's got caffeine that will do me fine. Do you have sugar please I have not had much food in the last couple of days and could do with a sugar rush?"

"Sure you can Mr Miller I think we have some energy bars somewhere would you like one of them?"

"So long as it is not a problem then please, that is very kind of you"

Lachie passed him one of the British Military Ration Pack Energy Bars. I let Mr Miller eat his ration bar and drink his coffee while I topped up my own coffee.

"Better?" I asked

"Much better Thank you?"

"OK I need to clarify some details with you. You said you met this woman at the airport and that you had to hold up a card with a Black Door on?"

"Yes that's right"

"Where did you get the board or did you make it yourself?"

"No I collected it from the Airport desk. Sorry I was told the card would be waiting for me in an envelope. All I had to do was to say which taxi firm I was and give my name and badge number then they passed it over and I held it up the exit gate."

"OK you said you went to Glasgow?"

"Yes she wanted to see the shipyards, a lot of tourists do"

"You say a lot of tourists, did you think that dressed like that, she would be a tourist?"

"Well no not a tourist. I did not really think of much except for the money I suppose"

"The Hotel where you stayed at what was it called again?"

"The Blairmore Hotel it is in the little village of Blairmore"

"Do you remember anything else about Blairmore the town or village?"

"Well it was almost night time when we arrived but it was like a Navy place."

"Blue?"

"No Like Royal Navy except there were a lot of Americans in Whites"

"When you were in Inverness, you went to a Marina?"

"Yes the South Kessock Marina. When I said, that she got on a flash boat, it was like really flash you know chrome and glass sort of thing. Not a clinker built"

"Did you get a name?"

"What her? Or the boat?"

"Either"

"Sorry no I did not."

"OK Mr Miller I believe you, what do you guys think?"

They all nodded and Abdalla took him across to the Rayburn and put the chair next to it for him to get warm. While he was there, I huddled with the others

"What do you think about Jane?"

"She's hot in a nice sort of way"

"For Fucks Sake Lachie"

"Sorry but she is, you all know it, but back to the topic. I think she is a pawn Andy. Just like the rest of us. I think she is honest. At least to the point where she has admitted her sins, right off the bat."

"I think she is holding back something" said Hans

"I think she is telling the truth" said Abdalla

"I tend to agree with you all including you Hans. There is something there that has not been said. So let's bring her out and give her the coffee and biscuit thing OK?"

Jane was brought back into the room this time all the restraints were removed and she sat down at the table.

"I would ask you not to look at your father, when you answer questions and I would ask your father to please stay quiet. Do you think you both could do that?"

They nodded and Jane turned her face from her father and looked at me.

"I am going to have Hans ask you some questions for a couple of reasons first he interrogates on a professional level and the second is that, both he and I feel you are holding something that is very important, back from the rest of us. Hans?"

"Hello again, Jane, Would you like a coffee?"

"No Thanks, Hans?"

Even I could sense the instant change in her mood

"I am not here to hurt you Jane. I just want to clarify some things. Like 'The Suit', 'The Man' and most of all 'The Mysterious Lady'. So first 'The Suit'. We saw you with him on a few occasions. You even went into an office with him. You must have noticed something. Tell me more about the telephone conversation was he talking to a man or a woman. Come on Jane you are a trained police officer. Use your training, remember the conversation. Close your eyes. Relax and remember."

She closed her eyes and relaxed a little. We waited in silence. She suddenly opened her eyes

"A contract for UKAEA something to do with research. So I presume it has to do with CDE Porton Down, Research Establishment."

"OK Jane that's good it's something tangible, even if it means nothing to us."

"So now tell me about 'The Man'."

"I don't understand Hans?"

"Well what is he like?"

"He seems genuine, in that he is dedicated to this country. He has a picture of him in his office with Prince Charles giving him an award of some kind. There is also a picture of him when he was younger and I think he was in the Queens Protection detail or something like that. I would say, if I thought he was on the wrong side of this, then I personally would have a hard time in believing it. I can tell from the way he is. That there are some things that he did not like about the whole operation. He had just had a telephone conversation from either 'The Suit' or his Boss. I know he did not like shutting you down. His anger at that was genuine. As he smashed a glass door at Brora when he slammed it shut."

"OK so now tell me, when was the first time you met with this woman?"

"I never met with her. I have only spoken to her on the phone, my own mobile phone that I use to contact my parents"

"What did she say to you?"

"The first time she just rang up and said "I know you are Black Door and we have killed your mother. If you ever want to see your father alive again, don't call anyone. Don't tell anyone. Go home you will find your mother. We have your father. So I drove down from Brora just after meeting with 'The Man'. I found my mother strapped to a chair and dead. There was a telephone number pinned to her blouse. I rang the number and I received a picture of my father alive but groggy and a shot of the Grampian News on TV so I knew it was a live picture. They told me they knew of your escape from Old Kinbrace, and from the house by Ben Graim and that you were now near Altnabreac. They knew I was working between you and The Man. They also have satellite images not always up to date. But they knew you were not Loggers. They knew you were going to attack them. They gave me one of their radios. And I was to pass over the messages that you had between you. I gave out your position Hans. I am sorry I Just wanted my dad back. So they came around the back of you while they also came at the front of you. I did not know about the fancy sights you had on your guns. The rest you already know."

"Thank you Jane. I might have done the same in your shoes were it my father." said Hans

"So where does that leave us?" I asked

"Fucked" Lachie said

"So, Hans and I do not exist and there is no record of us entering this country whatsoever, which makes us criminals, and illegal immigrants?" Abdalla asked Jane

"Better than professional Killers" said Lachie

"That is pretty much, the way things are at the moment" Jane replied

"So this can be fixed?" Abdalla asked Jane.

"I don't know Abdalla, but assuming they can create carnage like this and break the laws of this country with impunity. I would speculate that they can also repair things just as quickly."

"OK I am not one hundred percent convinced by what you have told me. I guess it will have to do for now. I don't really trust either 'The Man' or 'The Suit'. If you are as much of a pawn in this as we were. I guess only time will tell. I know that your father is innocent. And as soon as we can, we need to get him to safety." I said

"I can handle a gun, I was in the military and they have killed my wife" Mr Miller said

"I am sorry for your loss Mr Miller. But I can't have you here. I am sure you can use a gun. It is just that I can't have you on my conscience. So it is a flat out NO"

"He is right dad. We have to get you out of here. This is not just about people shooting at each other. There are other things going on. You heard the previous conversation. These men have specialist training and equipment that requires s special skill-set. I am sure they don't have the time to train you, or even the spare equipment. I would be of no use to them, if all the time I was worrying over you. I will be safe Dad. So when the time comes, then you have let me go do my job. The one I always wanted to do. I am a police woman first and all this shit second. Why don't we try, to work out what is going on, rather than trying to fight what is going on?"

"Yes" said Hans and continued.

"She is right, let us not look at the damage to lives, for which I am sad. But rather let us Dot the Joins. As you British

Say."

"It's Join the Dots, Hans." Jane laughed.

"All right, we have to make the connections between the Glasgow Shipyards, Blairmore, Fort William, South Kessock Marina, Dounreay, MOSAD, SIS Black Door and CDE Porton Down. We also have to find out who or what UKAEA is. Where do we start?" I asked

"We could try a Map first Andy" Hans said

"Fair enough Hans. Anyone of you have a UK Map in your back packs? The one we snagged from Jon got destroyed in the cottage explosion. We can't use our laptops as the power and phone lines are down. So no internet either. I would bet that the phone towers are out as they will have lost power too."

"Why don't you search this house Andy? You never know." Jane said

So we all set out looking through the house for a map. I was not confident that we would find one. We checked in all the drawers and cupboards. All of us came up empty handed. We reconvened in the kitchen. Abdalla set about heating up the rations. And then he put them all in the oven so that we could all eat at the same time. I made a large pot of coffee and finally found a tin of Carnation evaporated milk. Jane set the table and the six of us sat down. Abdalla brought the food to the table then we ate. It was not five-star food but it was hot. The caffeine and food started to make me feel more human. As there was nothing seriously important to do in the next five minutes I decided to wash up our plates. Lachie got a tea towel and started to dry the crockery.

"Lachie we know there is some form of a link between Mosad and SIS. We know there is a link between Porton Down and SIS. We know that Black Door is linked between all of them and GCHQ, because Brora is a substation for that. What though do Kessock, Fort William and The Clyde have to do with it? We also know that they have some connection with the Fishing boat in Keiss. And Dounreay fits in there somewhere as well. It seems, the more we learn the more there is to learn. It is like some kind of three dimensional spider's web. A web where they all, tell lies to each other. And we are supposed to solve it, without any help. Ohh and they want us to save the fucking world!"

"Where do they keep the whisky Andy? I think better with a glass in my hand"

"I don't know mate. I will go look."

I went looking and found some in a downstairs lounge. There was a glass fronted cabinet which had crystal glasses and a decanter of some unknown whisky in it. I snagged six glasses and the decanter then took them back to the kitchen.

"No Ice unless you want to go outside for some" I said

I started pouring when Abdalla stopped me

"No, not for me, thank you Mr Andy"

"I am sorry Abdalla. I never gave it any thought, are you a practising Muslim?"

"I am a follower of Islam. I choose when to follow and when not. Today is one of those days when I would choose not to. However, it is not that my friend, I just do not like the taste of whisky. I prefer Black Rum"

"Not a problem in a house like this, I am sure that they carry a variety of spirits. I will go and see what I can find. Back in a minute"

I went back to the room where I had found the Decanter. It was set up like a lounge come library with tasteful décor and quality furniture. There were Persian rugs scattered around the polished, real wood floor. Nice leather chesterfield sofa with matching wing chairs. Then next to one of the wing chairs there was a Victorian Globe bar. I opened it and there was a bottle of Havana Club 7. I was just about to take the bottle when I realised that whilst it had a world map on the outside it had a map of the UK inside the lid. It would be out of date but it was better than nothing. I closed the lid and ran back through to the Kitchen. I handed the bottle of rum to Abdalla.

"Will this do?"

"Wow my favourite, Mr Andy"

"Good now come with me quickly, all of you."

They all followed me to the lounge

"See? It has a map of the UK. Anyone have a Pen?"

"I do Andy" said Jane and passed me a Parker 45"

"Classy"

"It's not mine I found it in the kitchen and was trying to join up the dots on places"

"OK Jane let's see if we can do better on a map?"

ACT 30

"You're not going to draw on that map are you? It's an antique and probably worth thousands"

"Is it worth your life? Hans?"

"No I guess not, it just seems wrong is all to deface something as old and beautiful as that"

"Point taken Hans, but nonetheless, my need is greater than the antiques. So Porton Down is way down here. Kessock Marina is here. The Clyde Shipyards are here. Blairmore is here. Fort William is here, Dounreay is here. Keiss is here. So where are the common denominators?"

"Well apart for CDE Porton. They are all either coastal or accessible from the sea or inland waterways" Hans said looking at the map. Then he continued. There is another common link between The Clyde and Dounreay."

"What's that Hans?"

"They have both got something to do with Nuclear Power. Dounreay was a Fast Breeder Nuclear Power Station. Then on the Clyde apart from the ship building yards, you have Her Majesty's Naval Base at Faslane where they have the Trident Missile Program based. You also have the Holy Loch Base for the US Navy also with Nukes. There was also a Submarine Nuclear Refuelling base that was built at Dounreay, way back in the 1950's"

"Tell me Hans how is it you know all this?"

"I study all military set ups, throughout the world. Just because we only have a defensive Army does not mean that we don't take an interest in the political natures of other countries and their armament capabilities. The Arabs have a great saying. Keep your friends close and your enemies' closer still."

"You never cease to amaze me Hans"

"Would you like to know what else I have noticed?"

"Let me get your drink first as I want a big one now"

I passed him his drink and sat down on one of the wing chairs facing him. Abdalla chose not to use a glass but took a large swig from the bottle of fine Cuban Rum. I gave him an enquiring look?

"Mr Andy when we talk about Nuclear Weapons it makes me nervous"

"Go on Hans"

"Well apart from being on the coast"

He took the pen from me and drew a line across Scotland at about forty-five degrees.

"The canal, that goes from Fort William all the way to Inverness. This they call the Caledonian Canal yes?"

"That's right but what of it?"

"Imagine if you wanted to steal something Nuclear and get it out of the country without being seen?"

"Even boats are not invisible Hans"

"No but Submarines are. And I am not talking about one of the big ones. Suppose you had a decommissioned nuclear missile and wanted to make it a non-decommissioned missile, then where would you get nuclear material suitable for this to make it a proper nuclear missile again?"

"Dounreay" I said and continued, as it hit me.

"The only by product of a Fast Breeder Reactor is weapons grade Plutonium. Fuck Me!"

"But I thought Dounreay was closed down after they had some sort of problem in 1977." Lachie said.

"Yes Lachie. They were dumping waste on site at Dounreay, but after a hydrogen explosion blew the concrete lid off the shaft, scattering small quantities of radioactive material. Dumping ceased and ever since the shaft has been monitored for any build-up of explosive gas. So Just in case that was to happen, nitrogen would be pumped in to prevent a blast. But the deep hole on this remote Scottish cliff top, is one of Britain's two most awkward and dangerous radioactive sites. They were conducting research into how the Dounreay waste shaft can be made permanently safe. One option was to freeze it to a water filled depth of two-hundred-foot. There was always risk of a runaway nuclear chain-reaction. I know this because I attended a seminar in Reykjavik on nuclear waste and possible contamination sources to the sea. As you probably know the main industry in Iceland is fishing. There is a little known problem with the Dounreay site, and it is that, the cliffs, have underwater cave system. There are some, that say, some of the plutonium that also went missing, is down there. Now this Plutonium was never found. There are also rumours in the intelligence community that it never left the site but was hidden in the underwater cave system. Eleven Pounds of Highly-radioactive plutonium has apparently gone missing from the plant. There was also another, one and a half pounds of Enriched Uranium. I am sure all of you know what these materials are best designed for use in nasty bombs. Either, as a nuclear bomb or as a dirty bomb. The latter actually being worse in some ways, as the material they had here, was Plutonium 244. At this point, you are going to want to take a drink now. It has a life span of up to eighty million years. Meaning that if, it was used, in the construction of a dirty bomb. Wherever it was used would never be able to be lived in, EVER."

"Sweet Mother of God" I drank my entire glass of Whisky in one gulp

"My friends, this is very very bad" said Abdalla, who then took a large swig from the bottle he was holding.

"What are we going to do? We do not even know who to trust with this"

"I plan to be shit faced for the next eighty million years" Said Lachie.

Hans stood up and started pacing the floor, while we looked on. He stopped picked up his glass, took a sip and put it back down then went back over to the globe bar.

"If you managed to get a Nuclear Missile without the nasty bit, and then you would need a small submarine, to travel the length of the Caledonian Canal. It would have to be small because it is not a wide canal in places and you could not just take it out from the Military Bases on a surface boat as you would be seen. They have submarine nets which are to stop submarines entering from the sea but not from the canal. Then you would have to have a surface boat on the canal, because of the lock gates. So you hide a mini sub under a boat. You take a small boat with that mini sub then you get to Inverness. Customs and Excise people as well as the Police, always check boats but never check what's under them. Then presumably the underwater cave system at Dounreay can actually be accessed directly from the sea. However if they are not, openings on the cliff face below Dounreay. So the submarine would be no use there. Boats are not allowed too close to the cliff, but local fishing boats, fish just five hundred yards from the shore. You could swim to the cliff face, using SCUBA Gear. And then climb unseen from the top of the cliffs, to the cave openings. Then you would have to swim, back down into the underwater caves, in order to collect the material. This is always assuming, that someone has planned this out many years in advance. Again I am assuming that they stored it safely in special containers, if hidden down there. Then they would have to take it back to the boat. And either combine the missile with the material on site or take both out of Britain."

Hans filled his glass again.

"Hans surely there are easier ways of getting Plutonium or Uranium, say from Eastern Bloc Countries?"

"You are right Andy, but for years now, all radioactive material has like a DNA sort of Code. A bomb goes off and you know which country to blame instantly, well quite soon afterwards. So suppose you wanted to start a conflict and not to be blamed for it. Rather you wanted the blame, to be put on an innocent country. This would be a good way to do it, don't you think?"

"Yes I suppose so, but what is UKAEA?"

"In light of everything I have just heard. That would be the United Kingdom Atomic Energy Authority" Said Jane.

"There are still lots of pieces to this puzzle that I don't have a handle on Hans. Like why us and not some crack SAS team? There is not a single piece of the puzzle that fits directly with another piece. It is more like there are two or three complete puzzles, that have all been put in the one box, then shaken up. Then split into three piles and put back into the empty boxes. So no matter how hard we try, we can never get a complete picture."

ACT 31

"Andy whilst that may appear to be random. It's not really. You and Lachie are from the exact theatre of operations. So therefore have a local knowledge. And whilst you don't realise it your team was chosen for you and not by you."

"No way Hans I chose you. They did not put you on my team here. I asked for you personally."

"Andy, do you remember when the teams were set up by 'The Suit'?"

"Of course I do, we were at CDE Porton Down. It was 'The Suit' who chose the teams then, correct?"

"Yes but when we got up here, I could have chosen other people."

"Could you Andy? Who did you know and could trust?"

"I chose you and Abdalla"

"How did you come to trust me?"

"Because you found the bugs in my room"

"They knew I would look, as I once did the same in Iceland. I found listening devices in Assistant Attorney General's Office. I then reported what I had found, to him. I was given a commendation and it was entered onto my permanent records. So they knew I would look and that as you were my team members I would tell you."

"Yes but Abdalla? How could they know I would choose him?"

"Because there is only one man that you know, who can shoot better than you or Lachie. They knew you would only want the best long distance sniper. He is also battle hardened and fearless. He made you feel like a friend at CDE. He did this, not because of 'The Suit' but because it is in his nature to be friendly"

"Jon?"

"Someone had suspected him, so put they him on your team and it was better to have him in a controlled environment and let him show his colours. This is exactly what he did.

"And Jane?"

"She was ordered on to your team at Brora"

"Lachie?"

"He and you were put together using that fake incident on the Brecon Beacons. In the same way as I was. Seriously a soldier gets blown up with a grenade and ends up in a tree, with his clothing intact and the only injury you can find is that his ears are bleeding? Did you see flowing blood? Did you get any real time to take all his vital signs and do an X-ray? No I don't think so. The reason your boss was posted, was so he did not ask questions. Then all you have to do is get other people to tell the same story, unofficially of course, and you end up with a conspiracy. Next we have the class where we all met. We were told so much information about new and nasty biological germs. We were overloaded with the haemorrhagic fever story. Full of half-truths all smoke and mirrors which they perpetuated. At the moment you all think that, 'The Suit' is the man that has sold you out. I don't think so. I think this is more smoke and mirrors. I actually think he is the inside man, inside the organisation that are trying to get their hands on the radioactive material, or whatever it is they want."

"But we could easily have killed him in the fire fight"

"It would have been a risk, he was willing to take to save your countries embarrassment"

"But this mission is real right?"

"Yes Andy it is very real."

"You keep saying my team. You are not telling me that right from the beginning I was supposed to be the team leader are you"

"Yes"

"Why not you, you seem to be able to see things that the rest of us miss?"

"I could not be the leader of a team, investigation crimes within the UK, simply because I am not a British Subject."

"Again, I have to ask why me?"

"How many service men or women do you know from Kinbrace that already had a Top Secret security clearance? Did you get it because previously you worked somewhere sensitive? Lachie would have had a Secret Clearance level because his job was to guard secret installations."

"I guess only Lachie and me"

"Jane and I are investigators for want of another word. Abdalla and Lachie are soldiers and you Andy are a medic who is from the area. You had a Top Secret clearance, even before you were pulled into all this. People respect you because you are a nice person. See Andy, when it comes down to it. They had very limited choices who to choose for this mission. And you are it."

"I need another drink!"

"Hans? Where do we go from here?"

"We have to follow the dots and try to put a stop to whatever it is that is truly happening here."

"So Hans, are you saying that the CDE Stuff is a red herring"?

"What I am saying to you is that whilst we have no definitive proof, that any of these things are real. We do have more circumstantial reasons, to believe that the radioactive material that went missing, from Dounreay is the reason, why bad things are happening at the moment. Remember, we have no proof about radioactive stuff, nor do we have any proof about biological stuff. What we have, is just what we have been told or intimated by others" Hans said

"So Jane, how come we can't call in the cavalry, to come in and clean all this up? Get them to shoot all the bad guys and retrieve whatever it is that is missing?" I asked

"We have no one, that actually knows who we are. I did tell you that your entire life has been wiped from the record books. You don't exist as a civilian, and you don't exist as a member of the military. Andy they have wiped us out on paper. How can we, without any proof and nothing but theories, go to anyone and expect them to believe us. We would ourselves be treated as armed hostile militia. We have weapons that no civilian should have. All that would happen is that we would go to jail and the real terrorists would just vanish and then start up from a new location. Or worse they would actually complete whatever it is they have planned to do. We are the cavalry. When we have the proof, then we can do something about trying to convince the authorities." She replied to me

"Wow just great Jane, and do we have any kind of info as to the time scale involved in this comedic international James Bond shit?" Lachie said to her.

I could see he was getting close to the end of his tether.

"Lachie I wish I could give you the answers you are looking for. I really do. Would you rather give up and go away and hide or would you prefer that we catch these bastards? Then recover whatever it is that is missing and I can promise you this. I know that 'The Man" will give us our lives back."

"Why can't we go to him now? We know that he was at Brora"

"Yes he was at Brora. Though I doubt he is there now. But, there will be no official record of him ever having been there. They don't even know his real name. So we catch the guys, find the stuff and then and only then, we go public. In other words when we have proof, then someone may come to our aid. Sorry Lachie, it is just the way it is"

I mulled over everything, that had been said. I think I must have worn out one of the Persian rugs out with my walking up and down. I had a fresh glass of whisky in my hand, although I had not drunk it yet. The golden liquid splashed around inside the crystal. I put the untouched drink down on the coffee table. I still felt that Jane was holding something back. She seemed to speak confidently about certain aspects of this mess. Things that to me were just suppositions and tittle tattle, half-truths and rumour.

"OK folks. We are not all going to travel up and down the length of the Caledonian Canal. So we are going to split into two teams. Team one will go to the Clyde and then up to Fort William, and see what you can dig up. Team two will go to Dounreay and see if we can find a way to get into those theoretical underwater caves, and find out if anything is hidden inside them. If there is anything there, then we try to get it out of there, before anyone else can. Team one will be Jane, Abdalla and Mr Miller. I am including your father with you Jane, because he took the flash chick, down by Holy Loch. Abdalla is probably the best man to have as tactical support. No offence to Lachie and Hans. But Abdalla has a very quick eye and he scans the area around him, with a natural feel. Lachie and I know this part of Scotland and can blend in. Hans also has the feel for this type of barren landscape and rugged coast. So we will follow up on the Fishing Boat from Keiss. We will scope out the entire area above and somehow below the cliffs at Dounreay."

ACT 32

After, I had divided our little group into two. We started to formulate our plans with rough sketches and prioritised plans. Team one was to follow the itinerary taken by Mr Miller and they would buy as many burner cell phones as soon as they were able to get out. We had found a beat up old VW Passat 2.0td Sport. It was in an adjoining garage. I had Lachie have a look at it and see if he could get it running. If he could, then Team One could drive down and if not, we would have to find somewhere to rent a car. Lachie said that the battery was dead and that he needed to free up the engine, plus, clean out the injectors. Fortunately, he had loaded his basic tool kit onto the Snow-Cat. Abdalla had found a couple of Guitars and Hard cases. This he found with a little modification the cases would hold the AS50 along with a pair of Mini Uzi's and magazines. I took one, and also hid my AS50 in it. The back packs were likewise loaded up with a couple Sig Automatic pistols and along with preloaded spare magazines. We found a lot of clothing in the drawers and wardrobes upstairs. Which were suitable for Jane, but there were also some woollen jumpers and jackets that were a reasonable fit for us as well. Even though Mr Miller was a true civilian, the rest of us were not. We managed to get him to wear a KaBar knife in a sheath under his jacket. Although he said he would stay close to Abdalla. If we could get the car going, we would put spare guns and ammo in accessible parts inside of it. This was a 'just in case' scenario that Abdalla insisted on. Abdalla had, on top of his 50cal in the guitar case with the Uzi's, would be taking a pair of Mossberg 500 ATP 12Ga Pistol Grip Pump Action Shotguns. Complete with a mixed selection of shells including single slug. These would stop a car or a truck if fired into the engine block. Jane was rapidly trained by Abdalla, how to use one of these shotguns. Mr Miller said he had fired shotguns before but only at rabbits, and offered to have one have one of Lachie's. So along with some flash-bangs and smoke bombs, they were equipped for a small conflict. This was all dependent on Lachie getting the Passat to work and the roads being cleared. If and when they made it down to the shipyards, they were to gather info and pass it back to us. But all the phones which were to be bought, were to be the cheap throwaway variety. They would buy as many phones as they could as they stopped at garages along the way. They were to use cash only. Also we would all wear hats or caps when out and about. The UK has the highest percentage of security cameras per head of capita in the western world. So petrol stations, shops, takeaway food outlets and even road junctions we would be careful to try and avoid our faces, being seen clearly. This was all on the advice of Hans. Team two, this was to be my team. We were to scout out as much as we could, around the main Dounreay site. With special care taken around the top of the cliff top. The idea being to see, if there was any way we could rappel down the cliff face. We would have to find, beg, borrow or steal a small boat with a motor. This would be used if abseiling was not an option. Although Hans had packed a scuba kit we did not have a compressor to refill the two tanks that he had. So somehow or other in the Highlands of Scotland be had to find a Dive Shop. We likewise had the problem of the people that we had left at Altnabreac. And finally we had to see what was going on at Keiss. If the folks at Altnabreac had taken young Rosemary, what had they done with her? We had transport that was a good thing and as we had taken plenty of diesel with us, in the jerry cans. So we were not short of fuel for either the Passat or the Snow-Cat. If we could access it, we had still two ammo and fuel dumps, up by Altnabreac. We still had our 50cal with the advanced BAE scopes. And two micro Uzi's along with four Sig Sauer's. No one said anything as all the magazines were loaded and knocked on the table to ensure free operation when in use. We gave most of the spare 9mm ammunition to team one. The bulk of the 50cal we kept. I did not expect that Abdalla would have a situation down in Glasgow where he would be using a lot of heavy ordinance. But he could use the BAE scope and if they managed to get a suitable memory card they would be able to take still and video shots of locations and anything of a nature to do with our operation. We worked all through the night on preparation. This was done as much as was possible in shifts. Lachie though, worked for six hours straight and finally got the Passat running after a jump start, using the battery from the Snow-Cat. Then he came in and showered, ate a meal and crashed out on the chaise lounge. I let him sleep, he had worked hard and it had been a really shitty day. The sun was just starting to come up and it had stopped snowing, although it was still windy. The wind was whipping the powdery snow up and creating drifts and gullies. I loved Scotland and particularly the highlands at this time of year. When the sun shone on the mountains covered in snow. It made it look like a Christmas Card. My father used to say to me that the snow was a great leveller of gardens, in that it did not matter if you had the most beautiful garden in the world and your neighbour had a tip for a garden. They both looked as pretty, when covered in snow. He was right as it turned out. The dogs were going to stay with us. We found several large packets of breakfast cereal this would do as temporary dog food as we had left most of the dog food at the logging site. We all stocked up on as much food as we thought we would require over the coming days. Most of it came from the pantry in the house, mainly tinned soups and stews. If the worst came to the worst we could still eat them as cold rations. It would not be Michelin Star, but it would provide nourishment. Our overland transport was suitable for all weather and all terrain, so we would be setting off in a couple of hours. As they were relying on the main roads they would have to wait for the ploughs to clear them. During the time while they waited for that. Abdalla and Mr Miller started on clearing the driveway down from the house to the main road. A lot of the B class roads, tend to get cleared of snow, by farmers using tractors with a bucket fitted to the front. The A class roads, were cleared by the various County Councils. Jane was listening to the CB radio on channel 19. The truckers were calling out road and snow reports. The A9 north of Inverness was blocked along with the Struie Hill, but was in the process of being cleared. The snow gates were closed for the Drumochter Pass. The A9 north of Helmsdale was closed. And The Strath was also closed. All this meant that the crowd at Altnabreac were going nowhere fast. I am sure that given time, someone would come looking for them, then they were bound to come looking for us. What remained to be seen was who would find the other first and who would have the upper hand. If we found them, I wanted if at all possible, to get 'The Suit' and the mysterious woman alive. We needed information more than dead bodies. Team one, would be here for at least another eight hours. But we had to get moving. Lachie and I did not need a map to get around anywhere north of Inverness. But team one, would have to get themselves a map or a satellite navigation system. When they were in CB Radio Range we would use Sideband and use FM Upper frequency on channel 7. And only when out of range and for important or urgent messages, would we use a burner phone, which would then be disposed of. I had to hand it to Hans he really seemed to know his stuff when it came to all this covert shit. I, like all the others, took a chance to have a shower and to freshen up. Then I quickly caught some shut-eye. When Lachie had rested, we loaded up the Snow-Cat, said our goodbyes and wished each other luck. I silently prayed that we would all make it through this alive. But in my heart I doubted if any of us would survive. Lachie got in behind the driving column of the Snow-Cat, with Hans and me next to him. The two dogs jumped in the back.

"Where too Kemo Sabe" Lachie said as turned the ignition key

"We go North West to the coast Tonto." I replied

"You know Tonto in old Spanish Means Stupid right?

"If the cap fits"

ACT 33

We drove over farmlands mostly, but at times we were able to get on to snow covered road. The low farm walls were not too much of a struggle for the Snow-Cat to get over. Fortunately, due to us using a tracked vehicle we were able to travel in a relatively straight line. We talked tactics, as a way of passing the time. I had managed to get hold of an out of date booklet, at the house where we were staying, it was one of those books that gave photos of the coastline.

"I noticed there is some discoloured ground to the east side of the Dounreay complex. The three fields to the most eastern side are not as green as the rest of the fields surrounding the site. There also appear to be two large circles on the surface. Could this be where they were dumping the official contaminated material? I know they claimed, they had dug a single shaft into the rock and put two hundred foot of ice and concrete on top of it. Is it possible that they also dug a second hole like the first one and put the unofficial waste in there?"

"Andy you know the Government they never tell the whole truth. So I would say they probably buried twice the amount of toxic waste that they claimed."

"Lachie there were always stories around about leaks and missing quantities and they got even worse when Dounreay became a dumping ground for the rest of worlds fissionable, waste material"

"There is a rail line that goes right into the site and they have their own private airfield. However, there is a no fly zone except for military aircraft. And if we were to fly the chopper in, it will trigger a deadly response from either RAF Kinloss or Lossiemouth. They have automatic standing orders, to destroy any aircraft that enters that zone. There are two harbours at the foot of those cliffs. They used to refuel nuclear subs there. From the 1950's to the 1970's there was also a secret Naval Facility there for testing the reactors, that were be used by the Royal Navy on their submarines and ships. That was the Royal Navy Vulcan Project. So there is a good chance that there is still a lot of security there, even years later. This leaves us with only two ways in, we either come in from the sea or we somehow manage to get on to the site and go down the cliff face. Which would be your choice Hans?"

ACT 34

"Personally Andy I think the sea offers the best chance of seeing any opening at the bottom for the caves, but that would leave us exposed to any patrol boat or guards walking the perimeter. Let us have a good look during day time and then we can pull back and formulate a complete plan."

"OK Hans we still have to get some equipment, which we have to find from somewhere.

"Andy I think there used to be a Dive Club, based in Thurso. They had a Zodiac Rigid Inflatable Boat, that they use to dive from. There are a lot of folks that come up in the summer and they dive on the wrecks by Scapa Flow and the Pentland Firth." Lachie said

Scapa Flow is situated on the north east coast of Scotland. It is a large expanse of water surrounded by the Orkney Isles. It is a natural harbour providing shelter from the worst of the weather. It has been used as an anchorage since Viking times, and throughout both world wars. Scapa Flow is one of Europe's premier wreck diving centres. The historic site of the scuttled German High Seas Fleet, where you'll find the remains of seven large warships and four destroyers, which still lay waiting for folks to come and explore on the sea bed. It brings divers from all over the world, even though the waters surrounding it are freezing. Then, there is the Pentland Firth 'The Merry Men of Mey' forms off St John's point in the west-going stream and extends as the tide increases North by North West across the firth to Tor Ness. The worst part is over a sand wave field, about three and a half miles West of Stroma. The waves formed by this race, create a natural breakwater with relatively calm water to the East of it. Its is particularly noticeable when a Westerly swell is running. Tides in this area can exceed ten miles an hour. The race at the North end of Stroma, off Swelkie Point is known as 'The Swelkie'. It extends from the point in an Easterly or Westerly direction depending on the tide and can be particularly violent. The whirlpool of the same name was, according to a Viking legend, caused by a sea-witch turning the mill wheels which ground the salt, to keep the seas salty. The name derives from an old term, 'Svalga' meaning "The Swallower". The 'Duncansby Race' forms off Ness of Duncansby at the start of the South-East-going tidal stream. Initially extending East by North-East but wheeling gradually anti-clockwise until it extends about one-mile North-West some two and a half hours later at which point it is known as 'The Boars of Duncansby'. During the time of the South-East stream there is additional turbulence off Duncansby Head, particularly to the East. The race temporarily ceases at the turn of the tide before forming in an East by North-East direction in the North-Westerly going tidal stream before ceasing again at the next turn of the tide. The race is particularly violent and dangerous when the tidal stream is opposed by gales in the opposite direction. During the East-going stream a race forms off Ness of Huna. This race can be particularly dangerous in an easterly or South-Easterly gale. The 'Liddel Eddy' forms between South Ronaldsay and Muckle Skerry in the East-going stream. A race also forms for part of the time off Old Head at the South-Easterly part of South Ronaldsay. In addition to 'The Swelkie', races form at both the North and South ends of Stroma and Swona. Between the races there is a calm eddy which extends down tide as the tide strengthens. The races are highly visible with overfalls and whirlpools. Large swell waves can also be present, especially in bad weather conditions. When entering or leaving the eddies. Crossing the races, even large powerful vessels can be pushed off course. Such is the demarcation between the relatively calm eddy and the fast-moving tide in the races. There are other races in the firth particularly off Brough Head. The frigid waters in this area can vary between five and ten degrees. And can incapacitate an unprotected man in just one minute and kill in less than five. Without doubt some of the most dangerous waters in the world. Making it extremely difficult, to get a small boat close to the cliffs. Even if you do get close enough to dive from a small boat. The vicious tides will tumble you in and out of the rocky shore. Race tides, whirlpools, freezing waters, sharp rocks. Then there are the waves, of devastating power. I was not sure if any of us would even survive the swim let alone get to the underwater caves. If we were able to get the Zodiac, we would still require a bigger support vessel. Getting what we needed, into place before we could even make a move, in itself was going to be a difficult thing to do.

However first, we had to get as close to Scrabster as we could. There are many places up here where you see Snow-Cats, so getting close to the harbour with one, would not be too difficult. We parked inside an old disused barn on a run-down croft, near the village. It would seem that luck was on our side. On the Jetty slip and on a trailer was a Rigid Inflatable Zodiac boat. According to what was written it belonged to the Caithness Dive Club. It did not take too much searching to find the lock up unit that belonged to them. Nor did it take much to gain access to it but breaking a window to the rear. The entire rear of the building was obscured by a tall wooden Larch Lap fence. Diving equipment was neatly housed in cages and with suits hanging on clothing racks.

Amazingly they had not just wet suits but had the latest dry suits. They had the D1 Hybrid Dry Suits they were the world's first insulated constant volume dry suit that was tested in the Antarctic to give a perfect dry suit. They had Silicone neck and wrist seals are fixed to the suit. The neck seal is designed with a bellow in the back of the neck for easier movement of the head. A Neoprene Warm-neck with water drain valves and moulded Velcro tabs. The silicon seals holds a layer of warmed water around them. They also had a mesh lining that keeps you warm all over, two layers are kept apart by nylon springs like in a bed mattress that create a uniform layer of insulating air all around your body. Unrestricted Airflow from the inner lining provides a pathway for air and ensures that trapped air can escape. The mesh lining does not absorb any moisture and will keep you dry, and provides constant insulation at all depths.

These suits had a 10-Butyl layer trilaminate that is abrasion proof but still very flexible. Military Grade DuPont Kevlar fibre reinforced Kneepads. They even came with Kevlar boots. We found sizes that would fit us, we also found Air tanks and dive weights along with underwater torches. Lachie found a small and portable petrol operated air compressor. There was a set of wrenches with wrist straps. But still we could not find the helmets to go with the dry suits. Lachie found a carton of masks and asked Hans.

"Will these do or is this a Darth Vader play suit?"

Hans went over and looked at the Picture on the box

"Perfect"

According to the leaflet inside the box. They were the Ocean Reef's Neptune Space Predator, Full Face Dive mask. It looked the most futuristic piece of dive gear, since re-breathers. An easy crossover from normal scuba breathing system making this mask a definite part of the future of diving. I read more of the leaflet. The Neptune Space Predator Full Face Mask includes a state-of-the art regulator, reduced internal volume, an improved visual field and integrated surface air valve. Much more importantly was that it is compatible with a communication unit of the type we had, our Storno Radios and throat mikes. So we had Suits, Tanks and a boat. We loaded the dive gear into the Snow Cat. It was hard going in the snow which had drifted to several feet in places. By the time we had finished trekking backwards and forwards we were soaked in sweat. Next on the list was climbing equipment. I had checked the telephone directory and could not find a single shop in Caithness that sold climbing equipment. The closest was the Assynt Mountain Centre in South West Sutherlandshire. We did not have the time to go there and back. Not to mention the danger of being caught. Ropes were not a problem there was plenty of that around Scrabster, for use on the fishing boats. So unless we were able to get hold of other climbing equipment. We would have to free climb and make our own pitons which we could drive into the rock crevices. This was a back-up plan in case we could not get access from the sea. We would still need the rope to link us together if we dived. With so many variables and no solid plan to work to it was always going to be difficult. We went down the slip to the Zodiac. It was fitted with a trio of Honda 250 outboard engines. Whilst the fuel tank was full of petrol we would probably need more. After another search of the dive centre we still came up empty handed. We did find an empty twenty-five-gallon drum which we took along with the filler. We could buy some petrol. The next thing though, was to go to Keiss. The main roads were being cleared and we would require some ordinary transport. So after hiding most of our kit in the barn, we let the dogs out for a run, fed and watered them and we set out with backpacks on. We walked into Scrabster village to look for something to buy. There was nothing, so we caught a bus into town of Thurso. We found Dunnets Garage and bought a beat up old Ford Transit Van for £750 cash. The salesman wanted a name and address along with proof of identity. But he said an extra £250 would make him forget about re-registering for the time being. And that he would buy the van back for £500 if we brought it back within a week. Then we went back to Scrabster and picked up the dogs along with the rest of the weapons. We also took the empty petrol cans, which we filled up at the first garage we came to. Once again paying in cash, we had all decided to throw away our credit and debit cards as they were a sure fire way of getting tracked. Lachie fitted one of the CB radios to the van and a magnetic mounted aerial. Then we set off for Keiss. The plan being, first to try and find out what happened to Rosemary? And secondly get her back if possible. I wanted to know what sort of deal Sandy McKay the skipper of the Catherine May had struck with the group from Altnabreac. We followed the Main A9 across to Miller Point and then went down the B876. This road had not been ploughed, so at times we had to force our way through snow drifts. At one point the van almost slipped into a deep ditch at the side of the road, but Lachie managed to pull it back at the last moment. We drove on and then turned left at McAllister on to the A99 back up towards Keiss. Not the most direct of routes but it was where the roads were mostly clear of snow. At Keiss we turned right at the Sinclair Bay Hotel. On to the High Street and followed it down to the harbour. Of all the Harbours that I have been to, in the Highlands of Scotland, I think this is the most beautiful. In summer with the bright yellow Whin bushes blooming on the hillsides, contrasting with the clear blue water of the harbour. Many times as a boy I had fished for Mackerel and other fish that would swim close to the shores. In winter when the wind and the high tides would mix it up, I loved to watch the power of nature, as the breakers would crash up against the harbour walls. The sea spray would be carried on the wind up and along the High street over a hundred feet above. Where it would fall as salty rain, or be blown into your face and sting your eyes. We went down to the harbour and parked up behind a stack of creels on the edge of the dock. The Catherine May, was tied up and no one was on the deck.

"How do you want to do this?" Lachie asked

"Well I went down last time and had no problems also they seemed happy enough to see me, so perhaps I should try the same thing again. But if you could walk Kyla down one side of the harbour and Hans if you take raven down the other side. That way we will have the whole of the harbour covered. I am going to take a Sig with a suppressor attached, just because, it looks too quiet. Last time I was here Stuart was on deck working and Sandy was in the engine room."

ACT 35

The bilge pump was running which should have meant someone was on board. I held the Sig under the back of my coat as if I had my hands clasped behind my back. Although I was a right handed person, I actually held the Sig in my left. This was something that Abdalla had taught me, just in case the person I met was unarmed and wanted to shake hands. I had a throat mike on but no earpiece. Both Lachie and Hans would be able to hear as I had set my Storno to transmit, they of course were wearing ear pieces. I walked towards the boat. The harbour still had a covering of snow on it even though there was a lot of sea spray coming over the top of the granite wall. I carefully climbed the railing and snuck a peek into the wheelhouse. Nothing there

"Wheelhouse Empty"

I tried the door to the wheelhouse, it turned easily and the door opened with a slight creak. It probably was not loud enough to allow anyone nearby hear but it sounded like a foghorn to me.

Inside it was laid out as I would have expected any of the fishing boats around here to be. GPS, Ship to Shore radio and a CB Radio under. There was a chart on the small shelf that served as a desk for the skipper. A half-finished cup of coffee, which I put my hand too. It was cold. I opened the cupboards over and looked inside, nothing of interest. I looked at the chart. It was of the waters around the Pentland Skerries Isle and Lighthouse. The only inhabitant of that, used to be a lighthouse keeper. But there were three other tiny Islands in the group that were all uninhabited. It was also a very dangerous place to take a small fishing boat. The waters around this area, are always very unpredictable, sharp rocks can easily pierce a hull and sink a boat. Over the years this stretch of water had claimed many lives and taken many ships and boats to the bottom, after smashing them on the unforgiving rocks. The list of which reads like a war memorial, although most were lost in peacetime. Why would Sandy want to risk life, limb and livelihood to fish there at this time of year? To my understanding he was an experienced skipper. I am sure the lobsters and crabs in that area were there in abundance. But the risks surely outweighed the prize. I was having a good snoop around, when my foot crunched on some broken glass that was on the floor. It was the hip flask that I had seen in Sandy's shirt pocket, one of those half glass and half pewter things, that held about a quarter of a bottle. The Pewter part lay next to the broken shards of glass.

"We may have a problem here I whispered" Through my throat mike.

ACT 36

I changed my Sig Sauer from my left to my right and let my hand dangle next to my leg. Rather than going through the door down to the cabin below. I went out of the wheelhouse and removed my boots. Then I walked to the engine room cover. I could see both Lachie and Hans closing in from both sides of the quay. Lachlan had slipped the lead of Kyla who was walking at his heel. Hans did the same thing but Raven ran towards the boat that I was standing on. I raised my hand, the way my father would, to stop him, as I did not want to shout out. Raven stopped running but kept walking towards me. Carefully I slipped down into the smelly engine room. It was a mixture of fish, oil and salt water and it was not a pleasant odour. This would never make the inside of a cologne bottle. The light down here was poor and came from a single caged, low wattage bulb, which over the years had been coated in soot, grime and oil. This made it even worse than it would have been. Carefully I inched along, using my left hand now to balance. My socks and feet were wet from the moisture that always lines the inside of a working boat's, engine room. The engine was still warm so the boat had not long been tied up. The corridor towards the bunk area was barely thin enough for a man to walk, and I had to stoop a bit. I peeked inside the lounge come dining galley area. I could see that Sandy was bound up using duct tape and he had a nasty bump on his forehead. Another quick peek and it showed Stuart face down on the floor, similarly bound.

"Sandy and Stuart are tied up they but seem OK other

than that. I am going to check the whole boat before I give the all clear."

I had no sooner said this than I heard a loud commotion coming from the deck above. I heard someone yell, then I heard a shot and something heavy landed on the deck. I knew there was no point in shouting from here. I looked through the small porthole on the door into the galley and saw Lachie storming in from the wheelhouse above. In his hand was his own Sig Sauer with silencer attached. I pushed the door open with my back and checked that no one was coming at me from the Engine room.

"You OK? Lachie?"

"Yes Andy but…."

"Hans?"

"Andy, we are both OK but you better come topside quick!"

I took out my KaBar and slit the bindings on Sandy and Stuart. Then I quickly followed Lachie back up through the wheelhouse cabin and then through its door onto the deck. Hans was on deck with his gun pressed to the temple of a man who was laid down. His trouser leg was ripped and Kyla was growling in the man's face and he looked terrified.

"So you caught one then, Good Girl Kyla"

"Which one of you, bozos, forgot to attach his silencer until after the shooting?"

"Andy. That is not the problem."

"Why what's up?"

"Andy its Raven your dad's dog, he's been shot. This guy here was coming in behind you. Raven saw it and tore into him, before he could shoot you in the back. Andy, Raven's dead"

"What do you mean Raven is dead?" I asked

"He shot Raven at point blank range. Raven is gone mate" Lachie replied

My first reaction was to go and shoot this slime-ball in the face for what he had done. Lachie saw me move even before the thought had formulated in my own brain. He stepped between me and the man while putting his hand on my arm to stop me raising my own automatic.

"NO! Not here Not now. Help me get him below and we are going to have to move Raven's body" Lachie said

Quickly they dragged the man down into the galley of the boat. I walked over to where my father's Great Dane, lay dead on the foredeck of the boat. His tongue hung lifeless from his open mouth. There was a pool of dark red blood under his head. My father had owned Raven, since he was a puppy. After my mother died and I had left home, Raven was my father's companion. He was easily recognisable, standing almost forty inches at the shoulder and not a spot of white hair on him. He was as black as pitch. The dog had a wonderful temperament. He had been the epitome of the gentle giant and children loved him. My father loved him and I am sure that love was reciprocated in an honest and true way. I had absolutely no idea as to how I was going to break this sad news to my father, it would destroy him and it had all been my fault. I had only asked Lachie and Hans, to take the dogs with them, in order to legitimise their being out and walking around the harbour on a cold, wintry day. Raven had obviously sensed that I was in danger. I had never known him to ever bite anyone, he had growled at a few people over the years. People, that he felt posed some kind of threat to my father or his stock. Yet he had attacked this man with his dying breath in order to save me. I knelt down beside him and the tears of the emotional pain I was feeling, welled up and fell onto and then down his shiny black coat. I put my fingers against my lips, kissed them and gently touched him on his neck then I drew a nearby tarpaulin over him. I could not carry him ashore, so we would have to take him out to sea. The bastard that did this, was going to suffer, not just for killing the dog but for taking a piece of me and destroying my dad, even if he did not know at present. I climbed down in to the galley which was getting a little crowded. All the time I stared at him, the bastard, the dog killer.

"Sandy what happened to you?"

"Two men came on to the boat this morning, they had Rosemary with them, and they told us to take them to the Outer Skerries Lighthouse. About two weeks ago they came to our house and took Rosemary. They said they wanted to use the boat without others knowing, they promised that they would return her when all this was over. But then they saw you down here the other day and said that I had told you, what was happening. As you know I did not. But they did not believe me.

So they brought rosemary here. They made her watch as they slapped me about a bit and then they slapped her around they said they would cut her up if I did anything more. They forced me to take them to the Skerries. Originally they were going to put Rosemary on the smallest of the uninhabited Isles. That is the easterly Isle but the sea was too rough and the boat along with them would have gone down. So we went to the lighthouse Isle and one man took Rosemary and said he would kill her if I said anything to anyone. After that we came back here then everything went black until just now when I woke up. How's Stuart?"

"Like you he has a good bump on his head, but he is OK. Tell me about this man, why did he come back? Apart from trying to kill us that is"

"He is the one who first took Rosemary. He is supposed to be getting something, which they were going to use my boat to take to the Skerries. Now my Rosemary will be killed, I wish you had not come here Andy, I really do!" Sandy stared at me with tears in his sad old eyes. He was right I had in all probability, caused the death of his child. This was a situation that I had no control over, yet the people I cared about, friends and family, were all being put in dangers way. I wondered just how many innocent men, women and children, SIS were willing to sacrifice for the greater good.

"He is right you know, if I don't go there tonight, he will kill the stupid bitch, probably after he has had his way with her. Too bad eh" said the man

Hans backhanded the man in his mouth, causing a trickle of blood to run form the mans lower lip.

"Speak another word, before you are asked to, and I will gut you like a fish. Then will let you watch your own intestines, spill onto the deck. You won't die right away but you will suffer an agonising and slow death. That I guarantee you." Hans said as he held the man's chin tightly in his hand, His other hand had pulled his KaBar out with lightning speed and was now held against then man's belly.

"Don't worry Sandy you have my word you will get your lass back tonight. Do you know what time you are supposed to be there?"

"He said something about come after dark, but I did not

hear all of the conversation."

"You'll be too late as he will rape her and throw her body in the sea." The man said

Hans slid the KaBar with its laser cut edge, lightly across the man's shirt and a thin line of blood appeared. The man shut his mouth.

"Just say one more fucking word and I will cut chunks of flesh off you and feed them to my dog, and if you think the black dog you murdered was dangerous, well then you are sadly mistaken. My dog is pure breed Japanese Akita. They were bred to hunt down and kill bears. They will fight to the absolute death. She will bite then rip you to bits. Normally they rip the throat out of their prey. So just give me one fucking reason and you WILL regret it! A man of your size is not a problem to her. The Great Dane was a soft pet. She is NOT" I said in anger and then I continued speaking to Sandy

"We won't be too late I promise you Sandy"

Take your coat off and your trousers."

The man looked worried I grabbed Kyla by the scruff of the neck and pushed her forward a few inches. She bared her teeth, her tail went down, and her heckles went up, making her look even bigger and more menacing that she already was. She snarled and barked. It would not have taken much for me to let her go at that moment in time. I still wanted my own revenge for the death of Raven. But first I needed information from this man.

"Have you checked him for weapons?"

"Even in the secret crack" Hans replied.

I know Hans was feeling guilty about Raven. I could see the pain and guilt, in his eyes

"It was not your fault Hans. He was protecting his master's son. Even if Raven had not been off the lead, he would have dragged you along and still got to that tosser. If it was anyone's fault it was his."

I put my gun under the man's chin and pushed it up hard so that it was almost choking him and hissed in his ear.

"Get your clothes off now you bastard. I don't care if you take them off, or if I have to shoot you in the face and drag them off you, your choice at this point, but they are coming off and it's a time sensitive option. Got it?"

ACT 37

"Andy? Lachie? Just who are you? You are not in the RAF are you?" Sandy asked us.

"Sandy, I ask that you will trust me. We are the good guys and just take it on good faith. We will get Rosemary back. You have my word on it. You know Lachie and me. We are from here, and we are nothing like these other people. I can't tell you what is going on, I can't tell you much of it because, I don't actually know all of it myself. However, the bits I do know I still can't tell you, because it could put you in more danger, than you are already in. I am going to have to ask you to help us, because we need your help to get your Rosemary back. We will need you as well Stuart. That said you do have a choice, it's just, you know the waters, you know where the dangerous currents are. We don't. So will you both help us?"

"Just try and stop me" said Stuart

"Tell me how I can help." Sandy said

"OK Stuart. We have a white Ford Transit van over there. Lachie will give you the keys. In the back you will find a Guitar Case and three back packs, they are heavy can you fetch them here."

"Aye I can do that" he took the keys from Lachie and set off to the dock. The man was taking his clothes off too slowly for Hans who slapped him hard on the back of the head. The man fell forward and caught his head on the side of a cupboard, resulting in a small cut on the bridge of his nose.

"Today" Hans barked at him

"How soon can you be ready to put to sea again Sandy?"

"Just need to pump some fuel from the barrels over there, and we are ready, the tide is good"

"OK can you do it please?"

"No problem" he walked out of the galley which left Hans, Lachie, Kyla and the man.

"Down to you boxers now" Lachie said

The man, who had been quite cocky ten minutes previous, was now decidedly less talkative. Now he was down to his boxers and socks. I looked him up and down. He was a big man and fit. The thin line from the cut given to him by Hans now had little rivulets of blood. But he was just one man and we were now three, plus two, and a very nasty dog. He looked to be about Lachie's build and although the hair was not quite the same colour it was not far off.

"Lachie you like the prince you are, have a new wardrobe" I said with a smile and continued

"I think at one hundred yards you could pass as his twin brother"

"Don't think so Andy, his mother threw the best bit away, but I get where you are going with this" He replied

"I know in Iceland they say we are progressive when it comes to matters of sexuality, but I can't say I will be joining in with the swingers in here" Hans said with a wink to me.

I knew what he was doing he was trying to lighten the mood and I secretly thanked him for it. As the more I brooded on my father's now dead companion, then the less control I would be able to exert over my actions.

"Funny how Icelanders think they are not good swingers, my father said your mother was" Lachie retorted.

"Girls, please not in front of our esteemed guest here in the striped boxers"

Hans snorted. Lachie smiled, Kyla growled, and the man looked worried as well he should be, more so if he knew what I had in mind for him.

"I brought your stuff on board, I have stowed it in the forward hatch, by the way which one of you is the guitarist?" asked Stuart

"He is" Lachie, Hans and I, all said at the same time. Whilst pointing at each other. It got us a strange look from

Stuart. But he shrugged and went to the engine room where Sandy was just finishing refuelling. Both of them went on up to the wheelhouse and the engine started. Stuart came out and cast of the lines, then shouted down at us.

"Skipper wants to know where we're going."

"Tell him to take us two or three miles out. And I will be up to see him in a few minutes. I don't want us to be seen on deck until we are out of eyesight of the shore."

"OK You're the boss, can one of you put the kettle on? Skip says he is thirsty as hell and the new hands job is always tea boy." Smiling he raced off to the wheelhouse.

"Find anything in his pockets?" I asked to Lachie's

"Just a wallet, pack of cigarettes, lighter, couple of spare clips in his boots but apart from that nothing."

"Let me guess Noblesse cigarettes?"

"Indeed they are Andy. Give that man a Sherlock Holmes award!"

It was bad enough at times having to listen to Lachie's warped and at times twisted sense of humour, but now I had to put up with Iceland's answer to the Chuckle Brothers.

"Is there anything in the wallet?"

"Just a few quid and a girl's picture along with a piece of paper with some sort of telephone number on it" Hans said as he emptied the contents on the table, He even took the guys Zippo Lighter to pieces, to make sure there was nothing hidden inside of it. Lachie was now re-dressed in the man's shirt, trousers, and jacket. He had the coat laying on the bench seat, in what passed for a dining table in the galley. The boat was starting to rise and fall as it crested the bigger waves clearing the shore. When we hit the sea proper it would just be a swell that we would have to deal with. The physics of waves closer to the shore tends to make them more violent and damaging. But we should be out of that soon enough. I was changing, and I knew it was not something I could stop. The recent events had forced me to become more of a survivor. They had shown me how easy it would be for me just not to exist. I was determined that my friends and I would get out of this shitstorm that we had been forced into. But it was not just my friends and I that I held dear, it was my family and their families. We were just being used as pawns in some violent game of chess where the players never leave their gilded towers and the pieces on the chess board are the ones that die for the player's mistakes. Lachie had tied the man's hands behind his back and his ankles were also tied together with coarse blue nylon netting cord. I could see that it must be painful but I did not care any more about how hard things were for him, on the other side of this dangerous board game. Hans had found a dirty oily rag, it looked like it had just come from the engines sump and had stuffed it in the man's mouth. Obviously he no longer cared either. Sandy came down to the galley.

"We are just approaching the three-mile marker we can see the shore but in this swell they won't see much of us. Also thanks for the tea. You can have a job any day Lachie"

"I can just see it in big bold lights The Swinging Tea Boy Sailor" laughed Hans, at Lachie's expense

To which Lachie offered him the bird. It was like being part of the Marx Brothers or worse the Three Stooges.

"So where do you want to go too from here Andy?"

"Do you have a sea Anchor? Sandy"

"We do have but it's not something we normally use. We are usually in port of a night. I can dig it out from the stowage compartment. Do you want me deploy it?"

"If you could please Sandy, give us a shout if you need any help."

"No need Andy, we just tie it off and throw it in the ocean, the sea does the rest. Care to tell me what you have in mind?"

"Not yet, I want it to be a surprise for our distinguished guest."

"You have not asked him anything more than his name yet Andy, care to enlighten your brothers in arms here?" asked Lachie

"I hope you will just be a little patient. What I have to say and ask, cannot be rushed. You should know that when fishing you have to know when to apply the right bait and just when, to pull the line in. Trust me you are about to see a whole new side to me. Our friend here is to be my fish."

Hans and Lachie exchanged looks but said nothing. The man looked from each one of us to another.

Kyla just growled. Stuart came down and said

"Skips got the sea anchor out and it taking the boat to the wind so she is a bit more stable on the water"

"Thanks Stuart, we are on our way up. Which of you two want to bring him on deck?"

Hans shrugged so Lachie grabbed the man by the heels and dragged him none to gently up the stairs, bouncing his head of the steps on the way up. He then threw him down bodily, on the foredeck.

ACT 38

"What now boss?" Lachie asked

"Sandy do you have a long rope about hundred feet or so?"

"I think so Andy. It's in the aft, I'll get it for you now."

"Stuart, when he comes back with it can you loop it through the pulley, on the swing jib. Also I want a small weight of some form, and a small buoy. If you can get them for me as well thanks."

Lachie wandered over to me and spoke quietly in my ear

"Care to tell me where you going with this?"

I leant forward and said

"Did you ever see the mutiny on the bounty?"

Sandy and Stuart came back and Stuart threaded the rope through the pulley of the winch jib, and then tied a small marker buoy to the other end.

"Where do you want the weight put on?"

"About ten feet from the buoy please Stuart. And then take the buoy and the weight to the front of the boat and wait there, Sandy can you turn the props off please?"

Sandy said nothing but went up to the wheel house and engaged the clutch, leaving the engines running so that everything still worked on the boat. Then he came back to the deck. I tied the other end of the rope through the man's ankles

"Stuart can you drop the buoy and weight to the other side just in front of the pointy end of the boat. Lachie can you grab that hook and catch the buoy as she comes up on the side, then pull the rope up and chuck it on the deck, best tie it off when you have pulled up the slack"

"Are you going to do what I think you are going to do?" Sandy asked.

"Sandy these bastards have taken your daughter and his fiancé." I said pointing to Stuart. And then I continued.

"They will probably kill her if we can't get her back. They have tried to kill me, and my friends, they tried to kill my father. They are the ones that blew my home up. They tried the same thing at Lachie's, only we caught them first. They tried to kill us several times since then. They even just killed my dad's dog. They would kill every one of us here right now, if we gave them the chance. You can go down below if you don't have the stomach for this. I would think none the less of you if you did. You are a good man. I am not the man you remember. They changed all that."

"If it's just the same to you, I will stay" he said and stared intently at me with eyes that had seen many things in a long life. Some good and some bad. He knew this would be filed away in the bad section.

"Are you sure?" I asked, Thus allowing him a chance to change his mind.

"Aye"

"Stuart?"

"I know what you are doing and I am staying"

"OK folk's and for the benefit of our new friend, well friend, is possibly a bit of a stretch. We shall call you an unwelcome visitor. The Rhodian Code has the first record of this, as a punishment. However over the years and in every sea in the world, it has been used by almost every seafaring nation. In German it is Hellhole, in Swedish it is Kólhalning, in Danish and Norwegian it is Kolhaling. Of course we speak English here and it was probably most famously demonstrated in the film Mutiny on the Bounty. No prizes for guessing the punishment. It is Keel-Hauling. Now it would probably be much nicer for you if this was a modern fishing boat with a smooth steel hull, but alas for you, Sandy is not a rich skipper and has to make do with this albeit a very nice fishing boat. However, she is old, and of a clinker construction. And barnacles just love these old wooden hulls, and the skippers of these, unlike the owners of the steel hulled boats don't clean them off as often as they should. That would mean re-corking and bitumen paint and then a complete repaint of the hull. So Mr... We shall refer to you as Mr No Pants from now, as I don't know your name and even if I did, that would not be important. You will guess that the hull is kind of rough. In olden days, they would haul you under the keel a set number of times. This of course would depend on the crime you committed. And sailors were not always guilty. They had just to be accused of a crime to warrant the punishment. In order for you to know what you will be in for, should you chose at any point to lie to me or just refuse to answer me, then of course I have to show you what will happen. This means Mr No-Pants that you are going in the cold, cold, North Sea. By the way if you should see any damage whilst you are inspecting the keel. Please feel free to report it to Mr Sandy the Skipper, in order for him to carry out timely repairs. Lachie can you take his gag out as we don't want him to choke"

I untied the man's hands from behind him and retied them at the front then I tied the lose end of the rope, that was laid upon the deck and tied it off, through his tied wrists. The other end of the rope, which was looped through the pulley, I tied to his ankles. The man started screaming and throwing himself around the deck trying to get out of the way. We now had a complete loop of rope that went under and over the boat. Mr No-Pants was the link that kept both ends together.

"Please, Please, Please. You don't have to do this I will tell you whatever you want. I beg you don't please don't do it." He screamed at me.

"Start the winch please Skipper"

The winch lifted the man from the deck and he hung face down towards the deck. I eased the winch over the side of the boat.

"One of us is going to have to take up the slack up on the other end of the rope" I said.

Lachie came over to me and whispered in my ear.

"Are you fucking nuts? Andy this is not you, I don't even think it is me?"

"What would you do if someone hurt your dad?" I replied

"Sorry, point taken. I will take the other end of the

rope."

"Sure you two want to stay?" I said to Sandy and Stuart.

Both looked like they did not, but I had to hand it to them they stood their ground. This whole thing was changing many more people, including innocent civilians, who were about to take part in a punishment, that had formally been abolished since 1853. It was no doubt against the Geneva Convention, the one saving grace in that is that the Geneva Convention did not apply to private militia or to spies. I was actually sickened by what I was about to do. Although I had no doubt in my mind that he would not tell the truth until he had experienced this at least once and if he was a hard nut perhaps twice. He needed to know I was mortally serious about this.

ACT 39

The first written jurisprudence of the sea, was written approximately eight hundred years before the birth of Christ. It gave immense powers to the master of any ship. And although only tiny extracts of it still exist, it became the foundation for all the contemporary Maritime law that is known today. The Greek Island of Rhodes was a prominent merchant heart in a time before Roman Armies were marching across Europe and North Africa. When they did eventually take their war and trade ships to the seas they also took a mercantile law with them. This they referred to as Lex Rhodian, meaning, Law of Rhodes. In short it gave the captain of the ship, the power over all the people on his ship or boat. This was at the period of time and still to a certain degree, an omnipotent power over life and death as well as the goods and chattels on his vessel. It did not matter if the Captain was outranked by any on board, not even a King himself, had greater power when at sea. There were a few downsides to it though. If the ship was transporting a merchant's goods, such as Flax or honey, then the skipper would have to guarantee that no damage became of that consignment, and that none of his crew would steal it. For if that were to come about, it would be the captain that would pay the price. If nonetheless the ship were to founder in stormy waters, then the captain could jettison the Cargo, to lighten the load. Where upon reaching land, then it would be up to a court there, to determine if this storm had been caused by the Gods, or if the captain had either deliberately taken his boat into dangerous waters. If they found it was the Gods then there would be no price to pay, but if negligence were the cause, then the Captain would pay. Punishment on a boat for a crew member who had upset the captain or crew would be decided, and provided by the captain. This could be loss of pay for something like tardiness, to death for something like stealing. There were more minor punishments, like flogging with a cat of nine tails. This was less of a flogging and more of a flailing of skin and flesh from the bones of the unlucky sailor. Often men would die from this minor punishment. The Cat of Nine had nothing to do with cats or the number of strands in this whip. There was in fact no real name for it in the ancient world, for it. This was a whip whose long talons of braided and knotted leather of cotton. Often the strands were knotted around bits of broken pottery or glass and sometimes even arrow heads. The consequence being than when whipped against the bare flesh, it would literally cut to the bone and tear the flesh and muscle away. If the flogged person, did not die from the blood loss or shock, then they would most likely die from septicaemia. They would then just be thrown overboard, because they could no longer work and become food for the sharks. There was no space on a ship for a man who could not work. Invariably in the early days of shipping the Captain was the individual who personally delivered the punitive punishment. Around this time some sadist who never managed to get a place in the history books, decided that a great sea borne punishment, would be to Keel Haul the transgressor. This would involve throwing the convicted person over the prow of the ship with a rope tied around his hands in such a manner as they would be forced under the front of the ship. Then the rope would be let out the unfortunate individual would slide under the keel, to hopefully resurface that the stern of the boat. Were they to survive this ordeal, then the man would be considered to have been punished and the matter would be struck from the records. Many years later, some even more evil captain, revised this method of keel hauling. Such that the guilty person would be attached to a rope that went from port to starboard underneath the boat. This would allow for the time under water to be decreased. This did not however mean that the punishment was more humane. Because the said captain, also decided that the sailor could then be keel hauled several times for his crimes. They would even allow the person to recover between the hauling. Also this was the first true Hauling. As the rope would be kept taut by sailors on either side of the boat so that the criminals bare body would be dragged tight up against the barnacle laden hull. The result was not too dissimilar to a flogging or flailing. The sharp barnacles would scrub and slice the skin as they were hauled, from one side of the boat to the other. Then because captains did not want to witness the face of the person they were punishing. They modified this punishment by tying cloths or canvas bags over the person's head before they entered the water. In short this was the first form of water boarding. This punishment that is still in use to this day by numerous, modern and so called civilised countries. Although most would reject that they use this variety of torturous punishment to extract information, whereby their victim is allowed to feel that he or sometimes even she, is dying by drowning. It happens, no matter what government denials there are. So this is what I was going to do. Not just because I desired information. I craved much more than that. In an almost feral manner, I wanted pure vengeance. I wanted to inflict a natural inherent fear of him dying, a long and drawn-out death, and I wanted to inflict as much pain as I could. Any information that he might spew forth, would be a bonus.

"Sandy can you drop him about four feet!"

"You're serious?"

"Yes Sandy I am"

I went over to the opposite side of the boat and took up the excess slack, so that now his hands were pulled against the side of the hull. The remainder of the rope was now likewise flush up against the bottom of the boat. Sandy, let out the rope from the jib winch. The man started screeching and promising to tell the truth.

"They do say that most sailors died, while they were being Keel Hauled. Most drowned but some of them, their hearts just gave out from the fear, of what was just about to happen to them. Which category do you think you fall into Mr No Pants?" I shouted

He screamed and thrashed against the bindings. Then he puked all down the side of the boat. Lachie came over and whispered in my ear.

"Let me play the good cop, perhaps he will talk."

I looked my friend square in the eye, I was convinced he could see that I was filled with nothing short of maniacal hatred for the living thing, that was currently hanging upside down from the jib. Inside I was having a struggle with my own emotions. Two days ago I would have thought such a barbaric act, to be completely out with my thoughts, let alone my ability to carry a despicable inhumane action to it fruition. Who was I now? Was I Andy McPhee a compassionate and moderate man, with a care for his fellow mankind? Or was I now a monster of the human race, where all that mattered was the mission? Was it just pure and unadulterated vengeance? Was I doing this to rescue another soul, or because my own soul itself was dammed? I wanted to scream out and smash my own head against something hard."

"Please Andy let me try? Lachie whispered

I just looked at my friend, and let him do the right thing, I did not try to stop him, nor did I give any indication to Mr No Pants. Lachie went over to the jib and spoke with him. Then he came back to me.

"What say you just dunk him and not keel haul. I have told him you will do it. He is shitting himself. At this point in time, he believes he is going to be hauled. What if we tie a shirt around his face? So that he can't see. Then just dunk for just one minute. If his body is dunked to the waist, then the feel of the boat rocking on the water, will have the same effect as water boarding, without the reality of actually ripping him to pieces. What do you say? I know that the last week has not been what you signed up for. I also know, we are trapped in it. At some point this whole state of affairs will come to a conclusion. If we survive, do you want to be remembered for a monstrous act like this? It will make you hate yourself forever. PLEASE Andy?"

"I am sorry Lachie. I don't know what's gotten into me. You are right, do it your way, and have Hans help you. I will be in the wheelhouse. Send Sandy and Stuart in there too."

I watched as Lachie took a sweatshirt from Stuart, Then Sandy and Stuart joined me in the wheel house. Hans reversed the Jib hoist. Then Lachie tied the sweatshirt good and tight around Mr No Pants face. Hans then lowered the winch, until Mr No Pants was immersed into the frigid and cruel waters of the North Sea. Hans lowered him down until all that remained out of the water, were the man's knees to feet. I watched as he battled against the bindings. Thrashing about, like a large fish trying to escape from a hook. They kept him in the water for about one minute. And then they pulled him up for thirty seconds. When he was out of the water, Lachlan shouted and slapped the man. Then they repeated the entire procedure.

"I want to say how sorry I am to you Sandy and also to you Stuart. That you have had to witness the barbarity, and to see a side of me that I never knew I had. I know you thought you knew Lachie and me as respectable folks, but we have changed. Things have come about, that you would not believe, even if I could tell you. Things like this change a man into a monster."

"Andy you are still a good man. I know you are doing this out of anger, not just at this man and the things the he has done. But you are grief stricken for the loss of your father's companion. Lachie has saved you. He is a strong man, both morally and physically. Stick with him. I believe you will get my daughter returned to me. Just try not to be the man who has to do everything all by himself. You have friends, good friends. Let them be a guide to you. I, would have let you do what you were going to. I would have done it myself. However, I doubt if I could have lived with the guilt. But that said, I would do anything to save my little girl."

He put his weather beaten hands on my shoulders. I could see his steel grey eyes, were glassy with tears of pain, partly for his daughter, partly because of the man he thought he knew, was in danger of becoming a man he did not want to know. I put my own palm on his cheek a single tear ran from the corner of his tired eyes, then it rolled down his crazed and weather-beaten face, before it rolled over my hand and was lost. Then I pulled him to me, hugged him and said

"Thank you Sandy"

I went back out from the wheelhouse and onto the deck

"Pull him in" I shouted

ACT 40

They winched him up and swung the jib back over the boat. Then Hans lowered him down onto the deck. His boxer shorts were now down around his ankles. He lay on his back gasping and puking up sea water. I walked over to where he lay. And then I removed the sweatshirt from around his head. Laying on the deck with his hands tied together and his ankles similarly so, but extended above his naked and wet. The wind was approaching from the North East and blowing the crests of the waves into our faces. It was enough to make me shiver, and I was appropriately clothed for winter. He was not. His body was convulsing on the bare wooden deck boards. Under normal circumstances was I to come across a man in such critical distress. I would be attempting, to provide assistance to him. My anger had softened but not entirely. Lachie grabbed him by his hair and slapped him once again.

"Name?"

The man coughed and spluttered.

"NAME?"

Mr No Name, said nothing, he just lay there shivering. I knew without any doubt. He was in the initial process of hypothermia. This could kill quite easily.

"Last chance you mother fucker" Lachie shouted "Or you are going back in for good"

He whispered something that I could not hear. I knew he would lose consciousness soon, so we would have to work fast.

"I say we feed the fish" I said

Lachie grabbed him by his hair and dragged him over to the side railings of the boat. Hans started the winch motor. The man struggled and started screaming.

"No. No, no more PLEASE!!! Please don't I will talk. Quasim! My name is Quasim" he spluttered between trembling lips.

"Finally" I said more as a way of calming myself than as a statement to him.

"OK you bastard! Where is the girl you took?"

"She is still in the Lighthouse on the rocky Island"

"Who is the man with her?"

"I don't know"

Hans started the winch and the man's legs lifted off the deck

"Please I don't know"

"Why and what are you doing here?"

"We have to get something from the Rocks"

"What rocks?"

"The ones at the old nuclear station"

"What is it you are getting?"

"A box, something big, please that is all I know, please it is the truth. In the name of Allah and of his prophet Mohamed, peace be upon him."

"Get him down and get him inside please, but keep his hands tied. Then find a blanket and wrap him in it. He might actually have more use to us alive"

I turned and went to the wheelhouse

"Sandy can you pull the Sea Anchor and make for The Skerries? But if you could stay on the blind side of the Eastern Isle, at least until it gets dark. Can you do that?"

"OK Andy, what about him?"

"Let him warm up. Give him a cup of coco or something. If you have some old Oil Skins on board, when he is dry, He should put them on. Don't worry, one of us or the dog will watch him at all times. Just you concentrate on getting us to the Skerries in one piece. OK?"

He gave me the thumbs up and went about making the boat ready to get there.

I looked through the man's possessions, meagre as they

were. The picture of the girls was probably his wife as a high school sweetheart. It was about ten years old by the look of it. I was not up on my international dialling codes. So I would have to use one of our throw away telephones, then just make the call and see who answers. However, getting a mobile phone signal out here would prove extremely difficult, if not impossible. The Israeli cigarettes were also of some interest to me. The man we had in our custody was definitely not Israeli. If I was a betting man, I would have put his accent as American or Canadian. It was time for a little one on one, with Mr No Pants once again.

"OK Quasim, so you are a Muslim, but which country are you from? There are so many things that don't add up about you."

"I am Canadian, I live in West Toronto."

"So why would you want to come to Scotland and attack poor fishermen?"

"I used to work for Garda-World, but they would no longer employ me"

"Why was that?"

"Do you know who Garda-world are?"

"Please enlighten me"

"They are a company not unlike Black-Water services in America, or the Westminster Services in the United Kingdom."

"That means nothing to me."

"They are Armed Private Security consultants. Mostly operating in dangerous areas of the world, where kidnapping and ransom is a high threat. They are mostly made up of ex-military. They select their men from the likes of the SAS, Delta Force, Navy Seals and I was previously in the CSO. That is to say Canadian Special Forces. I was chosen for the Garda-world because my father is from Aleppo, in Syria. I am ahl as-sunnah wa l-jam-ah. You would know this as Sunni Muslim. I had been attached to a protection detail for a prominent Canadian businessman. He was there to oversee a contract for Suncor. We were attacked by a Shia rebel group working in conjunction with Ansar Allah. My charge was taken and most of our detail, were either killed or wounded. I escaped without injury. When I returned to Canada, then Garda-world sacked me. I then applied to an advert for Private security operatives wanted for an international project. The pay was to be £100,000 for one month's work, with half of the money to be paid up front, and the remainder on completion of the contract."

"But you are Canadian, and yet you have Israeli cigarettes? So that does not tally with you being a Sunni Muslim. From my understanding almost every person of Arab descent, hates the Israelis."

"I don't care about faith the way my father does. I have a family in Canada. I only want to provide a good life for my family, in as short a time as possible. It is Just about the money. The man I am working with. The man on the Lighthouse Island, he is from Israel. He gave me the cigarettes. He was in Shayetet 13. They are like your SAS only they have no morals."

"Are you saying they have no morals, because you are Arab and he is a Jew?"

"No, No, No I am saying it because he is an animal who enjoys his work. If he thinks that you will capture or kill him, he will kill the girl in front of your eyes, just because he can."

"What is his name? And what in the way of equipment does he have on the Island with him?

"He is called Betzalel, I do not know his last name. He had just an Automatic Machine pistol and a knife. He claims that he has killed more men with the knife, than with a gun, because he likes to feel a person die in his hands. He is sick."

"What is the mission?"

"I told you we are to collect a package and then it will be collected from us. I do not know what the package is. We are contacted by an intermediary. He tells us where, when and what to do. I do not know his name"

"How does he contact you?"

"A note or letter makes it way to us. I met him only twice. The first time was in Canada. When I attended the interview for this job, it was him that gave me the money. The second time was here in Scotland. That was two days ago. We took the girl about ten days ago. The man came here two days back and said something about another group working and they were getting too close. They knew you had been to see the owner of this boat. I was to make sure that the girl was used to force the owner of the boat, to comply with all the requests. I was given the paper with the telephone numbers on. This was to be given to another man."

"Who is the other man?"

"I don't know"

"Then how do you know who to give it to?"

"Just that he will come to me and ask for the paper"

"How would he come to you?"

"I don't know. In this profession you learn not to ask questions. Just do as you are told."

"Do you know which country this dialling code is for" I pointed to the numbers on the paper.

"No I don't."

"Tell me why I should not kill you? Or just throw you into the sea?"

"No reason, except if you were going to kill me. You would have done so on the deck of the boat. You are not a mercenary."

"And how do you know that?"

"Because you struggle with your conscience, I saw you on the deck and I heard the doubt in your soul."

I made sure that the bindings on Quasim were good and strong without impeding the blood flow to his hands.

"Watch him Kyla"

Kyla sat down directly in from of him.

"By the way Quasim, do not eyeball my dog. She will take eyeballing as a challenge. Trust me, that is one battle, you would not win, even if you were not restrained."

"I left the galley and went up to the wheelhouse. I could see Lachie and Stuart out on the deck talking. In the wheelhouse Hans and Sandy were having a coffee. Now we were out to sea proper, we were clear of the harsher waves that were pummelling the shoreline. Now out here the swell was steady, the boat rose and then would fall into the deep but smooth troughs. The wind seemed to have reduced somewhat. And the snow had turned to steady rain. I knew 'The Man' would probably not want us to jeopardise any perceived mission that he had for us, by attempting a rescue of Rosemary. However, in my newly elected role of team leader, I would be making an executive decision on this matter.

"How far is it to the Island, to the East of the Skerries?" I asked of Sandy.

"We are about one hour out."

"How much cover will that give us from the other Isle?"

"If we keep to the East we can't be seen, but I am going to have to go around the north side and lay too."

"Do you have a plan yet Andy?"

"Yes I think so Sandy."

I said looking at his charts.

"It's risky but has to be worth a try. I know that we can't use running lights. But if you had a pair of night vision goggles on do you think that you could get us in close enough to here" I said pointing to what looked like a natural harbour formed by high rocks on three sides. It was almost like a lagoon with the steep rocks on its sides forming a natural breakwater. A large ship could not make it in, so I was banking on Sandy's years of skill to be able to take this medium sized fishing boat in.

"I don't know Andy; I am not sure how much water is under the hull there. We can drop the large rubber buoys to the sides of the boat and hopefully they will stop us from being smashed to pieces on the cliffs."

"If you get us in there, can you hold the boat in there for about thirty minutes?"

"If I can get us in there I can stay as long as you need. Getting out could be a problem though. It is too narrow to turn the boat around, as you can see it is a long gully but not very wide. Boats are not like cars they don't steer well in reverse. If it saves my daughter, I don't mind losing the boat. Do you think you can save her?"

"I can't promise anything Sandy. We should have the edge on their man as there are three of us and we have the element of surprise. He would expect your boat to arrive at the other side of the Island. Consequently, that is where he will be watching for you."

"Just bring her back please"

"What do you want me to do Andy?" Hans asked

"I think the best use of our resources is to have you and me providing support, with Lachie on point. You have done Hostage rescue training so you can give Lachie some tips. The only training, I have had in that department was at CDE. So if you could make a plan. I would assume, he has her in the lighthouse, because he is not going to want to be out in this weather."

"A light house is not an easy thing to take Andy. He has the high ground and it will be a single entry building. If we enter through the door, he would cut us to pieces with his fire. And we would never even get a shot at him. Unless he goes to a door or a window the AS50 will be no use. Even if he does he will use Rosemary as a human shield. We have to draw him out somehow. If we can get him in the open, we can easily take him out. So whilst I think under normal circumstances you would be correct. However, I think we should use Lachie to draw the man out. He is already dressed in Quasim's clothes. It is dark and they do not have street lights here. So unless Lachie is very close to the other man, then he should pass for Quasim. I will go and get Lachie and we will work a plan out."

ACT 41

Hans went off to get Lachie, while I studied the maps and charts that Sandy had laid out. There were no trees or real vegetation for us to hide behind. But in our favour we would be coming at the Lighthouse from the blind side of the Island. On the down side Lachie would somehow have to work his way around to the front side of the lighthouse and trick Betzalel to come out into the open. When Hans and Lachie came back to the wheelhouse, I worked a rough plan with them. We could climb the rocks of the natural harbour. Then Lachie would go with Hans towards the south of the Island and I would go north, Hans would then break away from Lachie so that we formed a triangle, with Lachie at the bottom point. Hans and I would both be carrying our AS50's and Lachie would have a pair of Sig Sauer's. Hans and I would take up positions to either side of the lighthouse about two hundred yards out. This in effect meant, that we were both on the edge of the Island. We would have the door of the Lighthouse effectively caught in our crossfire. Lachie would approach from the front of the lighthouse door. He would attempt to call Betzalel out on some pretext or other. Then either Hans or I would take him out. God, there I was again, getting ready to kill another. Though from what Quasim had told me about his friend, the world would be a much better place without him in it. But who was I to be judge jury and executioner. My moral compass was completely broken or so it seemed to me. Hans, Lachie and I went back to the galley where

Quasim was sat and Kyla was still watching him.

"What do you call your friend on the Island?"

"I told you is name is Betzalel"

"I know you told me his name, but what do YOU call him?"

"I don't know what you mean."

Hans grabbed the man by the scruff of the neck and said to him

"If you can't help us then you are no use to us"

"Bez we call him Bez!"

"I can promise you one thing Quasim if you have lied to us about this, your death will be very slow and very very painful"

"In the name of Allah and his Prophet Mohamed Peace be upon him. It is the truth we call him Bez like the insect you know like honey bez. Say it like Beezs."

"You mean BEES?"

"Yes yes Bees."

"OK you got that Lachie? Can you say it like this shit?"

"Aye Hans, I have it, Beez!"

Stuart came down to the galley

"We are standing off, by the eastern Isle. The skipper says that it is actually dark enough to make to the inlet to the Lighthouse Island. And he wants to know if you can all come up. I have already put buoys and tires around the boat to protect it as much as we can"

"OK Stuart. Keep an eye on this fellow. If he moves hit him with this" I said as I gave him a cast Iron skillet pan from the stove, and don't hold back hit him hard! OK?"

"I got it. Good luck to you."

"Thanks"

I wanted to add we are going to need it, if there was to be any chance of us pulling this off without one of us getting hurt, or worse one of us getting killed or getting Rosemary killed.

"When we were inside the wheelhouse Sandy had already switched off the running lights and killed all the other lights on deck. We used Red light torches to look at the map and Hans equipped Sandy with a set of night vision goggles. We went over the plan one more time and Sandy set out for the

Lighthouse Island. I went down to the galley and gave Stuart a Red Light torch. I switched all the rest of the lights inside the boat off.

"Keep that torch in one hand and the skillet in the other, as I told you before, if he so much as moves, hit him really hard. We will be back soon with Rosemary."

As we approached the natural inlet, the three of us went on to the deck. Sandy had asked, that there be one of us on the bow and one each to starboard and port. Although there were protective buoys around the boat there could be rocks higher, and those that we could not see under the hull, that would pose a danger to the boat. Fortunately getting in to this natural lagoon proved a lot easier than we had imagined. Lachie made the four-foot jump, to the rocks, I thought for one awful moment he was going to slip and fall into the gap between the boat and the rock face. He regained his footing and set about tying of the bow and stern. By tying the boat on the at port side, we were able to hook ropes around the jutting rocks and then we added extra buoys to stop any damage to the boat. I tossed my AS50 over to Lachie and followed that with Hans's rifle. All three of us were wearing our Storno throat mikes and ear pieces. Then Hans and I made our jump for the cliff. We had to wait for the boat to be on the rise before jumping. We both made it without incident. Having climbed the rock face, we rested at the top and then did a full equipment check.

I had insisted, that Lachie wear the full body armour under his clothing. This made him look slightly fatter than Quasim. Lachie was the one who would be getting closest to Beez. If he was made, then I knew Beez would have no qualms in shooting to kill.

"Right as soon as Hans and I are in place. Then you will have to make your way around to the front of the Lighthouse. Keep as close to the edge of the cliff, because the front of the lighthouse is all open ground. As soon as you are in place we will have you and the front door of the lighthouse covered."

"Lachie, if you get made, the chances are in the darkness he will go for a body shot. If you get hit STAY down, even if it is just the armour that is hit. If he operates the way, I think he does then he will want to kill you with a knife. If this scenario comes in to play we will have you covered and will drop him before he can make it to you. If he has the girl with him when he comes out from the Lighthouse, unless we, that is, Andy and I, have a clear line of shot with no chance of any bullet going through him and into her. Then you should take a shot straight on with your Sig. If he does not have her with him, then that means that he either has her hidden in the Lighthouse or God forbid tied up somewhere outside. So if she is with him and we have a clear shot then we take him out with a kill shot. Don't mess around trying to take him prisoner if he has the hostage. On the other side of this same hostage coin, then we need him alive, to get the girl back so a wound shot unless he tries to kill Lachie then and only then we shoot to kill. Got it?"

"Yes I understand Hans" I said, and then Lachie said

"I understand too, but still don't like being bait for this nutter"

"Now Lachie you know that is what Rock Apes do"

ACT 42

I set off and crouch ran to a good vantage point, which put me at about a forty-five-degree angle to the right hand side of the Lighthouse door. While Hans and Lachie headed around the top.

"I am in lower position. I have a full sweep view of the front right side of the door"

I waited until Hans radioed in.

"Top side full cover. Lachie's heading down."

"Hans keep an eye on the door I will track Lachie."

I set the BAE sight to thermal and in this cold it clearly showed Lachie crouch running across to the dock area towards the front of the Lighthouse. Then he slowly moved towards the front using a worn footpath. He stumbled slightly a couple of times. When he was about fifty yards out I saw him put down his backpack and take out a Sig and tuck it in his waistband at his back. The other he tucked into the pocket of the coat he was wearing. I switched to night view and saw Lachie in high resolution black and white. In this mode he looked almost identical to Quasim. I zoomed out so that I had a better view over my field of vision.

I could see Lachie to the left of my sight and Hans to the right he was covering the door to the lighthouse as well as watching my back.

"You ready Lachie?"

"I would be more ready if you were the bait Andy"

"Ah the life of a Rock Ape"

"Hans?"

"Got you both, Lachie don't get any closer than 75 yards"

"Got it, here we go guys." Lachie replied

Lachie walked slowly towards the door. When he was seventy-five yards out, he shouted

"Hey Beez"

No response

"Hey Beez we gotta go man!"

I had to hand it to Lachie he even sounded a bit like our Canadian captive.

"Come on Beez the man says we gotta go" Lachie shouted

"Lachie try not to overplay the part, don't say too much" said Hans in our earpieces

A minute later the door to the lighthouse opened. And the light spilled out. I switched my sight back to thermal. There were two heat sources. The smaller of the two was standing to the front. He was using her as a human shield.

"Hold your fire, he has Rosemary in front of him and it looks like he has a gun at her back."

"Roger" said Hans

"Boats here Beez we gotta go" shouted Lachie

Rosemary took a couple of steps in front of Beez. I quickly switched back to high resolution and zoomed in a little. He had a rope or something like it tied around her neck and he held on to it with his other hand This made it impossible for Lachie to get a shot and the angle also made it difficult for shot Hans. I would not be able to take him out without the risk of harming Rosemary.

"Lachie see if you can get him to follow you back down the path that way when he gets level with us we could have a shot."

"Roger that I will try" It was like watching a ventriloquist. Lachie spoke to us without moving his lips."

"Come on Beez we have to go, bring the girl"

Beez took a few steps forward and Rosemary led the way then he stopped.

"I think he suspects" said Hans

"Why are we going early tonight Quasim?" Beez shouted down towards Lachie's back.

"What's he doing Andy?" Lachie asked

"Nothing he just stopped. Rosemary is about three feet in front of him. He has her held with the rope and what looks like a gun on her back."

"Ask the man he's on the boat" Lachie shouted

Rosemary took one step forward. The man seemed to be thinking

"Andy, can you zoom in on the arm with the gun?"

I zoomed

"Roger"

"You have a choice here, I can't hit him, without hitting the Girl, Lachie is probably blown. And you have the shot"

Literally in the blink of an eye, everything changed, it seemed to me that it all became like a slow motion replay from some Quinton Tarantino movie. I pressed the button on the Scope it put a dot on the man's arm. He looked at Lachie, and then he actually looked at the red dot that had mysteriously appeared on his arm. His knowledge and experience as a specialist soldier computed it in his brain. But caught by surprise his brain was just that bit slower than my finger on the trigger of the AS50. He made a half turn towards me about a quarter of a second too late. By the time he heard the shot and saw the flash his entire right arm from about midpoint between shoulder and elbow had separated itself from the rest of his body. The force of the impact, spun him back around in the opposite direction so that instead of facing me, he was now facing Hans. At the sound of the shot Lachie had already turned around and was racing full tilt up towards the front of the Lighthouse. Hans was up and running. I kept cover watch over them. The man was dropping to the ground and Rosemary was panicking and screaming. The man slumped against the wall. Rosemary could not run, the man seemed determined not to let her go. Beez saw his arm still with the gun in its grip. I could almost see him computing in his brain. The adrenalin of the sudden shock was not allowing the immense pain to register with his central nervous system. Lachie was about halfway towards Rosemary. I watched as he raised his gun and shouted for Rosemary to GET DOWN. Then Beez let her go and she ran towards me. This suddenly blocked my sight of the man

"Get down Rosemary for Christ's sake Get down" I shouted

But it was no use she just kept running towards me. I saw the man topple over and his uninjured arm reached out for the gun. I saw for a fraction of a second the gun come up. I could not get a shot because of Rosemary. I knew also that Hans was running down towards the doorway of the lighthouse. I heard a burst of small arms fire, and then unmistakeable sound of Hans's 50 cal. Then silence.

"Get down Rosemary for Christ's sake. Get down girl"

This time she did as I asked and I re-acquired the target at the door. Due to the fact, that most of his head was no longer there. I knew that Hans had provided a kill shot. I ran towards where Rosemary was now crouched. I knelt down next to her

"Hello Rosemary, you are safe now, your dad and Stuart are waiting for you."

"whhh-oo are you?"

"Don't you remember me Rosemary, it's me Andy McPhee"

"What are you doing here? I thought you're in the Army or something"

"It's a long story, but you're safe now that's all that matters"

ACT 43

"ANDY!"

"What's up Hans?"

"Get over here fast."

I stood up. Hans was now by the path that Lachie had been running up. Lachie was on the ground.

"No!" I shouted to no one

I grabbed Rosemary's hand and ran with her to Hans and Lachie.

"Rosemary this is Hans he will keep you safe OK?"

She said nothing but moved a few yards away from Lachie with Hans. Lachie was having trouble breathing and there was quite a lot of blood. I took out my KaBar and sliced open his shirt and then cut the webbing that was holding the body armour into place. From the look of things, he had been hit in the chest several times. All but one of them had hit the armour. But one had hit him just below the collar bone. The wound had bled down the front of his white shirt making things look a lot worse than they really were. I knew that when we removed all of his clothing he would carry some ugly bruising and possibly a few cracked ribs. I opened my battlefield medical pouch. I squirted some antibiotic powder into the wound and then injected the wound with Xstat. This was a new battlefield blood clotting agent. Then I attached a blast dressing to the wound after that I gave him an ampoule of Morphine. Lachie was just about able to breath and was coming back to full consciousness.

"Fuck! Fuck! Fuck, the bastard was fast. And Fuck me, this really fucking hurts"

"You are luckier than you know Lachie. If he had gone for a head shot you, would have bought the farm. Now I have done a temporary patch job on you and I have just shot you full of Morphine. It might make you feel a little sick and you will get a little high with it as well. I think Hans killed the guy, on account of Beez has no head. Rosemary can you come over here and sit with Lachie, while Hans and I go and do a quick check on things around here. Then we will get you back to Stuart and your dad, how's that sound?"

"What do I do for him? I don't know what to do. I don't think I can"

"Rosemary come and sit with me, I am OK just a little nick is all. I promise I don't bite" Lachie had a way with the girls that seemed to put them all at ease

"Come and sit with this war wounded hero"

Trust Lachie to lay it on thick. Still it had the desired effect.

"Just make sure he stays upright and that he keeps his arm in the sling. We'll be back in a minute or so." I swapped my rifle with Lachie for his pair of Sig Sauer's. After checking the magazines were full. I passed one over to Hans. I followed Hans to the Door where the body of Beez lay in a large pool of about seven pints of his life's fluid. It was not a pretty sight of torn skin shattered bone, and pulped brain matter. This was not the sort of scene a young girl should ever see. I picked up the Uzi and checked its clip. Empty he had fired a whole clip towards Lachie Taken in real time terms a tad over 2 seconds to send a hail of lead towards whatever was approaching. This fortunately was, a spray and run weapon and not all that accurate. All the same five or six bullets had hit Lachie in the chest and were we not better prepared, he would have surely died on this remote and thankless Island. Hans went through Beez's pockets and found cigarettes, lighter, two spare clips and some loose change. There were no communication devices on him. With Hans on one side of the door and me on the other,

"Remember house clearing at CDE. Just do the same here. You go low I will go high. On three, ready? One, Two,

Three"

I threw myself through the doorway and did a rapid check Left, Right and Up.

"Clear"

Hans came in behind me and went across to the far wall pointing his gun up the spiral staircase towards the first level. I ran up the first flight to the halfway point and brought my gun to bear on the opening to the first floor opening.

"Clear"

"Hans raced up past me to the edge of the opening and did a swift Right and Left of the open room on that floor. I ran halfway up the second flight towards the Light gallery of the light house.

"Clear"

Hans again ran past me to the doorway and waited whilst covering me I got to the landing, and then rolled in through the doorway going left, while Hans ran to the right.

"All clear" he called out

"So why would they have these guys, on here without communication. It makes absolutely no sense. They must have some way other than the boat to get in and out."

"Down there Andy"

"Ahhh"

There was a large white circle painted on the course grass to the side of the Lighthouse tower. With a large H painted inside it. Unless you were above it or it was a beautiful clear and sunny day you would not see it.

"They are planning on coming here at some point either to pick these men up or to bring something here. Come on Hans let's get Lachie and Rosemary back to the boat. We need to get him fixed up and we need to get ashore to see what is happening at Dounreay, then hopefully make contact with Jane and her team. We walked back down to the front of the Lighthouse. Down past the dead Israeli in the doorway, that was laid in a pool of his own blood. There was nothing we could or for that matter even want to do for him. It seems that I was becoming battle hardened in a very short period of time. I was more concerned with the health of my lifelong friend who had almost died, to save a young and innocent girl. When we reached Lachie we found Rosemary in full on nurse mode. And Lachie was lapping it up. He was the shining knight, who had ridden into the enemy camp and rescued the damsel in distress, and battled the dragon and other mythical monsters. I would have to make sure that Lachie cooled his ardour for the fair maiden and remember that she was betrothed, to the young fisherman on the boat.

"Time to go big boy" I said as Hans and I, helped him to his feet.

With his good arm over Hans's shoulder, and my arm around his waist, I handed Rosemary a torch and directed her to where her father's boat was hidden. Strangely enough it was a lot quicker going back to the boat, even with an injured man. When we got there we set up an improvised bosons chair. Now with the deck lights on it was a lot easier than it had been getting off in the dark. The wind had dropped even more and the swell had reduced. It looked like the storm was blowing through fast. Next across was Lachie followed by me. Hans untied the boat and the bosons chair and then made the jump landing firmly on the deck. Rosemary was being hugged and kissed by her father and her young man. We left them to it and carefully took Lachie down to the galley. I cleared the table and laid my friend on it. The morphine had kicked in and he was drowsy. I went upstairs to speak to Sandy.

"Sandy can we stay here for about an hour?"

"Andy for you and your friends I will do anything, hell you can even have the boat."

"Thanks for the offer Sandy but I don't want to be on the sea any more than I have to be. If I had wanted a life on the ocean wave, I would have joined the Navy. That said I may ask you to help us out a bit more before we finish this thing, whatever it is. Right now though I really need to go and see to Lachie."

"Aye, go and look after him and tell him I can never repay him for saving my daughter"

"I will do Sandy"

I went below and Hans was with Lachie. Quasim had moved to the furthest corner of the Galley and was trying to sink into its walls with fear. I went across to the table with Lachie on it. I grabbed my backpack with a proper medical kit in. Rosemary came down into the Galley.

"Hi Rosemary how are you?"

"I am fine just a little shaken up I guess. How is Lachie?"

"He will be fine but I need a little help. We are going to have to get this bullet out"

"Why don't you take him to the hospital in Kirkwall?"

"Trust me Rosemary we can't take him to a hospital, they would ask too many questions, that we could not answer. They would call the police. Again that would cause more problems than would be good for us. There is something going on that we can't tell you or anyone about. But if you are willing to help, I could use an extra pair of hand while I fix him up"

"I don't know anything about medicine Andy"

"Can you boil a large pan of water?"

"Yes"

"OK then please do that and when it is boiling can you put these instruments in and boil them for ten minutes."

"OK I can do that"

"Hans can you help me strip Lachie of everything above his waist. We will probably have to cut off the items that I have not already done so."

"OK Andy I am on it"

"*I feel good now I know that I would now...........*" Lachie started to sing in a James Brown voice. The morphine was making things good for him.

"Right, Lachie I am going to have to clean out all the Xstat clotting material and then I am going to have to find that bullet and any bits of cloth that may have got in there. I will give you a couple of injections in and around the area. When I first inject you it's going to hurt a bit OK?"

"No worries Andy I am floating" he slurred his reply.

I took off most of the kit I was wearing and stripped down to my Nomex. Then I put on a pair of neoprene surgical gloves, unwrapped a preloaded syringe of Lignocaine with adrenalin. I injected the local anaesthetic all around the wound and then a few more spots deeper inside the wound area. Most of the clotting sponge had gelled together into one large clot. I removed the larger chunks and flushed the wound with saline from my kit. This flushed out some more pieces of sterile clotting sponge. Fortunately, I had not gone too deep when I had injected the Xstat. I flushed the wound again which caused a fresh flow of blood. I unwrapped and laid out a sterile instrument sheet.

"OK Rosemary I need you to take the instruments from the boiling water and lay them on that blue sterile cloth next to me."

"Hans can you keep some pressure on the wound, while the instruments cool. Lachie I am going to give you another shot of local this time deeper into the wound. When it's done you should not feel any pain, when I dig around for the bullet. Its deep, but it does not look like he hit any major arteries or any of your bones. Lucky for you he was using a crap gun! You ready?"

"Go for it buddy"

"OK Lachie I am going to cut the wound to enlarge the entry, so that I can get my instruments in without causing any more damage than I have to. You are going to feel the pressure of the instruments inside you but if you feel any pain, just let me know, and I will give you some more local. Though you should be pretty numb by now"

I took a scalpel and made a lateral incision across the wound through the flesh and muscle, being careful not to nick any arteries. Then I inserted a probe following the line that I thought the bullet would have taken in a straight line. Luckily for Lachie it had, sometimes bullets enter a body and spin around and are difficult to locate without an X-ray.

"Lachie I have located the bullet and now I am going to take it out."

I took a pair of long handled artery forceps and carefully slid them into the wound until I felt them touch the bullet. Then I opened the forceps as much as I dared without causing further damage to Lachie's shoulder.

"Here goes Lachie. Please let me know, if at any point I am hurting you"

I slid the forceps forward another half inch and then closed them around the bullet, being very careful not to let go of it. I pulled it out in one slow and smooth movement. Then I dropped it and the forceps on the sterile instrument cloth that was laid out to my right hand side.

"It's out mate just got to clean it up and close you up, I'll only be another ten minutes."

I flushed the wound again and had Hans shine a light into the wound to make sure I had cleared all of the debris, that goes with getting shot through clothing. One final flush and dry off. Then I squirted some Neosporin antibiotic powder in and around the wound. Sutured him up and applied a topical dressing with self-adhesive sides. Then a larger dressing and bandage over the shoulder and under the arm. We helped him off the table and into a seat. I gave him a couple of 50mg Tramadol Hydrochloride capsules.

"These will help with the pain when the Morphine and local anaesthetic wear off. You were very lucky mate. Just take a look at the bruises on your chest and belly where the armour saved you. You are going to be sore for a few days. If you were in a medical centre, on camp. Then you would get two weeks off and a further four weeks' light duties. But I don't think I can offer you that, just take it easy for a few days if you can. Now lie down on that bunk and get some sleep. Rosemary, can you tell your dad to take us out to sea now?"

The next problem was Quasim. We had no facilities to imprison him, we could not just hand him to the police. We needed to talk. Lachie needed to rest. I waited for rosemary to return. When she did I spoke with her.

"Rosemary, do you think that you could watch over Lachie? And also keep an eye on him"

I pointed to Quasim.

"Yes if you make sure he is not able to hurt me"

I went over to Quasim and checked his bindings, then as an afterthought tied him to a hook on the bulkhead. Then I made a big show of cocking one of the Sig Sauer pistols.

"If he moves just point this at him and pull the trigger. Hans and I are going to talk with your Dad and Stuart. We will be in the wheelhouse if you need us OK?"

"Please don't be long"

"I won't, remember if he tries anything just point this gun at him and pull the trigger."

"OK"

ACT 44

Hans and I went up to the wheelhouse. Sandy had started the engine and was carefully extricating the boat from the natural rock harbour.

"Hello lads. How's Lachie doing?"

"He is sleeping. He will be sore when he wakes up. So long as the wound does not become infected he will be OK. Sandy we have a bit of a problem."

"What is that Andy?"

"Our prisoner, we can't take him with us. We can't leave him here in case a lighthouse man is sent here. We can't take him to the police and we can't just let him go. As he will just run back to his friends and tell tales."

"So what are you going to do with him?"

"I really don't know. Any of you got any ideas, on what to do with him."

"Technically he is a Pirate. As he came aboard my boat and forced me to take them here in the first place."

"What you gonna do Sandy? Make him walk the plank?" Hans asked him

"For what he did with my daughter I could easily do that"

"Sandy you are not a killer. Nor for that matter are Hans, Lachie or I. We are soldiers, battle is different."

"If you are not going to kill him, then what?" asked Stuart

"I don't know. Which is why Hans and I came up here to see if you had any ideas?

Nobody spoke for a long time. Then Stuart came forward.

"Why don't you cast him away on one of the many small rock islands around here? We could give him enough food for a week or so. No boat or ship would come near enough to one of these Islands for fear of getting holed. There's a small Island to the south of here that has a place where we could get close to the shoreline. And just put a life jacket on him and throw him over. Close to the shore the water is less than six foot deep. He would be OK for a week. There are some crags and caves there so he could find some shelter, providing he had enough provisions."

"I know where he is talking about, we used to drop creels there when the weather is calm in summer. There are a lot of un-fished lobster and crab grounds there." Sandy said

"Sandy can you show me on the charts, please?"

"See here? This spot Andy. We can get in there and be close to the shore and he can jump or swim to the shore."

Sandy took a ruler and drew two lines forming a cross on the chart.

"If you want to send some folks to rescue him at some time in the future they should go to these co-ordinates. 60°25'18.94"N by 0°43'43.12"W."

He wrote it down on a piece of paper and gave it to me. And I put it in my pocket.

"You sure you can get us in there?"

"If I can't then we are all fucked" He laughed."

"Let us just say that we are once again interpreting Rhodian's Law of the sea. Still I suppose it is better than attaching him to the prow of the boat and having him squashed as we ram another boat" I said

Sandy took the boat out into open water and we sat back and started to drink our coffee.

We were still talking when Rosemary burst into the Wheelhouse. Quasim was behind her with my Sig Sauer pointed at the side of her head he had his arm around her throat. Hans immediately went for his side arm. He had it halfway out

"Don't Fucking do it. Or I will put a hole through her

head that you can see all the way back to the beginning of time."

Hans let go of his pistol.

"So where do we go from here Quasim?" I asked.

"Take this boat back to Keiss."

"We were going there anyway Quasim. What are going to do when we get there?"

"I am going to call the man who hired us and let him have you. You three have been a real thorn in his side he will reward me. Then I am going home, to live in a life of luxury."

"OK it looks like you hold all the cards. Let the girl go to her dad. You have a gun on us and we can't move, sound fair to you?"

"Give me your fucking gun first."

Hans slowly took out his pistol. Ejected the magazine and then ejected the chambered round. Then he tossed it over on to the floor near Quasim.

"Now we have done that, let the girl go. You are holding all the cards. She is not a threat to you. Hell she could not even shoot you when you escaped. By the way how did you escape?"

"You forgot that a man has teeth in his mouth and if you let him have the ability to get to his hands then unless you are using wire or handcuffs then it is easy to escape"

"OK I will remember that in the future Quasim. Now let the girl go"

"Why should I do anything you tell me to?"

"Well I am not telling you to do anything. It would of course be your choice, and it would show you to be a powerful and brave man who has control. You are a brave Muslim man. Are you not Quasim? Remember your Quran. I have read the Quran, Quasim, and if my memory serves right, if you look at the passage 17:33. Then you will see that it says. Nor take life which Allah has made sacred except for just cause. And if anyone is slain wrongfully, we have given his heir authority to demand retaliation or to forgive, but let him not exceed bounds in the matter of taking life, for he is helped by the Law."

"What do you know of the law of Islam?"

"I know that Allah has said that the innocent must never be harmed. If you break his laws, you will definitely not get the seven vestal virgins and all that goes with it. You will go to hell, without redemption."

"Why would you a Christian, read our Quran."

"Was Jesus not one of the Prophets?"

"Very well you can have the girl. But now it is your turn to be punished"

He threw Rosemary towards her father, who caught her as she stumbled.

"Now Mr Andy and Mr Hans, we shall go out to the deck then you shall feel how cold the sea is when you are stripped naked. You will feel the same torture as you die as you have subjected me to. You, BOY come here, you will tie their hands."

We all moved to the deck area while Quasim covered us with my Sig Sauer. Hans whispered to me

"You got a plan to get us out of this one?"

"Let's see how it unfolds first."

"You know I can't swim?" Hans said

"But you do Sub Aqua training, and you live next to the sea!"

"Sub Aqua you don't have to be able to stay on the surface!"

"Oh well then you are fucked!" I said

"Thanks Andy that is a big help"

"SHUT UP. Stop talking, you two get over there."

Quasim pointed to the starboard side of the boat by the jib

We walked over.

"You Boy! Tie their hands with rope and do it properly"

"Don't bother Stu" I said

"I will shoot the boy. If you do not let him tie you up, and then, I will fucking shoot you both down like dogs. I am only going to tie your hands. Who knows perhaps you can tread water until some ship or boat passes." He laughed.

"I tell you what Quasim. If you give me the gun, I will not kill you. Does that sound fair?"

"You think you can move faster than I can shoot all three of you?"

"I know I can Quasim."

Both Hans and Stuart looked at me and then at each other.

"Quasim Have you ever played roulette?"

"What has that to do with anything?"

"Well like most things in a casino. The odds are always stacked in favour of the house. And when they can't have the odds naturally stacked in their favour. They cheat, its true Quasim. They use a magnet on the wheel and a ball that is just a steel ball painted white. Then they chose the number on the wheel that they want for the house. That would be the number with the least bets on. And the Croupier then presses a button under the table that corresponds to that number and Hey Presto! The ball goes there. And then you lose"

"Except Mr Andy I am the croupier here"

"You think?"

"Hans. KaBar!

Hans looked at me like I was gone out of my head

"Trust me Hans. Kobayashi Maru."

I started to walk towards Quasim. He pointed the gun at my head.

"Stay where you are or I will shoot you down like a dog!"

"No you won't Quasim"

"And why would that be? Do you think I do not have the will to kill you?"

"Oh you have the will Quasim. But like the Casino's I cheat. You just don't have the bullets. I removed the magazine before I gave it to Rosemary. You don't think I would give a loaded gun to someone who does not know how to use it. She could have hurt herself. So give me the Gun!"

"You think you can trick me Mr Andy? I will Kill the boy and throw his body in the sea?"

"It's not a trick. Hans!"

In a lightning flash movement that would not have beaten a bullet. But was fast enough to strike Quasim in the chest the KaBar knife belonging to Hans flew through the cold night air and embedded itself deep into the chest of Quasim. He fell to his knees and then toppled forward onto his face. The Sig Sauer fell from his grasp.

"Why did you let him think he had us?"

"Because he ended up, being his own executioner. He could just have remained our prisoner and we would have put him on the Island. But he chose to re-enter as a combatant. It was his action and his choice to die. Not yours or mine. If the gun had been loaded, he would have killed every one on this boat. Now the problem of where to keep him is solved and his mouth is permanently closed."

"What should we do with him." said Stuart

"You go back to the wheelhouse Hans and I will sort this"

Hans rolled Quasim over and retrieved his KaBar, which was a struggle, as it was embedded deep in the sternum. He was probably not dead when the knife struck him. But the fall onto the blade had definitely ended his life.

"What now, Andy?" Hans asked?

"Feed the fish"

We lifted his body to the side of the boat and let him fall into the waves. A few moments later I gently lifted Raven with the help of Hans, even though it was a mental struggle for me, then I let him slide from my grasp slowly into the waves to follow Quasim to a watery grave. Then we also returned to the wheel house.

ACT 45

"I am sorry Andy. I could not shoot him." Rosemary was crying

"I am glad you were not able to. It would have ruined your life. But no matter, we are all safe now.

Sandy is there any chance you can take us to Scrabster?

"I can take you anywhere you want to go. I am indebted to you for saving my little girl."

"We just need to pick something up so to speak. What time do you think we can be there for?"

"Probably about two or three in the morning"

"Perfect Sandy"

"Anyone want more coffee with a drop of the good stuff in?" Asked Sandy

"I thought your flask was smashed Sandy"

"Oh it was, but I still have the rest of the bottle. Rosemary darling, will you be so kind to go and make a big pot of coffee."

Rosemary headed down to the galley.

"So what's the plan when we get to Scrabster?" asked Hans

"Not a plan my friend we just have to collect something."

"The Zodiac?"

"Correct. Hans"

Rosemary brought a large pot of coffee to the

wheelhouse along with a tin of evaporated milk and can of sugar. Then she came back a few minutes later with packet of digestive biscuits. I had not realised how hungry I was and tucked into a handful of biscuits with my coffee. I had it black with sugar and a generous slug of whisky. I felt the warmth of the coffee and whisky flow. I had the instant effect of raising my spirits.

"Andy can you let me have a look on that piece of paper with the telephone numbers on. The one you took from Quasim?" Hans asked

I reached into my inside pocket and took out my wallet and then the piece of paper, and handed it to Hans. He took the paper and went over to Sandy, then came back to me.

"Andy? What if this is not a telephone number, with an international dialling code?"

"Go on Hans"

"What if it is a location to a GPS point as in a navigational reference?"

He walked over to Sandy and handed him the paper. Sandy pulled out a chart for the coast line across the north of Scotland. Then set about drawing two lines. Then he turned the chart so that it was facing me.

"It is a cliff face very slightly West of Dounreay. It actually refers to a point literally on the shoreline or cliff face. There is a marker buoy about one hundred yards from the shore. It marks the old entry lane for the Submarine refuelling station. Obviously they don't use it any more. They left the marker buoy. It has a light on top, so it will be easy to find in day or night."

"Thanks for that Sandy you have solved one part of a puzzle for us. Once we get to Scrabster and pick up what we have to get. I want you to take us all back to Keiss. When you drop us off there, can you refuel and then lay off somewhere out from the harbour? I don't want them to come looking for you again and keep Rosemary on board.

"I will do Andy. You know there is a private harbour just to the North of Freswick cove. There is a road down to it from Skirza. I don't think there are any commercial boats go out from there so there is no Harbour master. And it's a safe place if any storms come. Would that be OK for you?"

Sandy pointed it out on his coastal map.

"That would work for me and perhaps, we will bring our kit down there. I had completely forgotten about that little harbour."

We drank our coffee and made our way into Scrabster harbour. It was a little after three in the morning. There was no one about. Hans and I pushed the Zodiac down the slipway and let it float away from its trailer. Then we attached rope to the front and pulled it along the harbour wall and to the back of the Catherine May. Sandy took us back out to sea and headed back to Keiss. Just before we got there we woke Lachie and helped him into a sweater and threw a coat over his shoulders. When Sandy had tied up I sent Stuart with the keys to our van, then I had him transfer all our gear from the boat back into the van. We helped Lachie into the van. And Sandy set sail for Skirza. I told him we would meet up with him there, in the next couple of days. I gave him one of my throwaway mobile phones and told him I would give him a call when we were on our way to him. I also gave him one thousand pounds. To make up for his lost fishing. I told him to radio in and tell folks he had gone to fish further down the Moray Firth, just so that no one would raise the alarm that his boat had not returned to Keiss. I did not want an Air Sea Rescue search for a missing fishing boat, as it would draw attention to what we were doing. It would also place him in danger again from the others, who had previously taken Rosemary, and forced Sandy and the Catherine May to work for them. From my point this was good news, as they would have to find themselves another boat to do whatever it was that they had in mind to do. I gave Lachie another couple of Tramadol just until we could get to somewhere more comfortable. The Snow-Cat was still in Scrabster and we would have to try and get that back. For now, though I had to get Lachlan to a bed. The only place I could think of was Georgemas House. So with Hans driving we set off, I just hoped that the roads had been cleared since we had left. The rain was taking care of most of the snow but there were still some drifts and icy spots on the road. Our luck held and we managed to get to Georgemas, without incident. I let Kyla out for a run and for her to take care of her business. I scouted around the house before motioning for Hans and Lachie to come in. The Electric and phone lines were back on. This meant that we had the use of the internet. So I could do some research on the location of the co-ordinates that we had for the cliff at Dounreay.

"How are you feeling Lachie?"

"I feel like I have been shot, how do you think I feel?"

It would appear that without the morphine. His normal cheery self, had been stopped by the bullet as well.

"Sorry mate. I want you to go and lie down and then I will come and have a look at your shoulder."

"OK Andy. Thanks by the way. I am glad you were on hand to treat me."

Hans set about sorting out food by heating some tins of Lamb Stew from the well-stocked pantry whilst I went and got my medical kit. I tended to Lachie and then brought him a large bowl of stew along with a mug of coffee. The wound did not appear to show any signs of infection starting. But I would keep a close eye on it over the coming days. Back in the Kitchen, Hans had brought the rest of our kit in. He was stripping down guns and cleaning them. Refilling Magazines and then reloading the back packs.

"How is Lachie?"

"A lot better than he really has a right to be, all things considered. He will have sore and stiff shoulder for a few days. Fortunately, he got hit in an area where there are no bones, and he is right handed so can still hold a pistol if needs be. In the real world before all this shit that has happened to us. I would have written him off as not fit for work. I doubt if that is going to happen though. Let's rest up and hope that the other team, have had more luck than us. Apart from Lachie catching a bullet, we didn't do too badly. We got rosemary back safely and took them off the Skerries. They are another two men down, assuming they are part of the same team. And we know where they are going to look, for whatever it is that is down by Dounreay. Sandy is out of their clutches, plus we have a Zodiac, dive gear and now a supply vessel, which is the Catherine May. All in all, we are up on things again."

"Was it true what you said about Rhodian's Law of the Sea?"

"Some of it, I think I read about it in a Douglas Reeman book some time back."

"And the Quran?"

"I got bored once so decided to read the Quran just to compare it against the Bible. Did you know they have the same basic Ten Commandments as the Bible? Extremists of all religious faiths tend to only to select the parts that justify their own agendas. Christians choose parts of the Old Testament to justify wars and Islamic extremists chose the part that says all heathens or unbelievers should be put to death. Really though the Quran preaches peace. Much the same as the Bible does.

ACT 46

After the first full night sleep in what seemed like forever. I had the luxury of a piping hot shower which I stood in for a full ten minutes. Then I turned it all the way too cold to revitalise my body. I dried myself and shaved. Then I dressed in some fresh clothes and headed down to the kitchen. Lachie was already sat at the table and was tucking into breakfast of fried spam and beans. Hans was at the cooker.

"Want some?"

"What's the choice?"

"Take it or leave it."

"In that case I will take it."

I sat down at the table and poured myself a black coffee from the pot in the middle of the table.

"Good Morning Lachie. How's your shoulder this morning? Did you sleep well?"

"The shoulder is a bit stiff but not too painful. And yes mate I was out cold as soon as my head hit the pillow. Hell of a day yesterday."

"I am glad you are not in pain mate. I was not sure if you would even be up yet. And yes Lachie. It was a crazy day. I can't promise that there won't be more like it either, before all this is done. In fact, I am fairly sure that there is bound to be at least one more. I don't think the other side, are done yet."

Hans put a plate of greasy fried spam with half a tin of

beans next to it, in front of me and then sat down with the same, in front of himself.

"Don't suppose you found any Tabasco in the pantry Hans?"

"I never even looked."

"So we have to drive over to Scrabster and pick up the Snow-Cat and bring it back here. Which means at least two of us have to go. I think we should leave Lachie here in case the others come back or try to make contact."

"That works for me" Lachie said with a mouthful of spam

"Do you want to drive the Snow-cat back or the Van, Hans?"

"Well you know the land better than I do around here so I think I should stick to the roads. Are we going out armed for bear or just hand guns?"

"OK Hans, I agree. I think during the daylight hours whilst shotguns are a common enough sight around the Highlands, big heavy sniper rifles fitted with half million pound scopes is not. So let's just keep to hand guns and keep them out of sight of the locals. Anyone sees a handgun and they will call the police. I for one don't mind shooting it out with the bad guys but I am not willing to take pot shots at local police. So shoulder holsters under the jackets and nothing more. We have enough fuel to get to Scrabster and back and the Cat has an almost full tank. I am going to buy some milk, bread, bacon and some eggs on the way. Much as you are a great shot and super soldier Hans, a chef you are not" I said

Then I put my plate on the floor for Kyla, she came up sniffed it and then walked over to the bowel with dried cereal in it.

"I guess some dog biscuits as well"

"Eat don't eat, your choice. In the fishing village where I am from in Iceland we have Hákarl it is cured shark dish. It smells like urine and tastes like it too. If you ate shark fresh, it would be poisonousness. So we bury it in the earth for up to three months, then we hang it up to dry for another four to five months. It makes a man of you. So you will be strong like I am."

"No wonder you like greasy fried tinned spam Hans. After Hákarl it sounds like eating shit would taste good"

"Yes this is true."

Lachie was trying not to laugh, but was fighting a losing battle.

"Ohh ooh Stop please. Don't tell me you really eat that Hans?" Lachie asked

"No, I tried it once and never again. But some people say that it will mend a person's body when they have bad injuries Lachlan"

"Is that so? If that is the choice, let me die"

"The point I make to you Andy, is eat Compo Field Rations or Hot Spam and Beans"

"I will load up on carbs when we find a shop, Mars Bars, Potato Crisps, or even a McDonald's. Thank you for your effort Hans"

"OK Lachie, you have the High Gain Five, base unit and I have put the magnetic mount on the tin roof of the log store, and then used the cable from the TV Arial and connected it to the base unit using that, so you should get some good reception here. If you get word from the other team see if they want anything. We need to buy some more petrol for the outboard motors on the RIB. Andy it would probably be best to leave Kyla here with Lachie. She will give him an advance warning in case of anyone coming around the property. While we are gone, if Lachie feels up to it he can split up the spare ammo and any of the supplies that we can take from here. Also I could not accept it if another of your dogs was harmed."

"Hans IT WAS NOT your fault. Please stop beating yourself up about it. I think we should also leave aside some money for the owners to repay them for the things we have used and any damage we may have caused. I don't think we are going to be here much more after tonight. Quasim said that they were supposed to be picking something up from Dounreay soon. And we should try and get it first, whatever 'it' is. At the moment we do have an edge on them, I Think. However, I doubt that that edge will last for long. Lachie I hate to say this, but you need to try and keep the shoulder moving, nothing strenuous. Just light movements. I don't want you unable to move, because your shoulder is holding you back. Just don't overstretch it. We should use some the money to buy us some suitable clothing so we don't look like we are going to war. I will have to guess

Jane's size, the rest of us are all large guys Abdalla is a bit longer in the leg than the rest of us. We will just have to wear either our combat boots or grab something that fits along the way. We need to be ready and able to blend in with Joe public, especially if we have to make a run for it. I would not trust the passports that we were given by SIS as we know 'The Suit' looks like he is in, with those folks back at Altnabreac. I am going to leave Lachie to work out all of our finances once we get back. We will have to split up whatever cash we have, especially if this thing goes south on us. How do you two feel about that?"

"Suits me I can run off with all the money!"

"I see you are already feeling better Lachie"

"This works for me" Hans said

"OK when we have had another coffee, I think we should head on out. Remember, if its urgent and only urgent use one of the burner phones and NO NAMES to be said over the phones. The towers should be working now the electric is back on. Lachie can you, charge up all the mobile devices? I think you should charge up the BAE Scopes as well. I don't know how long they last between charges and we have used them quite a bit over the last couple of days. Same applies to the night vision stuff. I think that about covers it"

I put on a shoulder holster, being a right hander I set it to sit under my left armpit. Dropped the clip out from the Sig Sauer, checked it was full, then reinserted it, pulled back the slide and cocked it. Making sure the safety was on, and then I tucked it into its holster. Hans being Hans and a much more experienced hand at this opted for a double holster with one under each arm. He would have to be careful not to open his coat for anything other than the purposes of using his guns. The suppressors we put in the pockets of our bulky coats. Then we two headed out. Lachie stood at the door with Kyla as Hans drove us away.

ACT 47

We listened to the local radio station playing 'Buttons and Bows' Traditional Scottish folk music played by various accordion and fiddle bands. The song being played was 'Two by Four by Three' and it was being played by the 'Alisdair MacCuish and The Black Rose Ceilidh Band'. Apparently they were one of the better ones. Years ago as a boy I had gone along to dances, that were played up and down the Strath of Kildonnan, in the 'dry' village halls. Those were Dances that did not have a license to sell alcohol. That just meant we brought our own 'Carry Out', usually in the form of a flat half bottle or a hip flask, filled with your favourite spirit. I tended to like the dances where Hector McCrea and his Dance Band would play. They would even play pop tunes, but done on fiddle and accordion. I drummed my fingers on the steering wheel in time to the tune being played. I watched as Hans tapped his foot.

"You like this Hans?"

"It's OK and makes it feel like you are in Scotland, but I prefer Sororicide they are a heavy metal band from Iceland"

That was a real conversation killer as I doubted that that Caithness FM or Moray Firth Radio, would be playing it anytime soon, even if they could find a disc. We passed the rest of the journey listening to jigs and reels along with country music and the shipping forecast. There was nothing on the news about a big shoot out at the O.K. Corral, at Altnabreac. So either no one had heard it or 'The Suit' had managed to slap a gagging order on it. We arrived in Scrabster and I did a groceries shop for fresh and dry goods along with a big bag of Harrington's dried Dog food. Then we did a clothes shop and got denim jeans and warm shirts along with other clothing, suitable for the changeable weather like jackets with zip out inners. Then it was down to the harbour. There were only a few people around, but no sign of police looking for a stolen Zodiac. Hopefully it had not been reported stolen. And probably would not be until the next weekend. So we had a couple of days in hand. I got out of the van, near where we had left the Snow-Cat. There was some snow still laying around the area, but there were no footprints, other than our own and Stuarts. I reasoned then that it had not been noticed. After unlocking it I flicked a switch under the dashboard, which Lachie had told me was the modification to the silencer. Then I reached back under the dashboard and flicked another switch which was attached to the fuel line. Lachie had put this in to stop anyone other than ourselves using it. Then started it up and headed back to Georgemas. I knew that Hans would probably arrive before me, as the roads were now all clear. I had an uneventful trip back. When I got there I was happy to see that not only was Hans back, but the VW Passat was also parked up.

"Hi Jane, Abdalla, Mr Miller How are you all?"

"We are good, but it sounds like you managed to get yourself into some trouble"

Jane said as she poured me a coffee. Judging from the bags on the floor, I need not have worried about clothing. Jane seemed to have bought new wardrobes for everyone, from a store called House of Frazer.

"So what did you find out? And should I make myself more comfortable?"

"Well yes you probably should" Jane said as she passed me a mug of steaming black coffee made with fresh ground beans.

"Nice, thank you" I said and we all trooped through from the Kitchen to the lounge

I sat down in one of the wing chairs and sipped my coffee's

"So Jane, tell me all. I am sure Lachie has filled you in,

on what we know, so far from this end."

"Yes he has Andy. This is what we were able to discover. And we don't have exact dates for this. During the period when the Russians and the West were decommissioning and downsizing their respective nuclear arsenals, two totally decommissioned Trident Missiles went missing. Now at the time, the MOD were not too upset about this because all that actually went missing were the bare outer shells. The nuclear material and explosives were all accounted for and even the rocket fuel was removed, along with the guidance systems. These two empty shells were never recovered and it was put down to some joker stealing them for scrap metal, probably a sailor or tech working on site. But they are very large items and would be easily seen if moved across country by road. Although empty, they are still pretty heavy items. So not something you can throw in the back of a saloon car. Let us suppose that they managed to get it out of the yard, under one of the Private Supply vessels. And then that supply vessel managed to take it up the coast to Fort William. Then because the Supply vessel is much too big, to make the journey between Fort William and Kessock. They then drop it, just offshore from at Fort William. Then they use a small private boat atop, which no one would even notice on radar, not like they would, say at Holy Loch or Faslane. Then all they do is take a private pleasure boat down the canal from Kessock to Fort William recover the Missile and attach it to the Hull of this pleasure boat and then reverse the journey then out from Kessock and follow the coast up whilst staying within inshore waters all the way up to the north. From what Lachie has said they used the Light House Isle of the Outer Skerries. This is a place that has a small dock and apparently there is an H for a helicopter to land on. I would assume that it is either reflective paint or luminous paint. So that it can be seen at night, but only from directly above. At Blairmore a man and a woman, who sound a lot like 'The Suit' and 'The Woman' have booked two rooms at the Blairmore Hotel for three nights from now. I have also found out from a source of mine that I knew in Police Training, that the pleasure boat The New Sea Wave has left Kessock and is currently sailing down the Caledonian Canal. You were right about the UKAEA. They opened an investigation into missing quantities of Plutonium and Enriched

Uranium. The investigation which was being overseen by the Department of Defence was suddenly stopped about a year ago. Although no one seems to know which department managed to put a stop to the investigation? The Arab who owns the boat that my father saw in South Kessock is not in fact an Arab. From the type of the car that my father saw I was able again through my friend in the police, access CCTV cameras of Kessock for the day in question. I got a number plate and an owner. The registration is 274D899 and is registered to the Embassy of the USA. Not that this makes any sense at all. What might make a little more sense is that I was able to track it using the police PNR number plate recognition system. And he travelled down to Glasgow later that day. He got flashed for speeding but with Diplomatic plates on, he was not stopped. The local police followed him into Glasgow, where he met up with another car also with diplomatic plates, registration 187D912. This is registered to the Israeli Embassy. The police officer saw them exchange packages through their windows. Again he could not do anything because of their diplomatic status, nor was he able to write an official report as this would be seen as the UK spying on our friends. I think that just about covers it. Oh by the way I bought some clothes. I hope they fit."

"Nice work, I am impressed. Even if I am now more confused than I was before, it sounded easy, when we thought this was a radical Muslim thing, No offence meant Abdalla. But you said an Arab owns the boat?"

"Yes the Boat is registered to a minor prince from Qatar. He owns fancy boats and ships in just about every country in the world."

"We can't rule out that just because he owns the boat, that it is actually being used by him"

"I checked into that as well Andy. He is in the country but he is staying in London at the Lanesborough Hotel and he has the Royal Suite booked for two weeks. You could not even afford a single night with a year's wages."

"The question that now that sits in the back of my mind is, Did he book and pay for it? Or was he invited over here, so that the blame could be put on his doorstep? It all seems a bit too coincidental to me. Did you get any pictures or video while you were down there"?

"Yes but not all that helpful."

Jane passed me a couple of memory cards and I put them in my laptop, then I scrolled through them. I had to agree even with the use of the advanced BAE Scope they showed nothing that you could not get from the internet. The information we now had was even more confusing that it already was. There were links to both the USA and Israeli Embassy's, A rich Prince from the Middle East, The Outer Skerries, Dounreay, and the possible connection to CDE Porton, the involvement of the SIS and the use of one and possibly two teams of foreign mercenaries on British soil. We were out on our own, without any form of support. How could we solve the situation, when we were not privy to the full story? The SIS with their fucking compartmentalisation meant that the left hand, did not know what the right hand was doing. If we were stopped, by even some local policemen there was no way we could explain our way around how five civilians, two of whom were foreign nationals and had no legitimate reason to be in this country, were armed to the teeth with ordinance, some of which did not even exist on the books. The American term, Cluster Fuck, did not do it justice. So the way I saw it, that in order for us to get any kind of life back, we would have to finish the mission, even if at this point none of us knew what that was. Prioritise, was the only thing to do. So we had to find whatever it was, that everybody wanted. Dounreay held the key. According to the location of the longitude and latitude that was a point either on the cliff or at the foot of the cliff, right next to the shaft that Dounreay had dumped their contaminated waste. According to the public records there should only be one, and it was sealed, two-hundred-foot shaft. I had looked online and used Google Earth and there appears to be not one, but two areas showing as rings in the ground that covered that location, at Dounreay. Yet another mystery! Was there a shaft there, that should not exist? Was the missing plutonium and uranium, just dumped and not stolen? My head hurt from trying to figure it all out.

"OK folks. We have to throw any and all ideas on to the table. Anyone of you who thinks of anything we should be doing first, please speak up, most of you are far more experienced at the spy come anti-terrorism shit than me."

"I don't see why anyone would bother to try and bring an

empty Trident out to Fort William just to bring it back in and up the Caledonian Canal. It just to risky and complicated, too many places where boats could be checked at the lock gates. Lachie said

"So far, most of the clues, if you can call them that, lead to Dounreay. I say we take a look at that. See what the security is like on the site. See if there is access either from the top or the bottom. Then formulate a plan around that. I would say Lachie would have been my choice on the cliff but due to his injury that is out, that would leave Hans, Abdalla me or you" Jane pointed at each of us, as she said our names.

"I think we have the have the best chance of not being detected if we come in from the sea, rather than from the top. Lachie can stay on the Zodiac while the rest of us look at ways from either the shore or climb up the cliff. Also if Lachie stays on the boat he will be able to cover us from any threat either from the sea or the land." Hans said

"I tend to agree with Hans on that. Jane is also right we do need to check out the top side. Sandy has the Catherine May, moored at Skirza along with the Zodiac that we stole from Scrabster." I said

"You STOLE a boat Andy? Are you trying to get us caught?" Jane said

"And some dry suits from the dive club. We needed them. We will give them back when we are finished with them. So technically, they are only really borrowed." Lachie said with a smile

"We will need to look at the Dounreay Site during the day Andy. I say that first we drive by and see what is happening there. Then we should actually enter the site and walk around." Abdalla said as he paced up and down.

"How do you propose we do that Abdalla?" I asked him

"Mr Andy we go in as workmen. Apparently, they are doing some kind of regeneration project there. You and Mr Lachie have local accents, you two would blend in much better than say Mr Hans or me. What do you think Miss Jane?"

"I agree it is better to look before we act. But the choice is Andy's, we chose him to be our leader."

"Let's not call me a leader. Please we are all in this together. So we need to do a drive by, as close as we can get and take some pictures. If Abdalla will watch over us, when we are close to Dounreay, Hans can man the radio here and do further research while we are away. If we take the van it will look more workmen like. That is, IF we can get on site, after we have had a drive by. Agreed?"

They all gave their consent to the plan such as it was.

ACT 48

After removing most of the stuff from the back of the van, we put Abdalla's 'Guitar Case' in and just carried a single 9mm each in shoulder holsters, along with our KaBar Knives strapped to our calf's, under our trousers. Jane would do the drive by. Then if we could gain access, Jane should go and join Abdalla, at a suitable overlooking position, yet to be determined. We set off after a final brief on which radio channel to use and checked our Storno's. All four of us would wear them under our clothes. We drove to Dounreay then pulled into the Visitor Centre car park. Abdalla and I stayed in the van in the van. Jane removed her shoulder holster and KaBar, before she went in as a 'Tourist'. She came back thirty minutes later with a bundle of flyers about the history of the site and the regeneration projects, that were underway at the moment. I noticed there were gardeners working around one of the sites to the extreme right hand side where the circles appeared on the Google overview. All the gardeners were working inside the security fence. All of them wore plain green boiler suits. Each man wore a baseball cap, with the logo of the firm they worked for at the front. They all wore a security tag on a lanyard.

"Do you think we could follow one of those men and snag a security badge? Or have a look for another way in?"

"I think it would create a problem if we stole a badge. But if you look over there where the fence meets the edge of the cliff? It looks like there has been some subsidence there. Do you think, if we are careful you could sneak in under it? There is a building that hides it from view. Providing the building is unused, we will have an easy way in" Jane pointed to a brick and concrete building near the cliff. It's the one with the green roof"

"I see it" she replied

"D you think do you think you could manage to crawl under that?" I asked her

"I think so Andy"

"What are those two humps in the ground, over there Jane?" I asked as I pointed to where they were located next to the cliff.

"Apparently it is waste dating back to the 1950's. When they stopped the Uranium projects. It does not say much more than that. They also have a disused pipeline that goes out about five hundred yards to the sea. Which they used to use for liquid waste this they considered being of a low level. Again that is no longer used. But the killer finds, as far as information goes is this. And you want to be holding on to your arses. We thought that it was a few pounds in weight, of Plutonium and Uranium. They actually lost 375lb of weapons-grade uranium, enough to make several bombs. They also had a big accident. The result being that parts of the Sandside beach, are off limits to the public. People have recently been finding bits of spent nuclear fuel rods. Rolls Royce ran the Vulcan Nuclear Submarine engine program, here from the 1950. Most of that is still covered by the official secrets act, so information on that incident, is not available. Apart from talking to some of the older workers we cant get any info. The woman in the tourist office there said if we really wanted to know things, then we should talk to a crofter, who owns some of the land adjacent to that owned by the UKAEA. His land also comes down on to the beach. Perhaps he might have some useful information for a few quid? There are a lot of folks around here blaming Dounreay for causing cancers of all sorts." Jane said

"Thanks Jane, that makes me feel really good!! But you have given me an idea. I don't think we need to see anything more here for now. We should go see that old guy that has the croft. Probably with some cock and bull story, like writing a story for the Northern Times or something like that."

We set off for the croft next to Sandside. It was easy enough to find, even as trainee spy's, as there was a road marked Sandside Croft. We found the house and Jane knocked on the door. A man in his late thirties answered the door.

"Hello?"

"Hi there my name is Jane, and I am writing an article for the Northern times on the harm caused to people, who worked at Dounreay between the 1950's and 1970's. I understand the man who lived here. Was previously employed there?"

"Aye that'll be me Grandpa" The man at the door said

"Would it be possible for us, to speak with him?"

"Us?" He replied and looked at the van, where I was sat in the front passenger seat.

"Yes I have a man from Inverness with me. He is working on a compensation scheme, as we believe that Dounreay, has been responsible for the large number of sick people in the area, as well as problems with male sterility." Jane said, laying it on thick.

"What do you mean male sterility?" The man replied in a worried tone

"Well problems in later life, with men not being able to function. We are trying to get Dounreay, to compensate all the local men" she said, baiting the hook.

"What sort of compensation?" He replied

"Well, in a test case at Windscale Nuclear Power plant, one man in his 40's got over a million pounds" She said further baiting the now loaded hook.

Jane had showed herself to be a natural born spook. She lied with so much ease. Even I found it was almost believable.

"Aye well you and your man there, had better come in." The man said with the bait taken.

I followed Jane in and we took seats by an open coal fire. There was an old man sat opposite, with a crochet rug over his legs. He finished smoking a cigarette and promptly lit another from the stub of the previous one.

"Grandpa these folks are from the paper. They want to get you compensation for when you worked at the power station" The man said

"Why? Why they want to do that? I am old and fucked now. I aint got no use for their fucking money now, tell them to shove it up their arses!" The old man replied

"Grandpa tell them about when you worked there, when they lost all that metal stuff"
The old mans eyes flicked into life as he looked towards Jane and then me.

"Hahahaha the stupid bastards searched us all, when we were coming off shift. Like any of us were stupid enough to put Uranium, in our pockets. They lost the stuff themselves. Then again they did the same in the 1970's only it was the plutonium then. How the fuck can you lose enough stuff to fill a car. And still they searched our pockets for it." He chuckled, more to himself than to anyone else.

"Mr? I am sorry I don't know your name?" Jane asked him

"Why do ya want my name? I never stole their fucking radioactive shit. They lost it. They hid it" He said.
It was the last part of his statement that caught me by surprise. Even without thinking I asked.

"Why did they hide it?"

"Because, when they were changing some of their fucking fuel rods, some broke. Now I am telling you this, but I aint having my name in the papers, because, we all had to sign some form, to say it was a secret. Then they give us a bonus of an extra ten pound in our wages, the tight bastards. You know when I first started to work there, they never had enough safety equipment. I had to use my old rubber boots from the farm here. Then when we were going home, they takes me boots. Saying they are active or some shit!"

He finished his cigarette and again lit another then stubbed the old one out in an ashtray, on a small table next to him. The ashtray was long overdue emptying and its contents spilled over on to the table, which bore signs of previous still lit butts, that had fallen form the mountainous collection and burned the wood.

"So how much you paying for this story then?" He asked his eyes now not just inquisitive but filling with greed.

"That all depends on what you are able to tell us?" Jane replied

"Hahahaha you fuckers want to know, where the stuff is?" He chuckled and coughed, before drawing heavily on the cigarette, that was racing its way towards his heavily nicotine stained fingers.

"What stuff would that be?" Jane asked when the man had finished a coughing fit.

"The Uranium from the 1950's accident. From when they were working, on those Navy Submarines" He said as he pulled the crocheted blanket further up his body.

"If you could tell us about that. I am sure our readers will be interested?" Jane said. Pushing the old man to give us as much information as he could remember.

"Listen Girlie, I may be old and fucked, but I still got me wits. Let's see the money."

Jane nodded at me and I took out One Thousand in used twenty pound notes. I passed it to Jane and she passed it to the old man, but she did not let it go.

"Listen Mr, I am may be young, and I have been Fucked. So let's put our cards on the table. We are past the bullshit, so one thousand now and another thousand if the information you give me is any good. Is that fair?"

"Aye you're not really a reporter though are ya?" he cackled

"What makes you say that?" Jane said

"They wanted the story, before the cash as well" He replied

"Has someone else been here asking questions?" She pushed on

"About a week ago, some overdressed classy lady, not from these parts, sly like you, only more so. She was not a reporter either. She is supposed to come back in two days." He said.

Once again, it showed we were behind the game. I guessed that the woman that had visited and used the same rouse as we had, was the same lady that had been responsible for the death of Jane's mother. This mysterious woman was probably also the same woman that we had left behind at Altnabreac. I hoped that Jane would be able to continue questioning the old man about Dounreay rather than just about the 'Smart Dressed Woman'

"What's would it take for you not to be here tomorrow?

Say somewhere nice?" she asked the old man.

"More money than this" he said holding up the bundle of banknotes that were clutched firmly in his stained and claw-like hands before continuing.

"And a proper nice place"

"How much more money do you want, and where do you want to go?" Jane asked.

"Another four like this and I want to go to Glasgow. To a swanky hotel, all expenses paid five-star mind you" He said. His eyes were now filled with greed. This was something, that could work in our favour.

"Just give me a minute to talk to my friend sir." Jane said

"Take all the time you like but the next train for Glasgow leaves in four hours from Thurso. The clock's a 'ticking."

"How much money you got on you Andy?" Jane whispered in my ear as the old man looked on.

"About Three Grand on me and some more in my backpack" I whispered back.

"Sir, I am sorry that we cannot pay that much. But I would be willing to offer you another two thousand pounds. Plus pay for you to stay in a five-star hotel for one week. But as you said, the clocks ticking. We will provide transport to Thurso and help you on the train and even pay for your Son or Grandson to stay with you."

"Deal!" He said

He put his hand out for the money, which I had out of my pocket and in my own hand.

"Not until you tell us about where the stuff is." I said

"OK fair enough. Micky go pack me bags." The old man shouted at the younger man. The man left the room. And we sat down closer to him. He told us his story.

"When I first started there, this would be in 1950 something. It was when they first built the place. It was all secret shit. You know with the Navy people and Ministry Police. Lots of scientists and stuff like that. I was there, when they were first building the Submarine engine bay. One day the alarm starts blaring out. Apparently some of the stuff, that they have left over from them hot rods, well it spilled out. We all had to race out, take shower and all that stuff. When we go back in where they have those metal rods covered in water. Well there is one missing from the edge. It had broken and they took it out. Later in the day they replaced it. Now Rolls Royce owned them submarine engines, but it was the folks at Dounreay that made and tested them. No one told Rolls Royce about the broken rod, because they were frightened that they would lose the contract. There was this natural shaft in the rocks, on the far side of this place long before they built all the shit, that they have there now. Anyways there is this real deep tube like hole, that goes down from the surface, deep inside the rock bed. It's about two or three hundred feet deep. So they put the broken bits in barrels down there. And then they put a cap on top of it, then they puts earth on it and then grass. So you can't see it. So like, no one knows it's there. Most of the men that worked there back then are all dead. Some died from old age but more from the cancers. I was born and bred here about and this was my father's croft. He sold them part of our land so they could put some pipe out to sea. They made all the area around the cliffs, off limits to everybody. They put barbed wire around it an all. Now I was a young man back then. It being not long after they built Dounreay and chickens on the farm would not lay eggs. So we would gather and eat Sea Gulls eggs. The Gulls they nest on the cliff face. Anyways I climbs the cliff, early one night and I am collecting gull's eggs. I see this big opening in the cliff. You can't see it from the front or top or bottom, because it's set in like behind a rock wall. I just came across it. I don't think anyone knew it was there. It's about big enough for a man. So I looks in there, I could not see too well as it was almost night-time and it was dark in there, but I swear that there were several barrels down there. And they can only have been put there before they covered the top so that would make that the best place for the missing Uranium they call it rich Uranium I think." He paused only to light yet another cigarette, which he did so from the butt of the previous one.

"Enriched Uranium?" I asked

"Yeah that's the shite. Now do I get my money?" He said while coughing from the smoke he had just inhaled.

"Do you have a map of this area?" Jane asked

"Might have, you got more money?" he said. Greed

starting to get the better of him.

"Nope." Jane replied

"Then I might not have" He said as his eyes narrowed with the greed in his mind.

"I still have this to give to you and a place in Glasgow." I said waving the money

"Micky!" The man shouted at the young man.

"YEAH!" The reply came from another room in the house.

"Come here boy! And bring me maps of the land. The Ordinance ones"

Micky brought the maps and the old man sorted through them.

"Here it is. If you want to get to this hole in the cliff, you have to follow the line from Sandside cliff. There is a narrow ledge that actually goes all the way. Well it used to. I've not been there for twenty-five or more years. Now you gonna give me the money and a ride to the Station?" He asked as he passed me the now rolled up maps.

"Yes we are, as soon as you are ready." Jane said

"When do I get the cash?" He answered after another violent coughing fit.

"When you and your grandson on the train." Jane told him.

"Micky you get to ride in the back with me and my friend. Your granddad can sit up front with Jane" I said

We drove as fast as we dared to Wick. Got to the station and Jane went and bought two tickets, first class to Glasgow. She called the hotel in Glasgow and made the booking for the two men, then she helped the Man into the station and we waited for the train. The wait cost us two full three course meals and some whisky. But eventually the train was boarding. We helped them both on the train. I gave him the money along with another two thousand for expenses and hotel.

"If you stick to what we have said and stay away for a week I will give you another two thousand when you come back. But if you come back before then you get nothing."

"Make it three thousand"

"You Sir are a right chancer, two thousand five hundred. But stick to the deal." I told him.

"I will. I know the other folks are nasty. Think they would have hurt me rather than pay" He said

"I think you are right. So stay away as long as you can"

The train pulled out and we waved him off.

"They would have come back in two days and killed him and his boy. Without a thought, I am sure" Jane said

At least now according to the old guy, we have a fair idea as to where and how to get to the missing Uranium assuming that is what is down there. If we managed to get it, there was no way I was taking that back up to the surface. I was not even sure I wanted to be around it. We had no idea even if what went in the top of the hole, would come out the bottom of it, let alone if it was still there. I was unsure as to how this fitted in with things that happened, on the Brecon Beacons or how it connected with anything biological. Was all this about highly radioactive material. This stuff might kill you, just by being close to it. We had advanced NBC suits. And we had dry suits for underwater work. I could not imagine working with both on and I was not even sure it would be possible. We needed to get back to Georgemas house and rethink all the plans. Because none of the plans we had, could possibly work. We knew that the others at Altnabreac, probably had an inkling on where to find whatever it was. Just not exactly how to get to it. The old man had said that the entrance was invisible from the top, bottom and from the sea. They would come looking for answers from the old guy and not finding him they would look for someone else. He had said most of them were dead. He did not say all of them though.

"OK folks we gotta get back to Lachie, then we have a lot of work ahead."

The journey home was quiet and uneventful. I was sure we would all have ideas as to what we were involved in and how we would have to move forward. We arrived back and Lachie had made a beef casserole with potatoes and vegetables. It had been a long time since any of us had eaten a proper meal. Lachie had set the table and the smell coming from the kitchen, made your mouth water.

"Welcome back folks, have you all had a hard day at the office, can I get anyone drinks, let me see you all want a Martini, and you want it shaken not stirred."

"I tell you this Lachie, James Bond would have freaked today, I know he was supposed to be a Commander in the Navy, but he would not want to take the mission that we will have to."

"Let me guess. The world will come to an end and we all die" he said with a smile

"Yes Mr Lachie it will." said Abdalla

Lachie stopped smiling, and took the apron he was wearing off, being careful to use his right hand to pull it over his head.

"Let's eat first, I'm starving" Jane said and sat down at the prepared table.

Hans carried the casserole over to the table, and then fetched a large bowl of potatoes boiled with their skins on, along with a large bowl of broccoli and cauliflower florets. We ate heartily and all of us cleaned our plates. Lachie had saved some casserole for Kyla who ate it noisily mixed with her biscuits. I helped with the washing up and Jane put the crockery away. I let Kyla out for a run. She would not stray far from the house. Lachie suggested that we should all go through to the lounge, as we would be more comfortable. Also it had a large coffee table, where we could lay the old OS Map, that the old crofter had let us have, only after, he had relieved us of our cash. He had drawn points on it, where we should go to, and where the hole was. He used to collect Gulls Eggs he had said. But I doubt that he would have any of the equipment, that we would have to take with us. I sat down and helped myself to a large, no name whisky from the decanter. The others helped themselves to what they wanted to drink. Then we all settled in, to talk and to listen.

ACT 49

"So Andy what is this end of the world thing, that requires such a large whisky, and by the way you are very welcome to the dinner. I spent hours slaving over the hot stove making it for you. Your silence though, is starting to worry me a bit. Should I be worried or really worried, like more worried than being shot at?"

"Sorry Lachie. The dinner you made, was wonderful. Some day you will make a grand wife for someone. Thank you. Yes, you should be more worried than being shot at. So much so, that I think if I could get out of doing what we have to do. I would take being shot at." I replied

"That sounds bad, especially as I know you medics have such a low pain threshold."

"Funny! OK Today we found out that it is not a mere seven and a half pounds of plutonium. It could be as much as THREE HUNDRED and SEVENTY-FIVE Pounds of Enriched Uranium." I said emphasising the sheer numbers involved. I let the amount sink in to people's minds, before continuing.

"To make a bomb the size of the one that destroyed Hiroshima, they used a lower grade of enriched Uranium. They used U-235 and P-239 and the amount of Uranium they used was just one hundred and forty-one pounds. With Uranium enriched to a mere four percent. The stuff they have lost at Dounreay was ninety percent enriched. Which means a bigger blast and more radioactivity. Probably enough to make anywhere it is exploded, unusable forever! It is also likely that there is a lot more plutonium missing than was originally declared as missing. I have discovered there is plutonium contamination more than a mile down the beach. So much so, that people have been finding little pieces, all over the place. We are talking about pieces of plutonium, big enough to pick up in their hands. Not that you would want too, as it would probably kill you in a few weeks. Probably a lot of it is from the accident that they had back in the 1970's. However, there was also an unreported accident in the 1950's involving a Rolls Royce Vulcan engine. They were making engines and testing them for use in Nuclear Submarine. Rolls Royce will not comment on this and have referred any questions on this to the Ministry of Defence. Who are keeping it quiet, by using the extended version of the Official Secrets Act, no prizes for guessing where you will find those documents?"

"Pass me a large whisky please Andy! Lachie said. I could see his jolly disposition had gone. He took the whisky decanter from me and poured a large measure.

"So do you know where this stuff is?" He asked after drinking a large quantity of the golden liquid.

"We think we do Lachie." I replied

"Only think?" He said and drank the other half of the contents in the large crystal glass that was now empty in his equally large hands. While he set about pouring himself another large measure. I continued.

"Put it this way, we found a man who claims to have worked there at the time of both accidents. He claims to have seen them dispose of fuel rods down a natural hole at the top of the cliffs. And then seen them seal it off. He also claims that while he was collecting gull eggs from the cliff face, to have found an obscured natural entrance. He said this that went down, deep inside the cliff. Further to that, he claims that he has seen barrels or metal boxes, down there. He also told us, that a Smart Dressed lady had visited him and like us, she wanted to get his story from him. He said that she would be coming back in a couple of days to get it. It sounds like the Lady that we saw at Altnabreac and that Mr Miller saw in Inverness and then took to Glasgow. I think they know of it, but don't know exactly where to find it. They will be coming back to his house for sure. We have this old map here that he gave us, well sold to us. His story and the map cost us almost six thousand all in all. I would assume that the team at Altnabreac will have regrouped and no doubt got some more men, from murderer's for hire dot com. They seem to have no problems with funding in the same way that we do. We still have the chopper hidden up there, we have the Snow-Cat, the Transit van, the Passat, and the Zodiac we also have the use of the Catherine May. I think they had planned to get this stuff and take it to the Outer Skerries Lighthouse and then combine it with the Trident missile to be used somewhere in the world but to lay the blame, fare and squarely at the door of the United Kingdom. They could effectively start World War Three. I think 'The Man' at SIS is on our side but I think he is afraid, that if there is any mention of this, 'The Woman' will manage still to make a spin on it, to show intent on the Britain's part to start a war on some country or other. What I don't understand is the involvement of Israel and America. They are both supposed to be our Allies."

I poured myself another whisky, albeit a smaller one.

"Thoughts please folks?" I asked

"We are all Fucked" Lachie interjected, "I think I will just get drunk and await the end of the world."

"Seriously though Lachie. What way should we handle this?"

"OK Joking aside and the fact that there is no decent whisky in this house, I think once again we need to split the team. We need a team of two, to actually get to the place inside the cliff face. We need a team at the bottom with the Zodiac and we need someone on the Catherine May. Finally, we need Hans to get the chopper because, I have a horrible feeling at some point we are going to require a quick extraction."

Abdalla who normally said very little said

"Mr Lachie is correct. We can't manage to make this work, without air and sea support. So Mr Hans has to be Air Support, unless anyone else has learned to fly in the last week. Mr Lachie is out of action as far as the cliff face is concerned. That would leave Miss Jane or me to be with Mr Andy on the cliff face. I would love to say that I can get into small spaces but if I am brutally honest and this is not out of cowardice, I think that I should be on the Catherine May as Tactical support. I would be watching over you all, with the 50cal. So Mr Lachie would be in the Zodiac. To me this makes the best use of our resources."

"You are forgetting about me, I can drive a boat or help on the cliff." Jane's father said

"Mr Miller you are a civilian and have not been ordered into this situation" I replied.

"That is true Andy but my daughter is here and my wife is dead, because of them. I can not sit by idly while these bastards continue to create mayhem and fear." He said

"Andy, I could always use an extra pair of hands on the Zodiac. Especially if we have to haul anything out of the water. Beside I get lonely" Lachie started singing Lonely.

"*Oh so lonely...........*"

"Stop Lachie you are starting to make my ears bleed. OK I happen to agree with everyone so we split. Team One the Cliff Face, Jane and myself. Team two Hans and the Chopper. Team three Abdalla, tactical overview on the Catherine May. Team four Lachie and Mr Miller. Abdalla. Can you take you can take Kyla to the Catherine May?"

"Yes Mr Andy. I can do this."

"Can we drop the Mr Miller, and just go with what my friends call me, Dusty"

"OK Dusty you are with Lachie. So let us sort out the logistics of getting people and resources into place at the same time." I said.

We all sat down with pen and paper and made up out personal equipment checklist. I still wanted to get some Pitons, as I did not fancy going across the cliff face in the dark with nothing to hold on to.

Hans would have to take the Snow-Cat and dump it as soon as he got to the chopper. Lachie had asked him to disable it, so that the 'other side' could not have the benefit of it afterwards. Hans would also pick up extra supplies, from the equipment dumps. Those being the ones he had made that snowy night at Altnabreac. Abdalla would have to take the Passat with Kyla and any equipment he wanted on board the

Catherine May. I would drive Lachie and Dusty to the Catherine May where they would pick up the Zodiac. Finally, I would drive to Sandside Croft in the transit with Jane along, with our climbing gear, ANBC suits and dive equipment. This was not going to be easy. Jane and I would have to get the equipment to the mouth of the cave even before we could go in. This would mean multiple trips on a near sheer face, in the dead of night, for two inexperienced climbers. Somehow I had to find some fucking pitons. We needed to be ready to go tomorrow night. Furiously I scouted the internet for anyone selling used or new climbing gear, for next day delivery, by a set time. Finally, I found what I was looking for. They called them climbing Cam's. The sort of thing you squeeze and put into a crack or small hole in the rock face, then when you release the pressure on them the gripped the crack. When weight of the climber is put on them, they gripped the rock even tighter. But they were expensive at around £40 each. I did not know how many I would need, so more is always better. I also ordered body harnesses and quick release rings, and Five hundred foot of rope. A real climber would no doubt carry more and have hammers and bang in pitons, but I could not risk us being heard by security guards doing perimeter at the top of the cliff. This lot cost us almost four thousand pounds worth including delivery by midday next day and 5% extra, for cash on delivery. I opted for using a courier, rather than a local postman, who might call the police, as we did not own the house, we were currently using as a base.

ACT 50

Abdalla said he would take the Passat and drive Hans, to Scrabster in that morning and then return to Georgemas House. He would then load it up with whatever else they would require for the boat. After that he would meet up with the others, who were going to use the Zodiac. Lachie, Dusty, Jane and I, started to fill the transit. We had most of the supplies loaded and were waiting for the courier. The entire operation depended on that climbing equipment. I let Kyla take a good long run in the woods surrounding the house. It might be some time before she got to do it again. Spot on twelve mid-day, a small van belonging to an Inverness courier company, pulled up on to the drive. He had actually caught us by surprise and I had to quickly cover up some of the firearms that we were in the process of loading into the transit.

"Mr McKenzie?"

"That's me." I said.

I had ordered them, under the real name of the owners of Georgemas House.

"I have some big heavy boxes for you. They are C.O.D." The courier said

"That's OK, just dump them here on the drive and we

will sort them."

"Going Mountaineering?" He asked

"Something like that"

"Sign here please."

I paid him the money and signed for the goods, then thanked him. I waited for him to go before opening the boxes. I set about splitting the contents, into the extra-large North Face climbing backpacks that I had ordered with all the other bits and pieces.

"Have you done much climbing before?" Jane asked

"Nope. You?"

"None at all. Do you think we can really do it?"

"Ask me tomorrow Jane."

She left it at that. Then set about distributing the rest of the equipment, that we would have to take to the cave. I was seriously worried about my abilities. If the truth were told, I think the best man to do the climbing was Hans but none of the rest of us could fly a helicopter. The only other person would be Lachie, though I doubt in his condition he would fare any better than me. I was more frightened by the thought of this cliff climb, than I had been when the bullets were flying. I wanted to quit, I wanted my life to go back to its normality. I wanted so many things to be the same, as they were before. I knew in my heart that this was never going to happen. Even, if we managed to stop all this. Jesus it was ridiculous. Here we were trying to stop World War Three and save the world. How the hell could SIS think they had chosen the right people? Where was the cavalry? Were they all sat safely, in some underground bunker like the ones at CDE or Brora? Even if we could carry it off. Would we be alive to see the results? Or would we fall to a hired assassins bullet or knife? Failing that, would we suffer a fate worse than that, only to die a slow and painful death from radiation poisoning? A lot of questions without a single answer.

"We are truly fucked" I said to myself. It was not a comment meant to be heard by anyone else. Lachie popped his head from around the back door of the Transit.

"Andy. I have said this before but I will say it again. We have been friends for a long, long, time, and never have I seen you give up on anything."

"I am not giving up Lachie. I am just looking at the

futility of it all. We were fucked the moment they chose us. Looking back, I know that the incident at the Brecon Beacons was all staged for our benefit. The fake bullshit talk at CDE everything was set up for our benefit. I think we were meant to fail. In fact, the more I think about it the more I am sure. This is meant to be a no win situation. If they really wanted to succeed, then they would have used a squad of SAS. I don't even know who is running this operation, SIS or some twat in the Ministry of defence? Let's just suppose that the UK and USA along with Israel have made some form of a deal. Who would it benefit if someone made a bomb? Sure as fuck not them or us. Some of this is just smoke and mirrors. Trouble is I don't know which parts. My brain hurts from trying for figure things out. Every time we find something out and we make a plan, it just leads us to another something and we have to change plans, or make entirely new ones."

"I agree with pretty much everything you have said, but what of the now? Does it change what we are about to do?"

"No mate, it does not, I just don't know if it is worth it. I will do what we have to do, but I am really scared we will not all make it. We have been so lucky up to now. Even a winner's luck runs out sometime"

"You know I have your back mate"

"I know Lachie; I am probably just blowing off steam."

"Worried about the rock climb?"

"Of course I am mate. But I am more worried about letting the rest of you guys down. Dusty and me, we are not proper spooks or soldiers. You and the others you are."

"You are a better soldier then you think you are Andy. You have taken decisions that have kept us all alive until now. I don't know many that could do that. Or many that would do it, while putting their own lives in danger, whilst commanding. I would follow you mate, even if we were not friends."

"Thanks Lachie. That means a lot to me."

"Let's go and toast the mission before we all set out."

I closed the Transit door and went back in the house.

Sat around the table with the people whose lives I was directly responsible for. Lachie my lifelong friend who was more like a twin brother to me. Everything good I had done in my lifetime, he was part of. Abdalla the gentleman who had been battle hardened in Kenya. He had a kind and gentle way and was so protective of us all. He was a man who would always have your back even without being asked to watch it. Hans probably the most experienced soldier come policeman. He was capable of doing just about everything. Professional in whatever he did. Thoughtful, is the way I would describe him. Jane was part of the team, even though she had been flipped. She had been badly let down by her own handlers. She had lost her mother to this and almost lost her father. Her loyalties had been tested at Altnabreac. But I felt she was a full blown team member now. Her life would be in my hands, and mine in hers. Mr Dusty miller a civilian who had nowhere else to go, he was here not just for us, but to watch over his daughter. Then there were Sandy, Rosemary and Stuart, Last but not least Lachie's Father and my own Dad, more innocents, their lives were also in my hands. But without all of them, we could not win. If winning, is all we had to do. Though, I did not see this as the end of things. There was a glass of whisky for every person at the table.

"We are one short" I said and whistled for Kyla

"She drinks too she is a team member, without her Lachie and I would have died at Kinbrace."

Lachie poured another measure of whisky and put it down on the floor, we all laughed as she tucked into it. She had always had a taste for any whisky or beer. Ever since a pup she had stolen from anyone's who was dumb enough to put their glass on the floor.

"Gu soirbheachadh agus a 'tilleadh sàbhailte dhuinn uile" Lachie said

"Gu soirbheachadh agus a 'tilleadh sàbhailte dhuinn uile" I replied. And then I translated

"To success and a safe return for us all"

"To success" they all said.

Then we downed our drinks. I wrote a sorry note to the home owners and put it on the table under my empty glass. I also left an envelope with some cash in. We would really have to find a way to get some more money soon or we would end up robbing banks or something.

"OK let's go Mr Hans" Abdalla got up from the table "See you all later."

We watched Abdalla drive away with Hans, who gave us the thumbs up.

Later that afternoon when Abdalla came back. We loaded up and set out for Skirza harbour, where the Catherine May would be fuelled up and awaiting our arrival. Lachie, Abdalla, Dusty and Kyla climbed aboard. Jane and I waved them off after completing radio checks and promises of seeing each other later. I drove to Sandside Croft with Jane, not a word was spoken the entire journey. We listened to the shipping forecast and the local weather from Caithness radio station. We had promised to keep radio silence until we were actually on the cliff face, unless someone was in trouble. When we arrived at Sandside Croft, we went in and just sat there lost in our own personal thoughts of how we as unskilled rock climbers, we going to traverse across one of the most dangerous cliffs in Scotland. Any slip of fall would leave our bodies smashed and broken on the sharp rocks below. Then to have our bodies lost and washed out on the fast tides of the North Sea. If we failed, then everyone we cared about would also die.

"We need to get into our Nomex Suits before we set off" I said to Jane.

She did not appear to be listening to me. So I put my hand on her shoulder.

ACT 51

"Jane?"

"Yes"

"Are you OK?"

"Do you think we will be alive tomorrow?"

"You want the truth or do you want me to sugar coat it for you?"

"I would have thought by now Andy; I would warrant the truth. Don't you?"

"I would say that our chances of even getting to the cave are slim at best."

"And being alive?"

"Not good, if I am honest Jane."

"Andy what do you think of me?"

"I don't follow."

"Do you think in another life, I would have made someone a good wife and had kids?"

"I think so. Why?"

"Andy, can we go to bed for an hour?"

"You don't mean to sleep do you?"

"No Andy I don't"

I lay down on the bed with her. First we fucked and then

we made love to one and other. We dressed in our Nomex and kissed passionately. The darkness of night was rapidly approaching. We gathered up our clothes and took them out to the Transit. We drove as far as we could with the van. Then we ferried all the equipment, out and down to the point at the side of the cliff, from where, we would have to start climbing.

"I will have to go across first, with the rope and the Cams then you are going to have to start sending over our kit. When that is done, then you come over. If I can get over and then the kit, you should have no problems because the rope and pitons will already be in place OK?"

"I know this sounds fast, but I would cross over broken glass to get to you again Andy"

"Time for me to go Jane wish me luck."

Jane came forward and held me too her, followed by a long and lingering kiss. Then she let go of me and in that moment I saw the abject fear in her eyes.

"Catch you on the other side "

I called as I put the climbing pack on my back.

ACT 52

I walked towards the Edge of the cliff. My heart trembled as I put my first foot on the rock face. The pathway the old man had said went at an angle of about thirty degrees upwards for the first part, then along and slightly down with the final stretch was a steep upwards incline. I set the first cam at about six feet from the ground. Then clipped a ring to it and tied off one end of the rope. Another ten or so feet along, I found another crevice and slipped a cam into it checking first that it had a good grip of the cliff. I went along the first stretch it was quite easy with a good lip that followed the cliff around and upwards. Each time I checked to make sure both that, the cams and the rope were securely attached. About ninety yards from the point where the cave entrance was supposed to be. I had to search for hand and footholds. I wondered how the hell the crofter had managed to climb here for Gulls Eggs without a rope or any pitons. I suppose he had at some time, done it in daylight which was something we could not afford to do. I reached up and found a crevice and put the Cam in, tested it, and put the rope through. Then as I was trying for another hand and foot hold, I slipped and fell. The last cam, that I had set suddenly let go. I fell about fifteen feet and my face hit the rocky cliff first. I was suspended upside down on my rope, looking at the rocks and sea below me. I knew I had managed to gain a cut to my head as I saw my blood dripping down into the water below. I heard Jane in my earpiece.

"Andy Are you OK? Andy?"

I shook the clouds and stars, from my mind.

"Yeah, Yeah, I am OK. Just give me a minute."

I struggled to right myself, and then clung on to the cliff.

"I'm OK Jane just a little tumble the Cams work" I lied.

I did not want to tell her that the last one I put in had failed.

"Stay off the radio. OK"

I clambered back up to where I had fallen from, and found a better place for the Cam. Gradually I worked my way across. Then I found the pathway along. I continued without incident and put Cams in as often as I could. Probably more often, than an experienced rock climber would have required. I found the pathway up but could still not see the opening. Finally, after about an hour's climbing I found it. The old crofter was right there being no way you could see it from any angle until you were right on it. The opening went into a larger flat area. I took my pack off and laid it down. I had one of those automatic light bulb moments. I attached a second rope to the one I had.

"Lachie are you in position?"

"Roger"

"How close to my position can you get?"

"Give me a clue?"

I walked out of the entrance and shone my penlight out to sea.

"The tide is full in and I can get right under you"

"Let me know when you are there"

I heard the engines of the Zodiac faintly somewhere below. They were not being revved. They were just running on tick over.

"I am vertically below you" Lachie said in my earpiece

"I was not sure if you would be able to make it in this close, so this will make things a lot easier. Do you remember my start point?"

"Roger that"

"OK I am going to drop a rope, I want you to go back to my start point and pick up all the equipment that is there. Then bring it back here. I think it will be faster and easier to pull it up, rather than taking it across the cliff face. Message me when you get back"

"Roger that" He said

"Jane did you copy that"

"Yes Andy"

"Abdalla are you on station?"

"Roger Andy"

"I am going to signal you, let me know when you see it"

I flashed my torch on and off and on and off, while pointing it out to where I thought the Catherine May would be.

"I have you"

"Can you cover my three, six and twelve?"

"Roger that"

"Also keep an eye on Jane she will be coming in on your three"

"Roger got her"

"Thank you"

"On my way back Andy" Lachie said

I waited for the tug on the rope that would mean I had to haul up. It came about five minutes later. I hauled it up. Two back packs with ANBC suits. I dropped the line with the two empty packs back down. Lachie this time filled them with the two dry suits. Another ten minutes and I hauled up two compressed air tanks and the same again ten minutes later. The final lot was various tools and lights along with our small arms. I was drenched in sweat from all this exertion, caused by hauling up the fully laden backpacks.

"Jane I am ready for you to come over"

"OK promise you won't let me fall."

"Not a chance. I will keep you safe" I said and I knew she got the message

I could feel the tension on the rope, traversing the cliff face.

"Don't forget to clip on this side of the Cam before you unclip your side"

"Got it thank you"

Jane made good time and unlike me did not fall.

"OK folks keep us covered and listen out. We are going to kit up, and then go in."

"Roger" I said

"Got you covered" Abdalla replied.

"Your hurt Andy, let me have a look at that, it looks nasty." Jane said as she unclipped from the last section of rope and joined me in the mouth of the hidden cave.

"Well I can't do much about it at the moment. We are going to have to put on the ANBC's and if it is flooded down there we will have to get a dry suit on top of that. So there is no room for a bandage. Can you wipe it?"

"It's deep Andy"

"What the cut or this tunnel" I said with a smile

"Both, silly"

"OK in that pack over there." I pointed to the Blue North Face bag with my penlight.

"You will find a small Medical kit. It's in one of the outside pockets. There is a small blue and white tin. Bring it over here please"

Jane brought the tin over.

"Right I will need your help, because, I can't see the cut. Take the tube out. Now take the top off, but don't squeeze it yet. There is a pair of rat tooth tweezers in the tin. You will need to use the tweezers in your right hand and pick the tube up in your left. So you will have to nip the edges cut together, with the tweezers. Start at one end and work your way along. Every time you squeeze the edges of the skin together with the tweezers put a small blob of that paste behind it. But let it sit on the skin for ten seconds before you move the tweezers along another quarter of an inch at a time."

"What is in the tube?"

"Battlefield Sutures."

"What?"

"Super Glue" I replied

"Really?"

"Trust me it works. Ready?"

"No but I will do it anyway, scar-face"

Jane worked on my cut which seemed to be quite long. Then she finished and carefully wiped the blood away from below it.

"Thanks Jane. Now we have to get the funny blue suits on"

"Want to undress me?"

"I do but, we do have to get out of this shit first"

The very thought of making love to Jane again, caused an instant involuntary throb. We stripped out of the climbing harnesses and down to our Nomex. I glanced over at Jane. Lachie was right, she was hot.

I helped her into her ANBC suit, then she helped me into mine, but she could not get the zipper at the front to go up. I gave it a tug and it moved on up.

"I am not very good at pulling them up, I am much better taking them down" she said with a wink.

"Check your O2" I told her

"Hundred percent"

"Good"

I helped Jane on with the back pack of our dry suits. I carried two tanks and the tool bag along with the ropes that I slung over my shoulder. I pressed the transmit button.

"Going in guys stay sharp"

"Roger" said Lachie

"Roger" repeated Abdalla

The ANBC suits had their own intercom system plus we had our Storno throat mikes. I shone the torch ahead and started walking down into the rock below. The slope was quite slippery but we were able to hold on to the walls. I kept a check on my heads up display which was giving readings in RAD's. They were showing between one and two RAD's. Some of that could be naturally occurring in granite rock. So the levels showing were quite low. Then we saw a silver coloured barrel with the radioactive symbol on the side. I double checked my heads up display and it was registering just above two RAD's. I shone my light on the drum and checked it for splits or corrosion, but could not find any. Strange that it had ended up in this part of the tunnel system. I tried to move it and was surprised by how light it was. Perhaps it was empty. We carried on further down the tunnel. It opened into a large underground chamber. This had a great pool at the bottom. The water looked like it was fresh sea water. There must be an undersea fissure or small opening that allowed the sea to come in. Again I checked the

RAD's still around two. Whatever was down here was not leaking. I removed my face-mask being careful to avoid knocking the cut on my face. Jane looked at me. And I gave her the thumbs up.

"We are deep enough now that any light we shine, will not show on the outside. So let's set up some of the chemicals lanterns"

Jane removed her mask and started breaking chemical lanterns until the cave was well lit up. I broke two, shook them and then threw them into the water at the bottom of the cave. They seemed to sink down about thirty feet. Although we saw their light we could not see anything else.

"I am going to have to go down there, Jane. I need to take this suit off and then put the dry suit on. There is no radiation leaking. It is reading around two to three RAD's. Even so I want to have a quick look down there. Then I will come back up and we will see what we have to do then. Jane helped me out of my ANBC Suit. And then I helped her out of hers. I got into the dry suit and strapped on one of the air tanks. I attached the helmet and connected up the air. Then Jane tied a rope around my waist. I put on a weight belt and entered the underground pond. I could see my chemical lanterns and I turned on my torch then sank and swam down towards them. This may have been a dry suit but it was still cold water that surrounded me, even with the Nomex on, it was cold. I found myself wishing I had worn thermal underwear. Not so sexy I thought but definitely functional. Then the thermal properties of the dry suit started to work. I could feel the pressure being equalised automatically by this new form of diving suit. The water was clear and I swam deeper. My Lanterns had fallen on a ridge. So I picked one up and dropped it. I then watched as it floated further down into this underwater abyss. I swam down further. My depth gauge said I was fifty-five feet down. I could feel the pressure change and again the suit balanced it out again. I was not even sure how deep I could go on air alone. The lantern was now just a faint glow, so I swam further down. I was at nearly one hundred and twenty feet, when I came across the lantern. It was on another shelf just above the floor of the cave. There was a forest of kelp down here and it made moving forward difficult. I guess the floor was about one hundred feet across so this water chamber was like an upside down funnel, with the narrow opening at the top.

"I am at the bottom Jane and going to look around, I can't see anything except seaweed"

"Do you want me down there with you?"

"Not yet Jane I want to do a search first. No point in two of us glowing in the dark"

"Abdalla do you copy"

Nothing

"Lachie?"

Nothing

"Hans?

Nothing

"Jane I think the cavern is blocking my signal to the outside can you check and see if Lachie reads you "

"Will do"

I waited for what seemed like an eternity, and then she replied

"Roger they all read"

"OK Suit up, but stay up there for now"

"Will do, do you want me like a mermaid?"

"You'd freeze"

I started trying to find the middle of this underwater hole. Anything heavy dropped in from the top I would have thought would land around the middle or the lowest point. I nearly missed it. I was on another ledge. I shone my torch down into the blackness.

"Jane"

"Yes Andy"

"Please take up the slack on the rope, then measure of about fifty feet. And then tie it off to a rock"

I shone my torch around while I waited for Jane to get back to me. It was like being in a great Jurassic field of brown foliage. The kelp moved from the pressure of the water flowing in and then ebbing as it was sucked back out, no doubt the same as the waves on the surface. It was a strangely serene sight. The odd small fish would occasionally come into view.

"You are tied off Andy"

"OK Let it out slow please."

I took a step over the side. Without my torch it would

have been pitch black down here. I could feel the pressure of water on my suit and then again the suit made things level again. Jane let the rope out and I sank into what could effectively have been a bottomless pit. It felt colder here. I don't really know that it was, but it sure as hell felt it. There was no kelp down here just rocks and water, plenty of both. Then I saw them, lots of them, large barrels, all with the logo on their sides. My feet touched the bottom. It looked like they had only recently landed there, which was strange since they were supposed to be here from the 1950's. I walked over to them and wished I was still wearing my ANBC suit. I hoped that like the barrel on the top, that there was only two RAD's. I edged even closer shining my torch over the pile which just looked like it had fallen there this week. The barrels still had shiny labels. Slowly I walked around the stack there were about a dozen barrels. They were all pretty much all the same. They were labelled, not just with the radiation warning sign, but with silver coloured rectangular labels on the tops of the containers. Most of the Barrels had TRU written on them but I found one barrel that had HLW. Which I assumed meant High Level Waste. I silently prayed that this barrel had not split or corroded. Looking closer at the pile of barrels, it appeared that quite recently the barrels had previously been sitting in the cave where Jane was. And that this had been a completely independent cave, from the one above. There must have been a thin layer of rock that had kept the two caves separated. With the weight of the barrels and the erosion cause by the sea below, this roof had given way and the barrels along with the roof had fallen through and down to the sea floor where I was standing. The more I looked at the flat sheets of rock that lay around under and on the barrels, the more I knew this to be true. Fortunately for me, none of the barrels appeared to have ruptured. I tried to move the barrel marked HLW but could not budge it. Whatever was in it, was heavy. Being in this lower cave, got me wondering where the water was coming in and if there was a big enough access to it, from the ocean. If my thoughts on this barrel's designation HLW did mean that it was High Level Waste. Then it would be in barrels like this, that we would find the missing Uranium and Plutonium. This barrel had been fitted with a clamp on top and was quite new and shiny looking. The other barrels appeared to have screw on lids, which did not make any sense to me. As surely the more dangerous stuff would warrant a screw on top rather than a clip on one.

"Jane let me out another fifty feet of rope please."

"OK Andy"

I walked away from the barrels and made my way to where I thought was the open sea, judging by where the pressure of water movement was coming from. The fish I saw were larger than ones I saw above in the cave with the kelp forest. I wished there was kelp down here because then I could see flow and ebb which would tell me if there was an entrance and where it was. I walked and walked and could find no edge apart from the one I had come down next too. What if this was not a cave what if I was already in the open sea and at a depth of around one hundred and fifty feet, would I feel the effects of the gentle tide above? As now I could not feel the inward and outward pressure that I had previously felt. I needed a float of some form. Or some way of making something that could be seen from the surface. Jane was in the upper chamber above the first pond, there was no way she could drop anything to me that would actually get to where I was standing. There was equipment above that we could not leave behind. I had to go back up and get something myself.

"Jane I am going to come back up, start pulling up the slack please"

"OK will do" I walked back towards the barrels and then felt the rope tighten slightly. I swam upwards and followed the rope until I reached the lip of the first pond. Then I climbed over and went on up to the top where Jane was illuminated by the yellow glow of the chemical lanterns.

After removing my helmet and my almost empty air tank, I set them on the floor of the cave.

"I think I have found the stuff that everyone is looking for."

"Is it safe?"

"I think so Jane, but I am not sure if I am honest, can you put the ANBC helmet on and see if you can get a reading from the outside of my suit and tell me what the RAD count is from its heads up display?"

"OK Andy"

Jane donned the blue space like helmet and moved close

to me.

"Three RAD's Andy"

"OK thanks Jane. That is slightly higher than the initial background reading but still safe. I am sure the reading of the barrels on dry land would be higher. I think what I first believed to be a sub cave to this one, is in fact open sea. If I am right and can get something to float up to the surface, then Lachie just might be able to see it. Perhaps we could get a rope around the barrel and get it moved from where it is. But I don't think, the Zodiac will be powerful enough to lift it to the surface. But it might be powerful enough to drag it out into open water. When we get it there, we can use the winch on the Catherine May to get it up. So what I need now is something that I can inflate."

"What about this water bottle."

She said as she passed me her almost empty litre plastic bottle of Highland Spring water.

"Perfect" I said as I drank the final part of its contents. I broke another Chemical lamp and put it inside the bottle then screwed the top back on. Then I went to my own backpack and pulled out a ball of lightweight string. I tied one end to the bottle. It was only two hundred feet long, but if I was right it would be enough. Then I strapped on a new air tank and put my face mask on. Then took our last two hundred and fifty foot of climbing rope Tied that to the string and hung it over my shoulder.

"When I am down all the way, I will give two tugs on the rope. When I do that, tell Lachie to keep his eyes peeled for a light on the top of the water."

"OK Be safe Andy"

"Be back soon"

I knew where I was going this time, so hopefully I would not be down here to long. Once more I dropped down over the lip of the cave, into its darkness. I found the barrels almost immediately and then I turned, to face to what I thought and prayed would be the open sea. I walked to almost the full extent of the rope that connected me to Jane. After making sure the string was fully attached to the now glowing bottle and to the climbing rope. I released the bottle

"Jane?"

"Yes Andy."

"Call Lachie, tell him if he sees the bottle, go to it but don't pull it up until I say so."

"OK."

"Also let me know when he sees it."

"Andy! Lachie says he can hear parts of what you are saying."

"That's great Jane but I still can't hear him, so we will still have to pass messages through you."

"OK."

I waited what seem like an hour, but was really only minutes.

"He sees it. Andy you are behind him, in open sea."

"OK. Tell him to move to the bottle and wait."

"OK"

I checked the one end of my climbing rope which was tied to the string that was connected to the bottle and then I walked back to the barrel marked HLW. Then I secured the other end of the rope around the barrel using a slip loop figure of eight harness, so that any pull on it would only hold the barrel tighter.

"OK Jane tell Lachie to get the bottle, then slowly and carefully pull the sting up. Tell him it is attached to a rope. I need him to secure that rope to the Zodiac"

"Will do Andy"

I did not have to wait all that long.

"Andy. Lachie has the rope secured"

"OK. Ask him to move slowly out to sea, until the rope becomes tight. But he has to stop when this happens"

"Lachie heard you Andy and he is moving now."

I waited and waited, then the rope started to move, suddenly the line came up from the sea bed and went tight.

"Tell Lachie hold position and to call the Catherine May to him, and to let you know as soon as it is there. Tell them to hurry as I don't want to run out of air down here.

"OK"

I could not see my watch, which I had stupidly left under my dry suit. So just waited.

"Give me a sit rep, on when the Catherine May will be there?"

"OK Will ask"

"Andy they are two minutes away."

"Tell Lachie to get the rope to the boat. They are going to have to drag this out before they can lift it. So they need to attach it firmly to the boat."

"OK"

"Ask them to tell me when they are ready to pull it"

"OK Andy. How's your air level?"

"I am down to about half, so I still have some time"

I watched the rope then slowly rose higher. It went to about thirty to forty degrees.

"They are ready Andy"

"OK Jane tell them to slowly pull out towards the sea, but SLOWLY"

"Will do"

The line went tighter. Nothing happened. I touched my hand to the rope. I could feel the vibrations coming from the boat somewhere above. Then the barrel moved just a little to begin with. Suddenly it pulled clear of the pile and started out towards open sea. It scraped along the sea floor and I walked beside it until I was at the fullest extent of my own rope.

"Tell them to stop now"

"OK"

"I am coming back up now Jane, pull on my rope"

I steadily made it back up to the top cave. When I got there I stripped off my dry suit. Hopefully I would not require it again.

"Lachie can you hear me?"

"Roger Andy"

"Can you make it to the bottom of the cliff face?"

"I Think so, why, what have you got in mind?"

"I want to lower our equipment down and then rappel down to you. It will be our quickest and safest way out of here."

"Roger that, heading to you now."

"Jane let's get all the gear together and get the hell out of here."

We packed all the equipment into the back packs, and then carried them to the mouth of the cave. After which I tied my rope to the first two backpacks. I flashed my torch twice and got a double flash back from about one hundred feet below.

"Sending down the first lot of kit"

I lowered the first lot of our kit down. Then the line went slack and I pulled it back up again. I repeated the process three more times. Then I slipped Jane's harness and D-ring through the rope

"Remember take it slow. If you do that you will be fine. Take things nice and slow, use your feet to keep you off the cliff face."

"I can't do this Andy."

"You can. I have the other end of the rope. I will not let you fall. Put your feet on the edge and lean back then just walk backwards down. Remember I have the rope holding you."

Tentatively, she started down. I held the rope and gently let it out. It took her a long time to reach the bottom.

"I am down with Lachie and dad."

I had no one to hold the rope so I looped it through to the last Cam and prayed it would hold until I was down. Fortunately, it did and I joined them on the Zodiac. After which I pulled the climbing rope down I did not want any outward signs as to the caves existence or the fact that we had been there. There was nothing though that I could do about the line of cams that I had put across the cliff face. They would just have to stay there. We headed out for the Catherine May.

"Hans, do you copy?"

"Hans can't hear you but Sandy has him on ship to shore. Hans is on the cliff top by the Duncansby stacks. He is fully fuelled and ready to go."

"OK I will talk to him when we get on board the Catherine May."

The Catherine May was sitting just off shore with her lights off but we could make out her outline. It only took us a matter of minutes to get to her and another few to get everyone and the equipment on board, with the help of Abdalla, Stuart and Rosemary. Lachie secured the Zodiac to the stern of the fishing boat. Then we all clambered aboard.

"Sandy what is the weight capacity of your winch?"

"About two hundred and fifty pounds I think."

"That's a shame. Time for plan B"

"What band is Hans on?"

"Same as me ship to shore 16"

"Can anyone hear us on that?"

"I guess anyone with a ship to shore box or perhaps a radio amateur."

"Thanks Sandy"

It was too far, for our Storno radios without a proper mast. So I would have to talk in code and hope Hans understood.

"Iceland. Crab pots ready for you to lift. Over"

"On my way"

We waited. We heard him first and then saw him coming in just above the water. He came in and hovered just off our starboard. So I switched to our Storno system

"Hans somehow we have to get a rope to you. But we need to take up the majority of the rope that is attached to the barrel. Do you have any Ideas?"

"I have an idea" Sandy said

"Go on?"

"If I lose anchor, then I can use the anchor winch and feed the rope from below though that. The anchor winch can take up to five hundred pounds of dead weight. Then you will be able to attach it to the choppers winch"

I relayed that to Hans and he moved away from our boat so that the down draft did not move us about too much. Sandy and Stuart went to the forward hatch and down into the anchor bay. They disconnected the chain from the anchor chain block. Then they came out and Sandy went to the wheelhouse and released the anchor. The anchor splashed down into the water and the chain rolled out noisily then the end of the chain appeared and shot through the front of the boat. I went around the stern of the boat and untied the barrel. Let out some slack and took the rope to the front of the boat and handed it to Stuart.

"Don't drop it, or we are screwed"

"Don't worry I won't" He said as he went down into the anchor compartment. Then he went to the Wheelhouse to join Sandy, along with the rest of us which made for a very crowded room.

"Take it real slow Sandy. I am going to the front of the boat and when you see my hand go up, stop the anchor winch."

I ran to the front of the boat and hung over the side watching the rope come up. I was waiting for the barrel to just make it to the surface and then I was going to ask Hans to come in and hover over us. But I would need as many people, to help haul on the rope attached to the barrel. I saw the barrel just below the surface and held my arm up. The winch stopped.

"Dusty, Abdalla, Stuart can you come over here and be ready to pull on the rope, Jane I need you to relay messages to Sandy. So stay in the wheel house."

"Hans can you hover over the front of the boat about twenty feet up if you can"

"Roger on my way"

He flew an arc and hovered

"Hans. Let out your winch hook until it reaches us."

The hook came down swinging wildly in the rotor wash. Then it clanged against the side of the boat. Stuart grabbed it and brought it to me. I tied off the barrel to the winch hook.

"Hans take up the slack"

The wire took up and went tight

"Jane have sandy let out just a couple of feet"

The rope went slack but I knew it was locked inside the winch hook from the helicopter.

"Hans Move away to starboard about ten feet"

"Right every one grab the rope and pull hard."

We pulled and the barrel lifted clear of the water

"Keep the strain!"

"Hans move back"

The barrel dropped a little but we had one end of the rope and it was looped through the hook and fixed to the barrel so all we had to do now is tie it off to the hook and then cut the excess rope free.

We did that and it worked, the barrel was hanging from the helicopter.

"Hans winch up"

When the winch was fully retrieved, the barrel was snugly below the Helicopter

"What now?" Hans asked

"Now we get the hell out of here"

"Hans. What's the range of your chopper?

"With the fuel I have about two hundred miles each way. So total of four hundred"

"Can you make North Rona Isle?"

"I can make it there, but not sure if I can make it back"

"Sandy what is the range of you boat?"

"With the extra fuel barrels I have on board about six hundred miles, but remember we don't have an anchor to stand off."

"OK we can worry about those things later"

"Hans go to North Rona we will meet up with you there. Keep below the radar. Over"

"OK See you there. Out."

We secured all our gear and went down below. It was crowded the boat only had four bunks, we would manage. Stuart cooked up some fish and boiled potatoes along with a large pot of coffee.

"I think that is the hard part done" I said

"What next Andy?" Lachie asked

"Dinner and sleep."

I was exhausted, as I was sure the others were. Sandy had estimated that with the tides it would take us about six hours to make it. We all needed some sleep. So we slept, well more like snoozed, where we could. Jane came and sat next to me on the floor and laid her head on my shoulder.

"We did it"

"Did we Jane? I think we have some ways to go, before we see the end. All we have done is hopefully remove the Uranium to a safe distance. There is still the plutonium to find."

"How do you know?"

"There was an empty barrel in the top cave."

"Where do you think it is Andy?"

"I don't know, we will have to figure it out tomorrow, for now we have to recharge our own batteries, go to sleep Jane."

We locked hands and fell asleep against each other.

My mind continued to try and work things out. Who, What, Why? Along with all the other questions that I still did not have answers for.

ACT 53

I woke up several hours later. Jane was still sat on the floor next to me. Carefully as possible I put the blanket that had fallen from the bunk above, over her. Then I headed for the wheelhouse. Sandy was still at the wheel. Stuart and Rosemary were asleep in the corner.

"How much further to the Isle of North Rona?"

"No far about twenty miles or so."

"You got a plan?"

"Not fully, but I am working on it. Fancy a coffee?"

"That would be nice."

"I'll be back in a minute."

I went down to the galley. Lachie was up, as was Abdalla.

"Got another couple of cups in that pot?" I asked

Lachie poured two

"Let's go up on deck, I need to wake up."

The three of us went up. The cold hit us almost immediately, that and the sea spray. The dawn was an hour away but you could just see the start of light on the horizon. I went to the wheelhouse and gave Sandy his coffee and went to join Lachie and Abdalla on the deck.

"How do we finish this?" I asked Lachie

"You are asking the wrong man here; I am just a rock ape."

"Helpful, Lachie real helpful."

"Sorry mate I just don't have an answer for you."

"Abdalla?"

"Mr Andy that depends?"

"On what?"

"Mr Andy that would depend on what you are planning to do with the barrel that Hans took to this Island."

"What do you think we should do?"

"Mr Andy, I would hide it and go looking for the other stuff that they have. Remember they have that big boat near Inverness."

"At Kessock"?

"Yes there. I would go there and take them down or lure them out to sea, would be even better. Out here, there are no civilians to hurt, apart from the three on this boat. In a town or city there are way too many innocents. There would too much danger of a mistake being made, by us or them." Abdalla said.

"I have been thinking most of the night about the container we got from Dounreay"

"What about it Andy?" Lachie asked

"Well when I was down there effectively in a nuclear waste dump. The RAD Readings never even got above Three RADs"

"So they are safe" Lachie replied

"There is another thing that just does not add up. The barrels were supposed to have been down there since the 1950's Right? Or at the very latest from the 1970's?"

"Yes"

"Well there is no corrosion to this barrel its new. The other barrels are older but even they are not corroded. Don't either of you think that strange Lachie?"

"OK so this one is more recent?"

"No not just that Lachie, there was an empty one at the top. Which I think was left there to make us think that it was previously used for the missing plutonium. Or that something was previously taken. None of it adds up. It is like we are still being played."

"What's your plan now?"

"You are going to think I am crazy, and I mean completely off the scale sort of crazy. It could get us all killed."

"Go on Andy, I am listening and still breathing for now."

"There is a reason I wanted to take the barrel to North Rona. It's probably one of the most isolated places in the UK's territorial waters. The last folks to live on it left in the 1970's. Before that I think it was the Romans. If I am wrong then it could be another eighty million years before anyone can go there, and all of us on this boat will die a slow and painful death. If I am right, there is a good chance that everything on the Island and us will die a quick and painful death. But the Island should be safe in a shorter period of time."

"I vote the quick and painful death" Lachie said

"Given the choice, I would too, but that is only if I am right. Do you remember what happened with Gruinard Island on the West coast of Scotland?"

"Was that the Island that the Ministry of defence bought in the 1940's and moved all the residents off to the mainland, and gave them all a big lump sum?"

"One and the same Lachie, but I don't think it was that big a sum, they got paid. It was more like a compulsory purchase order by the Crown, and we all know what a generous bunch of bastards they are! What most people do not know, is that it was the UK's first test site, for biological warfare. Gruinard was the site of a biological warfare test by British military scientists from CDE Porton Down in 1942, during the Second World War. At that time there was an investigation by the British government into the feasibility of ending the war by attacking Germany using Anthrax. This was the brainchild of Winston Churchill. Given the nature of the weapon which was being developed, it was recognised that tests would cause widespread and long-lasting contamination of the immediate area by anthrax spores. To limit contamination, a remote and uninhabited island was required. Gruinard was surveyed, deemed suitable and requisitioned from its owners by the British Government. The Anthrax strain chosen for the Gruinard bio-weapons trials was a highly virulent type, called Vollum 14578, named after R.L.Vollum, Professor of Bacteriology at the University of Oxford, who supplied it. Eighty sheep were taken to the island and bombs filled with anthrax spores, were exploded close to where selected groups were tethered. The sheep became infected with anthrax and began to die within days of exposure. Some of the experiments were recorded on colour movie film, which was declassified in 1997. This is where I learned about it on one of the medical decontamination courses. One sequence shows the detonation of an anthrax bomb fixed at the end of a tall pole supported with guy ropes. When the bomb is detonated a brownish aerosol cloud drifts away towards the target animals. A later sequence shows anthrax-infected sheep carcasses being burned in incinerators, following the conclusion of the experiment. Scientists concluded after the tests were completed, that a large release of anthrax spores would thoroughly pollute German cities, rendering them uninhabitable for decades afterwards. These conclusions were supported by the discovery that initial efforts to decontaminate the island after the biological warfare trials had failed because of the high durability of anthrax spores. In 1945, when the owner sought the return of Gruinard Island, the Ministry of Defence, recognised that the island was contaminated as a result of the wartime experiments and consequently it could not be de-requisitioned, until it was deemed safe. In 1946, the Crown agreed to acquire the island and to take on the onus of responsibility. The owner or her heirs and beneficiaries would be able to repurchase the island for the initial sale price, when it was declared fit for habitation by man and beast. For many years it was judged too hazardous and too expensive to decontaminate the island sufficiently, to allow public access. Gruinard Island was quarantined indefinitely as a result. Visits to the island were prohibited, except periodic checks by Porton Down personnel to determine the level of contamination. In 1981 newspapers began receiving messages with the heading, Operation Dark Harvest, which demanded that the government decontaminate the island, and reported that a team of microbiologists from two universities had landed on the island with the aid of local people and collected 300lb of soil. The group threatened to leave samples of the soil at appropriate points to ensure the rapid loss of indifference of the government and the equally rapid education of the general public. The same day a sealed package of soil was left outside the military research facility at CDE Porton Down, tests revealed that it contained anthrax bacilli. A few days later another sealed package of soil was left in Blackpool Conservative Party was holding its annual conference. Starting in 1986 a determined effort was made to decontaminate the island, with 280 tonnes of formaldehyde solution diluted in seawater being sprayed over all 196 acres of the island and the worst-contaminated topsoil around the dispersal site being removed. A flock of sheep was then placed on the island and remained healthy. In April 1990, after 48 years of quarantine and four years after the solution being applied, a junior representative of the Ministry of defence visited the island and announced its safety, by removing the warning signs. In May 1990, the island was repurchased by the heirs of the original owner."

"Fuck a duck! I never knew the real reason for the Navy presence around that Island. I knew the Ministry of defence owned it, but not all that shit."

"So now imagine, just how much more deadly the bugs are, that they have created at CDE are since 1942. I have a hunch that what is in those barrels is not Radioactive Uranium or Plutonium. I think it is some nasty shit from Porton Down. I also have a horrible feeling that we might not be the good guys in this game. I think as we were originally told. Something they had created at CDE Porton Down, was stolen and that it was then going to be retrieved by the other team. That would be the guys at Altnabreac, who seem to have a massive amount of funding. This would appear to be an international team made up of members from The USA, Israel, Canada, UK, and possibly some friendly Arab nations. I believe that there was another team, as we were told. And that they were wiped out. They like us were also on the wrong side. We found what they had. They hid it under Dounreay."

"That would mean that 'The Suit' and 'The Lady' are really working for SIS and that 'The Man' who is at the top of SIS is the real criminal."

"Lachie that is what I think. It also means that the other team will have a definite shoot to kill policy on us. When they said we were on our own without support, probably means that they have orders to take us out. In order to stop us taking this to some faction or other, or in order to stop us from using it. History has taught us that the Ministry of Defence lied to the world about Gruinard and that they covered it up for fifty years. They sure as hell would not accept us going public. This means we are screwed. We can't call anyone, because if they get it back they kill us all to keep us quiet. Remember they have already wiped out our lives. We don't exist on paper. I would bet they have also wiped out Sandy, Stuart, Rosemary and Dusty, at least on paper."

"OK so what are we supposed to do?"

"First we find out what is in the Container."

"Jesus Andy!"

Abdalla, who had said nothing, threw the remains of his coffee over the railings. Then he shook his head.

"Mr Andy. Disease and pestilence has plagued my country for centuries, all of which Allah has found the time to create and give to us, for reasons known only to him. Your country plays God and makes this type of thing, just to threaten other countries. Why would any man want to do this? I am a soldier and I fight wars with other soldiers. I have killed innocent men in order to find this barrel. You have all killed innocent men, for this. Can we not make it go away, some way, so that no man can have it? I would be happier to die, if I did so, just to keep this from any General."

"So would I Abdalla. But first we have to be sure of what it is. One thing I am sure of though, is whatever is in that barrel is totally Toxic.

ACT 54

We had just come around the Southerly side of North Rona Isle, just as the sun was coming up. The sea was much calmer than it had been over recent days. Jane and Rosemary had prepared breakfast of bacon, egg, Lorne sausage and skirlie. Skirlie is a traditional Scots addition to the full English breakfast, made from pinhead oatmeal and onions fried off in the bacon fat. Breakfast was served with toast along with a fresh pot of coffee. We had to eat in two sittings around the small galley table. It was not what you could call a healthy breakfast but it was a filling meal full of carbs. I was sure we were going to have another long and arduous day ahead of us. I asked the women if they would save some for Hans who probably not eaten since the day before. As if on cue, Hans called in

"Hello fishing boat. This is the Icelandic Crabber. I landed on the Iceberg last night. I am standing on the top, and can see you sailing just off to the south. When do you expect to get here?"

"Hi there Icelandic Crabber, was it easy to find a landing

spot?"

"Roger, I don't want to give too many details over the radio. As I don't want other crabbers, to find our fishing spot, but I found it easy to land. I need you to send the small boat to the southern face, when you get close you will see a path that leads down to the sea. It's not safe enough to get the big boat in, but I think if you are careful about it you will manage in the landing craft. I will meet you there in one hour then I will help you to a safe place to put the mother boat."

"Roger that Iceland. I will come with young boy they have breakfast on the boat for you" I said referring to Stuart

"Thanks. See you then."

"Sounds like he got there OK" Lachie said

"Sandy what do you know about this Island"

"Not a lot really, the sea around it is too open most of the year for a small fishing boat like the Catherine May. It has some very dangerous rocks around it. I know it has a Lighthouse and some scientist bloke used to live there. The light house is an unmanned station. There are some sheep on the Island, and the Lewis shepherds come to check on their flocks once or twice a year. In summer there are some folks come here from universities to study the sea birds."

"I know some stuff about the Island" Rosemary piped up

"Can you tell me everything you know about it please?"

"Sure Andy what do you want to know?"

"Everything you do. Please and take your time."

"Rona or Rònaidh in Gaelic, Rona is often referred to as North Rona in order to distinguish it from South Rona, which lies north of Raasay, off Skye. It is more isolated than St Kilda. It is the remotest island in the British Isles to have ever been permanently inhabited. Rona is said to have been the home of Saint Ronan in the eighth century. The island remained inhabited for many hundreds of years. Then all of the people died in 1680, after rats reached the island, they were thought to have brought the Black Death also known as the Bubonic Plague. Then an unknown ship raided all their food stocks. It was resettled, but by 1695 in some sort of boating tragedy everyone left or died. So only a single shepherd and family lived there until 1844 when again it was deserted. Sir James Matheson, who bought Lewis in 1844, once offered the island to the Government for use as a prison Island. The Islands Celtic ruins of St Ronan's Chapel are still there. Legend has it that the Island was actually home to witches and also ancient Pict settlements. There are remnants of stone dwellings on the surface and also some small caves. The Island is just over a mile long and half a mile wide. Its highest point is three hundred feet above sea level."

"Wow Rosemary! How do you know all that?"

"I was working as a research assistant to an ornithologist, last summer for extra money. It was one of the Islands bird populations, he was doing a thesis on. Spooky Huh?"

"Not spooky, really handy, thank you Rosemary. I am sure, some of that will be helpful at some point."

She looked really pleased with having been able to help us rather than just making coffee. I was formulating a plan all the time, using as much new information as I could get my hands on. One hour later I joined Stuart along with Kyla in the Zodiac, and went to the area Hans had asked us to meet him at. At first I could not see him, as his Nomex suit blended into the dark near sheer cliffs. Sharp dangerous rocks surrounded the small island. We weaved our small craft between the cruel teeth of the rocks defending their island. Then I saw the path that Hans was walking down to meet us. The foot of which actually went into the sea. I threw Hans our bow rope and he caught it first time, then he pulled us to the cliff. I switched off the engines and took the triple props out of the water. Hans tied the boat to a large spike of rock.

"Good to see you two again."

"You too Hans. Were you able to land the barrel without damaging it?"

"Andy I am an expert with a chopper." he laughed and continued

"It was easy, as the wind has dropped. Did you know there is a Helipad here?"

"To tell the truth I knew nothing about this Island, apart from it was stuck out here in the North Atlantic on its own. That was until Rosemary filled me in on it about an hour ago. Have you had a look around the Island yet?"

"I have been here for five hours on my own, so out of

boredom I took a good look. There is a Fjord type of opening to the North West of the Island, where I think the Catherine May could tie off. I could not get right down there without ropes but it could be an underground cave, big enough to get the boat right in. It would offer protection from the elements and it would also be a good place to hide it if needs be."

"That's good thinking, have you found any ancient buildings? Rosemary says there were settlements here a long, long, time ago."

"Yes I have found a few, but if you are thinking of using them for shelter, then think again as they are nothing more than rubble."

"OK Hans, as soon as Kyla has done her business, let's get back to the Catherine May and then later, you can guide us to this Fjord you have found. After you have had your breakfast"

We climbed back onto the Zodiac and set off for the Catherine May, that was sitting off about five hundred yards. The sea was almost flat calm now and a clear blue sky overhead. We tied off to the stern of the Sandy's fishing boat. When we were on board, Hans went for his breakfast. I went to see Sandy in the wheelhouse.

"Sandy, Hans thinks he has found an inlet to the North West side of the Island, which he thinks you can get your boat in. He also thinks that it continues under the Island to a cave. However, he can't be certain of that. So once he has had his breakfast and a bit of a rest. My plan is for him and me, to lead the way in the Zodiac and go in first. Obviously we will need to check the depth of the water and the width of the inlet, before we even attempt to guide you in."

"That all sounds fine to me Andy, how do you plan to check the water depth?"

"I was hoping you could come up with some sort of device to check that from the Zodiac, because as I know we don't have sonar on it"

"That would be relatively simple we use a rope with a weight on it and mark off the rope in increments either with knots or tape, say one foot apart. That's how the old salts used to do it"

"Sandy if you could sort that out for us? That would be a

big help."

"Not a problem Andy, I will get right on it."

I went down to the Galley. Lachie, Hans and Jane, were there Abdalla was on deck keeping watch.

I quickly laid my concerns out, to the three of them.

"So what you are saying is that it might be 'The Suit' behind all this."

"I am not entirely sure who is actually behind all this, but in a nutshell, all the evidence we have so far seems to point that way. He was involved in some way with the death of Mrs Miller and also the kidnapping of Dusty. So that is my thought, if you all think back to the beginning. At least from where Lachie, Hans and I were thrown into the mix. Let us suppose that we were entirely duped at the Brecon Beacons. And that the SAS man had inadvertently, really been exposed to some of the nasty stuff, that they make at Porton Down. I know for a fact that CDE Porton Down asks for volunteers from the armed forces to test things on. They are given an additional payment to take part in experiments, sort of a danger money thing and to ensure that they keep their mouths shut, about the goings on there. I am just speculating here. What if this soldier was exposed to as superbug of the type that 'The Suit' was talking about? 'The Super haemorrhagic fever type stuff.' Remember he said that he had already seen it used twice. Suppose once was an accident and the SAS soldier that they sent us to collect, was one such person. Lachie will tell you that his injuries were nothing like consistent, with having been blown up by a grenade. The only sign of injuries I could see was that he was haemorrhaging from his ears. No broken bones and no tears or rips to his uniform. I know for a fact that they expose servicemen and women to these nasties at Porton Down. Most of the stuff they expose them to is relatively harmless stuff, like blistering agents. We know that according to 'The Suit' that some mad scientist had managed to combine a highly modified version of the Ebola virus and a modified strain of the meningitis bug along with the sap of the Giant Hogweed plant. We also know that they have made a new Advanced NBC suit like the ones we have and that we have seen used by the boffins at CDE."

"Furanocoumarins, that is the stuff they said they had

synthesized from the Hogweed and Grapefruit" Jane said.

"Thanks for that Jane I had forgotten what they called it. Anyway, 'The Suit' reckoned that it had made the Ebola stuff, more specific, so that it would just attack the brain. In the same way as certain strains of Meningitis does. When we were at CDE we found listening devices in our rooms. This obviously meant that someone was taking a specific interest in us. Our teams were chosen by 'The Suit' He told us that they previously had a team up here in Scotland, but that they had vanished. We were chosen for our knowledge of the local area. If I am right, we were chosen even before we arrived at CDE. I know for a fact that the SAS have their own medics. In fact I think every member of the SAS has some form of battlefield medical training. This story that we were later fed by 'The Man' about it being a possible theft of nuclear material from the 1950's just does not hold water. I have no doubt that the material went missing. Some of that would be due to clerical errors. However, in the 1970's they did have an accident at Dounreay. Some of the material actually blew as far away as three miles. They are still finding little chunks of Uranium and Plutonium, in and around the Dounreay site, so much so that the Atomic Energy Commission has declared Sandside beach off limits to everyone. The AEC are a civilian authority. But I believe that the SIS using their Black Door operations have twisted the truth, to suit their own purposes. The head of Black Door, 'The Man' told us that everything is compartmentalized to the point that, outside any particular operation, no one knows what is going on. If we assume that 'The Suit' was running his own operation, to gain access to and also to try and recover this new nasty super Ebola. He then knows, that we are working for 'The Man.' The previous group to ours actually managed to hide, what they had helped to take on the orders of 'The Man'. I don't know how they were all killed or entirely by whom. 'The Man' himself, he then finds out that 'The Suit' is on to him so he lays a breadcrumb trail for us to follow, so that we will recover this nasty shit. He already knew that they had hidden it somewhere around Dounreay. But when he went to the cave probably with another minion, all he finds is the Empty Container that we found in the top cave. He then thinks that the original team has taken it elsewhere and sets us, out to find it. By looking in all the locations that the previous team went. Where it went wrong, was that the Entire Black Door operation gets shut down. Probably by some funding committee made up of members of parliament. And then one other thing happened. Didn't it Jane?"

"I don't follow you Andy?"

"You were working for The Man?"

"Well everyone in SIS and Black Door works for 'The Man'."

Jane started to look very nervous and jumpy

"Except we were told there was one member of the team still alive and working up here. You are the only member of SIS. We, the rest of us that is, are not proper members of SIS. Up to the point where your mother died of a heart attack, you were still working for 'The Man'. Then you realised what was going on. You knew that 'The Suit' had figured you were the inside person for 'The Man' Then you questioned your loyalties to 'The Man', even though it was 'Suit' who had in part been responsible for the accidental death of your mother. Sandy was also forced to work for 'The Suit' even though it was as an unwilling, and unknowing role he was playing. 'The suit' needed to keep tabs on our team. Both 'The Man' and 'The Suit' will do anything to get their hands on what I think we have. Perhaps 'The Suit' is doing it for reasons of National Security but 'The Man' I think, has a completely different Idea. Whether he intends to use it in some way to extort the British Government or perhaps he is intending to sell it to a foreign power. I don't know. Jane you used me and all these other people. You would have continued to use us, until the end of whatever 'The Man' had in store for it. Then you started to question your loyalties. Or perhaps you realised that this was bigger than just a few people getting killed. How close am I to the truth?"

Jane had turned white and was fidgeting. Hans looked at me, Lachie looked at me and then at Jane."

"You are wrong Andy; I am as innocent in this as the rest of you."

"Then you will not mind me checking your bag?"

"How can you think this of me Andy, I am in love with you?"

"I can't deny it Jane, I have feelings for you. When you

started to give information to 'The Suit' I had my concerns that you were not with our group, then you changed back to our side. You knew that 'The Suit' would not harm your father or they would have killed him at the same time as you mother died. 'The Suit' knew you were working with 'The Man' so he put pressure on you to give him information on us. What has 'The Man' promised you Jane?"

Jane reached for her gun Hans was a lot quicker

"Don't do it Jane"

We seemed frozen in time for a few moments. Jane slowly removed her hand from the butt of her weapon. Lachie reached over and took it from her. Hans kept his levelled directly at Jane's heart.

"Jane I am not a cold blooded killer, you know that. We can fix this. Just tell us what you know. I know none of our lives will ever be the same as they were before all this started. Please help us to understand. The who? The what? And the why?"

Jane seemed to just shrink into herself. She lifted her head and looked me square in the eye.

"Andy everything I have told you about my feelings towards you is true. Yes, I have been working both sides of the coin. At first with the person you call 'The Man' his real name is Marcus Brown. He promised me, that what he was doing was to make sure that there would be peace in the world. He convinced me he was a humanitarian. His plan was to level the worlds playing fields, by selling this Biological weapon to as many countries in the world that would buy it. He said that he would be ruined and sent to jail if caught, even though he was doing it for the good of the world. He would use the money, to give us new lives, anywhere we wanted to go. He would make sure that we all had enough to live off comfortably. Then when the first team, who had been working inside CDE Proton, they took the entire contents of one of the Bio Stores. Marcus had managed to procure them jobs working security for the Level 5 biohazard Laboratories. They stole the stuff and then they decided that the deal which had been offered to them by Marcus was not such a good deal. They contacted Marcus and told him they wanted £5,000,000 each or they would take it, and sell it themselves to whoever would pay the most. Marcus told me he could not allow that to happen. As they might sell it to a hostile power and then it could be used against us. I believed him. I know he sent another team up to Scotland to recover they stuff from CDE Porton. They found the First team and there was a fire-fight somewhere near Altnabreac. The wet work team killed the entire first team. However, the first team had already hidden the stuff below Dounreay. The Wet work team told Marcus that they had the coordinates of the place where it was hidden, which was the top cave. They knew nothing about the floor having caved in. The wet team took Marcus there and they found the empty Barrel, so they assumed that it had been moved from there to somewhere else. He knew that it had not been moved out of the country. So he formed a new team to find it. That would be you. I was to contact him when we had it."

"And have you contacted him?"

"Yes. But I know I have been stupid."

"When did you contact him?"

"When you went for a stroll on deck this morning."

"Did you give our position?"

"I just told him we were heading for an Island in the North Sea"

"I can't tell you how disappointed I am in you Jane"

"I am sorry Andy. Really I am." she burst into tears.

"How did you contact him?"

"I have a Sat Phone in my backpack"

Lachie went to the backpack and undid the string and tipped it upside down on the table. He picked up the phone. I put my hand put and he passed it to me.

"Watch her" I said and went up to the wheel house.

"Sandy I need the charts. I need to find another remote and uninhabited Island as far away from here as your boat could possibly go."

"Why do you want to do that Andy?"

"I will let you know as soon as I do, but for now have you got some charts I can look at?"

"Sure, they are all over there, rolled up in the Chart Box"

"Can you pick the right ones out for me please Sandy?

Sandy rummaged through a large roll of Maps and charts. And found one

"Here you go Andy. See here there is a tiny group of rocks Islands to the North West coast of Pappa Stoor at approximately 60°22'28.07"N by 1°48'47.41"W. No one lives there. It is just bare rocks. I can't take my boat in there its way to dangerous. I suppose you could manage with the Zodiac, but I would not advise it."

"Thanks Sandy I just wanted somewhere remote and away from us."

I took the charts and headed back down to the Galley

"Jane I want you to call Marcus, and I want you to tell him, that we will be going to these coordinates and that the barrel is safe. And Jane, please don't fuck us over. I am offering you and your father a lifeline."

I passed the Satellite Phone over to her. Hans still had his pistol levelled at her. She took the phone and switched it on.

"Marcus, it's me, I don't have long to talk I am going to send you the coordinates of where they are taking it......No they have not opened it...... They are going to be at that location......"

I held my hands up with my fingers outstretched.

"At about ten o'clock tonight...........No they left all the guns on the mainland..........OK........ You promise dad and me will be OK and you will get us out of the Country...........Yes I will call you when we are there.......Yes I love you too." She hung up

"You LOVE Him?"

"We had a thing before this all started."

"Jane if you are playing us, we will ALL die."

"I just wanted it to sound authentic,"

"You know he will not let you live. He has probably planned for everyone to die, so that there are no witnesses. You know, I will not play you Jane? We did not have a choice. We were forced into this. You chose to do this. So I need to be sure, which side of the divide you are now on? And that you will not change horses again as you have already done twice."

"Andy I have my father here. Do you think I would be willing to risk his life?"

"Jane you risked his life the moment you started this thing with Marcus. If you really believe he will whisk you away, then you are a stupid girl. I thought you were smart. Now I think you may have been too stupid or too smart for your own good."

Lachie Who had said nothing all the time. Walked over to the table and sat down.

"You know there are two endings for us? One in which we die, and one in which Marcus dies"

"There is a third option Lachie." Hans said

"And that is?"

"Everyone in the world dies!"

ACT 55

There did not seem any point in restraining Jane she was already stuck on a small fishing boat out in the North Atlantic. I had kept the phone and removed its battery, so that it could not be used as a tracking device. I did not know what to believe about Jane, I doubted that I could trust her. She had seemed so genuine and passionate when we had made love back in Sandside Croft. I did not know if I loved her, or hated her. I was disappointed in myself for having been fooled, and for having feelings for someone so short a time after meeting them. She was stunningly beautiful, but had been willing to place all of our lives in danger. Perhaps she believed Marcus's promises to her. If this was as it looked to be. I was sure that we would all die. The question was how we died and where we died. Jane had lied to Marcus, when she told him we were not armed any more. We had a full complement of arms, including the Claymore Anti Personal Mines along with our AS50's and all the other small arms. We did have enough fuel in the Boat for about another four to five hundred miles. I needed to talk to Lachie, Hans and

Abdalla without Jane present. But I needed her to stay in my eyesight at the same time. I asked her to stand at the front of the boat while we sat down on the deck just in front of the wheelhouse. Sandy was at the wheel Stuart and Rosemary were back down in the Galley. Dusty was sleeping in a bunk. He did not fare well at sea and had been sea sick most of the time since we left Dounreay.

"Do you have a plan Andy?" Abdalla asked me.

"I do have a plan in my mind but it is continually formulating and I am not even sure if most of it will work.

"Try breaking your plan down into little segments, I have always found it is easier that way" Hans said as he toyed with his KaBar on the wood of the deck.

"Don't you think it would be better for you to lead us in this Hans?"

"I have experience this is true, as does Abdalla. But we are not British citizens. You are the correct choice as you are the highest ranking British soldier here."

"I also agree with both Hans and Abdalla, you are the correct choice to lead us. Andy you and I go way back and I have always trusted your judgement. So what do you have in mind for us?"

Lachie spoke warmly and with a confidence in me, a confidence that I truly did not have in myself.

"OK so breaking it down the first thing we need to do is in two parts. The first is to get the Catherine May, out of sight from any other boats or ships. And if at all possible out of Satellite viewing. I am sure that Marcus Brown will be searching for us, as will 'The Suit'. Hopefully for now they will be looking for us in all the wrong places. But at some point they will widen their search locations and they will check every inhabited and uninhabited Island between here and Iceland. So we have to either stop them or should I say, stop both of them looking for us. Hans has found an inlet which he describes as a bit of a Fjord and that the water, seems to flow into a cave at the foot of the North West cliffs on this Island. The second part is to move the helicopter and the barrel, preferably to separate locations on this Island. If we can find some way to hide the chopper or disguise it that would be of a great help. So let's get part one done. Did you get enough rest Hans?"

"Yes thank you Andy. I can work on just an hour or two of sleep at a time."

"Right guys, let's do part one. When we get close to the Fjord, Hans and I will go in first and make sure there is space for the Catherine May. Then if there is we will guide you in. Then we take it from there."

We all stood up and filled our back packs with items that we thought we would require, Torches, and the rope tied of in one foot increments with a lead weight tied to the bottom, had been made up for me by Stuart. Hans would man the outboards, and I would take the readings. It was almost midday on a beautiful clear and calm spring morning. The weather itself was a long way removed from the hell that was in my mind.

I instructed Lachie to keep a close watch on Jane, Abdalla would keep an eye out for any approaching craft or aircraft. Hans and I got in the Zodiac and cast of from the stern. We moved into the little fjord slowly and steadily. I took constant readings which varied from forty feet to twelve in the actual inlet. I could not see any opening for a cave as it was completely dark at the end of the inlet. I switched on my torch and shone it directly ahead. There was a cave there but I was not sure if there was enough height for the Catherine May. There was just about enough width and with twelve feet of water below, so there was enough depth. Hans and I entered the cave it was huge. I shone my torch to the ceiling and around the walls. Inside there was a small but accessible shoreline. We approached it slowly until the bow of the Zodiac touched the course sand.

"What do you think Hans? Will the Catherine May get in and more to the point will she be able to get out?"

"From the look of things the tide is in. When the tide is out the ceiling will be higher at the entrance but the depth of water below the boat will be less. I think the tide in here probably rises and falls about four feet. So yes I think the Catherine May can get in, if we drop her radio masts and take the life raft containers from on top of the wheelhouse, she should make it in. It is the perfect place to hide her and safe too. Due to the way the inlet comes in from the north and then swings to the east. It will be totally invisible to sight, radar and satellite. The beach area is big enough for people to get ashore and stretch their legs even though it's only thirty or forty feet."

"What's that over there Hans?"

I shone my torch to the right hand side of the sandy beach. There looked to be an old wooden jetty of some form. I got off the Zodiac and walked over. There was indeed a small wooden jetty, well what was left of it. There were some rough hewn posts and most of the planking had rotted, but there were still a couple of feeble looking boards left. I shone my torch around the area looking to see if there was a way up. Some carved stone steps had been chiselled out of the rock face. I walked towards them, then I saw it. There was a skeleton laid on the steps. The clothes were nothing more than a few strands of some canvas like material.

"Over here Hans."

Hans came over to where I was standing

"Who is he?"

"I don't have a clue Hans, but I think he has been here for a very long time, probably more than a hundred years. That wooden Jetty has rotted over many years, and judging by the skeleton, no one has been in here since his or her demise."

Hans looked around the area of the body and only found an old flask. There was a leather belt about the skeleton, with a large plain brass buckle. There was an old knife that had rusted to nothing so that just a stump and an ivory or bone handle remained.

"Do you think he got stuck in here Andy?"

"I think it is more likely that he was killed or died from the Black Death. According to Rosemary the Island was ravaged by the Bubonic plague and everyone either left or died. I wonder where those steps lead."

"You stay here and look around, I will go back to the Catherine May and see if we can clear the top of the wheelhouse. Then I will lead them in. It should be about half an hour."

"OK Hans see you soon."

I went up the steps, they were slippery at the start where the tide had come in. But after a few steps they became just wet from the moisture within the cave. I climbed up and then the steps just stopped. I would guess about two hundred feet above sea level. There appeared to have been an opening in the past.

Either someone had blocked it or there had been a cave in. So now there was no exit to the surface of the Island from here. I walked back down to the Skeleton and gave it a quick examination from the number of ribs it was a man. He had only a few teeth left in his mouth, not an uncommon thing from his era of time. But there was no obvious sign of murder. It was of course possible that he had been blocked in here and left to die. He would not have survived much more than a few minutes in the frigid North Atlantic Sea, if he had tried to swim for it. If he had stayed here without attempting to swim for it, then it could have been weeks before he died. I heard the Zodiac before I saw it, then I saw two spotlights close behind. I could make out the silhouetted figures either side of her with poles ensuring that the Catherine May, did not hit the sides of the entrance. The top of the wheelhouse had been cleared and the boat slid almost silently under the opening to this large underground chasm.

Hans powered the Zodiac up onto the beach and killed the three Honda Engines. We would have to find a way to secure the Catherine May, so that as the tide came and went she would not damage herself on the walls of this cave. I would leave that up to Sandy and Stuart to organise. He could use us, if needs be, to assist with that. I knew he no longer had an Anchor. So she would have to be fixed to at least one wall.

"What did you find out about our friend here?" Hans said pointing to the bones at the foot of the steps.

"Not a lot, just that he is, sorry, was a man. The steps lead up about two hundred feet and then it's blocked off. It might be worth a look on the surface? We know roughly where it is, in conjunction to the inlet."

"OK Andy I am going to start ferrying most of the folks to the shore. After that we can take a look around the Island. I still have the tarp that I used to cover the Helicopter at Altnabreac but we will have to do something to change it from being white. That or else we find another way to hide the helicopter."

"OK. If Sandy needs some help in tying off the boat, then we will do that, before we take off and have a look on top"

Hans and I pushed the Zodiac back into the water and he set off the fifty or so feet to the boat. He started ferrying people ashore. Lachie, Rosemary, Jane, Dusty, Abdalla and Kyla came ashore. They all had backpacks and also Rosemary had a Tilley Lamp which illuminated the entire cave. It was almost silent in there with just the gentle lapping of the water at the walls of the cave. The roof extended up almost at the same angle as the lie of the land above. So it was between thirty and two hundred feet high. With the narrow ledge which had the steps carved into the bare rock, going up to about two hundred feet and then coming to a sudden end. It was decided to set up some form of camp on the beach. Sandy managed to find enough points to secure the boat to one wall. So we ferried him and Stuart to the internal beach of the vast cave. Sandy gave us some netting that we could use in conjunction with the tarp to help hide the helicopter, as soon as we had finished doing what I had in mind. We took the Zodiac and went back around the coast to where I had first seen Hans, when we arrived. Hans guided the boat into where the pathway, led up to the top of the Island. After tying off the Zodiac, we had climbed the path and then over a piece of well grazed ground. Still walking upwards until, we could see the unmanned lighthouse in front of us. About fifty yards to the left of it was the helicopter. And next to it was the barrel. There was absolutely nowhere to hide the Helicopter. I walked around the Island looking for the Pictish settlement that Rosemary had told us about, without any success apart from mounds of stones. So we spread out and worked a full grid on the Island. Still we found nothing, except the sheep, that were the sole inhabitants of this barren Isle. The only standing building was the lighthouse.

"Abdalla do you think that between the three of us we could very carefully move the barrel into the lighthouse."

Abdalla and Hans were both big powerful men, much more so than me.

"I think Hans and I could carry it from the helicopter between us. It would be more awkward with three of us we would end up tripping. We could make a cradle from the ropes and cut some of the tarpaulin. But we would need some strong poles."

"Can we use the hand rails from the walkway of the lighthouse? They looked to be made from two inch galvanised steel tubing. The only problem is how do we cut it into lengths?"

"There has to be some tools in the lighthouse let's take a quick look in there."

Hans tried the door

"Locked" He said

Abdalla gave it an almighty kick with the full weight of his solid body behind it.

"Not any more"

"Subtle Abdalla, Real subtle"

"Mr Andy. It's open. You wanted it open and I doubt they left the key under the mat"

"You have been sitting to close to Lachie I think, Abdalla"

We walked in and it had the hollow and empty sound that functional but non domestic buildings have. There was a hallway with two more doors and a short flight of stairs to the actual light room. Power was from an array of solar panels along with a small wind turbine. Abdalla pushed his shoulder against the first door, forcing it open, and we went in. I tried the handle as I went past it, it was unlocked.

"Abdalla the door was not locked"

"So?"

"Nothing"

We struck gold there were a multitude of tools including a large hacksaw.

"Problem solved" Hans said as he picked it up along with a large ten-pound hammer.

"Mr Andy, we only need to cut one end then we can bend it until it snaps. Rather than expending all our energy sawing."

So that is what we did. We had two six foot lengths of heavy steel piping. We laid out the tarpaulin and carefully lay the barrel on its side on top. Then we doubled up the edged of the tarpaulin and cut holes with our KaBars so that we threaded the pipes through like a curtain pole. Then put ropes under the tarpaulin and barrel, for extra measure tying off both ends. Abdalla stood at the front between the two poles that lay on the ground. Then Hans went and stood the same way at the back. Each of them bent down and picked the poles up, until they had taken up the slack.

"Lift on three" Abdalla commanded and continued.

"One, Two, Three"

Both men groaned at the weight of the barrel. It came off the ground. Taking the weight on their shoulders as they straightened their backs, they started walking towards the lighthouse. I helped Hans on the back as we went up the three steps to the door, in order to keep the barrel level. Then we walked in to the main corridor. They carefully put it down on the floor of the hallway.

"Can we stand it up so that the sealing clamp is at the top? Sorry for asking you to do all the donkey work while I watch" I said.

They stood the barrel up and we went back outside into the sunshine

"Now what do we do?" Asked Hans

"Now we try and Hide the Helicopter, if we use the tarpaulin along with the netting. We should be able to gather enough clumps of grass to weave them into the fishing net. It won't be perfect but hopefully it will pass a cursory glance or a satellite image. At least if we use enough grass and any gorse and whin bushes we can find."

It took us almost two hours to cover the chopper. Not perfect but to my eyes it looked pretty damn good. It resembled a rock mound with crags filled with grass and other natural occurring plants from this Island.

"What now, Mr Andy?" asked Abdalla.

I think Hans had already figured out. What I had in mind to do with the barrel, but he had like me kept it to himself.

"We go back and eat, then sleep. The light will be fading soon. Hopefully we will have a worry free night, one without someone trying to kill us." I replied

We strolled back down the hill and down the pathway to our Zodiac. Then we followed the coast back into the cave. There was a small fire burning when we got there, the smoke drifted out the entrance. I supposed they were cooking on the beach or trying to keep warm. Abdalla jumped out of the boat as soon as we got there and quickly covered the fire with sand.

"What did you do that for?" Jane asked

"Miss Jane. Do you want to get us all caught. The smoke coming from that fire is drifting out of the opening and could be seen by satellite or passing aircraft. This is supposed to be an uninhabited Island. That means NO OPEN FIRES during daylight hours. If you want to cook them, we use the Boats cooker or you eat cold rations. If you are cold put more clothing on."

Jane looked really embarrassed and I thought she was about to cry. I could also see the disappointment on the faces of Rosemary, Sandy, Stuart and Dusty. Lachie also looked ashamed. I felt for him but I knew Abdalla was right to do what he had done. He was also right, to chastise them all for it. Our lives depended on us being invisible at the moment.

"Sorry folks but Abdalla is correct. Now we are back with the Zodiac you can go back and forth to the Catherine May as you like. I would suggest that we men, make a latrine over there behind the old jetty and Rosemary and Jane use the toilet on the Catherine May. As far as cooking goes I say we make a large pan of pasta, I saw that Sandy has some on board. If you want to wash use, the sea. We can't afford to waste the fresh water we have. It's just for cooking and drinking nothing else. Is that OK with every one?"

They all nodded their agreement to this. I planned to tell them later what I had in store for tomorrow and possibly the following day. But for tonight, every one deserved a rest. Time just to chill out. I still needed to have a chat with Jane. I knew my feelings towards her were true, but in light of her recent admissions I wondered, if she had just played me. She had said to Marcus on the phone, that she loved him. So I was not sure that she was being truthful about us. Perhaps she was one of those women that use men in the same way that some men use women. Would she remain loyal to our side of the divide and what would she think to my plan when I revealed it? I waited until she wanted to go on board to use the boats toilet and I went across with her in the Zodiac. It probably looked strange to everyone else. I had told no one about what Jane and I had been up to in Sandside Croft. I was not even sure if I wanted to tell my oldest and dearest friend. Though, I knew I would at some point, just not now. We tied off at the stern of the Catherine May and then I got on board and offered my hand to her, which she took. That electricity that had flowed between us at the croft was still there, but it was tinged with a feelings of betrayal.

"You are not here just to watch me pee, are you Andy?"

"No I wanted to catch you alone. I need to know where we stand. I don't just mean we, as in you and me, I mean the, we, as in you me and all of us here. What you did before, in using us. It was wrong. I know that you thought you were following orders, and that you were serving two masters as in Marcus and 'The Suit' and that the lines between right and wrong became blurred and the lines between emotion and loyalties also were crossed. You said you were falling in love with me. Was that just an act? Was the passion in Sandside another act? Was the confession an act? I have to know what is real."

"Yes I was in love with Marcus at least I think I was. It could have been infatuation. I think it was not so much me, but Marcus. He has a way of using people, to get things he wants done. Marcus told me not to trust 'The Suit' I really don't know his real name, I was just to get 'him' on the phone, or call the 'number two'. We only started calling him 'The Suit', after all of you, started to call him that. It just kind of stuck. So much so that even Marcus referred to him that way. As far as my feeling for you go, they are real. My heart flutters when you are close to me. I never planned for the thing at the croft. It just happened and I have not slept with Marcus. He kept promising to take me away with him. He was going to leave his wife. We were going to go and live in Mexico. He said he was going to buy a Hacienda near the beach, just south of Cancún. I realise now that he was just using me, as he used every one, including you and your friends. It was the same way he used the other team, before you. I should have told you before."

"Yes Jane you should have told me from the start. I need to be sure I can trust you, not just with my feelings, but because all of our lives depend on us working together."

"Andy, there is one more thing that you have to know."

"What's that Jane?"

"Remember being told that there might be a Wet Work team sent in to get you?"

"Yes that was just after we had a visit from Mervin"

"What I should have told you yesterday, or even the day before. When the Black Door ops were closed, you were all automatically placed on that list. They were only holding off, from killing you, to see if you found what had been taken from

Porton Down. 'The Suit' and his men are the Wet Work team. When they find you they will kill all of you."

I grabbed her by her wrists and stared her eye to eye

"What about the men from the Island and, those that wanted this boat?"

"They were hired by Marcus. To make sure he got the barrel"

"And you just thought you would keep that little bit of information to your fucking self! You know that because, you are with us. They will, Fucking kill you, and your dad as well. They will not come and say, we will kill him and him and then say, oh we will not kill her or her innocent father, or Rosemary. They will fucking try to wipe us all out, in the one hit. Jesus, Jane for a member of the SIS you have behaved like a complete fucking idiot. I don't even know how to feel about you now."

I must have been shouting because Lachie shouted over the water

"Is everything all right over there?"

I put my head around the side of the wheelhouse

"We are fine Lachie I have just a few disagreements with the way SIS have been playing us. I will be back over with Jane in a minute."

"Just go to the toilet Jane. I will wait here for you."

She came back five minutes later. I could tell she had been crying but had wiped her face. Her eyes were red.

"Come on Jane lets go. We will work it all out"

We got back into the Zodiac and went back to the shore. Rosemary and Jane then went back to the boat and cooked up a big pan of pasta with tomatoes and smoked sausage along with a bucket of coffee. And it was actually a bucket. Rosemary said that she had scrubbed it clean using sea water and then wiped it out and boiled up the coffee in it. They brought back bowls and cups for all along with the pasta and coffee. We ate for the greater part in silence, with just the odd bit of chit chat. I guess my shouting at Jane, had worried them all a little. I had decided to not throw all the blame at Jane's door publically. Lachie, Hans and Abdalla already knew. And it would have proved pointless to destroy her relationship with her father. I was however going to tell everyone, just how much danger they were in. My plan would initially place them in a very high level of danger, if not kill them outright. Rosemary and Stuart cleared the plates and washed them along with the pans in the sea.

ACT 56

"OK can everybody gather around, I want to tell you about my plans for tomorrow, I will be doing some things, that I feel need to be done. It is my opinion that the barrel, that we thought contained some form of radioactive compound, does not. I believe that its contents, are far more dangerous to the world. We have also been working for the wrong side. I have previously shared my suspicions with my military brothers that you all know. We have unwittingly been working for a man who is very high up in an organisation called SIS. This is not a new organisation. They have been around since before World War Two. Most of you guys will have heard of MI5 and MI6 on the movies all that James bond stuff, well SIS is the parent umbrella for them. We, that is to say those of us from a military, or even Jane from the police, were recruited to work for SIS under the guise of saving the UK from some kind of terrorist attack. It turns out that, the terrorist attack to be carried out, was by our boss. He is at the top of the Spy world. The team that has been chasing us and trying to kill us all, are the good guys in all of this. Due to the embarrassing nature, to the British Government, a sort gagging notice has been issued on us, a bit like those that they put on newspapers. Except the order that has been issued on us, is for us to be killed."

The faces of all the civilian members of our team went white and there were gasps, Sandy and Stuart both hugged Rosemary, and Jane hugged her father. I continued.

"I want to give you all an opportunity, not to take part in what I am proposing to do. You can go your own way and try to hide. All of us, including the civilians, cannot use our banks, credit cards, passports even our cars without triggering an alarm. That would result in a wet team, being sent to kill you. You can't go to your homes or the homes of your friends and families. The Catherine May cannot be seen without the risk of it being destroyed. All of this, is because of this Barrel of stuff, that was stolen by the man we work for. The rest of the world probably believes that we intend to use it either for financial gain or to cause World War Three."

I let that set in and then told them part of my plan. If that part worked then I would tell them what I would be doing, but only after I had completed the first piece of my plan. If it failed, we would all be dead anyway. So it would be of no consequence and would be moot.

"Tomorrow along with one volunteer, I intend to open the barrel to see what its contents are. I will be opening it inside the lighthouse building. Where there is no wind. If it is filled with Radioactive Plutonium or Uranium, then our Advanced NBC Suits should protect us long enough for me to replace the top. If it is filled with Biological material, then our suits MAY protect us. They will not protect you, assuming that the contents inside are in damaged containers from the rough handling that the barrel has suffered recently. If the contents are in SAFE and undamaged containers, then we will be fine. I am told that most Biological material made for armaments are either in fragile, thin plastic vials or glass ones. Assuming they are not damaged there will be no immediate danger to us or for that matter to the world. I can't call anyone to help us, without them sending people immediately, to kill all of us."

It was quiet before. But now the silence was palpable, so much so that the other noise of the sea blocked out even my thoughts for a moment.

"I will volunteer" Jane put her hand up as if she was in a classroom at school.

"Be very sure, because if I am wrong either way, if it is Uranium or some futuristic form of Ebola in a damaged container. Then we will die. It will only be a question of how long and how painful, that death is."

"I am sure Andy. A lot of this is my fault."

"The only person who can bear the full blame is Marcus Brown. So now you all need to decide what you want to do. I will give you all until tomorrow. If you want to leave then go, if you want to help. Then stay. The only chance any of us have of getting out of this alive, is to stop this entire operation, which is being carried out against our Country. Now we have had a busy few days, get some sleep. Tonight no one will shoot at us."

Lachie came over to me with Hans and Abdalla.

"You intend to destroy it somehow don't you?"

"Yes I think so, and we will need to figure out a way to do that, without a laboratory."

ACT 57

I woke in the morning, washed myself in the sea water. I even shaved. Rosemary and Abdalla were up before me and had been to the Catherine May and made a big pan of porridge and again a bucket of coffee. I ate mine and even had a second bowl. I now needed to know who was staying and who was going. I finished up my breakfast and loaded up the Zodiac with Two blue ANBC suits along with a bag of tools. Then it was time to ask, the big question.

"OK folks you have had a night to sleep on it. I will not force anyone to stay, but I have to ask you to tell me now. Are you staying or are you going?"

My gaze fell upon Lachie first. I knew he would stand by my side until death. That was just his way. He was my true friend, who asked nothing in return except honesty. If I was entirely truthful, I hoped they would all say that they were going as that would make my task a lot easier. Lachie's eyes locked with mine.

"I am surprised you felt you had to ask me. Besides I am

a Rock Ape and this is a Rock"

Abdalla the consummate soldier, he stood as always proud and tall, a Kenyan tribal elder who became a soldier, to protect his country from terrorists, both from within and without his homeland. This was not truly his fight. The soldier in him was telling him, you never leave a man behind. He had promised me his allegiance. His moral compass would not allow him to break that.

"Mr Andy I will stay" He said

Hans only wanted right to win over wrong. Like Abdalla he too was a soldier to the core and would stand back to back until there was no fight to be won or lost.

"I am proud to be a member of your team Andy. Team Seven will always fight until the end"

These men were my brothers in arms, they would stand with me not just as my friends, rather they would stand with me as a matter of duty. We would stand together until there was no blood in our veins to power our hearts and bodies.

The civilians and I had included Jane within that as she had never seen or been on a battlefield, excluding Altnabreac. I knew she was staying out of a sense of correcting the wrongs she had committed against her country and those she had committed against her friends. Also on a personal level against me. Because Jane was staying her father would stay and stand beside his daughter. Out of a fathers love and to avenge the death of his wife. That then left Sandy, Stuart and Rosemary. I would expect them to take the Catherine May and try to make a run for it perhaps find some remote Island or find fuel and make it to Iceland and claim political asylum. But I asked them all anyway.

"Sandy, are you in or out?"

"We are all in?"

"By all you mean Stuart and Rosemary as well"

"Aye that's right."

I looked at Rosemary with her arm linked into Stuarts. She was a beautiful young woman. I prayed a silent prayer for them to have the life they deserved.

"Is there anyone who wishes to leave? I will not think less of you. Every one of you has shown yourself to be extremely brave, in the face of exceptional danger. Loyalties have been challenged and expectations have been surpassed by all of you. If this goes as planned, then we will have just a chance at some kind of life afterwards. It will not be the life you would have chosen. But it will be a life. More importantly billions of others will have their chance of life. They will never know of the details. If we do this and we manage to stop it all. This will never be reported in the newspapers. None of us will be public heroes. All of you are heroes to me. I need one other volunteer to take Jane and me around to the other side of the Island."

"That's my job then" Lachie stepped forward.

"OK Mate it is good to have you at my back. I want everyone else on the Catherine May before we go. If we are not back by night fall, you will know we are not coming back. If that happens, then Hans you will be in charge and it will be your choice of where and how to run. If that happens, I want you all to trust his abilities as a leader. That's it, finish your coffee and Lachie will take you all over to the boat."

"Mr Andy. What about your dog?" Abdalla enquired

"Kyla will come with me. I trust her nose to be better than mine."

ACT 58

Lachie ferried all the rest of our group to the Catherine May and then came back for Jane, Kyla and myself. Jane and I put the ANBC Suits over our Nomex, leaving just the helmets off. We would put them on only when I was going to open the barrel. After clambering into the Zodiac, I whistled for Kyla and she jumped in. Lachie carefully reversed the motors and then turned the RIB around. Then we left the darkness of the cave, back out into the open waters of the North Atlantic. It was another glorious day. The sea was like a millpond and not a breath of wind. There was a slight frost in the air. Breathing pure crisp air into my lungs, for what might be the last time. I savoured its freshness. I smelt the salt of the sea. I don't know if there is ever a good day to die. But it was not a bad one. Lachie gunned the three Honda engines into full life and the bow of our Zodiac lifted free of the water, its wash and wake spreading out in white lines fanning out from the stern. I felt the spray of the salty water on my face, along with the wind created by our speeding boat. It was refreshing and I suppose I must have been smiling. Jane looked at me with the same look, I had seen back at Sandside. I felt that spark of emotion, pull at both my heart and my mind. All too soon we approached the pathway along the cliffs. Lachie let the motors run down to idle and we coasted to the shoreline.

I stepped off and pulled the bow line bring the nose of the Zodiac onto the rocks at the foot of the cliff face. Jane passed me the backpacks one at a time. Then she jumped down on to the shore. I whistled for Kyla and she bounded out of the boat. Her tail, erect and curled up on her back, wagging back and forth.

"Lachie Come back and pick us up at four p.m. If we are not back by four, take off and join the others. If you see my dad again, tell him I have always loved him not just as my father but as my friend. The same applies to you mate you are like a brother to me. Thanks for everything."

"I will mate Áitichairson mo charaid A-nis bidh sinn a 'coinneachadh a-rithist."

"And goodbye to you my friend and we will meet again, as you say Lachie" I replied in translation.

"Remember Lachie be here at four on the dot."

"I will be here."

We waved and headed up the path with me at the front, Kyla in the middle and Jane bringing up the rear. It was private now so I could talk openly with Jane.

"What sort of relationship do you have with this Marcus fella?"

"I thought he loved me to begin with. He used to take me to fancy hotels for meals and tell me how I was headed for great things in the SIS. I even ran some operations myself, under his supervision of course. I felt that I was needed and that I had a sense of belonging. I was doing good things, or so I thought. I knew he was married and he told me that when this operation was over we would have a wonderful life together and that we would never have to work again. We could go anywhere and be anything we wanted to be. I admit now that I was worse than a silly little schoolgirl. I know you don't trust me any more and I don't blame you either. I do want you to trust me and I know that can't happen overnight. I guess he selected me in the same way as he selects everyone. He would say, get this person, because they have this weakness, or they will do anything for money or power. Some people he would help get into powerful positions. Then he would ask for favours in return or ask them to look the other way, lose a file or other things like that. He said that the SIS, is like a multi-dimensional and complicated game. You would allow someone to make a play on the level and then trap their piece from below. I think I did love him to begin with and I was also infatuated with his power. I thought he was doing good things. I was wrong. I think I knew he was bad, a long time ago but would then convince myself that I was wrong, and he was right, because he was an experienced high level man in our countries intelligence service. I know I am directly responsible for the deaths of quite a few people and that I could have been responsible for all of our deaths."

"How do I know I can trust you?"

"I don't know, but I will do anything you ask. I know that this is much bigger than us. Just tell me what you want me to do."

"Soon Jane, we have something that we have to do together."

We walked on and up to the lighthouse. The Chopper appeared at first sight, to be a grassy knoll near the light house buildings. The camouflage would suffice from a distance. Then I heard it, a long time before I saw it, that unmistakable double whoop, coming from the twin rotors, of a Chinook heavy helicopter.

"Quick Jane, run for that knoll"

I ran as fast as I could, literally running for our lives. I got to the knoll first with Kyla and lifted up the edge of the tarpaulin and slid under. I held it open so that Jane could get under.

"Did they see us?"

"I don't know Jane, we are pretty visible in these bright blue suits."

The Chopper had come in at sea level, and I only hoped that by us being higher than they were that their line of sight was blocked by the high sheer cliff face. The chopper sounded a lot closer, almost overhead, and then the sound receded. We stayed where we were for about another thirty minutes, just in case they or others came back. I had automatically put my arm over Jane's shoulders in protection. I realised my arm was around her and withdrew. I lifted the tarpaulin and could hear nothing. And I could see nothing. I guessed that they were searching for us and were looking at all the possible places where we could hide out. I was sure that Lachie would have been back with the others long before the chopper did its fly by.

"Time to go, Jane."

We walked to the lighthouse door and entered the narrow hallway where the Barrel was standing.

After taking off my back pack I helped Jane off with hers. Then I rolled out the tool kit I had borrowed from Lachie.

"What now? Andy"

"Now we see how trust works."

"I don't follow?"

"You will Jane, you will. Put your mask on and connect your O2 bottle, then put your gloves and boots on."

We both finished getting into the last parts of our ANBC suits. I connected up my own O2. Then I took a seven-pound mallet and a two-inch cold chisel from the toolkit.

"Jane, hold the barrel steady. I am going to remove the clamp that holds the top on."

"Why Andy, why do this?"

"Because I have to know Jane, I have to know about you, and I have to know about what we have been risking our lives for."

"OK what do you want me to do?"

"Just hold the barrel and watch your heads up display. If it is radioactive Uranium, then your RAD Count will go all the way into the red. If this is Biological and any part is exposed, then the green meter at the bottom of your display will issue a WARNING sign by flashing red letters on a green background. If that happens, then we put the lid back on and I shoot you, Kyla and then me. Because any biological material will be on our suits and we don't have a proper decontamination booth. I am not going to risk the lives of the others. Lachie knows what to so if we are not back by night fall. Jane this is not a joke. And there is no getting out of this.

"Can we not just hide it again Andy?"

"And risk some Sheppard finding it or a maintenance crew for the lighthouse, no Jane that is not an option. It is just you me and of course Kyla. Please hold the barrel. If I am wrong about this, then a bullet will be a better death, than being killed by anything that is in there."

"Andy I am scared."

"Me too Jane, I am bricking it. It has to be done. It has to be us."

With trembling hands I placed the cold chisel on the latch for the lid

"Hold on to the barrel as hard as you can"

She did and I looked at her through my mask. Tears streamed down her face. And she mouthed I Love You. I hit the clasp as hard as I could and metal band holding the top shot off. Jane jumped back. The read out on my suits heads up display showed no change from before. I tapped the edge of the lid with the chisel and it gave easily.

"Time to find out, what the future holds for us? Shall we lift the lid off together?"

Jane said nothing but she stepped forward and placed both her gloved hands on the lid. I did the same.

"On three Jane, One…. Two…. three."

The lid came up and off. I held on to it and laid it down against the wall of the corridor. I looked inside. There was a polished stainless steel framework inside, with a thick polystyrene layer all the way around the barrel. In the steel frame, there were approximately one hundred long, thin glass or clear plastic cylinders. Each one was filled with a purple liquid or gel. There was still no reading from my heads up display. I picked the lid up from the floor and put it back on top. Then I removed my hood and mask. Kayla followed me as I walked back out into the beautiful sunlight of the day.

Jane joined me a few moments later. She had also removed her hood and mask. She came and stood by Kyla and faced me.

"Did I pass the trust test?"

"It was not just about trust Jane. I wanted to know if you knew what exactly was in there. You didn't I could tell from your eyes. You also gasped when you saw it. You knew some had been stolen but you were never told how much. Also if I had to die today it was going to be with a beautiful woman."

"So you were not going to shoot me then?"

"If there had been a single broken vial in there? Then yes I would have shot all three of us on the spot."

I took out the Sig Sauer that I had been tucked into my utility belt, behind my back and released the hammer.

"Jane if this is the stuff that they were talking about on the first day I was at CDE. Then this is a doomsday weapon. This, if used on a country would kill all the people and animals within an hour and then the virus would die and an army could just walk in and take over a country."

"So what are you going to do with it?"

"Destroy it?"

"How?"

"At this point I don't know. Let's get out of these suits they are too damn hot to wear on a day like today."

ACT 59

I started to strip down to my Nomex and Jane did the same. I looked at her body in the figure hugging Nomex. If ever there was a military uniform that made a slim woman look good it was Nomex. It had been designed not to have any loose parts that could get snagged, on a branch or a wire. It was like a tough Lycra outfit. She turned away from me when getting out of he ANBC and I could not stop myself from imagining her naked here on the grass of this Island. I reached over and touched her arm, and she stood up with a start.

"Sorry I did not mean to frighten you."

"That's OK I am just a little nervous after seeing that stuff."

I pulled her to me and kissed her passionately on the lips, pulling her so close that the Nomex barely seemed to be between our bodies. My fingers ran down the outside of her back, tracing a line from the nape of her neck, to the top of her buttocks. Then I reached down and held one firmly in my hand I pulled her upwards towards me, and then I reached down with my other and took the other buttock. I lifted her up and her legs wrapped around me. We stripped off and made love, right there on the top of the Island. After our orgasms she turned me on to my back I made to move and she put her hand on my chest.

"We have plenty of time yet. Let's stay here naked for a while. The world could end tomorrow, but for now let's be natural. We don't need our clothes on for another two hours yet. I want to enjoy the free feeling now."

"If we stay like this for ten minutes I will want to make love to you, I want to have you again. Jane."

"Mmmmm that sounds wonderful."

Time had stood still for us. I walked over to where the Chopper was hidden under the tarpaulin and took one of the water bottles that were in the main cabin of it. I walked back over to Jane and we shared the bottle as a shower wash. Then we dressed and kissed deeply again.

"I have never known a woman who gives herself so completely during sex Jane."

"Why should a woman not like the physical and emotional act of lovemaking as much as a man?"

"You have a good point there, Jane. Just I have never met anyone who is honest about sex as you are."

"Andy you know it's not just sex between us? There is something else there. I know it is not just a physical thing. There is an emotional bond there as well. I feel that bond Andy."

"I know Jane."

ACT 60

I looked down at my Omega SeaMaster it was almost three thirty in the afternoon.

"We have to get going, Lachie will be waiting."

I picked up my back pack and then helped Jane with hers. She reached for my hand and I took it as we walked back down to the pathway to the shore. Lachie was just arriving when we got there. We climbed on board the Zodiac with Kyla and Lachie just smiled and said nothing. I was not sure but I think I may have blushed.

"Home James, and don't spare the Horses" I said in a fake posh English accent

He turned the Zodiac around and we headed back of around to the other side of the Island and into the cave and up to the beach.

I got out and pulled the Zodiac up on to the dry ground, then helped Jane out of the boat. Lachie tied it off, to the old jetty. We walked across to the others and sat down on the sand. Rosemary passed coffee around to us all.

"Did you hear the Chinook?" Hans asked

"Yes I think we managed to get out of sight just in time." I sipped my coffee and continued.

"Lachie did you manage to get back before the chopper buzzed the Island?"

"Yes mate I was having a coffee here when it flew over."

"I would say that they went on the message, that Jane sent them and that they are checking all the uninhabited islands, anywhere north of Scrabster all the way up to Iceland. So we will have to be ultra-careful when up on the top. The same applies to going out of the cave in the Zodiac. I would also guess at some point they will actually send boats to check the Islands."

Then came the question I was dreading and waiting for, it came from the most unlikely person in the group. Rosemary, she seemed to have grown and matured in the few days that we had been with her.

"Did you find out what is in the Barrel?"

"We did. But I need to talk with Abdalla, Lachie, Jane and Hans first, before I can discuss it with you Rosemary. I know we are all in this together, but you have to realise that this is still a military operation. I will tell you when the time is right and I hope that you will understand that."

She started to say something else but stopped when her father put his hand over hers and gave it a gentle squeeze.

"What's for dinner?" I asked

Rosemary's face brightened up. She had taken it upon herself to be the Head Cook and Mother Hen, to our little band of warriors. This was a good thing not only because she was a very good cook, but because it gave her lots to do and filled her time, which helped to stop her worrying, about all the other stuff that was going on. Her father said that she learned to cook from her mother, who had been a chef to some member of the Royal Family. She had even worked at Mey Castle, for the Queen Mother. So Rosemary had learned which herbs and spices to use with different meat or fish dishes. Tonight would be no exception.

"Tonight we have Fisherman's Pie, served with Creamed Duchess potatoes and Samphire."

Samphire is a succulent plant that grows around the shores of Britain and many other countries. Some people refer to it as Sea Asparagus, because it has a similar taste and texture to it. Personally I loved the taste of it.

"Fantastic, Rosemary really looking forward to it. Now I need to talk to my military friends."

I called my team together and we moved away from the rest of our party.

"I need to talk to you about this barrel. As all you know, I have had my suspicions about the contents of the barrel. I went and opened it today. And yes before anyone says it, I know I could have killed all of us by doing so. I made an executive decision. I was not prepared to ask any of you to do something, that would later come back and bite us on the arse, and that I was not personally willing to do myself. So I just went ahead and did it. I can tell you that it is no way radioactive. Nor does it contain the items required to make any form of atomic bomb or missile. We have followed the wrong leads, which were laid our for us like breadcrumbs. This was done so that we would make our own a cock and bull story. We have also been working for the wrong master. I personally have killed an innocent man because of all this. I have been complicit in the killing of other innocent men. We do not actually work for the British Government per sé. We are actually working for a rogue senior agent of the SIS. The man we originally suspected in this 'The Suit' and 'The Lady,' are in fact working to get this item back. However, we can't just roll up and say oops sorry, here is you missing weapon of mass destruction, let's all be friends again. What I believe to be the truth is, that there is an international mandate to recover this item. It is made up of members of the UN and other friendly states. The person known as 'The Man', who I now know to be called Mr Marcus Brown, he is the current head of the SIS. He used the Black Door operations, to first steal and then to take the items, up here to Scotland. The first team he used either wanted more money or they were going to steal the item and sell it on to unknown parties. He had a wet work team take them out. Unfortunately for him he did not know the exact location, other than it was somewhere around Dounreay. I suspect that the Arab that Dusty saw was really from Qatar, and not as Jane was told. Qatar is one of the friendly nations, who were afraid that this would fall into the hands of a nearby, not so friendly nation. The USA Embassy involvement, probably indicates that the CIA are involved. The same would apply to Israel, they had even managed to get a Mosad agent onto our team. Unbeknown to them he was also an infiltrator from a hostile nation. Fortunately, when he tried to take us out, Kyla manage to get in first. Both 'The Man' and 'The Suit' have laid a trail of bread crumbs for us to follow, both of them for alternative reasons. Quasim and his friend were both part of a wet work team, sent to take us out and retrieve the barrel by 'The Man'. The 'Suit' is using UK agents and independent contractors from various Black Op agencies farmed out by SIS, CIA, MOSAD and probably several other letters of the alphabet in the intelligence communities from our allies. 'The Man', used Rosemary to get to us. 'The Suit' used Dusty to get at Jane. All the information about Lachie and me, that was in our records, including that I had lived in Keiss. It would not have taken much to find out that I used to go to school with friends from here. Or to find out that Sandy knew Lachie's parents. Every single thing we were told, was back to front. The orders as they stand regarding us, at the moment and I mean internationally. Is a Shoot to kill policy. We are wanted by everyone. We are also wanted, by the bad guys who were originally planning to buy the stuff, that is in the barrel and they got shafted. Jane previously was working for 'The Suit' and then 'The Man' until recently though she was working for Marcus Brown. Before you all get bent out of shape about her continually changing sides. Bear in mind she was being played as well. She was a willing participant at the start. However, her mother died as a result of this. She no longer has any loyalties to either 'The Suit' or Marcus Brown. Her loyalties are completely with us. I understand some of you, who may question this, but I tested those loyalties today, she was with me when we opened up that barrel. I can tell you had any of the contents been damaged we would not be having this conversation now. Now for the sixty-four-thousand-dollar question that you all have. What is in the Barrel? It has around one hundred vials of a purple liquid or gel, locked into a solid stainless steel frame. This is why the barrel was so damn heavy. The contents, which I believe to be some form of Bacteriological weapon, probably the nastiest of the nasty. When we were at CDE Porton Down, and as I have said before, we were told of something that was made from a highly dangerous form of Ebola type Virus, which had been genetically modified, with an extremely strong version of a Furanocoumarins. This works not just as a blistering agent but when the DNA was modified and then combined with the other nasty bits. It then allows the modified Ebola type bug, to attack a singular organ, like some strains of the meningitis. This bug directly attacks the membrane of the brain, resulting in an extremely painful and nasty death. So this nasty bastard kills by turning the brain to liquid and then in a matter of hours the bug itself dies. What we have is enough stuff to wipe out entire countries, if used as a vapour or a mist. Now I need to hear what you think we should do."

"Run very fucking fast" That was Lachie

"Seriously though, please."

"Andy! Seriously we all need to run really fucking fast!!!"

"You say we can't give it back to them Andy?" Hans asked

"No Hans we can't, because we are on a hit list just for having it. We go anywhere near them they will kill us. As far as 'The Suit' is concerned we are working for and with Marcus Brown."

"Can't we call the Americans, and have them collect it? They are our allies."

"No because our country does not want the Americans to have it either. They want to keep it for themselves. I doubt that they have told the Americans as to what it truly is. They will be perpetuating the Uranium story to all our allies. Plus, the CIA ergo the USA also wants to eradicate us."

"Mr Andy. Can we destroy it?" Abdalla asked

"Abdalla I think for that we would require a battlefield Atomic weapon. Something like, a low yield Tactical Nuclear bomb. And we have a nice arsenal of hand held weapons, but we are severely lacking, in the nukes state." I replied.

"Is there any way at all that we can get out of this alive?" Hans asked

"None, I can think of Hans."

It was Jane that really laid it out for us.

"The thing that puts us and anyone else in danger, is the contents of that barrel. The British government want it back and they don't want any other Country, to know what it is. All the other Countries want it, so they can either replicate it, save it or use it as a weapon. That also includes our so called allies. We can't hide it, in case someone discovers it. So that leaves us with one choice, we destroy it, here on this Island and we all die. Better that than billions of people. The weather forecast for the coming days is that the wind will drop. Which is good, because then it will not carry to other lands. If it has an air life of an hour or so, it seems to me we have to destroy it." Jane looked terrified as she said it. She knew it was not just her life but her father's life.

"How do we tell the others and what if they don't want to stay?" Lachie asked to no one in particular.

We sat quiet and sullen. Jane was right, we could not chance it getting into any hands. The British government had breached the Geneva Convention. They knew this was not something that you could send out a cure for, because anyone exposed to it would be dead in under an hour from exposure, probably a lot less than an hour. They would kill, even if they got it back, because they would know, we knew what it was. Any of us who went out into the world at this point. Would no doubt have a heavy price on our heads? There was no safe haven for us.

ACT 61

"What about a Thermobaric Explosion?" Abdalla said

"A what? What in the name of God is that?"

"Mr Andy. It would be the next best thing to a Tactical Nuclear Weapon. Something that gets so hot that it burns everything including nasty shit bugs. Some people wrongly call them Vacuum Bombs. Because first they explode and then they burn all the oxygen around them and then they suck in more air to create an even hotter fire. They are a bit like a Fuel Air Bomb, except they use less explosive. You have to generate enough heat in the middle of the bomb to super heat the fuel and then you explode that and the fuel, which can be Petrol or Diesel, turns from a liquid to a super-heated vapour and the very air, catches fire. The oxygen in the air burns, like it was a fuel."

"Abdalla Are you sure that would kill all the germs?"

"Mr Andy. If we build it correctly, it will kill anything that is even close to it, and by close to it, is a relative thing. Depending on the size that could be as far away as one or two miles. The Americans tried using Napalm and that was good but this is way, way better. And Yes I think it will kill everything within five hundred yards, perhaps as much as a mile. The down side, is that it will be seen and probably felt a long way away. It will give our position away."

"Tell us more about how we could manufacture such a weapon with just the resources we have."

"Mr Andy. First I think we should eat and then we should talk to your friends, we should tell them the dangerous position we are all in. Also if we do it, could we convince the SIS to remove the Kill order on us? Because if not what is the point."

We walked back over with a conspirator's silence. The food Rosemary had completed on board the Catherine May. Was beautiful the fish pie was made from lobster and crab, white meat in a thick and creamy sauce, with a flaky pie covering. The duchess potatoes made from mashed potatoes and piped in swirls, then oven cooked until the tops were browned. The Samphire was lightly steamed and then tossed in butter. In short, this may have been cooked on board and in old fishing boat's galley. But it was presented and tasted as good, as any meal I had had from a five-star restaurant. We all chatted amicably about the things we enjoyed doing, and some of the things, we would like to do in the future. I tried not to dwell too much on that part of the conversation, knowing the subject, we would be talking about after dinner.

"I think that meal calls for a wee dram" Sandy said and seemingly out of nowhere produced a bottle of Glenfiddich fifteen-year-old single malt. Unlike the normal Glenfiddich single malt whisky, this was not in the easily recognisable Green bottle. This was in a clear glass bottle with a brown label instead of the normal Green Label. We rinsed our cups in the sea and dried them off and Sandy poured a good measure for everyone. The entire bottle was used up, even Abdalla accepted a drink.

"To what shall we drink?" I asked Sandy

He sat deep in thought for a long time and then said

"We should drink to a world of peace"

"That's a great toast Sandy, sìth an t-saoghail"

"A world of peace" everyone said and Lachie also added "sìth an t-saoghail" as I had done in the Scots Gaelic.

"Now we need to talk to everyone, as we have to make a decision that will affect us all. As you all know, there are dangers, from which at the moment, none of us can escape. Some of what has been going on, you may well have guessed correctly. Some of it you will have no knowledge of. It will be a difficult choice for all of you to make. We five have already made our choice. Not that we really had a choice. In my honest opinion, no one here, had a choice in anything that has happened to them so far. This is the one thing. that you will have a choice in. What I will shortly tell you, will frighten you. There will be two choices for you. One is to stay with us and see this through to the end. The other is for you to cut and run. If you chose the latter, we cannot protect you. There is an almost certainty, that without our protection, you will be killed by someone within forty-eight hours. We have already had a cursory fly over. But soon men with boats and guns will come. I just wanted you to know what the situation is."

I sipped my drink and prepared to tell them, of all the things we knew and had discovered over the past days. The Idea that I had broken the Official Secrets Act now seemed superfluous. The only thing that mattered was, could we destroy this evil and could we get our lives back, or at least some semblance of them.

"I am going to let you talk about it amongst yourselves. Jane you can stay, as it concerns you and your father. I am going to talk with Lachie, Hans, and Abdalla."

I wandered over to the Jetty with the three other military men, who I now thought of as my close friends. I knew that they would have each other's backs and that they looked out for me, in the knowledge that they were combat trained men and I was not. We were nonetheless true brothers in life and in arms.

We sat down on the coarse sand next to the broken down jetty.

"Abdalla You said something about a Thermobaric device or bomb? Do we have the materials to build it? If so will it work for sure?"

"Mr Andy."

Abdalla had taken to calling me that, I took it as some form of respect. He continued.

"Your question has three parts to it. So I will take it one

part at a time. First a Thermobaric device or bomb, is as its name would suggest. It gets its name from a combination of two Greek words, 'Thermo' meaning to heat and 'Baric' meaning to apply pressure. So a Thermobaric device applies great heat and pressure at the same time. In order to do the first, we must have fire and in order to do the second part we have to apply pressure from an explosion. On paper it is probably a very simple thing to produce. But to produce one that will supply, a super intense heat and pressure might prove to be a bit harder. To move on to the second part. Most Thermobaric devices rely on liquid fuel as the main part of the explosive and heat. Some are entirely made from just fuel. Some are a mixture of fuel and explosives. Yet some others are fuel triggered by explosives. We need to supply a concussive blast to shatter the vials whilst at the same time or almost instantaneously generate a heat so hot that it will turn everything within a minimum 500 hundred yards to ash. If we can generate a pressure wave of about four hundred and fifty pounds per square inch we could theoretically obtain a fire air temperature of somewhere between four thousand, five hundred degrees, up to five thousand, five hundred degrees Fahrenheit. Or if you want that put into context almost twice the boiling point of molten steel. So on to the second part of your question. Do we have the materials to make such a device. The short answer to that is yes we do, although most of it will require some modification. We have the main ingredient which is Petrol and Diesel. We have some air tanks that can be used as pressurised fuel tanks where we can actually heat the fuel inside to an explosive point. It is how we heat this and the control of this that we will have trouble with. We have some claymore mines that contain C4 explosive so we can create a shaped charge. We would require a triggering mechanism that explodes everything towards the centre. If we could build a framework, that would allow all this. Then yes we can make such a device. Finally, to the last part of your question Mr Andy. If, and it is a big If. If we can make it work as a Thermobaric device, then yes it will kill every living thing, in the blast radius. It will become a sterile zone. Even the ground below the crater that it will create, for tens of metres will be sterile."

"Wow. Where the hell do you learn things like this?"

"Mr Andy, I study all weapons. I am not just an expert

on firearms. I just happen to excel with a rifle."

"What do you think Hans?"

"I have seen them used on training films, I think they are similar to the ones, they use to clear underground structures. The fire rushes outwards but then, as the fire burns its own oxygen. There is so much heat, that the very air itself burns So much so, that it requires more oxygen and it sucks the fire back in, as an inward fireball. It is this part that is the most destructive. I say that we at least try. What have we to lose? We will be dead anyway"

"Yes you are correct Mr Hans."

"Lachie?"

"Andy we are friends yet you still need to ask me?"

"I know we are friends, but I don't want you to do it for me. You have to make the choice for you"

"I say HELL YES. Rock Apes DO what the rest of the RAF only dream of doing."

"So is everyone in agreement, that we make this super fireball thing?"

They all nodded their ascent.

"OK We have made our choice, let's see what the others have chosen to do. Then we tell them what we need and ask for their help to build it. I say we put Abdalla in charge of making it and we just help him. We don't question him, what he says goes and gets done."

We walked back to join the others. The mood had changed since we had our drink, after the dinner Rosemary had made for us.

"Have you had enough time to discuss all that we have told you? And have you made a choice? If so is it the choice of all of you?"

Sandy stood up and looked around at Jane, Rosemary, Stuart and Dusty. The all nodded at him

"Aye, we have Andy."

"And?"

"We have decided to stay with you and to trust your judgement. If we die it is by OUR CHOICE and not by theirs. If you need our help just ask"

My eyes glazed as I thought about these people, who had been pulled into this in order to entrap others, to doing the bidding of either Marcus Brown, or 'The Suit' from SIS. The people here were good people, ordinary people, innocent people. They had survived extraordinary circumstances. My heart was with them all. I let my tears fall openly. They say that greater love has no man, than he lays down his life for his fellow men. These innocent people were willing to lay down their lives, for people they did not even know, and who would never know of their courage, or sacrifice. If I were going to die, it could be with none better. I wiped my face on my sleeve. Cleared my throat and continued

"Thank you. We do have a bit of a plan and Abdalla will be in charge of it, whatever he asks for, please just do it. We may yet survive this. So let's work together. Tonight rest. Tomorrow we begin"

ACT 62

I went over and sat down beside Jane the light from the Tilley lamp shone from under her face and made her face look sad and gaunt. She had every reason to be sad. We laid our sleeping bags down next to each other. She drifted off to an uneasy sleep. I lay awake for hours, with thoughts of what if, running around my mind. We would be offering ourselves up as sacrificial lambs, in a war of which country would create the deadliest Virus, Bacteria or Chemical and then hope that the other side, did not have an even worse bug in some doomsday battle. I knew this went on, even long before I went to CDE Porton Down. Although I have to say I never understood. We had an Arms race first to see who could have the most Nuclear Bombs. Then they decided once we had enough to destroy the world a thousand times over, that enough was enough. So all the big nations sat down and said, that they would decommission X amount from Y amount and end up with Z amount. The truth was probably a long way from Y minus X Equals Z. It would probably be Z equals what Y used to equal, less just a few. Now the race was on for the most destructive short term mass killer, that they could produce. Even though the majority of those countries, who were still manufacturing these banned microscopic murderers, were signatories to the Geneva Convention that banned the use of them. It also banned the stockpiling of them. They were according to the non proliferation treat that they had signed up to, supposed to destroy them. But it did not ban them from making them. This makes it, a real back to front treaty. Because the crazy countries, who would actually first strike using them, were some of the North Africa dictatorships and some of the more fundamentalist and extremist, Middle Eastern Countries. It was the Regan administration, who through Donald Rumsfeld, that actually supported Saddam, against the Kurds and helped him to build his chemical arsenal. Rumsfeld who at the time was an executive of a 'Pharmaceutical Industry' that allowed Saddam, to source from American Suppliers, Anthrax and Bubonic Plague. The CIA at the time used a Chilean front company to arrange for Cluster bombs, to be sent to Saddam. The USA also shipped dozens of Biological agents under a licence from The Commerce Department. The USA was not alone in this. Many European countries were also complicit in one way or another. Back then it was just a simple question of the enemy of my enemy is my friend syndrome. Some say it was far simpler than that. That it was about Oil. Some even more cynical folks said, that it had more to do with the profits, that a war would make for companies involved in the supply, of weapons and hardware. Companies that definitely profited were the likes of Halliburton and Black Forest who worked covertly for the CIA some individuals made literally Billions. Bush, Cheney and many more. War is Big Business. So selling the likes of what we had, in the container, would not be worth just a few million. It would be a game changer in armed conflict. As such it would be valued in the thousands of billions, or even the tens of Trillions. People kill for a lot less than four figures. What we had was something in the region of a number with twelve zeroes'. So our lives, to the people in charge of our country were worth less than, that of a gnat.

The next day we woke to a mini spring heat wave. We

breakfasted and then busied ourselves, while Abdalla spent most of the morning cooped up inside the wheelhouse of the Catherine May, making drawings and working calculations on the back of Sandy's sea charts. I know, I did not sleep much and I doubted if Abdalla had slept at all. The only time he stopped was at sunrise to say his prayers. It was Friday. A day when Abdalla, should have been in the Mosque, however Abdalla believed that so long as he said his prayers, Allah would understand that he was working for the good of mankind, He had told me previously that he had Joined the Kenyan Army as a boy, in order to protect innocent people from being killed by extremists. He later became a Tribal elder. He was a soldier but he was a soldier with strong morals. He was a Muslim that believed in his God, but he was also a worldly man, just the right combination of faith and common sense. We would be pinning all of our hopes and aspirations on the plan that Abdalla had come up with. Perhaps, I wondered if he was not just holding our lives in his hands, but that of a large portion of the world. It was a lot of pressure for one man to bear. Yet I had never seen him angry. If he disagreed with you he would say so, but not in an aggressive or an argumentative way. He would tell you the benefits of his side and show you the comparisons to whatever it was you were trying to do or say. He would have made a great politician. I felt that we were blessed to have him with us. Lachie my friend who was strong and bold, he would give his life in the blink of an eye to save a friend. He would always find a funny side in anything even in this, Lachie was a comedian and could even see the funny side of death. Hans who possessed a great analytical mind he taught survival, and was also a pilot, as well as being a great soldier. If we were to live through all this, then one day he would probably be a great statesman or a leader of NATO. Men respected him. Then back to Abdalla, who I would have chosen to lead us in anything, he had lots of battlefield experience. He knew when to fight and when to hide. Most of all though, he knew how to fight, using guerrilla wars. Hit and run. He would never give up on anything he believed in. Today he would have us build a device that would destroy the abomination that CDE Porton Down had created. Created no doubt at the behest of our government. The same government, who would fight other nations, for daring to try and make their own weapons of mass destruction. It was a double standard world, where first world countries, were allowed to break the Geneva convention. They in turn would condemn third world countries, which attempted to make, such weapons, even though these third world countries, were not signed up to the treaty. It was not about world justice it was about world power and being a bully. This was in order, for first world countries to remain at the top of the woodpile. We, that is, the Governments and not the people, of first world nations, had to keep the third world, as the third world.

I had a plan for the civilians in our group, that hopefully would keep them busy when not helping us. Building our thermobaric device, strangely enough, another weapon of mass destruction. This one though, would be used to destroy the other. I walked over to where Sandy was talking to Stu.

"Sandy, can I have a quick word please?"

"Sure you can Andy. What can I do for you?"

"You know that set of steps that go up from the jetty and then suddenly stop?"

"Yes."

"Do you think that you could get Stu, Dusty and Rosemary to help you to dig it out at the top. I am sure that it must lead to the surface of this Island."

"I am positive we could, mind telling me, why you want us to do it now?"

"Two reasons mate. One is it would keep you all busy and take your minds off the situation we have found ourselves in. The second reason is that it provides us with an alternate escape route if required."

"We don't have much in the way of tools. Just a couple of iron bars, that we use for freeing up machinery on the boat."

"See what you can do Sandy, judging by the height of this cave there could not be more than ten feet to the surface. It may be rocks or just soil that has blocked the exit. When Jane is finished doing what she is doing. Can you send her over to me please?"

"Will do and I will get Stuart and Dusty and we will get right on working on the entrance."

"Thanks sandy."

I walked back across the coarse sandy little beach to the

Jetty, where Lachie and Hans were waiting.

"I have another addition to the plan that we have made. At the moment we only have one way out of here, and that is by boat. Then up to the surface of the Island by using the cliff pathway. We need to give ourselves a backup plan. We have a helicopter which can take us all, if we leave behind most of the equipment. In order for that, we need to move the chopper from the blast zone, closer to this side of the Island. I have asked Sandy and the other men to try and dig up through to the surface from the cave. I think those steps once came out on top. The chopper is also the fastest way away from the Island."

"That's not a bad Idea Andy. People working hard don't worry as much. I will go with Lachie if you work with Abdalla. We should be gone for about an hour as we have to take the camouflage off the chopper first."

"I have asked Jane to come over and help us, take her with you as Lachie will need some help, moving the tarp. Then if you can cover the chopper again when it if relocated. See if you can set it down as close to where you think the top of this cave is."

"My shoulder is fine Andy, I can manage."

"I am sure you think it is Lachie, I don't tell you how to defend an air base. So trust me on medical matters."

"Point taken I will be careful and take things slow."

"So Jane goes. OK, now let's get started on things. You can take me to the Catherine May on the way out and pick me and Abdalla up, on the way back.

ACT 63

The Zodiac ferried Sandy and Stuart back to the Catherine May and then took them back to the beach with their tools. Then they took me to the boat and left to move the Helicopter. I joined Abdalla in the wheelhouse. He was bent over the map table drawing on the back of charts, whilst making long calculations at the side of the drawing that he was working on.

"How's it going Abdalla?"

"Mr Andy. It's going, as to how well it is going? That can only be revealed when and if, it goes boom."

"Have you had any sleep since last night?"

"Sleep is a luxury that I cannot afford. I can sleep when this is completed. Or if Allah decides for eternity"

"Surely you can think more clearly when you have rested?"

"Mr Andy my friend, this device has to be set just above the barrel, in order for the contents to be vaporised. It is not the device that is causing me problem. It is how do we create a cradle for it and how do we detonate it"

"Can we not just shoot it using an incendiary round from one if the AS50's?"

"We could but the shock wave would probably kill the person. This is a small Island and we are detonating inside the lighthouse. The line of site would be less than two hundred yards to the doorway. If a person were that close, they would be incinerated, even if they were behind some form of barrier, as the very air would be burning. If they were in the open, even as far away as 500 yards, they would die from damage to their internal organs caused by the following shock-wave. If the exact spot were not hit, it might cause the device not to work correctly. So I am trying to find another way with the items we have at hand. This is what is causing me problems."

I looked at his drawings, all of his notes were made in Arabic, as such I was unable to make head, nor tail of them.

"Can you explain your drawings to me, please?"

"Just give me a few moments to do these calculations and then I will do so Mr Andy."

"What say, I go and make you some strong coffee then?"

"Mr Andy. That would be very kind of you."

I went down to the galley and put a pot on to boil, then added some ground coffee to it. We were running low on supplies like coffee and sugar, I guess when folks are bored or worried, they drink more caffeine. Which in turn makes their minds work harder. One of lives vicious little incomplete spiralling and ever decreasing circles. The black coffee made, I took a jug and two cups, back up to the wheelhouse.

"Coffee"

"Thank you Mr Andy."

I had tried on many occasions to try and get Abdalla, just to call me Andy or Mate. Obviously they had fallen on deaf ears. He was a polite gentleman, who was always courteous to all the men and women. He was a man, who men really wanted to emulate and women loved to be around, yet he was still a man's man. With his deep bass voice and broad white smile combined with his strong muscular body. The tribal scars gave him a hint of the mysterious world of native Africa. Well educated and with a quiet self-confidence. I had to say I admired him as a soldier and a man. I passed him a steaming hot cup of aromatic black coffee.

"So, break it down for me please. When you do so, bear in mind that I am not an expert on these things. So try to keep it simple for me please."

He sipped his coffee, and then put his cup down next to one of the upturned charts that he had been drawing and writing on. Abdalla stood for about a minute, though it seemed much longer. Then he spoke, with sincerity and the authority of knowledge.

"OK Mr Andy. We have the barrel here" he said pointing to the base of one of his drawings and then continued.

"The first thing we have to do is build a cradle that is capable of holding the weight of all the eight O2 tanks, not filled with air, but filled with fuel. They have to be set with eight of the tanks set equally around the area above the barrel, and all facing towards the centre. We also have to set shaped charges here, here, here and here." He said pointing to areas to the outside of the O2 Tanks.

"Because we don't have a proper casing for a Thermobaric bomb, we have to super heat the fuel in the O2 tanks, this will serve two purposes. The first being, to make it more compressed and therefore more explosive. The second being, that when they do explode, the liquid fuel itself will become a preheated vapour, that will literally burn with the oxygen in the air. It will then be compressed with the shaped charges, that will be all around it. These will explode a nano second after and will force the burning fuel air mix inwards, as a compressed fireball. Now it is a far more destructive force. By using a shaped charge, the explosion goes inwards. This then draws even more oxygen in behind it, which will add to the intensity of the Fuel Air mix. The result being, an explosion of such intensiveness. that the heat in the immediate area of the explosion, can only be matched by that of an Atomic Bomb. This is the WHAT, of the bomb or device. The HOW of making it all happen? At the same time, is what is giving me a headache. We have to heat the air bottles without them prematurely exploding, and without detonating the shaped charges ahead of time. And all of this has to be done over a barrel, of dangerous bio-chem weapon. If something falls into the barrel and breaks one of the containers in it then. We die, the explosion goes wrong and we have released this toxin. So we first have to make the cradle that holds everything in place. Then we have to fix all our explosive bits to it. Then set up a heat source, or a way to detonate the fuel, and then set up the charges. Finally, we have to work on a trigger mechanism. I think we should discuss it with Mr Hans and Mr Lachie. They might see something that I have missed through tiredness."

"What do you need to build the cradle?"

"We need some metal rods and ideally we need some welding equipment?"

"Would the steel hand railing that goes around parts of the Lighthouse do?"

"That would help we could make it in sections and then bolt or clamp it together. But the O2 Tanks will have to be clamped or welded to the framework. We have to empty them first of course. We will need to unscrew the valves from their tops, as at some point we have to fill them with Fuel. Probably a mixture of Petrol and Diesel. Then we have to refit them. They are designed so that if they are over pressured, the tops will come off, before the rest of the tank explodes. This is a safety feature of most gas cylinders. It is something that should work in our favour. Providing, we put the exact amount of identically balanced fuel mixture in each tank. But I will come to that later."

"Work on the last part Abdalla I am going to ask Sandy to see what equipment he has on board. I will be back in about fifteen minutes."

I left and shouted to the shore and finally got a message up to sandy at the top of the steps. First I asked him how to get one of his life rafts from its sealed container. He shouted instructions back to me. I threw one of the heavy containers over the side of the Catherine May and ensured that I had secured its line to the boat. The Container hit the water and exploded out into a circular eight-man life raft. I clambered down the side of the fishing boat and into the life-raft, and then paddled furiously for the shore. Totally out of breath, I called Sandy to me.

"Sorry sandy this was the only way to get to you with the Zodiac gone"

"That's all right Andy, I am sure it is something important for you to use it."

"What engineering tools do you have on board?"

"Well we obviously have a full toolkit for the boats engine, Hammers, spanners, screwdrivers, wrenches and the like."

"I don't suppose you have a Welder do you?"

"We do have one of the old gas type ones."

"That's OK Sandy, what about hand operated winches?"

"I have a basic block and tackle winch"

"Great mate, I need you to come on board with me and show Abdalla all the tools you have and I mean all of them no matter how daft it may be. By the way how's the digging going?"

"We have shifted about six feet of dirt, but now we are finding boulders, so we are getting there."

"Sounds like you are all doing a really good job. We won't keep you too long on the boat just show Abdalla where everything is and he will take it from there. Now climb aboard."

With two of us paddling the life raft it was much easier returning to the Catherine May. Sandy climbed aboard first and gave me a hand up then we went to Abdalla. I finished my now cold coffee while Sandy and Abdalla went rooting around the fishing boat, in search of the items that Abdalla would require. It was agreed that the welding would be carried out on board the fishing boat and that the sections would then be bolted together using whatever could be scavenged from the lighthouse and the boat itself. Abdalla came back to the wheelhouse and modified his drawings, splitting them into sections, with exact specification made for each part. Our thoughts were interrupted by shouting coming from the beach. Stuart was covered in dirt and was jumping up and down and yelling something at us. I left the wheelhouse and went to the foredeck.

"We're through to the surface. There was a big rock blocking the entrance but it's free now"

"Make sure the top is safe, I will be over shortly"

"OK will do"

He turned and ran up the steps and to the top where I could see some light coming through. I left Abdalla to his drawings with a fresh pot of coffee, then Sandy and I rowed back to the shore. We tied the raft off to one of the last remaining posts to the old jetty. The steps up to the top had been cleared of earth and there were large boulders strewn about everywhere. I got to the top and Stuart and Dusty were enlarging the hole with their bare hands and old bits of broken timber. Rosemary was busy clearing off the top steps. She moved aside to let us pass.

"At some point someone had deliberately rolled a large rock over the surface of the hole, we dug around it and it fell down there"

Dusty said pointing to an enormous boulder that had rolled down to the far side of the jetty. Had it hit any of them on the way down it would surely have crushed them.

"See Andy, you can see the top of the light house from here."

ACT 64

I went up through the hole, and the fresh clean air hit me as soon as my head passed the grassy surface. The view from here was beautiful, looking up and across the Island gave us an unobstructed view of about two thirds of the Island, and you could see the tip of the lighthouse. What was even better was that about twelve yards away, I could see the large hump, which I knew to be the camouflaged tarpaulin covering the chopper. Had Hans, set the chopper down a little closer. He would have been in severe danger of falling through the roof of the cave and down on top of us all. Hans Lachie and Jane must be on their way back in the Zodiac. Having this hole in the surface of the Island, would mean that we could quickly take parts of the device to the lighthouse, much quicker that we would have done by taking in the Zodiac.

"Great job Dusty. Now we have a lot of work ahead of us. Go get yourself some food and a coffee."

I walked back down with Dusty to join the rest of them.

Hans Lachie and Jane had arrived back and were tucking into some food that had been prepared by Rosemary. Rosemary, the mother hen to all of us, making sure we were all well fed. She always had a hot pot of coffee going. By taking the top off the paraffin Tilley Lamp she was using it to keep the pot of coffee going night and day. She was a great cook too and could fabricate a meal from just about anything. Every member of our little crew, were pulling their weight, there were no slackers. Whenever someone finished their work, they would automatically offer to help in another task. Team Seven truly were working as a team.

Abdalla waved from the Katherine May and Lachie went over with the Zodiac and collected him. They returned to the shoreline of our underground harbour. Abdalla jumped ashore and pulled the boat up onto the sand. Then he reached into the boat and picked up a roll of charts that he had made his drawings on the back of. They both walked across to where the rest of us were sitting. Rosemary handed each of them a mug of coffee, along with a plate of beef sausage, beans and sliced shallow fried potatoes. When he had finished his meal, Abdalla refilled his mug from the coffee pot and then sat back down. Picking up his drawings he laid them flat on the ground, and then pointed to one that looked like a frame to hold a giant Fabergé egg. He cleared his throat and said.

"I have finished the design for the cradle, to hold the fuel and explosives. We will need a lot more tubing than just from the hand rails though. So I could use some help with any ideas, that any of you may have, as a way of building this framework."

Each of us took turns in looking at the drawings, and we discussed it between ourselves for about fifteen minutes.

Jane stood up and came back across to the drawing.

"What about the Solar panels that power the lighthouse?"

"Miss Jane I don't follow you, I don't need panels I need tubular steel."

"Sorry Abdalla, I did not explain myself correctly. What I meant was the solar panels, are all held up by a framework of tubular steel, which is held together by the same sort of brackets that they use when they put scaffolding up on the outsides of building when they are repairing, or building them. There are dozens of those large solar panels. Could we not remove them? The idea is to blow up the barrel in the light house, Right?"

"That is correct Miss Jane."

"Well The lighthouse will not need power if we are blowing it up. So can't we dismantle the array of solar panels then and use the steel and the brackets to build your bomb cradle?"

"Thank you Miss Jane. You are correct we will have more than enough by doing it this way."

Abdalla went back to his plans and made a few notes.

"We might even be able to do this, without having to weld anything other than the O2 tanks to the frame. It will also be quicker and easier to build using the bolt on brackets." He said and rolled up his drawings.

ACT 65

"Abdalla what would the time scale be, to build and make this device ready and complete for detonation?"

"Mr Andy. Now we have the hole to take things up to the surface. We can get tools there faster. Also we don't have to waste fuel from the Zodiac so we will have more Petrol to mix with the Diesel that we have. The more petrol in the mix the lower the boiling point that is required for the Fuel Air explosive. So it becomes easier. I think that I can build the frame in about five or six hours and another two to set the Thermobaric device up, so eight hours or so perhaps less, with us all working together on the separate parts. We should not start dismantling the Solar system until it gets dark, because if the light does not shine tonight they will send someone to check on it."

"Thank you Abdalla, so there is a slight delay, in us doing this. However, we should be well rested for the work we have to do tomorrow. Today you can all go up to the surface and enjoy the last of daylight. Please do not stray far from the new entrance hole to this cave and be vigilant. If you see any boats on the horizon, come straight back down. The same applies if you hear a plane. We will start at to build Abdalla's device dawn tomorrow, and with some luck be safe by dusk. Go and get some fresh air."

"Hans can you get Dusty and Sandy and join me on the surface, we can start dismantling the frames for the solar panels in about an hour or so. It will save us a lot more time tomorrow. Even if we just loosen up the bolts of the frames."

They went up to the surface in ones and twos, and relaxed for the first time in a long while.

The next morning, all but Rosemary went to the surface via the steps and the newly cleared exit. We shared the load of tools out amongst ourselves so that the weight of them was distributed evenly, and then made the half mile trek, to the lighthouse. The first job was to strip down the scaffolding from the solar panel array, which we had previously loosened off the night before. We split up into pairs, Hans with Stuart, Sandy with Dusty, Lachie with Me, and Jane with Abdalla. Jane would help Abdalla to build the cradle whilst the rest of us would work as scavengers. The work of undoing the frames for the large solar panels went well and we rapidly had two large stockpiles of tubular steel. They were stacked in two heaps in lengths ten foot and six-foot long. There was also a large pile of adjustable scaffolding joining brackets, the sort that could be set at any angle. When required, we would take lengths to Abdalla. He would then instruct one of us to help Jane hold them in place, while he would securely bolt them together above the barrel, which had its top replaced to protect the contents from any accidental damage. We had the first part completed by nine that morning. It was made by interlocking four of the ten foot piles in a three dimensional X shape over the barrel so that each pole rested on the ground and crossed over the barrel. Then using the six foot poles Abdalla made a cube shape over the top of the X shape. It made it look like a Box frame. By mid-day Abdalla had constructed is so that now there was another three dimensional X but inside the box shape. We all took a break for lunch and traipsed back down to the cave, where Rosemary had made a meal of a creamy chicken dish, made from using pre-packaged dried field ration Chicken stew along with boiled rice. This was accompanied with the now ubiquitous bucket of steaming hot black coffee.

"Is the framework finished now Abdalla?" I asked between mouthfuls of the savoury chicken stew.

"Yes Mr Andy, now we need to empty all eight of the O2 cylinders and I need to remove their release valves after we have removed them. We will remove the internal poles of the cube one at a time and then weld two cylinders to each. For now the internal double X is only lightly put in place. My plan is that when the cylinders are attached to the poles. We fill each one with the same mixture of fuel and then attach each of the modified valves to them, which will have a very small charge, this will be used as an igniter for the fuel in the tanks. They will then be detonated at that same time. The modified valves will then explode from the end of the tanks. The fuel inside the tanks will already be boiling due to the internal explosions. This will project the flaming fuel which will be in the form of a flaming boiling hot gas. Each tank will be directing its super-heated gas at its direct neighbour. As such all the eight bottles will fire towards the centre point. I will also have shaped charges, by using the claymore mines set to the outside of the frame. This will then create an added explosive pressure wave directed directly towards the centre of the burning fuel air explosive. This will happen, a fraction of a second after the fuel from the tank explodes. The result will be a super-heated super pressurised fireball that will burn all the oxygen in the immediate area. Then after it has burned that air, this will happen, in the blink of an eye. It will immediately draw oxygen from the air around the outside of the initial explosion. This in turn will add more compression and intensity to the fireball. The resulting explosive fireball will destroy every single thing in its vicinity, and the surrounding area."

"Wow how big is the following blast zone going to be?"

"This I do not know for sure, it might just be a few hundred yards, or it could be a mile, but the shock-wave could be several miles. I would think everything on the surface of this Island, will be destroyed. Mr Andy we should not be here when it happens. The shock wave might also cause this cave to collapse."

"If we can't be on the Island when it explodes, then how do we detonate it?

"This is the only problem I cannot solve Mr Andy. We do not have radio detonators nor do we have fuse wire. So it will have to be done manually"

"Do not worry Abdalla. We will sit down later and see if we can solve this problem."

After dinner Abdalla and Hans hauled the gas welding kit up to the Lighthouse. The rest of us emptied the Air out from our dive tanks and I unscrewed the brass release valves. Abdalla deconstructed one of our Claymore Mines and removed the explosive putty. This he then separated into two and then one of the half's he made eight small balls of explosives. After modifying the release valves which had two wires with their bare end exposed. He then attached the explosive to the wires to the base of the valve. The next job was to weld each tank to the scaffolding poles. Then they will be filled with a mixture of petrol and diesel, capped off with the now explosive release valve. This made each of the cross poles, carry two tanks with their ends facing in towards the centre of the three dimensional X shape. The end result was a complete framework now built over the barrel with the eight fuel air bombs pointing towards a single point. This was about three feet above the top of the Bio Barrel.

"Now we have to take the final eight claymore mines and fix them to the outside ends of the double X that carries the Air Tanks. We have to connect the firing pins that would normally be connected to a trip wire, to a ring on the centre of the X. This way, when the tanks explode, they will then auto detonate the claymore mines, at exactly the same moment. Making our Thermobaric device complete."

Abdalla pointed to all the places on the framework where things would go.

"I have an idea Abdalla but I need to have a talk with Jane first."

I left the team working and took Jane aside.

"Apart from the telephone, do you have any other way of contacting Marcus Brown?"

"There is a website he uses on the Dark Web, it is a type of chat room, but we don't have any internet here"

"If you could get internet access, do you think you could get him to come in person for the Bio weapon?"

"Originally he was supposed to get it from the boat"

"What boat?"

"Our boat, the Catherine May."

"Jane this is really important. Would he have come in person?"

"I think so, but he would have a protection team with him, and possibly a buyer."

"Jane, can you convince him that you are still on his side?"

"I think so"

"Tell Marcus I will also be here and that I will give him the stuff back, IF he gives us our life back. If he does not, then I will sell it to another buyer. Tell him I am serious. I want a face to face with him. I want new passports for all of us and I want Ten Million Pounds which is to be shared between us all so we can start a life elsewhere. Make sure he knows we just want out OK. I am tired of running around the countryside just to get my arse put in a sling."

"It would be nice to have a life with you Andy" She said giving my hand a squeeze and then said

"You know once he has this, he will still kill everyone on the Island. He will not keep his promise to you."

"I am banking on that Jane. Let me talk to Hans after dinner. Perhaps we still have a chance."

With the device completed. I went and asked Abdalla for a private chat.

"Abdalla if I found a way to have someone else detonate this device. Would that make that make things easier in your mind?"

I knew Abdalla to be a sincere and thoughtful man. I also knew that he would be the first to volunteer to be the person to detonate the device in order to save the rest of us. He was the sort of individual who would always, put innocent lives above his own. He would make his peace with Allah and then die in the explosion.

"Please go on Mr Andy?"

"Could you, booby trap it so that if someone opens the door that would set the device off?"

"Yes I suppose I could"

"Could you also make it so that if they found a booby trap wire, that if they interfered with it, that it would cause a secondary anti tamper device to set off the explosion?"

"Yes we could make the trip wire carry a small electrical charge. Using a couple of the torch batteries, which if interfered with would then cause the explosives in the air cylinders ignite. What is it you have in mind?"

"I am not sure yet but if you can set it up in the way I have described that would be helpful. If it works, we will all leave this Island safe."

Next I went to Hans, to have a chat with him

"Hans, can I speak with you in private please?"

"Yes Andy, what is it you want?"

"I want everyone off this Island. So I will want you to take them. But I need to know how confidant you are at getting the Zodiac across the open sea, on your own? There is no navigation device on it. I know you are a pilot I just wondered if you can navigate by the stars."

"How far will I have to travel?"

"That I don't know until I speak with Sandy"

"Would Sandy not be the better choice to send in a boat, as he will know the waters better than any one of us?"

"Under normal conditions I would say yes to that Hans. We have to remember that he is a civilian and it is not his place to do so in a military operation. Also it might be dangerous. He has his daughter to worry about as well. I will be asking Sandy where we should go to. I will also want you to take Jane to a different Island with telephone and internet."

"Do you trust her?"

"Not entirely, but I have no choice, if I want to save us all."

"OK Andy I will do whatever it is you ask."

"Thank you Hans, we will talk more, a little later."

I went to see Sandy who was talking with Stuart.

"Sandy where is the nearest big Island or landfall to here?"

"I suppose it would be either the Butt of Lewis or Cape Wrath on the mainland of Scotland. Both are about eighty or ninety miles away?"

"Thanks Sandy"

I needed to find out what the fuel situation was for both the Zodiac and the chopper. So I went back to talk with Hans.

"I have to get everyone away from here as you know Hans, what is the Fuel situation for the helicopter?"

"I think with the little I have from the tank I took on board, when we came here, about two to three hours flying time, why?"

"What does that mean in real terms, as in distance?"

"Andy that would depend on load and on the height that I fly at it would also depend on the speed."

"Let's say you made a flight to as a round robin of about 200 miles fully loaded with passengers for about 120 miles and make a drop off at an 80-mile point and then again drop off all but yourself a further 60 miles across and then back to here."

"It would be close but I could top up my tanks by carrying any spare fuel we have."

"I think I have a plan"

"How would I get back?"

"You would sail the Zodiac south to the mainland, where we would meet up."

"Am I to assume I drop Jane off first?"

"Correct. And you would fly at wave height all the way, including your return to this Island. Then you would sail the Catherine May and tow the Zodiac just outside the cave and tie her off and drop the sea anchor. Finally, you take the Zodiac to the bottom of the Island and sail due South. Then we will meet up with you."

"And what happens after that Andy?"

"In truth I don't know Hans, but we have to get as far away from here as we can. Do you think you can do it?"

"I think I can, if Sandy can turn the Catherine May around so that it points out towards the sea."

"We will find a way of getting a beacon for you to see. That will help you find us. You will know it when you see it."

"Let us all go and eat and I will explain my plan to all our military brothers. When you get back here after dropping us off, I want you to leave the Chopper partially covered. I want it to look like we are all still on the Island when they come to look for us."

"Who will be coming?"

"Hopefully Marcus Brown and his friends and if Jane is still working for him she will be there. If not, then she will not be with him. And then we will find her and get her back to us."

"If Jane is with him will she not just tell him we plan to blow it up?"

"Yes if she is still on his side she will, which is why I have asked Abdalla to set a double booby trap on it."

"This is a complex plan Andy, with a lot of variables and what ifs."

"It is the best plan I could make in a short period of time. If you know a better way to get rid of that shit and get us out of this mess, then please let me know."

"I can't."

I talked the entire plan over with Lachie. He said he should be the one to take the Zodiac home. Had it not been for his shoulder injury which was causing him severe discomfort from the exertions of the day's manual labour, he had even managed to pull one of the stitches resulting in it bleeding profusely until I had re-stitched it. There was a good chance of further injuring it, taking the Zodiac out to the open sea, which not rough would still have a swell, resulting in the little boat bouncing and putting a strain on whoever was manning it. So over dinner the plan was set for this evening. The device would be detonated by whoever opened the door to the lighthouse. They would not send a repair crew to the lighthouse tonight but they might tomorrow. I was betting that Marcus Brown would arrive with a full team of killers as soon as possible, after Jane contacted him. I gave her one of the throwaway cell phones and gave her the number for mine. I told her I would switch it on after we got back to the Island. In reality I would switch it on when I was on the mainland of Scotland. At least then we would have some running space. We would still have our rifles and small arms. I got Sandy to turn the Catherine May around on the pretext that. When we had to come back to the Island, It would make for a quicker escape. I gave our last cell phone to Hans and told him to keep it with him, whilst it would be no use out at sea, he could use it as soon as he came close enough to the mainland shore say about one or two miles. Then he would call me. Most of the matters concerning our removal from the Island were kept secret from Jane. She would be under the impression that we were just dropping her off and then going back to the Island to the Catherine May. Everyone else was just coming along for a Helicopter ride to relieve the boredom. Hans had stowed our guns in a compartment behind the seating bulkhead within the helicopter. This was so that Jane would not see that we were taking everything with us. Either way the plan should work.

Most of the gear apart from our weapons was left behind on the Island including all of our rations, bedding and clothing. We were to leave in the clothing, we had on, which for Lachie, Hans, Abdalla, Jane and myself were our Nomex Suits. For the others it was the clothing they had worn that day. The only people that knew all the details of our departure were Lachie Hans Abdalla and me the rest thought we were coming back here. I let Kyla have her last free roam of the surface of the island and then we all walked up to the chopper. We removed the tarpaulin covering, that we had on top of it. Hans went around all the external lights of his Helicopter and smashed each one, including those on the rotors and also on the belly below. The idea being that we would fly under the radar and also not be visible to the naked eye. Hans clambered into the pilot's seat and put on his night vision goggles. Then he started the motors. It was a bit of a squeeze but we managed it. I slid the side door closed. I needed this plan to work not just for me I had the lives of my friends to worry about. I prayed that Jane would remain as one of us, but I could not take the risk that she would flip once again. I wanted to tell her the full plan. I wanted to trust her. I think I did trust her in my heart. It was my mind that was having trouble in accepting the word of someone, who I had strong emotional feelings for, but who had let us all down before.

ACT 66

Hans took off and tilted the chopper forward then followed the slope of the Island, within a minute he had dropped to the gentle wave height and was speeding towards the Isle of Lewis. We were heading to The Port of Ness on the North West peninsula. Hans would land at the extreme tip and then drop Jane off. Jane would then make her way on foot to the small village there, where she would find a land line and an internet connection for her own laptop. She would then connect to the Dark Net Web chat rooms at Deep-dot-web and connect up with Marcus Brown. She would tell him, that the barrel was hidden inside the lighthouse. Also telling him, we were all still there waiting for him to come with the money. As we flashed over the water I was sat next to Jane, I could feel the warmth of her body next to mine. I looked over and could see Lachie and Abdalla both looking at me, I probably blushed but fortunately in the dark interior, no one would see it. I had grown close to Jane over the past week or so, I wanted a relationship with her. In truth though, nothing could break the bond between Lachie and me. That was a bond formed throughout boyhood and as men. This was a bond of brothers that nothing I could imagine could break, not even the love for a woman. We approached the cliffs forming the Port Ness peninsula on Lewis. I thought for a moment that Hans was not going to slow enough and that we would all meet our deaths as a result of the Helicopter smashing into the cliff face. At the last moment he pulled up and set it down gently on the grassy top. The door flew open by the hand of Abdalla and Jane jumped out. I never had a chance to say good luck as Abdalla had just as quickly closed the door as he had opened it. Hans already left the ground and I watched as Jane ran towards the houses about three quarters of a mile away. Hans turned to the east and back down across the watery surface of the North Atlantic. Forty minutes later Hans was setting down in a small beach to the East of Cape Wrath. The beach was in Kearvaig bay. It was sandy and a perfect place to guide Hans back to, especially as he would know what to look out for. This area of the coast did not have that many beaches to choose from. Kyla was the first out from the chopper followed by the rest of us. We took all the guns and munitions. Hans asked that he only have a spray and run gun along with his knife. We said our goodbyes and wished him luck and then he was gone within one minute of our touchdown. I watched him as he shot back out across the waves until I could no longer make out the shape tearing up the waves. There was a large rock right in the middle of the beach, we set this up as our fall-back point with guns and munitions on the top. Then we set a defensive ring, around the edge of the sand. Whilst we were spread out we were all within sight of each other. Abdalla had given Rosemary and Stuart a Sig Sauer each, after explaining quickly how to use them. Mossberg pump action to Dusty and Sandy. Abdalla had an AS50 as did Lachie, who was at one end of the defensive line, as I also had, at the other end of the line. Lachie, Abdalla and I also had Motorola throat mikes and ear pieces.

"Everyone keep quiet unless you see anyone approaching our position and please don't shoot unless you are in immediate danger. Lachie and I have your positions covered and Abdalla has our backs so you are in safe hands. We could be here for some time. Lay low and try not to move. Now we wait."

The night remained cool, whilst there was no wind from the sea the damp coming up through the ground in this springtime air was cold and the Nomex suits did little to keep it at bay. I was tired and cold and was sure, that this was the feeling of the others. After about four hours the mobile phone on my hip started to vibrate. Jane's number flashed up on the screen.

"Yes?"

"Messaged him"

"And?"

"He wants to go and inspect it himself"

"Good"

"Don't trust him Andy."

"OK Jane talk soon."

I closed the phone off and removed the battery. I kept the call quick for two reasons. One was I did not want it tracked, and two was I did not want to accidentally give my plan away at the moment.

"Hey guys according to Jane, Marcus is going to the Island to check the item for himself. Jane said also that we should not trust Marcus, which of course we don't. I don't think we will have to wait much longer now." I said into the throat mike.

Hans should have managed to get the Catherine May to the opening of the inlet in the fjord like cliff of the Island. Sandy had told him to switch the light inside the wheelhouse and also the boats running lights. So that she was visible. Then he had to get into the Zodiac and head for our rough positions, just as fast as he could. Abdalla would occasionally be using his laser from the BAE sight on his AS50. Sweeping the water, any boat within one mile would get an occasional glimpse of the red light. But only if they were close to the surface like the Zodiac would be. I heard him before I saw him. The three Honda engines screaming at full power were driving the lightweight RIB Zodiac through the water. Hans raced the Zodiac up onto the beach. And then ran past Abdalla on his rock, without even seeing him. I flashed my penlight a couple of times and Hans ran to me. He had made the round trip in just less than six hours. He had opened the triple Honda engines up to full power and must have been getting close to sixty miles an hour out of them. The Zodiac was light and Hans being the only person on board it would just fly over the waves. So much so that when he did hit the beach, where we were, the momentum had carried him almost to the grassy banks where the rest of our team lay

"Good to see you Hans"

"Nice to be back but I will miss the Helicopter"

"Nice to have you back Hans, you are better off without it. As soon as they see it, they will destroy it for sure and the same applies to the Catherine May. I have not told sandy yet, because he would have wanted, to take too many pieces from it and we could not carry anything more than the kit we had."

"I guess you are right" He said stroking Kyla's fur. At that point I realised that I was actually better off than any of the others as I had Kyla to help keep me warm.

"Time to leave this place, let's get everyone together, and hide the Zodiac."

I Called Lachie and got him to move towards me and I moved towards him, picking up the members of our team along the way. When we were all back together we moved back down onto the beach and behind the large rock, where we were joined by Abdalla.

"We are going to have to find somewhere to hide out"

"I know this area Andy. I grew up around here." Sandy said and moved to the front.

"There is a Bothy, just about three hundred yards inland almost due south from here. Last time I was around this side fishing, some people from the south, were starting to do it up as a summer home. I don't know if they have finished it yet, but it has a roof and we could light a fire and at least be warm. The nearest road to it is about a mile further inland. So there are no neighbours. It would be a good place I think."

"OK let's hide the Zodiac as best we can, let's make sure it can't be seen from the sea. So probably behind this rock will be a good place. It does not look like the tide comes up this far. We can hide the engines for it over there under that overhang of turf. Then we will make our way to the Bothy."

A Bothy is a traditional small cottage, with just one or two rooms, often used by shepherds during the lambing season. But many of them had been converted to small holiday homes, with the advent of modern ATV's, whereby the shepherd can quickly go out and find his sheep before returning home. In the old days they would spend all the lambing season, cooped up in this little house. Before joining their families at the end of the season. All of us helped to pull the Zodiac up the beach and behind the large rock, and then we carried the engines up to the back edge of the beach and tucked them in under the overhanging grassy turf.

"Sandy, do you want to lead the way. If you put these on it will be a lot easier for you" I said as I passed him a pair of NV Goggles.

"Let your eyes get used to them first and take it slow. If we all keep close together we will have no problems. Now if we all pick up some of the gear we have and let's go."

Our packs were shared out so that each person was carrying the same sort of weight, most of which was in the form of guns and ammunition. Sandy was right. The little house was exactly where he said it should be. From the look of the outside someone had spent some time and a lot of money renovating it to a good high standard. Instead of turf roof it was fully tiled, the small wooden windows had been replaced by shiny new double glazed units. There was a large propane gas tank to the side of the home. And it appeared to have been extended to the rear of the property. The front door was one of those new white plastic things with a combination of ten locking bolts. I had no clue on how to open this. I was just about to smash one of the side windows when Hans stopped me. He took out his Sig Sauer and attached his suppressor, then levelled it at the lock and from about two inches away he put a round into the lock mechanism which shot back into the room. I tried the handle, still locked. Hans took out a Swiss Army penknife and poked it into the lock hole and then turned it as you would a key and the door unlocked.

"Remind me to call you next time I lose my keys."

"Ahhh but you should see my call-out fee's I have to travel from the North of Iceland"

"Where did you learn to do that Hans?" I asked

"I learned it from a thief in Iceland. He would rob houses and be gone before we arrived. So we set up a sting for him. We were waiting outside and watched as he broke into the home of one of the richest people in Iceland. So I saw how he did it and since then I have taught the SAS how to do it this way rather than wasting time trying to break down a door you can do this in two seconds. Even though there is some noise from the lock being knocked out, it is not as loud as a door breaker, also door breakers only work on old wooden doors. Modern doors have as many as sixteen bolts. They will hold a door against an elephant. But once you have the lock barrel out you can turn the locking bolts with a screwdriver or a penknife."

"And you are the good guys? Rosemary asked with a laugh

"Sometimes and sometimes not so, but right now yes we are the good guys. Now can we go in before someone sees us?" I said

"Who will see us here?" asked Sandy.

"Them up there" Lachie said pointing to the sky

ACT 67

We went in. Lachie went around the house pulling the blinds shut and closing the curtains behind them. Then he switched the lights on. It was beautifully decorated, with quality furnishings and fittings. There was a central heating boiler and the house had mains electricity and water. So Lachie started up the gas boiler. We set our bags and rifles down in the centre of the floor. It was surprising just how much equipment we were able to carry, when we looked at it all in one spot.

"How did Jane get on?" Hans asked

"I got a message just before you arrived to say that she had been in touch with Marcus, and that he had agreed to come to meet us on the Island in person. He was going to bring a load of cash with him along with new passports for all of us."

"Do you believe her?"

"Yes I think I believe what Jane said. No I don't believe that Marcus will keep his word. I think he will send a team there to kill us. I have to say sorry to you now Sandy."

"Why are you sorry for saving me and my daughter?"

"I am saying sorry because it will be at the cost of the Catherine May. I think they will assume we are on it, or see it as our method of escape so they will destroy it. They will also destroy the Helicopter. Then and only then will they go on to the Island. I hope that Marcus will be with the team that goes to the Lighthouse. They will see that it is booby trapped and disable the booby trap but that in fact will be the trigger to make it all explode. Anyone or anything on top of the Island will be instantly killed or destroyed. Along with any helicopters in the sky within half a mile, they will also be destroyed. So I am sorry I did not tell you about your boat. I was afraid that there would be many things of sentimental value aboard and we could carry no more weight. I also needed Jane to believe, that we would be coming back to the Island."

"Don't worry about the boat, call it a debt paid. You got my Rosemary back, the boat was old and so am I. You do not trust Jane?"

"Sandy I want to trust her, just she was with Marcus at the start of all this. Dusty knows I want her to be true to us, and I think because her father is here, she will be."

"My daughter will, Andy"

"Why are you so sure Dusty?"

"Because, you're a stupid young man, can't you see what everyone else here can see? She is in love with you."

"You think we did not notice?" Lachie said

"There is none so blind as those that don't want to see" Abdalla answered

I was embarrassed both by their admissions and by my own lack of trust in Jane, even though I had feelings of my own towards her.

"OK I get the picture I am a piece of shit. But I am only a shit because, I care for all of you, so let us let it go at that. So let us get some food, if there is any here. use it. If not then its power bars and black coffee. After that we rotate guard shifts. That means everyone, we will pair up Lachie with Rosemary, Abdalla with Sandy, Hans with Dusty, and I will pair up first shift with Stuart. One hour then shift change. We keep one person doing rounds outside for thirty minutes and then swap with their partner. Does that work for you all?"

Everyone nodded and they set about getting food and coffee. Rosemary opened a cupboard full of Tinned soup, Tea Coffee, sugar and Shortbread Biscuits. So she set to cooking up, the better part of a gallon of Heinz cream of chicken soup, which we all ate greedily.

"OK Stuart you get the first watch outside, keep close to the building and always face out from it as you walk around, anything suspicious no matter how small come and get me. I am giving you a Sig with a silencer attached, try not to kill a friendly neighbour, or a sheep. You use it only if you fear for your life or ours. Got it?"

"Yes I understand"

"Good lad." I cocked it and chambered a round and switched the safety to off. No point in you having a firearm if you don't know how to cock it, or get the safety off. BUT Stuart please be careful it's all ready to fire"

"I will be careful I promise"

"OK off you go and be safe, remember we are just in here if you need any help."

Stuart zipped up his jacket and went outside.

Most of the team went off to find whatever comfortable place they could to lie down and get some rest. There were only two beds in the house one a double and the other a single. Rosemary and Stu would have the double, Sandy took the single. The others took the armchairs and sofa. I turned the lights off and pulled the curtains open on a small kitchen window. I watched out the front from there. After thirty minutes I went outside and called Stuart in.

"Keep a watch out the kitchen window and don't switch on any lights." I said as I took Kyla with me and I did my rounds keeping a good watch for any sign of interest in us from either land or sea, nothing. At the end of my shift I went in and woke Lachie and Rosemary. I took the Sig from Stuart and passed it to Rosemary.

"Listen to Lachie he will keep you straight. Do you want Kyla with you Lachie?"

"Why not she has been cooped up inside a cave for days she could do with the exercise and fresh air"

"OK Mate see you in a few hours I am going to grab the Sofa."

I needed a shower but I was so tired I just went and lay down. I did not have a deep sleep. I dozed and watched as each shift changed over, thirty minutes in and thirty out. Then team changes. All too soon it was Stuart's and my turn to stand watch again. We got the graveyard shift. That is the four in the morning shift. Again Stuart went out first followed by Kyla and me. I was doing my second walk around the house when I heard them, two or perhaps three light helicopters. I quickly went in and roused everyone.

"There are some choppers heading up from the south west. I have not seen them yet but I just heard them, the air is still out there so they are probably five or ten miles out."

The dawn was just starting to break and all eyes went to the windows around the little house.

"Behind us." called Hans.

Hans and Abdalla both raced for the stash of arms in the middle of the room, each of them locked on to their AS50's.

"Don't get seen, let's stay cool for now and see where they are going" I said

We did not have long to wait a few minutes later a pair of McDonnell-Douglas MD500 small helicopters flew over from the west of us heading out to sea. Both were kitted out with a pair of rocket launcher pods to the sides of their landing skids.

"Do you think they are going fishing" Lachie in his now normal humour said.

"They are going fishing for sure, just not for fish I think" Hans said

"I think we are supposed to be on the menu for them, let's hope that Marcus is on one of them."

There was no way we could see the Island from our location, nor would we hear the rockets strike. But if I had to bet the first target would be the Catherine May and that would be quickly followed by the Chopper Hans had left there. After they attacked they would circle the Island and then if they felt they were safe they would land. Perhaps only one would land to begin with to see if they could draw out survivors. They would not fire on the lighthouse because Marcus would know that the Bio weapon was being stored in there. Even though, he could not see it from outside of the building. He would know it was there. He was probably in the second chopper. No doubt in a Blue ANBC Suit. He would have a team go in first to check. In no incertitude, under his direct supervision from less than one hundred yards away. Perhaps he would land to watch them open the door. Possibly he would be even closer than that. We all stared intently out of the windows to the front of the house looking towards the sea. Our natural navigation skills built up and honed over the last few days showed us which direction to watch. Had the sky been any brighter we would not have seen it. A sudden bright orange flash on the skyline followed shortly after by a small mushroom type cloud from beyond the horizon. This was followed a short time after by what to other people would have sounded like a distant clap of rolling thunder. There was not a great cheer to our success, more a quiet resignation that the greatest part of the danger to us had been vaporised. And a silent wish that the man responsible for all the deaths and struggle over the past couple of weeks may very well have been vaporised and turned to dust with just the odd fragment of bone, or tooth surviving to show that he had once existed. I silently wished that no person would have that evil stuff in their hands, to threaten or hold a country to ransom. I was sure that they would no doubt have some idea of how to recreate it once again, at CDE. I could only wish that they would not. Abdalla had rolled his prayer mat out and was facing the west and would be giving thanks Allah. No one had ever paid any mind to him saying his prayers in his way, we just accepted that he was a man of faith. Each had his or her own way of talking to their outer or inner gods, and giving thanks, that an evil had been destroyed and along with it, with any luck a greedy and thoughtless man, with yet another group from rentakiller-dot-com, with him. It was time for me to call Jane.

ACT 68

"Hi Jane"

"Are you all safe, Marcus went to the Island, how did you get away? Where are you?"

"Slow down Jane we are all safe and we all got away clean. We will come and find you, stay where you are. It might be a few days. Do you have enough money?"

"I am so happy you are safe Andy I wanted to tell you how much I love you."

"That's OK Jane I know."

"How?"

"Everyone but me saw it, so where are you"

"I am in a little Bed and Breakfast house, next to the harbour, and yes I have enough money. The Lady here is sweet. I told her my boyfriend left me stranded, after we were Kayaking, and that this black Nomex suit, was my Kayak suit, hence lack of a change of clothing, she gave me some of her daughters, and they fit."

"OK Jane sometime in the next week, I will come and find you. I don't know how yet, but I will find a way. I hope things will be safe by then, if not I will need you to help us sort things with SIS. I will call you tomorrow at mid-day exactly. Only switch your phone on then. At all other times, take the sim card and battery out. Got it?"

"Yes but…."

"Please just do as I say. I have to go now be safe and I will call tomorrow. Bye."

I hung up and put the sim card in my wallet and the battery in one pocket and the phone in another.

I called everyone together, and had them sit down wherever they could.

"I never wanted to be your spokesperson or the one that gave orders, if you can call them that, because I don't believe I have done more that make suggestions, to which none of you have ever complained. I have not always told each of you what I may have told to others, but this is only because I thought things would work better this way. Dusty you will know that I have had occasion to doubt Jane. These were not so much personal doubts but more a way of being extra careful in my protection to all of you. Had I voiced openly some of my doubts at an early stage, I doubt if we would have worked well as a team. I can now tell you, that Jane is safe and well on the Island of Lewis. She still does not know exactly where we are, because when she left with us, when Hans put her down on Lewis, Jane thought we were all going back to the Island. This was because, as you know I had concerns at the time that Marcus might suck her back into working for him, using some lie or another. The reason I have not told her where we are now is still for your safety. I know that GCHQ listen to all conversations and flag certain names and words. If they locked on to our calls, which I have deliberately kept too short for trace, but if by chance they did manage, if I gave out where we were, I am sure it would not be long before we were not alive. What you have to remember, is that until we can clear things up with the SIS, they will see us as aiding and abetting Marcus in his dirty little plan. They will still have all of us on a Blacklist. Wet-work teams will still be looking to wipe not just our bodies out but every little document that proved we actually existed. I have asked Jane if she can find a way for us to contact 'The Suit' at SIS so that we can prove our innocence in this. Until we can do this, we are and will remain fugitives. This means you can't call anyone, talk to anyone or write to anyone until I can fix this. At the moment we have a roof over our head. I suspect that this house is only used in summer, it is far enough out of the way and remote enough, that no one should bother us for some time. There were some Utility Bills addressed to the owners of this house so if you are seen outside by any of the locals, you are to say that you are friends of either Mrs Watts or Mr Watts. Looking at the photographs there is one of the Corn Dolly in Oxford. I know this Pub because it is just down the road from where I stationed at RAF Abingdon. So you say you are friends of the Watts from Oxfordshire. That should actually work with anyone, who actually knows the owners. Try not to lay it on too thick. Now we have some of our money left. It's only a few thousand but it should be enough to buy us some normal clothing and a van of some form. Sandy I am going to ask you to find a way to the nearest town and buy basic clothes for all, if you take Rosemary with you. Also see if you can find a van for sale in the local papers, something like a Bedford or a Transit if possible a Box Luton cab. Pay cash give a false name and address, just nowhere near Keiss or any of our homes. Rosemary you will also buy basic foodstuff. Buy some basic dog food, Kyla will eat most brands, and it is something a genuine crofter would buy. Again don't give out names and addresses, if they ask, just say you are in a hurry and don't have time, nor do you want spam mail. I know shops are always trying to add people to mailing lists. Sandy can you get some black paint I want to paint that orange Zodiac, black. They will be looking for it. Abdalla can you take the covers off the three motors, we will paint those as well. If Sandy can get some Yamaha vinyl stickers from a Motorbike dealer, we should be able to disguise the engines. So that the boat looks completely different from the way it does at the moment. Make sure its spray paint if you can Sandy. Also if you get a van, drive around a bit and if you see a similar van, copy the number plate down. You can buy Blank number plates at Halfords or somewhere like that. Then if you can buy some Black letters and numbers to match and we will make up fake plates here. The best thing is for you to make it to the nearest village and then get a taxi or bus to Scrabster. If you see someone you know, walk away. Do not talk to them. It's a lot for you to take on board I know, but all of us here are relying on you. Don't forget to buy as many burner phones as you can. No more than two phones from any one retail outlet. There is £6,000 here which leaves us with just short of £4,000. They are all in used non sequential bills so they are untraceable. If you leave now hopefully you will get back here sometime tonight."

Sandy took the money and put it in his inside pockets of his fisherman's jacket. He would not look out of place in Scrabster. Hans spoke up

"Wear hats and caps and keep your heads down when in towns, especially in shops and garages. They all have video cameras these days and I am sure that SIS can tap into them. I don't mean to frighten you it is just better to be safe than sorry."

"Hans is right. Lachie, Abdalla, Hans and I will sort things out here. Now finish your coffee and be safe."

"What about me" Dusty asked

"Dusty your face will be plastered on every TV Screen and newspaper. Your wife was killed and you have vanished, your daughter is high up in SIS and is the number two suspect in an attempted act of terrorism. You have to stay close by us until this is sorted. Sandy and Rosemary will blend in

They will also be looking for Stuart to be with Rosemary and her father so they will be looking for two men and a woman not one man and a woman. Stuart will stay here with you as well. I hope that covers everything. We will work on a plan to get Jane back to us Dusty, I promise you.

ACT 69

I worried all the time Sandy and Rosemary were away and with each hour my worry grew. But at three twenty in the afternoon a big, old and somewhat rusty but mostly white, long wheel based Box Luton van rolled up, under the watchful eyes, of Hans and Abdalla. The van pulled around the front of the house and Sandy killed the engine. He and Rosemary got out to greetings from us all. Stuart greeted Rosemary more than most.

"Sorry it's a bit rusty Andy, but it was the only Box Luton, I could find for sale anywhere up here."

"Believe it or not, that is Perfect Sandy. It will blend in a lot better than a new one? Did you manage to get a number of another similar van?"

"Yes Andy and I have the blank plates and numbers in the back, with everything else. This van only cost us just over a grand, the exhaust is blown, but I figured that Lachie or Stuart could fix that up. We got almost all of the things on your list. We spread the money around rather than paying lots of money in one shop."

"Great thinking Sandy"

Stuart went around the back and pushed up the roller door, to reveal all the contents, neatly stacked in cardboard boxes. We ferried them all into the house. Sandy had managed to buy a dozen cheap burner phones, which we would have to charge up and keep charged. There was a sack of dog biscuits which sandy had actually managed to get someone else to buy for him. I would mix them, with scraps from our plates. Sandy had got the paint and blank number plates from Halfords along with stick on numbers and letters, on the pretext that he needed them for his tractor trailers. He had also copied down, the registration plate from another van of the same make and year as ours. So we could clone them. That would mean if we were ever caught on traffic cameras it would not lead back to us. The down side would be if we got stopped for any reason we would not be able to produce documents. We would cross that bridge if and when we got to it. Rosemary had managed to get lots of clothing, for all of us. This was great because apart from our Nomex requiring a damn good wash. We would not look so suspicious when out and about. We still had to work out a plan on how to get Jane back and how to clear our names. We now had food and clothing and it is amazing how great it feels to dress like normal people for a change. We took turns showering and changing into our new apparel. Then there was a fashion show, to show how well they fitted. I had shaved and Rosemary was even offering haircuts and restyling. I settled for an all over number one. Which changed my look dramatically? Real food, proper clothes, all that was missing was a real plan. We would work on that and the other things tomorrow. The next morning, I woke showered shaved and went into the kitchen. Rosemary was already up. She was busy cooking up a storm.

"Where is Lachie?"

"He is outside under the van with dad. They are repairing the exhaust."

I took my coffee along with two other cups for them. They had jacked the van up from the front. Lachie slid out from underneath and took the coffee I offered to him.

"Where is Sandy?"

"He is going through the trash to see if there is a baked

been tin in there. There is a hole in the exhaust, on the front pipe, where it is blowing. I am going to use a can wrapped around it and a couple of jubilee clips. That should do as a fix for as long as we have this heap."

"Will this do?" Sandy said from behind, and then offered a Heinz Soup tin, to Lachie.

"Perfect Sandy, if you take the bottom off and split the can down the side, then it will do a treat."

"Lachie what are you doing under this?"

"I just told you Andy."

"I mean should you not be resting that shoulder, rather than scrabbling around under this?"

"It's healing great mate, and I am taking it easy. Sandy is doing the grafting. I am just overseeing it" He said with a wink at Sandy.

Stuart appeared from the beach with several empty cans of black paint.

"Boat is done and the engines. I am just going to make up the number plates, what do you want me to do after that?"

"You seem to have it all in hand Stu, Thank you"

The only person on our team, who looked like he did not fit into the local picture, was Abdalla. They do not get many giant men up here who are black and have tribal scars. So I had asked him if he could keep out of sight as much as possible. If the police were looking for us they would definitely spot him. Abdalla busied himself stripping down and cleaning our weapons and refilling our magazines. Then he made bug out packs for all of us. He split the cash evenly, along with ensuring that each pack had a throwaway mobile phone with the numbers for each of the others logged in on speed-dial. Between the original firearms that we started out with we had also captured several. So each backpack also had a hand gun of some form in it along with a full magazine and spare preloaded clips. Abdalla took time in teaching each one of the civilian members of our crew. How to safely use them, how to attach a suppressor, if required? They were also taught how to load and fire the Mossberg's. Although they did not actually, use live ammo. It was more for them to learn how to defend themselves, if and when, we were not able to do so. One of the AS50's he dismantled and put into his own pack. The others were loaded back into their guitar flight cases. There were actually too many guns to go around so Hans made a small ammo dump in the sand dunes, but kept the firing pins separate. He said just in case some child found them by accident. No one needed to be told do a task, they all just seemed to know when and what was required and just got on with it. Time flew by. I still worried about Jane, and I worried about all the people under my care. We were into our third day and it was almost like we had settled in as a large family. The phone in my pocket vibrated. I opened it and the caller ID showed eight zeroes'. Was this a trap? What had happened to Jane's phone? The only way anyone could have got this number was from Jane or her phone. I let it ring while everyone looked at me. I held the phone up so that everyone could see the screen.

"Do I answer it?"

"Yes but keep it under thirty seconds" Hans said

I looked at Abdalla and at Lachie they both nodded. I pressed the button to receive. And stared at the Omega Sea master on my left wrist, watching the second hand as it swept around the inside of the orange bezel.

"Hello?"

"Is this team seven?"

"Who is this?"

"I think you know who we are?"

"We?"

"We are the people, who can give you your lives back"

"If I was team seven, how would you help me?"

"We can bring you in"

Twenty seconds gone by and ten to go.

"Who are you? What's your name?"

"I can't give that out. But I can help you."

Twenty-five seconds

"I need to know who you are"

"We are the Government"

Thirty seconds. I pressed the red disconnect button.

"Who was that?"

"They just said they were the government, he wanted to know if we were Team Seven Lachie, and that they could help us. He said he could give us our lives back. But they never gave a name or said anything about Jane or the stuff we blew up."

I was interrupted by the phone ringing again

"Just tell them to call you tomorrow at a set time then hang up" Hans said

I answered the phone

"Why did you hang up?"

"Call me back on this number at exactly two, tomorrow afternoon. And not before, then and only then I will speak."

I hung up and looked at all the others.

"We need to make a plan Andy"

"Any ideas Hans?"

"I do have, but we will have to do it away from here and possibly at a train or bus station, or something like that. That way we can keep it public and see any reactive force, if they are playing us. Because if they are just trying to capture us they will have the IMEI or MEID number of the phone you just used so you need to remove the battery and sim until tomorrow, before they track it. We can use that in our favour if we are careful and get the timing right."

"How do you know all of this spy shit Hans?"

"Its basic police and undercover work, Andy I teach it. Also I have seen lots of American films" he said, with a wink and a big smile.

"So in that case Hans, I would be grateful if you could set up a workable plan for us. If you need anything just ask. I don't mind being at the point, but I will take your advice on what to do when I am there."

"Andy. Do not worry I will have a plan, with another plan built into it, by tomorrow afternoon."

So that night we went through the plan several times. It would involve Hans, Sandy, Rosemary and me. Abdalla, Lachie, Dusty and Stuart would stay behind. The next afternoon, we set off. This time I was in the front with Rosemary. Hans and Sandy were in the back of the van, out of sight. Hans had told us to head into Scrabster and down to the harbour. There were two small holes cut in the sides of the van about one inch in diameter, these would allow Hans and Sandy to view things around us. They were both wearing the Storno throat mikes as were Rosemary and I. We parked up at the side of one of the fish warehouses. There was a lot of other transport there. Trucks and Vans like ours. Most were either local fishmongers or

Heavy Goods Trucks, that would be taking the days catch down South after the daily sales. At exactly one minute to two, I re-assembled my phone and at exactly two, the phone Vibrated.

"Hello" I said

"If you are team seven, we can help you."

"How can you help?"

"Just tell us where you are and we will bring you all in"

I kept a close eye on my watch. Hans had told me to let them have exactly two minutes this time.

"Where is Jane?"

"She is safe with us, she came in yesterday"

"Can I speak to her?"

"She is not at this location. But I can arrange for her to come to you. If you just tell us where you are?"

"How do I know I can trust you?"

"I know you are Team Seven. So that should tell you that I know who you are"

"I have a bit of a trust issue. As I am sure you will know."

"Mr McPhee. That is who I am speaking with? Is it not?"

"If you know who I am, why can you not tell me who you are?"

"I am sure you know why Mr McPhee."

"No I don't, you tell me why?"

"Mr McPhee, we are going around in circles. I am trying to help you get your lives back, along with putting an end to all this."

Rosemary who had been keeping a check on her own watch rotated her index finger. I looked down at my own watch. Time was almost up.

"I don't know you. I will only talk to someone I know. You said you have Jane. I want to speak to her." Two minutes and five seconds. Time to end this conversation, I closed the phone, opened the back and removed my sim card. I left the battery in the phone. Rosemary took the phone, all the time being watched by Hans on one side of the van and Sandy on the other. I was sat in the front watching and the rear of the van was hard up against a wall. So we had all sides covered. Rosemary walked casually over to a large van with its back doors open.

Two men were transferring boxes of fish that they had just bought at auction. They put a box of fish, into their van and then went back inside to get another. As soon as their backs were turned, Rosemary tossed my mobile phone into the back of their van. Then she took a casual walk back to our van. We drove away and found a good vantage point overlooking the harbour and with good sight of the other van. I was using one of the BAE sights to keep an eye on them. They closed the back door and got in. then they drove up from the harbour. We followed the van from Scrabster to Thurso and then down to the east coast. We were about eight or nine cars back when they eventually turned on to the A9. Then we followed them down past Helmsdale, Brora and Golspie. They were still eight cars in front of us when they turned on to the Dornoch Bridge. Cars were being directed away from it by workmen dressed in Hi-vis Jackets. The traffic was being sent on the old part of the A9 that took a much more circuitous route towards Inverness. However their van got to the junction, they were flagged through. There was no traffic coming from the other direction across the bridge. The cars in front of us were redirected to go on the old road. I kept my head down as we reached the diversion point.

"What do I do Andy?"

"We follow the main line of traffic until we can get a view of the bridge."

We went past the diversion with the rest of the traffic. Then we pulled into a passing place. I waited for the road by us to become clear and then jumped out and let Hans out the back of the van.

"Sandy, please go and sit with Rosemary. Drive up the road for about two miles then park up. Come back here in thirty minutes."

"OK Andy will do."

They drove off Hans handed me my Guitar case and we both descended the hillside until we had a clear view of the Dornoch Causeway. Hans had his AS50 out and was surveying the firth below him. I opened the guitar case, and took out my AS50 with BAE scope on. The far side of the bridge was closed as was this side. The van was stopped, at a set of traffic lights in the middle of the bridge. Effectively they were the only vehicle on the bridge. I looked at both sides to see if I could see a police car or any emergency flashing lights. There were none. There were only wooden barricades with diversion signs. This did not look good. Hans fitted his suppressor to the barrel of his AS50.

"Andy it's a trap, and not the sort that you get to walk away from. Keep an eye on the sky from all sides of the firth. Zoom out with your sight so you can cover a larger area and switch it to thermal"

"Why thermal?"

"Because I think they are going to use a missile or something like that, on those innocent folks down there. They have tracked the phone and have had plenty of time to cross refer and paint it from above."

I waited and scanned the skies. Then I saw it about a mile out and closing fast. Hans was right the thermal signature showed first on my scope.

"My ten o'clock Hans"

"Got it Andy, don't wait for me just shoot at it, I can shoot when you reload"

"I zeroed in on it and fired five shots in quick succession. Then dropped the magazine out and Hans fired his five shots and also dropped his magazine. I fired three more in semi auto mode. I don't know which one of us hit it. The reaper drone exploded in a fireball. It was a much bigger explosion that I would have expected from just an unarmed drone. I assumed that this either flew out from RAF Kinloss or RAF Lossiemouth. Even though, it was probably being controlled by someone in RAF Waddington in Lincolnshire. I knew that they actually controlled the drones used in the Middle East, from Waddington. Hopefully they would not have seen the shots fired at it, as their cameras would have been locked onto the target on the bridge. But the result of the drone explosion had caused the roadblocks on either side of the bridge to be removed. Hopefully they would send in a ground team and discover that it was just the phone in the back of the van and let the innocent men get on with selling fish. What we knew was that the man who had called us pretending to be a friend, was not. I also now suspected that they did not have Jane. This was both good and bad. Good because they had not found her, bad because they would now be looking for her as an individual rather than as part of our group. This would no doubt be reported as an unmanned practice drone that or either had a malfunction and had crashed into the Firth of Dornoch or that they had detonated it themselves after it developed some fault or other. Either way it would not be reported as a deliberate attempt, on innocent civilian's lives, or for that matter as a deliberate attempt to kill us.

I broke and cased my rifle, after checking both sides of the now unblocked bridge, all clear. Hans broke down his rifle so that it could be carried in his backpack. We scrambled up to the edge of the road and awaited Sandy and Rosemary's return. They arrived precisely on time but Hans and I waited a few minutes until the road was clear of traffic. Then we clambered into the back of the van and quickly pulled the shutter down.

"Take us home, please Sandy" I said through my throat mike. Then as a bit of an afterthought I said "Turn on Moray Firth Radio and listen for the News"

"OK. Andy I will do."

"What now?" I asked Hans

"Well I do not think that was meant as a warning. They want us out of the game altogether. I don't think they want any witnesses, to all that has happened. I would say that your government wants anyone who even knew about this, dead. I cannot see a way out for us."

"Hans. WE WERE THE GOOD GUYS! We stopped Marcus Brown from getting the bloody stuff. We destroyed it all, so that there could be no physical evidence. We saved this country and probably a lot of our allies a great deal of embarrassment. It's not like we saved any of the doomsday stuff. So what is the reasoning behind trying to kill us? Even if we all stuck to the same story, we would have no proof that it ever existed. We are not a threat."

"I have to say Andy that I don't know either, other than they want loose ends tied up."

"OK so we need a plan to first get Jane back and then I suppose, we have to draw out the folks who are trying to make us Ex Servicemen for real. We should talk it over with Abdalla and Lachie, when we get back."

I tried to get a little rest on the way back. The continual adrenalin rushes of the past days were taking its toll on me. I was not just becoming physically tired, but I was mentally drained. We had been drawn into this thing and then sucked down an ever deeper vortex, without any end in sight.

We arrived back home without further incident, much to my relief. Kyla greeted me with her usual exuberance. All the folks wanted to know what had gone on. I needed to talk to my military brothers in arms first, and then to our civilian charges after we had at least some semblance of a game plan.

Hans and I had recited the events of the day to Lachie and Abdalla. I asked for their thoughts.

"I am glad Andy, that you followed the advice of Hans. Sounds like, they whoever the, they are. Have not been told, how we saved the world." Lachie said.

"We know it is not Marcus, as he is bound to have died in the explosion. So it is either 'The Suit' or a third faction with military connections. It would not be the first time in history that high ranking military people have worked with civilians and other countries to steal, their own countries secrets for money or some political agenda. I have seen it happen in Kenya, where Generals sell out for a few thousand dollars. We know that this would have involved an item worth billions of dollars. People get very upset if they have lost out on that sort of payday. And on top of that they would do anything to protect their position and identity. What I am saying to you Mr Andy and also to you Mr Hans and Mr Lachie. You must assume that where your security agencies were involved, that some military individuals may also have been involved. We know Marcus had access to Royal Air Force Chinook's. Also the Reaper Drone came from a RAF base, controlled by the RAF. It was also on a live fire mission within British Air Space. This sort of thing takes a lot of clout, from a very high level. We should be looking in your military for the other player."

"Abdalla, I think that is the most I have ever heard you say."

"That is because Mr Andy. I have not had to say much before. Your leadership up to now has kept us all safe. I think now, that it is time to fight a different kind of battle"

"Abdalla I have always respected your thoughts and deeds. So if you have any other thoughts on how we can move forward. Please do so."

"Thank you for your kindness Mr Andy. I am a soldier. I

think at this point the most experienced person, and the man you should be taking advice from would be Mr Hans."

"I agree, with Abdalla, Andy. Hans is the man to help you here."

"Thanks Lachie, and of course Abdalla I have to agree. Hans you are an investigator. You have skills that none of us have. Can you come up with a plan?"

"I shall think on it Andy If that is alright? But we should first get Jane back."

"OK let's go talk with the others and let's eat. I am starving."

ACT 70

We ate and listened to the news on BBC Scotland. They had described it as a drone, that had gone off course, which had been safely destroyed, without harm to property or life. Fortunately. The newscaster said, the bridge had been closed for repairs at the time. So whoever was perpetuating all this was able to manipulate the media. After dinner, the thoughts, of us all, but especially Dusty and myself, turned to getting Jane back into the fold.

"Have you been able to contact Jane yet?" Dusty asked as he sat down in one of the two armchairs. He was looking weary. Not surprising given the circumstances added to the fact that his wife had been killed and his daughter, to all intense and purposes was M.I.A.

"I am going to call her just now. If she is smart like I think she is she will have discarded her old phone and bought a new burner set. Six on the dot I called her number. It rang three times and then.

"Hello?" It was Jane's voice

"I am going to keep this short and to the point." again I deliberately did not use her name

"OK?"

"Are you where we left you?"

"Yes"

"Every night, between now, and when we pick you up. Be at the exact spot, where we left you. Keep your sim and get another burner every time you use the phone. ONLY call us in an emergency. If I do not answer immediately, I will return your call. Got that?"

"Yes."

"We will come to you soon. Bye"

"Bye."

I removed my sim and broke the phone I had been using into bits. Then I opened a new burner package and set another on charge. I would not insert the sim until I needed to.

"She is safe. Now we need a plan to get her back to us, so your ideas please?"

"Well we can't use public transport, and Dusty can't be involved as his face is plastered all over the news. Same applies to Abdalla. So why can't we fly in and get her?" Lachie asked

"All planes have transponders on them and tracking devices so the moment we take off, assuming we don't get caught stealing the plane, then we will hit the radar. Also landing a plane where we left Jane is impossible. We dropped her on a cliff top. So you can't land anything but a helicopter there."

Hans replied to Lachie.

"Not quite the sort of plane I was thinking off. I was thinking of perhaps a hang glider come Microlight type thing. Both Andy and I have a lot of Parachuting experience. Perhaps looking at something like that?"

"Great thinking, Lachie if you can start looking on the internet that would help"

"We could drive the Zodiac over to the nearest coast in the van, and try that way" Sandy said

"Or somehow she smuggles herself out?" Dusty said

"We are looking at about thirty miles each way, from where she is to mainland Scotland. Think that might be a bit much for a Para-Glider." I said and then continued

"But it might not be too far for a Microlight. Lots of folks have them around the cliffs. Perhaps we could 'Borrow One' for an evening? Then just leave some cash inside for the owners? Lachie can you also search the internet for anyone who offers joy rides in a Microlight. If you look around the N.W. Coast and see what you come up with. I have told Jane to be at the spot we dropped her at every night at six. But it would have to be Hans to fly it. Do you think you could manage one of them Hans?"

"If it flies Andy, then I can fly it."

"OK so if the worst comes to the worst we use the Zodiac, assuming we have no other options. Though I suspect that it will have been reported missing by now. They probably will not be looking in the skies for us as they know we lost the chopper."

We worked through the night and argued the merits of using the Zodiac, against the risks involved in stealing a Microlight. Which Lachie had found a firm offering flights but it was about thirty miles inland from the closest point to point that we required. This added an extra sixty miles to the return trip, assuming that we would return it to the owners. If we did not, then they would report it stolen and it would bring the search back down on us. We could risk the Zodiac and hope we would not get caught. But we would have to cast it off or scupper it after we used it. In the end we decided to go with plan 'A'. We would try and see, if we could get a Microlight first. If that failed, we always had the fall-back plan 'B' of the Zodiac. We set out early in the morning on yet another unseasonably sunny day, Hans, Sandy, Lachie and myself. It was decided that if the Zodiac was to be used then Sandy would go with Lachie, but if they managed to secure a Microlight. Then the rest of us would still go to the closest seaward point. I would provide cover to either option with an AS50. Lachie was truthful enough to say that with his shoulder injury, he felt that I, would be the better choice. We got to the Airfield just outside. Kinlochbervie and found the hanger belonging to LiteFlight. However, there were far too many folks there with Hang Gliders and other Microlight aircraft, too many people around for us to be able to steal a microlight. We could not hire one without getting caught out, So we all opted for plan B which was the Zodiac. We estimated that the trip across would take about an hour and a half and about the same back give or take depending on tides and winds. As Hans would be free, I opted for him to go with Sandy as he could use the AS50. Lachie could provide back up support to me in the way of watching my back as I would be watching over the sea. We decided to find a place outside Kinlochbervie that was remote and also easy for us to get the Zodiac down to the water and that would give a good vantage point towards. Oldshoremore Beach, was perfect but it would mean that they would have a slightly longer trip. The advantage was I could set up a proper Hide and there were no people around at this time of year. They would be able to race the Zodiac, up onto the beach. The disadvantage was that the Honda now branded Yamaha engines were heavy and we had a long walk with them from the van to the water's edge. There was another advantage and that was there was a wooded area just up from the beach where we could stash the van. We would have to set off at four thirty at the latest. I would not call Jane before six. By which time the Zodiac would already be racing over the sea to The Butt of Lewis. They would not be showing any lights but Sandy said he would have the lighthouse on Lewis as a guide direct to the Butt. Time was chasing us down when we got to Oldshoremore Beach. We raced down to the beach with the Zodiac and then Hans. Lachie Sandy and I staggered the half mile through soft sand carrying the out board engines. We carried one engine between two and then on the last trip Hans and I carried the third engine while Lachie and Sandy carried the fuel. I could see Lachie was in great pain after helping me carry one of the outboards.

"How's the shoulder mate?"

"I will be fine it's just a little stiff"

I pulled his jacket aside and saw the crimson flower appearing on his t-shirt.

"Shit Lachie you have pulled the stitches again! And I don't have my full medical kit with me just dressings and superglue"

"Sorry Andy use the Super glue until we get back and just slap a dressing on top"

"I would prefer you did nothing more for a couple of

weeks' mate, but I guess we don't have much of a choice at the moment. When we get Jane back Lachie. You are on strict light duties and I mean you sit and watch TV or surf the web but nothing physical."

We sat in the back of the Van and I patched him up as best I could with the assistance of Hans. The look on Hans's face told me what I already knew, when he saw the wound, the start of an infection, with angry red lines tracing outwards from the wound. I said nothing to Lachie nor did Hans.

"OK Lachie all done. See if you can find a place to watch my back and a good place for me to set up I am going to help Hans fix the motors to the boat."

"OK Mate"

Hans, Sandy and I walked across the beach. We let Sandy walk a bit in front of us.

"Andy. Lachie needs to be in hospital"

"You think I don't know that? I have eye in my head. I can see the wound is infected and the infection is radiating out." I replied a little more harshly then I had intended.

"I was sure you did; don't you have any antibiotics?"

"I just have, topical antibiotics, but he needs fluids as well. We used up all the saline and glucose in my kit, at the start of all this. I need proper antibiotic in injection or drip form as well as a course of tablets. There is only so much medical stuff you can put in one field kit. The idea behind a field kit is you treat on the battlefield and then Evacuate to Hospital. However that is not an option for us. We send him to hospital they find him they will torture and then kill him. We would not get far from a hospital before they caught us either. I will think of something. Best thing I can do for now is keep him close to me, so I can watch him. I will not let my friend die. Not if I can help it. Hans, not a word to anyone please."

"OK Andy I know you two are close, just I have seen infection from gunshot wounds take a man down almost as fast as the bullet that did the damage. I am sure he is in good hands."

"I will help you drag the boat into the water. And wish you a safe trip. Sandy will get you there and back OK. I will contact Jane in a short while."

I waved them off, then I made my call. Slightly earlier than I was originally going to. I just prayed that Jane would answer. She did on the second ring

"I am going to keep this short and precise. Before you go to the beach. Find a VETS and find some Penicillin in an Injection and in tablet form, this will also mean you will also require some sterile water. I also need Liquid Glucose, in the form of an intravenous solution. It is for our lifelong dog that was hurt in a dogfight. Got That?

"How much"

"As much as you can get, you will have to borrow it as they will not give it to you, do you understand"

"I think so"

"It is very important, or our dog might be destroyed and I need the accoutrements that an addict, would need to inject" almost thirty seconds

"I love you"

"I love you too" I hung up

I could not use names. I took my phone to bits and put the sim in my wallet, and then I threw the parts of the old phone into the sea after the Zodiac, which was disappearing rapidly over the waves. I jogged back up to where Lachie was. I took our equipment out from the back of the van and left them in a hollow with Lachie. Then I drove the van into the wooded area. I then went back down to where Lachie was.

"Slight change of plan mate, I want us to use the same hide, you still keep watch from behind me and I will cover the sea."

I took my KaBar and cut lots of branches and shrubs and made a halfway decent hide with roof. Then set up my AS50 on its Bi Pod legs, checked that the mechanism was clear from sand and attached the BAE scope. Lachie had gone for overkill by attaching his advanced BAE scope to the Sig Sauer. But it allowed him infra-red capability. This should mean, we would not be caught blind-sided. I was worried about my friend and another of the reasons that I had kept him close as one of the signs of blood poisonings is sweating and shivering. So I would know if things took a serious turn, well more serious than they had done so already. The only thing in my kit I had close to a glucose drip were glucose tablets, which I sometimes took when running long distances. So I gave Lachie them along with a Mars Bar.

"I need you to let me know if you feel sick Lachie and I need you to be honest with me."

"I am fine mate just a bit tired, been a tough week or two."

"Yes it has Lachie. I just hope it reaches an end soon, as I am tired of all this dangerous shit"

I kept him talking until around a quarter past seven. My ears piqued and at first I thought I was imagining it. Then I heard it for sure, a pair of motor bikes or off road quad bikes racing towards where we were hidden. Lachie had heard it too and had repositioned himself, so he could look towards the sound. Was it possible that they had managed to get my position from that short call to Jane? Had she played me again and told them when I was going to call? I had no idea if they were hostile or innocent, but it was approaching the time when Sandy and Hans would be returning, hopefully with Jane. Two dirt bikes with boys who could not have been older than thirteen on them, raced right by our hide and disappeared over the sand dunes. I silently and metaphorically slapped myself for being a Doubting Thomas.

"Fuck me, Andy. I almost shot the little fuckers"

"Let's hope that they don't come back this way."

Another sound blew in from the ocean. At first I thought it was just our Zodiac with the three outboard engines, racing flat out, which they were. But there was another sound. There was another boat giving chase. I turned my scope to the sea, I could see our Zodiac weaving and another RIB chasing her down fast. There were flashes of suppressed gunfire from the chase boat.

"Target their engines" Lachie shouted at me

I zoomed and fired but their boat was bouncing and weaving so I think I missed completely, with the first two shots. The third shot must have struck one of the engines as there was trail of black smoke. I fired twice again and this time, fire erupted from the rear of their boat. I put a new clip in and fired five rounds directly into the front of the chase boat, which was now slowing. I could see the four men on-board trying to put out the flaming fuel. I put another full clip in and fired another three rounds into the side of her hull. The destructive force of the 50cal, even at this distance was plain to see. The sides were deflating and the fibreglass rigid hull was completely shattered along one side. The men on board here did not appear to have been hit. And they were not returning fire, nor were they shooting at our Zodiac which was racing away from them and towards our beach. For good measure I fired my last clip of three 50cal rounds into the sinking vessel. This time I think I hit one man who seemed to do a backwards flip into the sea. The boat sunk. I could see the three survivors in the sea. They had no life preservers on and I knew they would not survive more than a few minutes in the sea. If we tried to save them, they would try to kill us. I was sickened by my lack of empathy towards them. Our Zodiac hit the beach full tilt and slid over the flat sand for about twenty five yards. Jane was out and running before it stopped. Hans helped Sandy out. I ran down the beach past Jane, to help Hans with what we had to do next.

"Sandy, follow Jane to the edge of the sand"

I ran to Hans and tilted the out board motors up and then helped him drag the Zodiac back to the sea. It was an outgoing tide. We got it into the water, then we dropped the engines, Hans climbed on board and started the engines. Then tied off the wheel and engaged the engines and sent the Zodiac back out to sea, before diving into the water and swimming back to me.

We ran back up the beach and picked up his backpack from where he had dropped it, when the boat had come to a halt.

"Are you all OK? Where did you find the tail?"

"Yes mate we are fine. About ten minutes ago they came at us from the North. They must have been scoping out the waters around the highlands. I think these guys were SAS Andy. They were all wearing the same cap style badges. Only the cap was green I think."

"More like SBS"

"SBS?"

"Yes Hans they are like the SAS only they are Special Boat Service, they are more like Navy Seals. SAS are more like Delta Force. If they are in the game against us, then the strings that are being pulled have to be by a very high up puppeteer."

"Not good then"

"No Hans. Let's go join the others and get the hell out of here before the SAS do come"

I got to the hide.

"We need to get to van like now, they will have called this in. and I want to be on a main road before they get here"

I could see Lachie was starting to sweat, even though it was a chilly clear night. I was really getting worried. We got to the van there was a lot more space in the back without the Zodiac. Sandy and Hans were in the front, Jane and I helped Lachie and then we followed him into the back. Sandy drove us out onto the main road without the use of light. When he hit the main road, he turned them on and stayed within the speed limit, meanwhile in the rear cargo space.

"Jane, did you manage to get the stuff I asked for?"

"I think so, I broke into a vets and raided their store, then I ran for the beach" she put her back pack in front of me."

I tipped it up and grabbed a Penicillin bottle and a bottle of sterile water, there were packets of syringes and a variety of needles, some of which were actually meant for horses, so were somewhat big for a human. I chose a needle of the correct size and filled the syringe with sterile water. Then I injected it into the Penicillin bottle and gave it a good shake up, after which I drew it back up in to the syringe.

"Where do you want it arse or arm?"

"You have to be shitting me Andy. That stuff is for animals, not humans"

"I am reliably informed that it works on Rock Apes too."

"Ohhh Fucking Funny Andy, you should become a comedian."

"Lachie it is the same fucking stuff, most of it starts out as human medicine that is technically outdated. So they sell it to vets. It's still good, just stupid laws over sell by and use by dates. So where do you want it?"

"Are you sure about this mate?"

"Lachie, we both know that your wound is infected, I can't risk taking you to a hospital. If I don't do this Andy, things can go south really quick, like in a matter of hours. Do you understand? What I am telling you is, if I don't do this you could die mate."

"Arse then, in my fucking arse"

"Turn over and drop them"

"Really?"

"Yes really, I am sure Jane has seen plenty of big arses

working for SIS"

He dropped his trousers and shorts revealing a little heart shaped tattoo, with an arrow through it and the name Suzanne written in script below it. I must have laughed out loud because he gave me the bird.

"What?"

"Ohh nothing mate" I said as I put the needle into his buttock and slowly injected the contents of the syringe, next to Lachie's tattoo.

"Oow that fucking hurt"

"Not as much as it would in the arm, and I am sure it did not hurt as much as being shot Lachie."

"I would rather be shot. Than be stuck with a needle."

"As soon as we get back Lachie, I am going to have to put you on a drip for a couple of days and I might have to go digging in that wound of yours. If I do, I will give you a load of pain killers that will probably put you out for a while."

Almost three hours later we made it back to the house by the beach. As soon as I got inside I commandeered one of the beds for Lachie and set up an intravenous drip of glucose. We took turns watching over him during the night as at first his condition worsened. He became delirious. I was afraid to go rooting around inside his wound until he stabilised. I would do that tomorrow. I gave him another line set up with sterile water and penicillin. His temperature spiked at one hundred and four degrees Fahrenheit. Then fortunately it started to fall, just as the sun was rising. He was soaked in sweat and the bedding had to be changed. I had with the assistance of Hans stripped him of all his clothing during the night and filled pans with cold water and laid them on him, to try and force the heat from his body. Jane came in as I was changing the glucose drip.

"How is Lachie?"

"I think he is going to make it, but we are a long way from the woods yet."

"You love him don't you?"

"We are like brothers, we are as close as any two brothers could be. We grew up together, partied together, joined up together, and we are still fighting side by side. So yes I love him."

"I hope you will love me like that one day Andy"

"I do love you Jane, but it will never be like the love I have for Lachie. That is a brother's bond."

"How did they find us?"

"They were just searching all around the coast, looking to see if we made a run for Iceland."

"Did you manage to contact 'The Suit'?"

"I tried but got no replies."

"You look tired Andy" She stood next to me and massaged my neck. It felt good.

"I am it has been a scary couple of days."

"Want a coffee?"

"That would be nice Jane. Thank you.

"Mmmmm" Lachie said in his sleep

Jane turned with a bit of a start "Can he hear us?"

"I think he is just dreaming"

Jane came back with two coffees and a cold flannel, which she placed on Lachie's head. We sat like this for another two hours. Just chatting and Jane fetching a fresh cold compress every fifteen minutes. The others were up and I could hear Rosemary in the Kitchen making breakfast for all. The smell of frying bacon wafted through to the bedroom where Lachie lay. I had nearly lost my dearest and oldest friend. I was not even sure if I could ever be whole without him. Jane seemed to notice my thoughts. She put her arm around my waist and laid her head upon my shoulder.

"He will recover. He needs you as much as you need him. I know he will not leave you.

I went and grabbed a few hours shut-eye. I awoke and grabbed a coffee and went to check on Lachie. He was sitting up in bed eating a bowl of Chicken Soup that Rosemary had made for him. So I left him with Rosemary fussing over him. I went outside and found Abdalla, Hans and Jane sat together. Another beautiful day with bright sunshine it felt good to be alive on such a day. There was a swell developing so I guessed we were going to be in for another spring storm sometime soon.

"Morning all, we need to talk. My mind has been going around in circles." I said as I sat down next to them.

"What troubles you Mr Andy"

"Where do you want me to start Abdalla?"

"With the biggest problem"

ACT 71

"OK. The biggest problem is the WHO? See we already know that Marcus was the man in SIS, that was selling this deadly toxin. We know that people are still trying to kill us. Like the Royal Air Force and the bloody SAS or SBS. What if there are still two groups at war here? What if the people that were selling this, went higher than Marcus Brown, who was the head man of SIS. In order for him to have the resources, he would need someone much higher up the food chain."

"Like who Andy? I worked with Marcus and he never said anything about anyone else."

"Jane we know that he liked to keep things compartmentalised. So he would not tell you, purely for personal security. If you had been captured and interrogated by say 'The Suit's friends. So Marcus could not let you have information, that could kill his deal. We should start looking at the top of the tree. The Queen, highly unlikely, the Prime Minister again highly unlikely. So the only person between the

PM and the heads of the military is the Secretary of Defence. This is the only other person from our country that could use the military on home soil, to act offensively against us. I am not that up on politics, but I am sure you know who that is Jane?"

"It is Sir Peter Ramsay and he has met with Marcus quite a few times. When I think about it he has even been to his home several times."

"I don't suppose you know where his home is?"

"Yes I went to it once. It is in the Chiltern Hundreds in Buckinghamshire. He also has an office at the Ministry of Defence, in Whitehall, London."

"Thanks Jane. What do the rest of you think about this?"

"It is the only thing that makes sense Andy. He would have access to high up individuals in foreign powers and it would not look suspicious. He could also rubber stamp orders without any questions being asked, especially if he said that he was combating terrorism in the UK." Hans said as he threw the sediment of his coffee away.

"Thanks Hans."

"Mr Andy. He would also be able to contact other Nations Embassies, here in the UK. This would explain the Israeli and USA involvement. He could use them to be on the side of 'The Suit' to track us down, to both stop us exposing him. So that effectively the good guys and the bad guys are all after us. But he must also have help from someone other than Marcus."

"I agree Abdalla. I just do not know who"

"Andy it would have to be someone with access to the level five contagions. This means that it is a high ranking military officer who is stationed there. Probably not someone in an administrative role, I suspect that it will be the Army General. The Station Commander is the Royal Air Force, Group Captain. He just runs the day to day military base. The Army General is in charge of the biological research."

"OK Hans, I think we have to go after the head of the snake, or in this case the two heads of the snake. It is the only way that we will ever clear our names. But I think we have to make some kind of contact with 'The Suit.' There has to be a way."

"Andy I think I have an idea."

"What's that Jane?"

"If I contact SIS direct and give my name and Marcus Browns name. Then ask for the new head of SIS, which is bound to be 'The Suit' to contact me, at a set email address. Perhaps we could get him to listen to us. Perhaps even to call off his men and give us a chance to clear all this up. He is bound to know that we were used as pawns by Marcus. Then if we can prove, that it is the secretary of defence who is behind all this"

"Jane. Is this the same dark-web mail as you originally used to contact Marcus?"

"Yes Andy, but SIS use a bunch of Dark-Web chat rooms and Chat forums, that they use for agents to check in, or to receive messages on. If we can get a message to him and then get him to call one of our phones. Then so long as we keep our conversation short and to the point they will not be able to track us."

"OK Jane if you can set that up. BUT I will want to arrange a face to face with him. Do you think he would go for that?"

"To be quite honest Andy, I don't know. But anything is worth a try at this point."

Jane went to try and contact SIS on her laptop, which she connected to her mobile phone. I sat on a log with my coffee. I got up and walked over to Hans.

"Hans I need to have a private word with you"

We walked towards the beach then I stopped and found myself looking out over the sea.

"Hans I have a job that I would like you to take care of, if you would be so kind. I would like you to go to Golspie. There is a small Bed and Breakfast place, on the High Street. It's near the Stags Head Hotel. It is called the Sea Kraken. Take three thousand of the money we have left, and give it to my father, he is staying there. I moved him and Lachie's folks without letting any other person know. I told him I would be sending you if I could not do it personally. If you take the van, you should be back here for six tonight. Also if you could fill the van up with fuel, I think we are going to need it."

"Not a problem Andy. I can do it."

"One more thing, please don't tell him about his dog. I will do that myself when things are sorted."

"OK. Is there anything else I can do?"

"No that's it I think. I have to figure a way out of all this. A way, that sets us all free."

We walked back to the cottage and Hans collected the money and drove off in the van alone. I went in to see how Lachie was getting on. Kyla was sat by his bed, where he was sat up drinking coffee as Rosemary fussed over him.

"Can you give Lachie and me a minute please Rosemary?"

"Of course, if you need anything Lachie, just call out. OK"

Lachie gave her a thumbs up, and I sat down next to him.

"How are you feeling?"

"A bit washed out, but loads better than I was mate. Thanks for everything you did. So what's the deal now?"

"That I don't know Lachie. I am trying to find a way out, a way that will make us all free men and women again. I have asked Jane to contact 'The Suit'. We know he is on the right side. We also know we were duped by Marcus Brown. We destroyed the shit from CDE. Not only that, we killed Marcus and a bunch of his men. We have talked things over when you were resting. I actually think that the real top man behind all of this shite, is our own Secretary of Defence, Sir Peter Ramsay."

"Fucking Hell. Andy."

"The only way out, is to convince 'The Suit' and then, we see what happens after that. Jane is trying to contact him at the moment and then I will arrange a meet. But I want him alone. Not him and an army."

"Let me know how I can help"

"I will Lachie, as soon as I have a plan. By the way, I have sent Hans off to give our folks some money. I have our parents stashed away in Golspie."

"You never said anything to me?"

"Sorry I did it when they said 'They' said, they would move our folks. So I moved them first. They have enough funds for a couple of weeks. I hope this will all be over by then."

"Thanks for that Andy."

"OK Lachie I am going to work things out with the others. Get some rest."

I went and called all the others to an open meeting, to see if we could work a plan.

"Any ideas anybody?"

"Mr Andy you said you want to try and get a meeting, with just you and 'The Suit'? Do you think it wise to do this on your own?"

"Abdalla I will not be on my own. I will have you and Hans covering me, possibly Lachie, if he is recovered enough by then."

"What about us?"

"Sandy I want all the civilians to stay here. It is safe here. We will leave you the shotguns and I will be leaving Kyla with you. If it works out, we will only be away for a day."

"Jane have you had any replies from SIS?"

"Nothing yet Andy, but I have left messages on the Chat forum, and emailed SIS directly. So they will know we are still alive and kicking. I would expect a reply soon."

"OK so for now it's a sit and wait game."

"I will make some lunch for us all. Do you want to help me Stu?"

Stuart blushed and went with Rosemary into the house. Dusty went with Sandy and chopped up some wood for the Rayburn.

"How do you want me to play this, when they reply?"

"As soon as you get contact with 'The Suit' I want him to give you a telephone number, so I can call him. Then I plan to ask him to meet with me. I will give him a run-around. Just so we can make sure he does not have an army with him and when I am sure, I will direct him to a place that we will have already set up, and can control."

Just for the safety of our group. I did not tell Jane where, I wanted to have the final place for the meet. I did want to trust her. Had it been just my life, it might have been a different story. The reality though was different, I now had the responsibility for more than a dozen people, including Lachie's folks and my father. So I would discuss the final location only with Hans, Abdalla and Lachie.

ACT 72

Jane made contact at four that afternoon. After a bit of a palaver 'The Suit' finally, gave out a telephone number. I dialled the number using one of my burner phones.

"Hello"

"Who is this" A female voice answered

"The next time I call the guy in 'The Suit' better answer of all deals are off" I hung up.

I dialled two minutes later.

"Hello"

"Who am I talking too?" at last 'The Suit" I recognised his voice. I knew I had to keep this short.

"Andy McPhee. I want a meeting, just you and me. No others just you and me alone. I will call you later with the where, and the when." I hung up.

"OK Folks lets work this out." I said as I rolled out an Ordinance Survey Map of our area.

"Jane I am going to use you as a spotter. I want you to

get to the top of Kearvaig Hill. That is the one at the back of this property, if you follow the road for about half a mile and then head west from the road. Climb to the top of the hill and set up a look out post. If you use the blanket Abdalla has made up for you as your cover. If you head out now, you should get there in good time."

Abdalla had made a lot of camouflage blankets by first covering blankets that we had found in the house, with peat mud, and then covering them with clumps of heather, which had been poked through the material. He had then used duct tape to secure a thermal blanket to the other side. When laid on the ground even from close inspection they were hard to find. Due to the metallic thermal blanket under it would also hide the person under it from thermal cameras. As such they provided perfect cover with near invisibility. Jane left with her backpack, plus a pair of binoculars that we found in the house. She had her Storno radio, along with her throat mike and ear piece. Jane would have a good view of the Road from both east and west. She would also have a good view of the bay to the south and the country side to the north. I had told her, if she sees more than one vehicle, then we would assume 'The Suit' is not alone. If Jane were to see anyone else, then she would let us know and we would all pull back. I pointed out position on a large map that we had rolled out on the kitchen table.

"This is where I had asked 'The Suit' to leave his transport. From there he would have to walk the five miles down the road towards the Bridge at Inshore." I said as I pointed to the map.

"Lachie this is where I want you to set up. There is a large knoll to the south west side of Loch Inshore. There are two rowing boats there. I contacted the owners today. I checked on the pretence that I was looking for a week's fishing. The owners said that it has not been booked for any fishing this month. So we will have it to ourselves. Out of the two rowing boats there, I will already have taken one and have it hidden around the Eastern side, of the small Island that sits in the middle of the Loch. I will ask 'The Suit' to strip butt naked when he gets there." Again I pointed to the point on the map where that would happen. Then I continued.

"From there, I will direct him down the road to the south

of Loch Inshore. He will walk for a mile, where I will have a boiler suit left for him along with a pair of Wellington boots. You will cover him at all times with an AS50. You will also have a complete three hundred and sixty-degree view of the land for a couple of miles. Abdalla you will be on the eastern side of Loch Inshore. You will set up under the grassy bank of the beach. This will give you a complete view of the North, West and south of the small Island."

"Hans there is a disused and broken down house on the road to Inshore. If you can set up a hide to the east of that about two hundred yards from the Loch, you will then have a view of North, West and South of the small Island. Like Lachie, you and Hans will have AS50's. I will have already left some hand guns on the Island, just in case 'The Suit' wants to be difficult. I will then ask 'The Suit' to walk back to the Loch and take the one rowing boat that will be left there. He will then row out to the western side of the Island. I will not show myself, until I get the all clear from each of you. If any of you, see ANYTHING, that is ANYTHING at all suspicious, then we call it off. Remember I am going to give him the run around. If he fails to do anything I tell him to do, then I will ask one of you to fire a round at his feet. If it looks like, he has any form of radio, we call it off and regroup back here."

I got Sandy to drive us, as close as he could get to our locations. We passed Jane five minutes out from our cottage and waved at her as we passed by. Just out of safety she would have no idea where the rest of us would be located. Lachie was first out and he headed up the hillside. then Hans and me. Dusty then drove a mile further away and let Abdalla out. At the end of this road Dusty did a U turn and returned to the cottage to sit and wait for us to call him, to come and collect us. It was a perfect day. There was a slight chill in the air this morning. There was some good but high, cloud cover. That would help to obscure us from any satellite coverage. We would still have a good view of any planes or approaching helicopters or even any unmanned drones. I took one of the two small rowing boats and rowed out to the eastern side of the island. I pulled it ashore and covered it in large clumps of heather and grass. I set up my own hide near the centre of the Island.

"Everyone ready?"

"Roger" said Jane

"Ready" Said Lachie

"Roger" Said Hans

"I am ready Mr Andy and may Allah be with you and protect us all" said Abdalla

"Listening in" Said Sandy

"OK Sandy. Stay silent please unless I call you"

I dialled the Suit. He picked up on the fourth ring.

"Hello"

"Go to the bus stop at Cearbhag road. It is in the middle of nowhere. Come by car and park it exactly at the T junction. Get out and walk south on to the hillside. Then sit down and wait. Come alone. We will be watching. Do not wear a wire, or any tracking device. Do not bring a gun, just your telephone. Be there in two hours." I hung up. I knew from previous telephone conversations that "The Suit" was at Brora Radio Station. So I knew he would have to race to the point I had asked him to be at, if he was going to make it on time. But it gave him no time to do anything else other than drive to us.

"OK guys now we wait, stay vigilant." I got Roger's all around.

The last two weeks had been a roller coaster of running from death. None of us had deserved to be targeted. Each of us were innocent, with perhaps the exception of Jane who had been involved with Marcus, at the beginning of whatever this really was. They chose to fight this battle, in the remote Highlands of Scotland. That was probably their downfall. Insomuch as Lachie and I had walked this land as children and then as young men. This was our homeland. We knew how to survive with little or nothing. We could read the signs of the land and know when something was approaching. We also knew by the wildlife signs when things were safe. Sandy knew the coastal waters like the back of his hand. Without his knowledge we would surely have died a long time ago. The expertise of Hans and Abdalla in the art of camouflage I hoped would save us now. I was sure that they would try and get a satellite over our area at the time of the meeting so it was imperative that we were well hidden for as long as possible.

"Small car approaching from the west, following the road to Cearbhag" Jane said

"Roger let me know if it stops at the bus stop"

"Will do"

Three minutes of silence

"I think it is him he is parking up by the bus stop"

"Roger, keep a good watch"

I dialled his number

"Hello"

"Get out of the car walk due south for two hundred yards and sit down and wait for my next call"

"He is walking away from the car"

"Roger that let me know when he stops?"

"He has stopped and is now sitting down"

"Roger that"

I dialled another number on my phone. This was connected to a bomb that Hans had made and set by the bus stop. It connected, and the car was lifted ten feet into the air and then landed as a burning heap at the side of the road. I redialled the number for 'The Suit'

"What in the name of fuck, did you do to my car?"

"I removed it. Now remove all of your clothes and walk back down towards the road."

"I am not taking my clothes off for you, or anyone else"

"Lachie"

"Roger"

"Now"

Lachie fired a single suppressed 50cal round aimed at a point just inches from 'The Suit's right foot.

"The next shot will go into your head."

I ended the call.

"Lachie is he getting stripped?"

"Roger that 'The Suit' is changing into his birthday suit."

"Let me know when he is butt naked?"

"Roger"

I waited for Lachie to message me.

"Naked as the day he was born."

"Can you get a close up with the BAE scope Lachie?"

"Ughhh! Do you realise I will need a lifetime of therapy, after this?"

"You wanted to be a Rock Ape?"

"OK Andy. I have him on full screen, and boy is he white, he needs to get out of the office more, but he is not wearing a wire"

"Keep a good watch on him while I call him"

"Roger that"

I hit the redial button on my phone. He took some time answering, on account that his phone was in his clothes I guessed. After fumbling it out of his jacket pocket, he answered.

"Hello!" he did not sound so happy, nor did he sound as confident as he had a few moments before.

"Put your arms out to the side and slowly, very slowly turn around in a complete circle"

"Is this really necessary Mr McPhee?"

"Ask another question like that or give me more attitude and you will lose several toes. Now just fucking do it"

"Lachie?"

"He is rotating slowly, and now he is turning towards me. Makes me proud to be a Scot"

"How do you mean?"

"Well he is not what you could call well endowed. But I am still feeling scarred for life."

"Suit? Do you have a real name?"

"Just call me 'The Suit' as you have always done"

"Fine, before you do anything else, take off your watch and your ring. Then put those items along with your phone down on your pile of clothes. Then walk back up to the road and keep walking eastwards along the road. You will find a boiler suit and another phone. I will call you again when you have done that. Now move before one of us decides to shoot you just for fun."

I hung up. I had deliberately, not, put a pair of Wellington boots out for 'The Suit' as I had originally intended. This I had done out of spite, for all the hardships we had been put through by him.

"What's he doing Lachie?"

"It looks like he is removing his jewellery, and putting them on his clothes. You know he has folded his clothes neatly. Like 'who' after being shot at and asked to strip, folds their clothes?"

"Lachie when he is out of sight of you. Can you go

down to his clothes and set fire to them?"

"Why?"

"Just in case there is some form of tracker in them."

"Good thought."

I waited until Lachie told me 'The Suit' was in his boiler suit.

"Lachie When you have torched his clothes can you get back up to your position and provide cover again?"

"Roger that Andy."

I rang the suit on his new but far less glitzy mobile phone.

"Now what game do you want me to play?"

"No games today, I am deadly serious, especially about people who have tried to kill me."

"So what happens now?"

"Now I want you to jog down the road for about a mile. You will come to a small bridge over a Burn. I suppose you would call it a stream."

"But I don't have any shoes on!"

"So jog on the grass verges or the grass in the middle of the road, but watch out for thistles or worse Adders"

"Snakes?"

"Don't worry most of them are hibernating at this time of year. I will call you when you get to the bridge. But hurry. We will be watching you. Now GO!"

I ended the call.

"Let me know when you are back on point Lachie"

"Almost there."

"OK let me know when he is at the bridge please"

"Roger that."

I was already sat in the middle of the small Island of Loch Inshore. It was only twenty yards long by ten yards wide. But it was sufficiently grassy and undulated to hide my position well. I wondered, if when 'The Suit' finally got here, would he try to kill me or would he listen to what I had to say?"

"He is just approaching the bridge. By the way, he just tried to call out on the phone"

"Roger that Lachie. Keep a watch on us from above please"

"I have all your positions covered"

"Thanks Lachie"

I dialled 'The Suits' new phone.

"Now what?"

"Did I forget to mention the there is no dial out on that phone?"

"You Bastard. Where are you?"

"In the words of the song WE are all around you, and WE will show ourselves, when WE are ready.! Now if you jog down another half mile you will find a deserted house. It will be on your right. There is another Burn there. I want you to follow that Burn, to the Loch you can see. Do not deviate from the stream. When you get to the Loch, you will find a rowing boat. Get in and row it to the small Island. When you get to the Island I want you to stand right in the middle. Do you understand?"

"Enough of the games show yourself."

"Lachie make him move please"

"Roger that."

It is quite amazing the amount of damage that a 50cal round can inflict upon a hard surface like a road. Lachie had placed the round quite close to 'The Suits' naked left foot. The soft nosed round flattened on impact with the stony surface of the road, causing the road to have a new large pot hole where none had previously existed. 'The Suit' leapt back a good yard.

"All right I am going."

"Andy he is double timing it, to the next point."

I hung up the phone.

"Roger that Lachie."

"Abdalla are you ready?"

"Mr Andy. I have your position covered."

"Hans?"

"Got you covered from the other side"

"Thanks guys."

"He is at the boat Andy" Lachie said in my earpiece.

I waited and I watched as the boat slowly came into view. He handled the oars with a high level of proficiency. He had probably rowed at University for Oxford or Cambridge. The intelligence services had a habit of recruiting from one or other of these great learning institutions. Even though he had his back to me I could see how he used the oars in perfect symmetry.

"You should have a visual Andy"

"I have him. Everybody listen in, any tricks try to shoot to wound."

"Seriously? Andy we are using big guns, if we hit him he is dead"

"Well let's hope it does not come to that. Out"

I had my Sig Sauer tucked into the waistband of my jeans. There did not seem any point in fitting it with a suppressor. There was no one around out here, except for us and some wild game birds.

He walked to within feet of where I had set my hide. Then he walked past me and stood on the highest part of this little Island. He did not even notice me or so it first appeared.

"You have learned some new skills or so it would appear Mr McPhee. You can come out of your hide now. I know you are about twelve feet behind me."

I stood up and pointed my Sig at him.

"Do you mind lowering that I am sure your comrades have me well and truly covered from their positions, I am guessing from the sides of this Loch and from the high point over there, near where you blew up my car?"

"I don't even know your name. But what I do know, is that you know we were not working voluntarily with Marcus Brown. I can tell you we did not have a clue until we found the stuff, which as I am sure you already know, we destroyed along with Marcus. What I think is this. You actually used us as bait. I think you knew Marcus was involved, but as he was your boss, you needed absolute proof. Then you found out what we have now worked out. Which is, that Marcus Brown was not working on his own?"

"Go on Mr McPhee."

"It was not you who tried to kill us using a Reaper Drone, was it?"

"No, it was not me that authorised that"

"Or the attack, by the Special Boat Service?"

"No not that either."

"But you did try to kill us several other times?"

"I made it appear so."

"I don't follow"

"Mr McPhee don't you think if I had wanted you dead, I could have had you killed at Altnabreac. At the Logging site you set up. Which by the way was a stroke of genius? And we did lose you for quite some time"

"So correct me if I am wrong Marcus was doing this for money?"

"Yes and he was going to run away with Miss Miller."

"Your men killed her mother."

"That was a most regrettable accident. She had a weak heart that I was unaware of."

"My father's Dog."

"I believe you took care of the individual responsible for that"

"I have killed men and been responsible for the deaths of many more, including some of the men that you hired"

"They were not my men they belonged to the agent from Mosad, she hired them. She was supposed to steal the barrel back from Marcus."

"So what is the situation now?"

"You continue your operation."

"Excuse me? Are you out of your fucking mind? I arranged this meeting today. In order for you to accept that we are all innocent. We want our lives back."

"What? You think you can just walk away? When you are so close to completing this?"

"We never asked for any of this"

"Who do you think is responsible?"

"I think it is Sir Peter Ramsay."

"Then you would be correct."

"So you go and get him"

"I can't because of political reasons. My office is directly overseen by his office. I am sure that he has his moles within SIS. This was one of the reasons that I agreed to shut down all SIS Black Door ops. There is no point in us arresting Sir Peter because he has friends in extremely high places and by extremely high. I mean as in certain Royals."

"So what are we supposed to do?"

ACT 73

"Simple, you are to kill him."

"You are stark raving mad. You want me to murder a serving Peer of the Realm, who just happens to be a close personal friend, of a member of the Royal Family. I don't think so."

"As I said Mr McPhee, my office has more leaks than a Welsh Rugby field on cup final day. Technically you are no longer in any form of existence. Sir Peter is, or should I say was, supposed to be meeting with Marcus Brown, on a country estate near here. He would also be meeting with an American industrialist who was also involved. The CIA has been working with us on this, as have MOSAD.

It would be better for all the countries involved, if we were to take care of our own domestic problems, without foreign nations committing. Should they interfere it could technically be deemed as an act of war. The murder of our Secretary of Defence would be classed as that, were it ever to come out."

"What happens to us if we manage to end this?"

"You get your lives back and will be financially secure for the rest of your days."

"What about my home?"

"You would have a new one built, which we would pay for of course."

"And the rest of my team?"

"The same, they will be well rewarded."

"Sandy's fishing boat?"

"I will personally see to it that he is given a brand new fully equipped fishing boat, even better than the one he had."

"What is to stop you reneging on our deal?"

"No doubt, the recording that you are currently making on your mobile phone, I am sure you will have copies made for all your team. So that in the event of a sudden and unexpected death, would be made public?"

"What protection and support can you give us? I am sure you are aware that we are a little low on funds?"

"None until the completion of this operation."

"Where and when?"

"Where and when? What?"

"Where will Sir Peter be, and when will he be there? Also who is the other person?"

"He will be staying just one week, on Gruinard Island. The American is making a play to buy the Island. He wants to turn it into a golf course or something."

"I think I know who you mean. If I am correct, he is the Billionaire Douglas Crump? The man who has major shares in Halliburton and Black Forest not to mention owning half of Wall Street"

"One and the same, they need to have a fatal accident preferably without any further casualties."

"Can you lift, the 'Be on the Lookout for' from us? It will make it a lot easier to travel."

"I can state that you have all died in a mysterious accident, will that do?"

"So long as the there are no reaper drones and SBS type folks looking for us. It will make things a lot easier for us to move around. What happens when it is done?"

"We bring you in, debrief you and then you are free."

"Again how do I know I can trust you?"

"Mr McPhee. I came here unarmed and there were no bugs in my car or my clothing, not in my watch or my ring. I came on trust."

"OK let's meet with all of my friends. Please tear the sleeve off your boiler suit."

"I don't follow"

"I need to blindfold you"

I rowed back across from the Island with 'The Suit' in the boat. Jane had contacted Sandy, who was driving the van to collect us all. I walked 'The Suit' up to the road, still keeping a steady eye on him. When I got to the road the van was waiting. I rolled the shutter up and helped 'The Suit' in then I sat him down at the back. Lachie was first to join us, followed closely by Hans and finally Abdalla. We drove back in silence, past the burned out wreck of 'The Suits' car and then down to the Cottage. All of us piled out of the back and then into the house. I put my finger to my lips, in order that no one should speak, apart from me.

"Get everyone in here please."

I sat 'The Suit' down on a kitchen chair. We all stood and sat around, looking at him. I removed the blindfold and he blinked his eyes a few times, to get used to the light in the kitchen.

"This is the person, who is the current head of the SIS. He has promised to give us, all our lives back. Providing we do one more thing. That thing involves us killing the men who were working with Marcus Brown. These men were going to sell and or use the material that we destroyed. So I am going to record this conversation and I will mention all of our names. Is that OK with you all?"

They all indicated yes. I pressed record on the phone.

"All the following people are innocent of any and all charges levelled against them. They were all unwilling pawns used by the previous head of SIS, Mr Marcus Brown and the Current Secretary of Defence, Sir Peter Ramsay. They, along with the USA Industrialist, Mr Douglas Crump. The Current Head of SIS only known to us, as 'The Suit'" Click "I have just taken a photo of him to go with this recording. He has stated, to us all here, that if we finish this operation, we will all be free. We are.

Sgt Lachlan Henderson, Colonel Hans Gunnerson, Major Abdalla Mohamed, Miss Jane Miller, Mr Sandy McKay, Miss Rosemary McKay, Mr Stuart McCormack, Mr Dusty Miller, Mr Mark Henderson father of Lachlan, Mr Craig McPhee father of myself Flt Sgt Andy McPhee. Can you please state for the recording and video, that Miss Miller is currently filming? That we are completely innocent of any and all charges. State your Name Rank and Position within the British Secret Intelligence Service."

"I am General Sir Philip Reeves-Johnson, also known to these people as 'The Suit'. I am the senior officer in charge of counterterrorism and current head of the SIS, including MI5 and MI6 as well as any current and previous Black Door operations. This recording and video is not made under any duress"

"Thank you, though I kind of liked calling you 'The Suit' OK Folks do you all wish to finish this?"

"Hell yes" said Lachie

Everyone else said yes, even though they knew we still had to kill two more men. I started out thinking all life was sacred. And I was now actually plotting the deaths of two men. My life would never be the same I know that. I just hoped that some of the others here, could go back to some version of their old lives.

"Dusty can you take Sir Philip to a village so he can call home."

"What about my clothes, and my watch?"

"Sorry Sir Philip. I burned them" Lachie said

"Why?"

"Just in case, and you are lucky you were not in them at the time" Lachie finished

I was not sure but I thought I saw a smile cross the face of Sir Philip as he left the room with dusty.

I played the recording that I had made on the Island to the others. There were gasps and groans. And finally some sighs as we knew that the end was close.

ACT 74

This part of the operation would not involve any of the civilians. 'The Suit' had arranged with Dusty on his way to Cape Wrath, that he would send a package to a post office box, that would include ten thousand pounds as a temporary payment for services rendered. So they would be comfortable until we were able to return. We filled the Van and took as much equipment as we could. Lachie, Hans and Abdalla in front, Jane and I rode in the back with Kyla. Using as many side roads as we could we drove through the night down to the beautiful beach at Mungasdale. We would have to 'Borrow' a boat and get over to Gruinard Island, without being seen. There was bound to be security of some form surrounding Sir Peter and other officials at their meeting. We would have to find some way of staging an accident, whereby they both died without any innocents being hurt. As it turned out we were able to steal a small fishing boat that had obviously been tied up for the winter. There was a green tarpaulin covering the entire wheelhouse and decking area. The boat would be big enough for the five of us. However, I only wanted to take Lachie and Hans with me on to the Island. For reasons known only to the Government there were no accurate maps of Gruinard Island. No doubt it still held some secrets from the past. Some might say that is was judicious that this Island would be the end point, of yet another story in the biological war game. Once again this remote Scottish Island was to play host to evil men, bent on destroying the world with the use of refined germs. These germs although naturally occurring were killers, but when modified were more than just killers, they were genocidal. We looked across the short distance of water between us and the Island. We could see a newly built large bungalow with a decking area to the front and what looked like a heated swimming pool. There was an enormous marquee to the side of the sprawling house. The house seemed to have been made from great logs no doubt felled from some forest on the mainland. There were a lot of people working around the grounds. It looked like something you would expect to see in Northern Canada. There was a Helipad to the rear of the Property. The small floating dock was next to the sandy peninsula on the southern tip of the Island. I could see supply boats bringing goods and then leaving and going back to a large container ship anchored to the North of the Island I zoomed in and saw the name of this ship 'Sea Osprey'. It looked like they were setting up for a big party. Whilst the Island was open from all sides, which made it easy for us to see what was going on. The down side was that we would easily be seen if we went onto the Island. The first thing that we would have to do is to identify the two targets. It was easier for me now to think of them as targets, rather than as fellow human beings. We would first have to try and get a little closer in order to see the lay of the land. Hans and I would first take the boat out and do a little fishing, using the two rods that the owner of the boat had left in the little cabin. The Fuel tank was full, but the battery was dead. Hans found the starter handle and cranked the motor into life. The boat was registered to a man in the village of Little Gruinard. This was a couple of miles down the coast from here. Being so close to the Island I am sure that the security services already knew about this boat and therefore it would not arouse suspicion if see fishing in the area. Hans and I would sail up from the south and then across the north and down the west and finally back to the shore. All the time we would be fishing. I knew from my childhood that fishing for mackerel was simple. Just throw in a shiny hook and the Mackerel would bite. We found an old fish box and took that on board. We decided not to take any guns or military knives. The reason being if we were stopped, we could talk our way out, rather than a shoot-out at the OK corral. Lachie would cover us along the east of Gruinard Isle and Abdalla could keep watch on the western side. Jane would take each of them, to their locations. We had no radio on the boat and we could not risk being caught with Storno Radios. Jane would act as base for Lachie and Abdalla. Kyla would stay with her and the Van. I did not like flying blind, so to speak. Being out of radio contact, while we checked out the Island and the support vessels, that were supplying them. It would also appear, bringing guests from some rather posh looking yachts and other larger pleasure crafts. Whatever was happening on this Island looked like it would be happening tomorrow. My reasoning for that is you don't normally have the workmen present when you have a party. They are only there, to set things up and afterwards to clear things away. We started the motor and gently pulled into the deeper water. Both Hans and I put rods over the stern of the small fishing boat. I actually got a bite within seconds of dropping my hook into the water. It was not long before we were pulling fish in every couple of minutes. All this time we were circumnavigating Gruinard Island. As we rounded the northern tip a small RIB craft approached and gave us the once over. We waved and pulled in a couple of fish as they watched. They seemed satisfied and went back to the shore.

"What do you make of that Hans?"

"Low level security probably someone like G4S. They do security at all sorts of places including Unemployment Benefit Offices, Prison Transfer Vans, and some of the Open Prisons. They were not carrying guns."

"What about around the House on the Island."

"So far I can only see two proper security guards, one on the dock and another one at the front of the house. Let's see what we can see down the eastern and southern sides"

We sailed on and kept fishing. We had almost reached the southern tip of the Island when two RIB craft raced out from the Islands dock and headed in our direction.

"Shit, what going on?" Hans said

"Stay cool we are just two men out fishing for Mackerel and we have a box of them to prove it"

One boat came in on our port side and the other on our starboard. I could see no guns but these guys looked like proper professional security, rather than the minimum wage G4S guys.

"Please stop your boat. You are in restricted waters" One man said to us.

"Bollocks, this water has nae been restricted since the 1990's after they cleaned the Island. Next thing yae's will be telling us all, that we canae eat the fecking fish. Yea guys need to feck off back doon to England where yea all belong" I said in my best west coast accent. Hans looked at me in shock.

"Sorry to tell you Sir but this is a restricted area"

"I will write to ma member of parliament. How the feck is a Mon supposed tae make a living. Ya bastards ruined ma grandfather's farm, with your poison. Now yea want tae stop me at the fishing. Where is your proof, that I cannea fish? I fished here all ma life and I never heard such shite. I am going tae fish and if yea dinnae like it, then yeas can just go and feck off. Ya hear me, now get the feck away from ma boat. Yeas are scaring the fish. Fucking Sachanach's."

"Sir we are willing to pay you for the loss of the fishing just for two days"

"How much ya tight bastards?"

"How much do you earn in two days fishing Sir?"

"Yea twat's have been watching us ever since we started today, and as yea ken, we have only been on the water for an hour. We have an almost full box of fish and at today's prices, we would get forty pound a box"

"Sir we would be happy to pay you eighty pounds for two days' loss of fishing"

"I said forty a box, yea fecking numpty. Do yea take me for a dummy? There's eight hours in a day and that would be eight boxes in a day, twa days, is sixteen boxes ya ijid. Now that would be, six hundred and forty pounds. So unless yea's have that much in yer wallet, Yea can just feck off"

"I am sure we can manage that sir." The men in both boats started to empty out their wallets

"We have just over six hundred pounds Sir, would that be enough to keep you from fishing for two days?"

"Aye it would. But show me the cash first"

They passed over six hundred and twenty pounds

"I am keeping the fecking fish I have caught jist noo yeas ken?"

"Off course you can keep the fish you have caught up til now. Have a nice day Sir"

"Aye up yer arse"

We headed back to the shore.

"Andy I understood very little of what you said to the men out there. Why did you get so verbally aggressive with them? It is hardly a low profile"

"Hans imagine if you were a poor fisherman here who's grandparents lost their land and living to the British Government. How do you think you would react to them trying to do the same to you now? If I had given in, and just said OK no problem Sir. Then that would probably have looked much more suspicious to them. Now these guys, were proper security guards. They had money to burn. Sure they will claim it back from their employers. But they will describe us as two very disgruntled local fishermen, who ripped them off. It gives us total believability."

"Point taken Andy, also we have had a good look around the Island anyway. I guess it's mackerel for dinner"

ACT 75

We all regrouped near the beach. We cooked some of the fish over an open fire on the beach. I have to say, the fish was wonderful. However, we had to come up with a solid plan as soon as we could.

"OK Folks, we went around the Island. They are setting up for some kind of swanky party. There is low level, as well as professional security teams, on and around the Island. It will be damn near impossible, to gain access to the Island during the hours of daylight. I suspect that they will also patrol the perimeters after dark. My guess is that the two main players in this are not actually on the Island at the moment. There are several swanky yachts anchored to the north and a large container ship, which seems to be the main supply vessel. There is what looks to be a new semi permanent building in the centre of the Island. They have also erected several marquees. So the question I suppose is when and how?"

"Mr Andy. Can we not attack the yacht that these people

are on?"

"We could I suppose Abdalla, assuming that we can get out there without being caught by their security. We would also have to be sure that the targets were on board the one vessel."

"In my opinion Andy, we should wait until they are on the Island and target them there."

"How do we access the Island, Hans?"

"We don't Andy. We use our skills from here."

"I am sorry Hans; you have lost me?"

"We have not one, but four long range snipers. All of whom can hit a target cleanly at a mile. The Island is closer than that. The only problem I can see is that we have been told to make it look like an accident."

"OK Hans, do you have any ideas on how we are to pull off that miracle?"

"That is for now. That part I have not yet solved"

"Lachie. You have been quiet? Do you have any thoughts on this?"

"Sorry mate I have been racking my brains, thinking about how we are supposed to get both of these men together and then kill them in an accident."

"Jane?"

"Sorry Andy I cannot think of anything."

"Mr Andy, you said before that your house was destroyed by an explosion, which was made to look like an accident. Can we not do the same back to them?"

"That would be poetic justice indeed. However, there are a lot of innocent people on the Island. How would we be able to target just them?" I replied

"I have an Idea but I will have to contact the suit" Jane said

"Then please do it Jane, as I am clean out of ideas and the clock is ticking away from us."

Jane took my mobile phone and placed the call and then she put it on loud speaker.

"Hello" It was 'The Suit's' voice.

"This is team seven" Jane said

"What do you want?"

"A contact number?"

"For?"

"Tango one?"

The call was disconnected. I was seriously getting tired of people hanging up the phone on me whenever I asked for help. Then the phone vibrated. A simple text message or so it would seem.

"AHH I ACE FIG I"

"OK I am assuming that the message was not that gibberish. Call 'The Suit' again please Jane?"

"Wait a moment please Andy, Can I have a look at the phone please Jane"

"Sure Hans, but it will still be gibberish."

"Let us suppose that the private telephone number for your Secretary of Defence, if sent as a standard number text message would be immediately picked up by GCHQ? 'The Suit' would know this, so he has sent it in code."

"OK Hans how do we decode it?"

"We need pen and paper please"

"I have some in the van, Hans. I will get it, back in a moment"

"Thank you Jane."

I had never been great at word puzzles. My mother loved them, that and number games, a long time before Sudoku became popular. She possessed a great deductive mind. I hoped that Hans was the same. Jane brought the pen and paper to Hans. He wrote the letters out in a circle and started writing numbers next to them.

"Just as I thought it is a simple number to letter conversion."

"Doh! Simple for you spy types. Can you explain it to this dumb medic?"

"You do yourself a disservice Andy, just because you do not see numbers and letters as I do, does not make you a stupid man. You have solved many quandaries along the way. You have saved us on many occasions by solving them."

"OK Hans I get it. So what do the letters tell us?"

"A equals 0, I equals 9, so all the letters are in alphabetical and ascending order. As such AHH I ACE FIG I equates to 077 9 024 596 9. This would be a UK mobile telephone number. How is it you plan to use this to help us Jane?"

"I looked through one of those BAE sights and I saw the Marquees but at one side of the house, there is a large area which looks like they are setting up as an outdoor cooking station. It has a Bar-B-Q to the extreme right of that." she replied

"Great I love Bar B Q's do you think if we bring the fish they will swap them for some nice beef burgers" Lachie piped up

"If we could convince the two men to stand by the cooking area then we could kill them in an accident"

"Ahhh food poisoning, might take a little too long though"

"Joking aside Lachie, we can kill them. There is no mains electric, on that Island."

"So?"

"Well they will have a generator for the House, but I doubt it will be powerful enough for all that fancy catering equipment. This means they will be using gas, as in large propane gas cylinders. Which they are bound to have next to the cooking stations and the Bar B Q. We take out the cylinders with them standing there, and we will have taken them out as well."

"OK, I can see the plan working Jane. But like I said before there are a lot of innocent folks there, like the catering staff. I am sure they will be an outside contracted civilian company. So how do you plan to get them next to the gas tanks? More importantly, how do you manage to get them there alone?"

"That is why I wanted the telephone number, for Sir Peter and the American Nutter."

"OK I will ask the question, how?"

"We call him and tell him we still have the Biological weapon. And that we will meet him by the Bar B Q. We ask him to bring the American with him. We pretend we want to deal with both of them. He will first send his men to check the area. Then he will clear the area and with any luck. The pair of them will stand close enough to the tanks. Then we put an incendiary round into the tanks and Boom. Then we are all free."

"Anyone else got a better Idea, no? OK we run with this plan. We will have to wait until they start their party or whatever it is they are doing over there."

We finished our fish. Then Kyla had her fill, the rest back into the sea for the crabs to eat. Nothing wasted just the way I liked things to be. There would be some poetic justice after all. This had become real for Lachie and me the day they blew up my home. And now it would end the same way as it had started, with a gas explosion. Only this time we would be the ones responsible for it. We took shifts watching the Island. Nothing much happened the first night. Just more supplies were brought to the Island. Dozens of cases, of no doubt fine wines and champagne. There were barrels of beers and more cases of spirits. A large container was moved onto the Island. From which they pulled out a very large mobile stage, which was built up with Lights and speakers by an equally large crew of sound and lighting engineers. A band set up on the stage and ran through some practice numbers. All while another crew laid a wooden dance floor.

The catering staff, were busying themselves over pots and pans, set on their mobile kitchen. A large fire was set with burning logs and a complete pig was being turned over it on a rotisserie. We had split up once again to enable us all to have a good view of the Bar B Q area, which now had a pair of large red propane gas tanks. These gas tanks were housed in a metal cage, set about six feet from the burners.

"Jane is it you who will call them?"

"No Andy. It has to be you. I have no doubt, he has been told every single aspect of your life. He will probably have listened to recordings of you speaking. You will have to convince him and the American, to stand at a spot that will allow the others a clear shot at the propane tanks. He will have to die in the explosion and not by a bullet."

"It sounds easy when you say it Jane. I am still not comfortable with killing. I know it has to be done. I just don't like the idea of being the person responsible for it."

"It will never become easy for a man like you Mr Andy" Abdalla said

"Is it ever easy for one man to kill another, I have never done it myself. I do know men who do it for a living. Marcus was one such man. He enjoyed it. What you have to remember, is when we do this, that these two men would probably have been responsible, for the deaths of thousands of innocent people. They would say they were making the world a safer place. They might even say they would have killed dictators. What he will not tell you is that in order to kill one man at the top of the dictatorship, he would be willing to wipe out an entire city. You would not kill everyone on that Island over there, just those two men. But you would kill these men to save your families." Jane said

"No Jane I am not doing this to save my family. They are already safe. I am doing this to give life back to us all and to stop an evil man."

"Whatever reason you tell yourself Andy. I know you will do it because it is the right thing to do, in order to protect innocent people. This I know."

I kissed Jane on the cheek and walked long the sand with her and Kyla. There is nothing as relaxing as walking along a quiet beach with a dog. Dogs only offer kindness and loyalty to their families. There is a pack order within a dog's life, irrespective of the breed. This becomes much more visible, the closer the breed is to the original wolf. So in Kyla's case, she was not so far removed. Akitas are a pack mentality dog. The order is there, bred into their very structure. In our pack, when it was just me and dad and our two dogs. The pack order went this way. Me, Dad, Kyla and then Raven, who was no longer with us. Then anyone else. Here and now it was much more set. Me, Kyla, Lachie, Abdalla, Jane, Rosemary, Hans, Sandy, Dusty and finally there was Stuart. This was our pack and God help any person that was to attack or threaten that pack. It's strange as humans we think that we have a structured society. In truth it is not as good as that of dogs. The pack is set in stone. Yes, there can be challenges for leadership, usually by a young male. These challenges are normally quickly and violently put down. Then the peace is restored. This was the way I had now justified, what we would have to do in just an hour or so. I would be protecting my pack from a challenger. It would be a swift and final battle, that, order and structure could resume. I walked back towards the van. I told Kyla to get in the back. I closed the door down so that there was only a small gap at the bottom for fresh sea air to get in.

"OK are we all set" I said into my throat mike

ACT 76

"Overview good" said Jane

"West Clear" said Lachie

"Centre good" said Abdalla

"Coast clear" said Hans.

I made the call.

"Hello?"

"Sir Peter?"

"Yes who is this?"

"I am the man you have been looking for. I still have the item you want. I did not destroy it all. I need to meet with you and Mr Crump. I will call you in ten minutes. No point in trying to track this call I am on the Island at your party."

I hung up. I hoped that it was enough to put the wind up him and panic him into going to see Mr crump.

"Anyone have a visual on him yet?"

I got negatives all around. I could really do with a pair of eyes on the far side of the Island.

"There is a speedboat leaving one of the larger yachts."

"Roger that Hans"

I looked through my own scope. I could not see it as the Island obscured the yachts from me. At least until the boat came around to the front of the Island. There were three people on board. Two of them were the men who stopped us from fishing. The other man was big and fat. He wore expensive clothes, even from the distance that I was from him, the BAE sights showed him clear as day.

"I have a visual at the dock, Jane can you confirm that this is Douglas Crump?"

"Just taking a look at the moment, he has his back to me so I can't tell for sure. I will have to wait for him to turn around."

"Roger that."

I watched him as he went up to the front of the house. He was met by a tall man, with a military styled moustache. I zoomed in closer to the man's face. I had seen him on television before talking about home grown Islamic terrorism. I still could not get a good view of the other man's face. The two men seemed to be having a very animated chat, which involved a lot of arm and finger waving. They were interrupted by another man who seemed to calm the situation down. It was the Fucking Suit!

"Anyone else have a visual on what I have at the front of the house?"

"What the Fuck?"

"Yes Lachie that is what I thought."

"That's the Suit" said Jane

"Now why the hell is he here?"

"Perhaps he is here, to witness this Mr Andy?"

"Why would he do that, Abdalla?"

"That I cannot say, Mr Andy."

"Perhaps, so he can say it was a terrible accident. I mean the head of the intelligence services, says that it was an unfortunate accident. Then the rest of the world believes it?" Hans said

"I think that could be closer to the truth than you know, Hans" said Jane

More guests were arriving on the Island which was now lit up like a Christmas tree. Small motor boats would pull in and guests would decamp. Ladies were dressed in ball gowns and the men in Tuxedo's. This was a formal affair. I am sure there would be mini royals here as well. Given that Sir Peter was well in, with them. The band started playing and some of the guests took to the dance floor. Waiters went around the crowd, with trays of drinks. Other guests stood at a western style bar that had been set up to the left of the house. The Bar B Q was set to the right of the house.

It was time to make another call.

"Keep an eye on the fat man Jane. I am going to call Sir Peter. Watch both of them and keep me in the loop."

"Roger that"

I dialled

"Who are you?"

"I told you before Sir Peter. I am the man you have been looking for. I have your germs. I want money and lots of it. I know all about the deal you have with Mr Crump. I will meet with you but I will not do it in a crowd. You have far too many security people there for me to show myself."

"Where do you want to meet? And when?"

"I will let you know. Bring a cheque book and I want it made out for cash. Five million pounds for your bugs and my silence." I hung up

"What's Sir Peter doing? Jane"

"Him and the fat guy are talking. Sir peter is leading him away from the house. I see the fat guys face it is Crump."

"Thanks Jane."

I picked up my own AS50 and lay down on top of the sand bank, at the top of the beach. I zoomed the BAE sight in on the location of Sir Peter. I zoomed further and his face came into focus. I could kill him with a single shot from here. He would be dead. But it would be deemed a murder. This is what we were going to do anyway.

I checked the area around the Bar B Q. there were chefs preparing food, that I guessed would be served later. The hog roast was sizzling over the open fire. The vast majority of the people were up on the dance floor. 'The Suit' was nowhere in sight.

"Jane, come to my position."

"Roger that."

Five minutes later Jane arrived out of breath, having run to where I was set up.

"What's up Andy?"

"Are you one hundred percent sure that is Mr Crump the Billionaire?"

"Yes Andy I have seen several files on him and Marcus had lunch with him before."

"Call him. Tell him to meet us at the Bar B Q. if he argues tell him there are other buyers from Israel and the Middle East. If he asks who you are, tell him. OK?"

"What are you going to do Andy?"

"I am going to end this."

I pressed the dial button and passed the phone to Jane.

"Hello Sir Peter...............I am Jane Miller I used to work for Marcus Brown. .... I need you and Mr Crump to meet with us. We will be at the Bar B Q. In five minutes......One moment"

Jane mouthed to me "He wants to speak to whoever is in charge" I motioned for her to pass the phone to me.

"Listen, Sir Peter. I don't like you. I don't like what you do. You have ruined my life so now I want money. I want a cheque made out for cash for five million and I want it signed in front of me, by you and your American friend. I am sure you have various companies with with offshore funds. If you are not at the Bar B Q in five minutes, then I will disappear forever with your bugs. You know I can hide because you have spent the last three weeks trying to find me, without any success. Then I will sell this toxin, to your competitors. There is a Prince from Qatar, who wants to buy it, as do the Israelis. There are several other countries from the Middle East. Your choice, come and buy it or we will be in the wind again. No tricks just you and Mr Crump. I am sure a man of your capabilities, can clear that area of everybody, apart from you and us. I will call in one minute if you are not there, then its bye bye." I hung up

"Give him just over one minute and then call him. If he is standing too far from the gas tanks spin some story to get him closer"

I settled down with the AS50, which had become part of

me, as much as the guns that I had shot as a boy and then as a man. I remembered the training that Abdalla had taught us at the firing range. My right leg fully extended, with my left leg bent at the knee. My left hand was under the rifle and my right hand was on the pistol grip. I pulled the stock tight into my right shoulder and lifted it slightly off the ground. The barrel was balanced perfectly on the bi-pod legs. A straight line from the toes of my right foot, to the end of the barrel of the AS50. I cocked the rifle and a 50cal incendiary round with its blue tip, slid into the chamber. A perfect fit of brass to steel. The bullet would speed to its target at three thousand, five hundred feet per second. So it would cover the one mile in a little under, 5 seconds. This distance I was shooting at it would take about 3 seconds. I steadied my breathing and slowed it deliberately. Even though, the natural reaction, at the thought of killing two men, wanted my heart to race. Gradually it slowed and I looked through the scope.

"Jane when you call him, can you stand behind me and tap my foot when they are close enough to the tanks? They will have to be within ten feet. My sight will be totally focused on the target which will be the gas tanks. I don't want to see them die. I just want to see the tanks. Do you understand?"

"I understand Andy. Do you want me to call him now?"

"Please."

Jane pressed call.

"Sir Peter do you and Mr Crump want to deal or not………...It is a simple question yes or no?………. Andy and I will meet you at the Bar B Q…………….No Just US!………That's right…………………If there is ANYONE else there. Then the deal is off and we sell to the Arabs……Yes of course we are on the Island and we are watching…………...I can see you. You are standing with Mr Crump at the front of the house……………..You figure a way of making sure we are the only ones there…………...I don't give a shit about the cooks clear them out as well……That's right I can see you………..Good now the chefs………...If you both stand there we will walk to you………..."

I felt the tap on my foot. I clicked the safety off with my thumb and slid my index finger from its position on the outer guard, allowing my digit to smoothly slide down on to the trigger. I looked at the dot that was in the centre of the tank. Even if he saw it now it was going to be too late. The pressure increased as I felt the metal of the trigger push against the pad of my finger. The slack of the spring taken up and then that point just before the firing pin reaches the fullest extent of its backwards travel. Then the rifle exploded against my shoulder. The firing pin hit the back of the priming cap and the spark was generated. Then the larger charge housed in the shell case exploded with its full power. The micro second as the explosion swelled in the case, before it forced the bullet from the crimping. Now the bullet left the chamber and forced it's way down the barrel of the rifle, all the time picking up speed and spinning ever faster as it followed the rifling of the barrel. Now it blasted clear of the rifle with the flaming explosion behind it. It flew on its way unimpeded on its way over the water. The bullet would strike its target a long time before the sound of my shot would. The following explosion would also mask the sound of my rifle. I removed my eye from the sight. And for what seemed like an eternity nothing seemed to happen. The bullet was already over half way to its end point. Flying in a slight arc to it's own demise. Then the sky to the right of the house lit up as the gas cylinder exploded. Unexpected to me the second tank next to it also exploded a fraction of a second later. I returned my eye to the scope. There were several people that had been blown over by the concussive blast. The Bar-B-Q Area was completely destroyed. I zoomed back out a little. What was left of the two men who had been next to the gas tanks at the time my projectile struck, was not a lot. There were some burning remains on the ground. Security men were rushing to the scene. The band had stopped playing and the hog roast was now currently laid on the fire, it having been blown off its rotisserie mechanism. I looked to the front door of the house. And there, framed in the doorway, standing on his own was, 'The Suit." He was looking directly at my position. The bastard knew this was how I would do it. His hands would appear clean in all of this criminality. This unfortunate accident, as it would be reported. 'The sad demise of Sir Peter Ramsey. Much loved friend of the Royal Family who along with his lifelong friend and business partner. The flamboyant American Billionaire Douglas Crump'. I slid back from where I had fired the shot, being careful to collect my brass. I joined the others who were now down at the van behind the sand dunes.

"You did not have to take the shot my friend Mr Andy. I had a clean shot. I was just awaiting your call."

"I know you had the shot Abdalla. But the responsibility for this had to be mine, not just for revenge, but because it was my duty, to you my friends and to you my comrades."

"Andy what do we do now?"

"We go back to the cottage and rest Lachie. Then tomorrow we talk to 'The Suit' Tonight we get drunk and celebrate the fact that all of us are still alive"

We all climbed into the van and drove down the road without the lights on, until we hit the main road. When we arrived back at Kearvaig bay, it was already early morning. That said as we pulled up the lights were on in the house. As we piled out of the van Our friends filed out of the cottage to greet us. There were hugs and smiles all around. I wandered off to look at the sea with my beloved Kyla by my side. Even she seemed to know it was all over. She ran down the beach and then in and out of the waves. I was not sure if this was a time for celebration. But I knew it was a time to at least relax and let the last three weeks' fade. I would call my father in the morning, to let him know that we were all safe and well. I would tell him he could return to his life.

If not his home. To be continued…………………………

In The Return of Seven…………………………….

Books by Kenn Gordon

Altered Perceptions
Return of Seven
Dead End
A Short History of Chaplin Films
Audio Book – 9/11 The Firefighters

Albums By Kenn Gordon & 1916
Volumes 1 – 20
https://kenngordon1916.bandcamp.com

FaceBook
www.facebook.com/kenn.gordon96

E-Mail
kenn.gordon@yahoo.com

Printed in Poland
by Amazon Fulfillment
Poland Sp. z o.o., Wrocław